- MAROBOODUS -

THE GOTH CHRONICLES
BOOK 1

BY: ALARIC LONGWARD

HARDHILL
ADVENTURES

TABLE OF CONTENTS

The the fellow authors.

To Woden, Freya, and the old gods who are still everywhere in our lives.

A WORD FROM THE AUTHOR

Greetings, and thank you for getting this book. I hope you enjoy it and also read the **my other series below**, especially The Hraban Chronicles, that are related to the story of Maroboodus. When you have completed the story, I would appreciate if you could take the time to rate and review the story on Amazon.com and/or on Goodreads. This will be incredibly valuable for me going forward and I want you to know how much I appreciate your opinion and time.

Please visit
www.alariclongward.com

and sign up for my mailing list for a monthly dose of information on upcoming stories and information on our competitions and winners.

   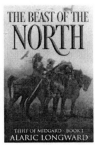

OTHER BOOKS BY THE AUTHOR:

THE HRABAN CHRONICLES – NOVELS OF ROME AND GERMANIA

THE OATH BREAKER – BOOK 1
RAVEN'S WYRD – BOOK 2
THE WINTER SWORD – BOOK 3
THE SNAKE CATCHER – BOOK 4 (COMING 2016)

GOTH CHRONICLES - NOVELS OF THE NORTH

MAROBOODUS - BOOK 1

GERMANI TALES

ADALWULF

THE CANTINIÉRE TALES – STORIES OF FRENCH REVOLUTION AND NAPOLEONIC WARS

JEANETTE'S SWORD – BOOK 1
JEANETTE'S LOVE – BOOK 2
JEANETTE'S CHOICE – BOOK 3 (COMING LATE 2016)

TEN TEARS CHRONICLES – STORIES OF THE NINE WORLDS

THE DARK LEVY – BOOK 1
EYE OF HEL – BOOK 2
THRONE OF SCARS – BOOK 3

THIEF OF MIDGARD – STORIES OF THE NINE WORLDS

THE BEAST OF THE NORTH – BOOK 1
QUEEN OF THE DRAUGR – BOOK 2 (COMING AUGUST 2016)

'Yea, you mortals,
hear the gods chortle.

Twigs and skull,
and an old, rotten hull.

The Bear shall choose,
between a woman and a noose.

A surprise for the crow lord,
and death at the end of the sword.

Victory for the beast,
but there shall be no feast.'

MAP OF THE GOTH SHORES B.C. 30 (SWEDEN)

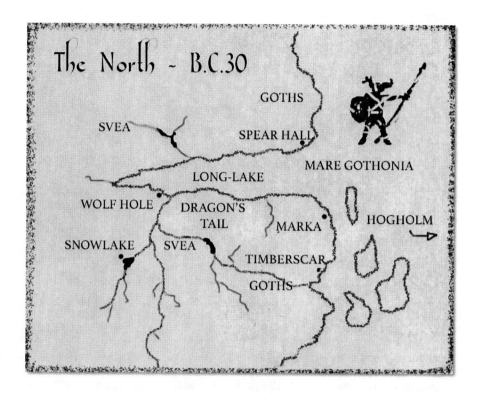

NAMES AND PLACES

Agin – son of Gislin, a Svea Lord and rival to his father, brother of Saxa

Aldbert – the poet friend of Maroboodus

Bero – Lord of Marka, the supposed Thiuda of the Black and Bear Goths

Boat-Lord – father of Hughnot and Friednot

Bone-Hall – Bero's hall

Ceadda – the Saxon ally of Maroboodus

Cuthbert – a Lorf of the Saxons

Danr – champion of Bero

Dragon's Tail – the hills where Hughnot and Maroboodus fought

Draupnir's Spawn – spawn of Draupnir, Woden's ring, the influential ancient ring of Maroboodus's family

Dubbe – champion of Hulderic

Eadwine – champion of Bero

Friednot – father of Bero and Hulderic, Lord of the Black and Beart Goths

Galdr – rhythmic spell singing

Gasto– champion of Bero.

Gislin – Svea Thiuda of Snowlake gau

Gothonia – home of the Goths, an island in the Baltic Sea

Gothoni – old Germanic tribe from the Baltic Sea

Harmod – champion of Hulderic

Hild – völva of Agin

Hraban – son of Maroboodus

Hrolf the Ax – son of Hughnot

Hogholm – home of the Boat-Lord

Hughnot – Lord of the Black Goths

Ingo – champion of Hughnot

Ingulf – champion of Hughnot

Long-Lake – a stretch of water on the coast of modern Sweden, stretching far inland from the Baltic Sea

Ludovicus – champion of Friednot

Maino – son of Bero

Marcus – daughter of Fulch the Red, lover to Hraban, then Wandal's wife to be

Mare Suebicum – the Baltic Sea.

Mare Germanicum – the North Sea

Marka – the home of the Bear Goths

Maroboodus – son of Hulderic the Goth

Njord – the Saxon and brother of Ceadda

Osgar – champion of Friednot

Ragnarök – the final battle of Germanic mythology, the end of most of the living things, the gods included

Saxa – the Svea princess, daughter of Gislin, sister of Agin

Seidr – magical power of Freya, the war goddess, mistress of seduction

Sigmundr – champion of Hulderic

Spear Hall – the home of the Black Goths

Suebi – a vast confederacy of Germanic tribes stretching from Sweden to Danube River

The Three Forks – rivers near Wolf Hole

The Three Spinners – norns, the Germanic deities, or spirits, sitting at the foot of the world tree, by the Well of Fate, weaving the past, the present, and the future of each living creature. Also called Urðr, Verðandi, and Skuld

Vaettir – Germanic nature spirits

Vitka – priest

Völva – priestess

Whisper- vitka of Gislin

Woden – also known as Odin, the leader of the Aesir gods, one of the creators of men and the world.

Wolf Hole – home of Gislin the Svea

Wyrd – fate in Germanic mythology

Yggdrasill – the world tree, where the nine worlds hang from. Source of all life

RAVENNA (A.D. 37)

It's called the city of silence.

While no city is truly silent, Ravenna is certainly different from the many hideous pits of villainy I've had the misfortune to tour in my time. The city is deserving of the title, though, and by that I mean *silence,* not villainy. Ravenna's well-built streets do not echo with the jubilant screams of the street urchins, there are few street vendors hawking their wares, and the general chaos of humanity seems strangely subdued as you cock your head and try to catch a hint of the hour of the day. You do so by listening carefully to the clues, you judge it by the way the people around you attend to their business, like I know the harried, crooked-nosed teacher's schedules, the man who dismisses his class when it gets insufferably hot on the street corner where they sit down to learn the basics of writing and reading. I know it's midday as he is right now screaming at his unhappy class of middle-class boys, and he is getting ready to spend his few denarii on wine and kneaded bread down the street. Also, at midday there is a steady stream of people moving around the piled streets below, as midday is the time you often meet your friends and clients, but still, even at that busiest of hours, Ravenna is peaceful.

I shake my head, taking a long, suffering breath. I'm to meet my guest at midday and so I prepare.

I stare across the room, calming my surprisingly wrecked nerves and try to focus on the silence. The insulae—the many-storied buildings that house many families of different means—are certainly calmer than they are in Rome, the people somehow more … severe. Yes, that is right. Severe is the right word. People are afraid to show too much emotion. I don't know why that is, exactly. It might be the effect of the long, winding canals? The water has a calming effect on the easily dazzled human mind and water is plentiful in Ravenna, the sea embraces the city, surrounds it, provides for it and guards it. Perhaps it's the far-reaching swamps, the barren lands that surround the city that remind people they are truly isolated. Perhaps that solitude from the rest of the Roman world gives them a level of *gravitas, dignitas*? There *is* something disquieting about the sad, deadly morass that stretches around the city for miles and miles, reaching to the west like a punishment of the gods, nearly uninhabitable and ugly. That might be so, the reason for the calmness of Ravenna. I've seen plenty of swamps in my lifetime—and it's been a long lifetime— and I can say they, like the vast deserts of scorching sand, the deadly northern plains of ice-white snow, and the never-ending woods filled with whispering spirits and strange animals all can change a man. The solitude and the lingering danger remind you just how small you are in the great game of life. Living by a vast wasteland brings you closer to your gods. Yeah. The swamps around Ravenna are like the deserts of snow and wastes of sand and they are god's fine works to keep the pride of men in check. The swamp and the sea forces men to see things from a different angle to those who rarely suffer the ravages of the elements the gods gave us to get along with.

I jump as someone opens a door below. I hear voices, a woman laughing shrilly and decide it is not my guest yet, after all. It's the short harlot who lives on the first floor, probably laughing at something that would make me cringe, like a funny-looking turd on the doorway. She is always cheerful, and I should probably admire her for it, but cannot. Not this day. Nor any other. Fun and Ravenna don't mix very well.

Well, I'm not being fair.

Yes, *of course* people have fun in Ravenna. I'll not pretend they don't, even if I cannot join such fun. They go and see the plays of best Greek drama—mainly lesser spectacles than in Rome— and they drink their Falernian wine to an excess and gorge on fine dishes, and these feasts end usually by *quarta vigilia noctism*, the dawn. Yes, and they gleefully celebrate the many Roman festivals, and god Woden knows they have far too many such festivals, as most any foreign celebration quickly finds a welcome home in the Roman calendar. Any excuse to enjoy life is easily embraced, even in the sterner Ravenna. The people even go to the gladiator games set at the theater and indeed, some of the best schools for this sport are here, in Ravenna. There's a match coming up, a fight to the death, between The Old Hand, a fighter of Cruxis, the owner of the ludus called "Spirit's Luck" and a lesser champion of a smaller, but aggressive house, and their man is called Clion. Their sandals will stomp the dust and the stone of the theater for a while, people will cheer, but they will cheer … politely.

As I said, gravitas and dignitas govern how they enjoy life, and it is a calmer life than they might live in decadent Rome or even Alexandria.

So now I shall try to be like them. Calm, dignified, as my executioner arrives.

I was not born here, but I too, was born in the wasteland. I should know how to be dignified. Calm. I will smile politely, slouch on the couch, and keep my head steady. I'm old as shit, but still formidable, and few old Germani nobles will let their enemy frighten them into shudders and tears, when they come for him with ready swords and spears. I am Maroboodus, *the* Maroboodus, and I'll not shed a tear as they make an end of me.

I can hear footfalls on the stairway. Perhaps the man entered with the whore, and she was laughing at some joke the man made? Perhaps. There is subdued speech, and I sense they forgot something. A man is running down, the rest waiting.

Should I run?

No.

I'm living on the top of the insula on the corner of Ninth Street and Hound Street. It's a fine, huge place, and while many lesser creatures live in the apartments the further down you go, the guards on the next floor are always alert and young, and no fools. They will never chance the Bear escaping his gilded cage and if I did, they would pay a hefty price. They know it. Tiberius would cut off their cocks. I hear their respectful voices now, speaking with reverence to the man who arrived from Rome last night. They told me I'd have a visitor from the capital. I rub my shoulders briefly, begging for the ache to disappear, at least for a moment. It's the stress, the forgotten fear, the long wait that pains my body, presses on my chest with a heavy foot of a jotun. I should not be surprised they finally came. I should have known better than to hope and I did know better, once. I have merely forgotten the death sentence that has simply not been put into effect.

I was there, wasn't I? I was there when Tiberius gave it to me.

I was brought here to die, eventually, but first to be forgotten, not to be made a martyr of, to live silently under the huge shadow of my gigantic failures, by the orders of Princeps Tiberius. For long years and then even more years I have been waiting for him to finally reach out and get rid of me. Did I not kill the one he trusted and loved? His *brother, Drusus. It was a good day,* I thought. He has taken his time, cruelly torturing me those first years, sending people to check on me and I remember I feared those footfalls on the stairs back then.

Then, for many, many years, there was nothing. The stairs were silent as … a grave. I chuckle at that and wince as my heart beats painfully, like a struggling butterfly.

For years I've been waiting for this day, but also hoping for him to die and hopefully unexpectedly, a victim of murder or illness, and that Maroboodus would be forgotten. But he did not die, and I've waited, even if I have allowed myself to relax, occasionally. I've done so patiently, as patiently as a former Germani king, a famous warlord, and a lord of so many nations might, but they have been long years. As the years passed, I began to believe I'd live. I lied to myself, but it was a pleasant lie. The rumors said he has been going mad, growing more and more sadistic and he was always dangerous, paranoid even, though perhaps a princeps should be paranoid and he certainly has his enemies. Plenty of them, in fact. Fear and distrust are the ingredients of a life lived in the hilt of power and I know, as I was once a lord of a land. I had so many enemies I could hardly count them all, and I count very well.

I believed he had forgotten me or in his madness, decided to spare me. I let myself even think Hraban, my son had relented in his hatred for me, and made Tiberius believe I was dead.

I am a fool.

The footfalls continue. They echo and some are soldiers, as I hear the hobnails scratching the stone.

The man is nearly up the stairs. I hear no clank of the fetters, nor the tell-tale thump of a spear hitting the walls and the butt dragging on the stairs, but they could be there, nonetheless, careful, ready to kill me swiftly or patiently, depending on their orders. I gaze over the white and red rooftops and enjoy the relative silence for a few more moments. Birds skim the treetops, and as it is spring, they are happy, joyful, free. *Perhaps I'll join them in a bit?* I have grown old here. It's not a bad place to die, to be honest. The waiting cell for my death could have been much, much worse, like some shit-hole of a dirt-covered hamlet in the deepest Gaul, or a forgotten frontier town of the Egyptian desert, where I would have lost my sight, my senses, tottering around with flies nesting under my eyeballs. Tiberius had a great imagination when he wanted someone to die miserably, but in this one case, he let his enemy live well. I could have died like Julia did, of hunger in a sad, barren island. Poor Julia, poor girl.

Ravenna is beautiful. For that, I must thank Tiberius, even as I hate him.

I eye the windows, and curse softly. I will join the prisoners who have died here previously. Armin's wife was imprisoned here. Thusnelda. She did not leave, bless her bones. His son is here, and he won't go anywhere either. He'll die a gladiator one day. Thumelicus, they call him.

The door opens with a creak and I struggle to remain calm, my hand groping for a sword that is not there, has not been for long years.

I turn my old eyes to the man. At first, he stays out. Instead, the guards come in and I tense, despite the decision I made to stay still like a brooding king, and I try to look indifferent and spiteful, but the guards do not carry swords, but perhaps wine in amphorae and a sturdy, comfortable chair, that they set near my desk. I ogle them with confusion, and they give me a brief smile that I take as somewhat good news.

The man enters. He has well-groomed hair, brown and black with thick, perfect ringlets around his ears, though perhaps they are natural. His skin is olive, so he is probably a Greek? *Yes, a Greek.* His clothing is simple, only a white tunic, serviceable sandals, a practical belt, and he carries a stylus and ink as if they were the most precious treasures in Midgard. They are, probably, to him.

He is a scribe.

'Are you ready to hear my proposal then, my lord?' asks the scribe with a smooth, respectful voice.

'Nobody told me you would have one, my friend,' I answer, biting my tongue, as I'm surprised. *A proposal?*

His eyes light up with brief confusion, but then he nods as he gives the departing guards a speculative look. 'They seem to have forgotten to inform you why I arrived here yesterday. They are good men, but still just soldiers.' I had a sudden hunch someone would pay for the oversight.

Oversight. Bah.

I'd have whipped the soldiers for having failed in their duty, I thought and kept an eye on him. They did it on purpose. The dog fondling bastards probably let me think it would be a blood-handed Pretorian rather than a scribe. Then I bite my lip. Scribes can be as dangerous as executioners. I quickly take stock of his face, and decide he is the sort of man whose true feelings are hidden under a heavy blanket of decorum. He will take care to give nothing away, but they are there, the feelings, nonetheless. Men like that annoy me. I'd rather see a spitting, roaring drunk charging me with a sharp spear, aimed for my gut, than a scribe of Tiberius, whose face does not seem to be made of skin, but marble. He is dangerous, scribe or not. *But then again,* I thought, *he's not here to kill me, at least immediately.* I frown. I cannot remember his damned name, even. I should, since the same guard who forgot to inform me of the man's business in Ravenna, did mention it at least three times. The curse of the old age is to know you should be able to remember many things—like the names of such dangerous scribes—but you cannot and instead you will pretend it is not the ravages of years, but the wine you drank the night before. I snort and he smiles. *I'm turning into an idiot.* I'll be one of those odd things you see in the corner of the street, playing with sticks and stones amongst vermin and trash, covered in shit and piss, speaking animatedly with a dog that is dying of hunger. It would be best if one so afflicted would sleep soundly until the Valkyries finally fetch them, dreaming pleasantly, but no. I can hardly sleep at all. The pains of my old wounds and my shamefully weak bladder force me to walk about every night and that cannot be changed. I'll sleep in the halls of Woden, in Asgaard, Valholl, when I go that way, perhaps soon. Or perhaps

I shall be whisked away to the home of Freya, the Red Goddess, in her golden Sessrúmnir? I shake my head and decide I am not dead yet and it's not wise to dwell on my future accommodations.

I make a brave attempt. 'Julius—'

'Marcus Pomponius Dionysions, master,' he said patiently and there was no mockery in his voice. I was used to mockery. It was the standard treatment I receive from the house slaves, the dogs, the whores who saw to my needs, but who in truth robbed me and spat in my food. Not so this man. And that is why I don't trust him. He is eyeing me with a gracious, wide smile, waiting patiently as a wolf for a prey to make a wrong move. He is a creature of the Palatine Hill, and there are no men there I would ever trust my life with. I've been serving there previously, haven't I?

I'm no damned prey. I'm Maroboodus.

'Julius. If you would be so kind as to fetch me some of that splendid …'I gesture for the wine.

'Vinum Pramnia,' he states helpfully.

'Vinum Pramnia, and I'd be very happy to discuss your business. By your refined, practical looks, you brought some good, practical wine, so let me sample it,' I told him with a voice that made it clear I was not making a request, but giving an order. And I felt better, as I would be enjoying something that was not from Ravenna. Something different. Something to make the ache less. I subtly massaged my chest and resisted the urge to press my belly, where there was a throbbing pain. The scribe saw that and I stared back at him mulishly.

'Yes, master,' he said with a small bow of his head, and got up to fetch me some of the wine. Maliciously, I thought I might ask him to bring me the whole heavy amphorae, but it would do no good to be drunk so early in the morning and so I decided I'd be happy with what he brought me and I'd give his business some thought. I eyed him, as he poured the drink expertly, not spilling a drop. He was a freedman, a former slave, and now a much higher creature of Juppiter's than most of the common Romans, of the nobilitas even. He served Tiberius, the Stone Jaws, the Princeps of all of Rome, the man who was my very old enemy, and also the demon who was the patron of my damned son Hraban. I tore my thoughts off Tiberius and

20

Hraban and gave him a good look-over. He was no fighter. A poisoner, perhaps, but certainly not the sort to stand in a shieldwall, or to run forward while clutching a bundle of javelins with the bloodthirsty intent of impaling men's faces and bellies. He didn't have the … ferocity? No, he didn't have that at all. *Nor the constitution*, I decided. The man was tall and thin as a willow, his face was coldly handsome, and there was clear, curious intelligence in his dark eyes. He had money. I was sure of it. Most freedmen who work for men of power are richer than a king of the east. But he wore nothing to make that apparent. That also annoyed me. He was rich, but did not flaunt it. I shuddered. *What a waste that is.* A Germani loves practicality, is married to prudence, but a man should also boast and a rich one would boast shamelessly, showing his merits to all who hail him, his fame read from the silver and gold he carries and few high lords would hide his wealth. I had loved mine.

Gods, yes, I had. I had loved it dearly.

But this one hid it. *He is a snake*, I decided, a man who enjoys the shadows and would butcher villages of innocents to silence a single voice, and never feel terrible after. At least I had, when I had had people killed, those who deserved it, and those who didn't.

The man seemed to know I was thinking about him and his many shortcomings, and flashed me a brief smile as he poured me another drink from a tall glass decanter. 'Water to wash it down. It can be an acquired taste.'

'I piss water, I don't drink it,' I informed him and he, ungraciously, did not laugh at the joke. *Didn't know how*, I thought, the Palatine Hill having purged him of the ability to give an honest smile.

'Are you doing fine?' he asked dryly.

'I'm not. And I'm not going to do anything you ask.' I waited for his rage.

Instead, he approached me and set the goblet with the water on a desk, not exactly near, but close enough so that I would be able to reach it, should I so desire. He handed me the one with the wine. 'I do think I have an exceedingly good taste in wine. I think you might as well. A king would and should know wine from piss. And you have lived in Rome for years, they tell me, when you served with the *Germani Corporis Custodies.*' He emphasized the name of my former unit and I nodded at him, carefully, wondering what he would want from me. Yet, as he mentioned my former military unit, I straightened my back instinctively. I didn't *feel* like a solider, but I did react immediately. My hair was red, streaked with white, and my shoulders had plenty of muscle, still, even if I had—or age had— allowed my belly fat to accumulate. I was strong and proud still, and as he looked into my eyes, he smiled wistfully, as he probably saw a warrior sitting before him.

I cursed him, as he had, just by uttering the name of my old unit, managed to pull me from my morose, stubborn mood and I had indeed done what he wanted me to do. It had been a very subtle retort to my obvious reluctance to help him out. I slouched no longer and he also knew I could be manipulated. Gracefully, he looked away and let me slump back and I decided I should not underestimate him. Nor should I drink too much of his wine. He knew of the time I had served with old Augustus, his daughter Julia, and the rest of the once powerful dynasty. He would know more. And so it was truly Tiberius, who had sent the man there.

The man bowed gently as he sat, speaking softly as if to an animal to be calmed down. 'I guessed you might enjoy this.'

The thought that had sprung to my mind sobered me, and I hated to be sobered. Perhaps he was trying to calm me down, and perhaps the wine had been spiced with something to make it a lasting calm? 'So, this wine—'

'Is not poisoned,' he said with a polite laugh, dry as the sands of Judea. 'This is pressed not far from where I used to live as a boy. My grandmother worked for the estate, and pressed the grapes for twenty years. She had a taste for a good wine, so I also knew very much about the business. I used to think I'd live there, our home, and I'd raise a winery and a family of my own. But Zeus in his indifference determined our lives would change and here I am, a former Roman slave. But I do still enjoy a good, strong aroma on a wine. This one? It's rough, tough, arid, and a bit sad.'

'A wine can be sad, you say?' I mused with a small laugh, fully aware he was hard at work to put me at ease. 'I shall have to trust you don't mean to poison this old Germani, though few would weep if you did. It would be a happy day for so many men and women out there.' I looked at him carefully, trying to catch a hint of his feelings, but I didn't have to. He spoke plainly.

'You are right, lord Maroboodus. There are still many men and some women who would rename this wine the "Nectar of Unmatched Joy" should it become your bane. And yes, I work for such men and women. But not as a poisoner, no.'

'Let's keep the vintage sad then,' I agreed and sighed. 'What do you want?' I asked him, going to the point, though I knew by the ache in my body I was also afraid of the answer. He nodded heavily, as if loath to speak of it, and picked up his pen. I counted to ten as I was sampling, relishing the bitter taste. *Yes, perhaps a bit sad*, I thought.

'I wish to speak of *you*.'

'Of me?' I asked, surprised. 'What about me? You wish to know how I am doing? Didn't you just ask that? You wish an account of my wellbeing? I'm ill. Old. I fart and it smells of ancient cabbage and I piss far too much. I should probably see the sun more, and sleep longer. I've not had a woman in years. Not sure *it* works, even, if you care. I've not even had the slaves, and did it only once with that terrible servant who smells of onions. Can't remember her name either. She has buck teeth. That's years past. Come to think of it, I haven't seen her in months. Perhaps she is dead? Surely you know all of this already?'

He shook his head. 'I know all of this. And I know you lie, because you had it twice with the woman.'

'It was the same night! That doesn't count.'

He chortled. 'Like the wine, you have a story to tell. The wine over there whispers of the land it grew on, my lord Maroboodus,' he said with a wistful smile. 'It whispers of the secrets of the soil. It's made up of tears and blood, they say. One can taste it, I think, the blood. And the tears, as well. The older the land, the more stories the wine has to tell. And you, like the wine, reek of old stories. And Rome, as you know, documents everything. We hoard information, my lord, and even pen down those tales we might hate and fear. I'd hear your sad tale.'

'Why now?'

His smile disappeared. 'Because time is growing short—'

'For me? For Tiberius?' I insisted.

'For both,' he said without emotion. 'Both, my lord, will die soon. First one, then the other, but your death, like the death of many others like you, is linked to his. One follows the other like lighting follows thunder. You know this.'

I tapped my hand on the couch, then checked it. I let my eyes travel the fine wall tapestry of faded animals, trees, and people who looked like they had hit their heads, falling from a horse. Their eyes were emotionless, dead, and I let my eyes go to the ceiling. His words were a death sentence. He would sit there, penning it all down, and then one day he would not come up, but a soldier or two and the apartment would no longer be occupied. *Had Augustus killed my best son like this? Yes.* And perhaps, like it was with me, this man, or someone like him had sat down with him to pen his words down. It was their way. They loved death. We deal death, the Germani, and enjoy a proper bloodletting, the sound of weeping widows, but then, later, we would salute the enemies, grant them honor, for their valor made our valor and we shall all meet again.

Not so the Romans.

They will mock you in your death. They will strike down your statues, erase your name and fame, hunt your family to poverty and slavery, and read such final words while smiling triumphantly, feeling perversely superior to the poor being whose testament they own and hold in their greedy hands. They wish to dominate, to rob, to suppress, and then enjoy the deaths of their enemies in silence, alone, and such men we don't understand. Warriors should die with honor, hailed by all.

I squinted my eyes at him and he cocked his head gently.

But my story was a long one. And the longer it was, the more time I had to learn of Marcus, and to plan. No king dies willingly, like a pig led to be sacrificed. No.

And so I agreed.

'You bring me sad wine from a sad land you knew,' I smiled. 'And you'd hear me speak of my people, men and women of a similar land?

Why not? It's far, Marcus, the land I hail from. Do you have time to hear such stories?'

'I have some time spared for this. They have a room for me below,' he informed me modestly. 'But of course, only the gods know how much time I really have.'

'Gods,' I said. 'I hate the lot and let the denizens of Hel hump the unfair fucks in their sodden rear ends.'

He ignored my coarseness. 'Gothonia? This is the land you were born in? You are son of Huldric the Goth, the lord of the village of Timberscar? In the gau of—'

'Hraban?' I asked him, naming my cursed son. I gauged his reaction and decided he had spoken with Hraban. I scowled at him, while contemplating on bashing the goblet over his head just to draw some reaction out of the statue-like scribe, but relented. *What does it matter, what indeed? Fuck Hraban as well,* I thought. 'Matters not.' I nodded and he seemed relieved, just for a tiniest moment. 'And my father's name was *Hulderic.*'

'What do you remember of your land? What is the one thing that comes to your mind?' he asked and I wondered if he tried to make sure I was not senile.

I nodded towards the north. 'That way, far, far away, if a jotun jumped over the Alps, a frog swam over and hopped beyond the Danubius River and a bear hiked across the thick woods of my former kingdom, there is the mysterious land of Germania. There, over the mountains and the endless hills and beyond the secrets of the dreaded Black Forest, far beyond that, over the flats of the Chauci and over the sea, the Mare Gothonium, there is a land of snow. And the one thing I remember about that land is how it broke my heart.' His eyes looked out to the windowsill, where a bird was sitting, and I stiffened at the sight. It was a beautiful creature of yellow feathers and bobbling head, as it feasted on the crumbs of bread from my last night's dinner. I had never seen a bird like that, I was sure, and yet, it reminded me of Saxa. It reminded me of a happy day, a similar bird that had marked our love, and a wedding feast and how I had loved her back then, when my heart had been young. Wind rustled the drapes, the bird disappeared in a eye blink and so I was left with Marcus.

'Was it a woman, my lord, who broke your heart?' he asked and I noticed he was already writing. I nodded slowly.

I thought back and remembered the days when Hulderic and my uncle Bero had served Friednot, my grandfather. We were rulers of hamlets, lords of the woods, and had so little. Later, in deeper lands of Germania, the wealth of the many nations like the Sigambri astonished us, but in the north our wealth was jealously guarded, the clans war-like, our men harsh and unforgiving and still, we were only men. We succumbed to illness, hunger, and … love. I waved my hand that way again. 'It *was* about a woman. But there was more to it than love. It was a subtle mix of many ingredients. It was greed, fear, love, fear of losing.'

'You are very eloquent,' Marcus said with a wistful smile 'Like your son.'

I frowned at that and nodded heavily, and continued, though with an angrier note. Mention of Hraban's name did that to me. 'It was also about our family and its honor. Or lack of it, rather. I wanted it all. I sought love and found it, but I honestly thought I could create a strong nation out there, up there, far away, and I was so young. I was like a duckling learning to paddle along and like such a duckling, I didn't know what I was doing. I paddled into grave danger, many ducks and fucks died, and all of that broke my heart.'

He looked out again, musing. There was a strange look in his eyes and a small, wistful smile and probably he thought of some girl he had lost, but given up for his high position in the court. It was often so with such men as Marcus. Power and love do not mix. Power poisons a man, curses love, and the gentle thoughts many of us harbor when we are still young, of a peaceful life with a gentle woman's touch on our cheek every morning are but high, fleet clouds if we attain a position of power. *Curse power*, I thought.

'But you loved, yes?' he asked.

'Yes, why do you doubt it?'

'Your son claims you are unable to feel love,' he stated bluntly.

I sat up. 'I didn't love *him!*' I breathed hard and cursed my son. I had *not* known him. I had not known *my wife*. Thanks to Hulderic, my father, I was a Roman more than a Germani and Hraban knew this. Had we not spoken of it the day I killed Drusus, when he had me under the sword? I came home and found a family I didn't know or trust ... or love. I saw my wife die, and while my father Hulderic had fallen as I had planned, I had wanted Sigilind to survive my plan. But she didn't, thanks to Vangione king Vago's evil, and that was her fate. And Hraban still sulks for what I did? And he still wonders if I ever loved him? 'Love,' I stated hollowly and noticed I was covered in sweat. 'It's a deadly emotion, isn't it?'

'It is, lord,' he said with a smile.

'Yeah. I loved this woman. It was doomed. Of course it was. There are old stories of ancient Goth heroes who ride their brave horses deep inside the pine forests, braving vaettir and small gods of the night just to visit a grass mound where their former dreams have been buried. Gothonia is a veritable cesspit of woeful stories and tales of fools seeking out their *wyrd*—'

He frowned and stopped writing. 'What is this word?'

'Has my son,' I asked spitefully, 'not spoken with you about *wyrd*? He has wept how bad a father I was, but—'

'You assume your son knows I am here and that I ...' he began, but noticed how my eyes twitched aggressively and smiled instead. 'No, lord. He told me nothing. Not a thing, really, unless what I might expect from you and he cursed you as a father and a man. He told me to be careful with you.'

'Careful?'

He fidgeted. 'He said you might crush my skull on the floor tiles, but I think you are lonely, my lord, and wish to have this slightest of chances to get your story told, and told out there.'

'My story won't leave some moldy archive,' I stated bluntly.

He nodded and gave a small, dry laugh. He leaned forward. 'Of course, we know that is so. There are rooms in the *Tabularium* none enter, and this will end up there. I know what happened with you and my lord Tiberius. I know what you did and for whom, and Tiberius has not forgotten. Our lord will never forget what happened to Nero Claudius Drusus and I half think he is still hoping to understand the events that so changed his life to what he considers Hades, and wishes to hear the story. From your lips, my lord. But he doesn't wish to see you.'

'I thank him for that!' I said. 'But if these texts are forgotten, left to molder in a room full of such confessions, it might be so that one day …' my voice trailed off, as I wondered how much I wanted to have my tale told.

'Who knows, my lord?' he answered dutifully. 'Anything can happen, I suppose.'

'Wyrd,' I said, happy with his explanation, 'means fate. Like you Romans, we think our souls a loan from the gods to inhabit Midgard. We are bound … our story woven as we speak, and our choices will determine what kind of tapestry we will see when we die. It might be dark and short cloth, coarse to the touch, but it might also be long, and full of knots of a life lived, with misery and happiness both. Few are fine and rich with no ugly marks of sorrow. Some parts of the tapestry will be dark, black, badly knotted and thus bear marks of our worse decisions. And Gothonia, the north in general is a place to make such terrible decision. Hunger, lord, forces men to act, often harshly, with no hope of success. Lords grasp at power, adelings to gain fame, and men who would serve them. Yes, it's a sad land, it certainly is and I am its man, no matter my later travels. The Gothoni lands made me a harsher man. And broke my heart, indeed.' I smiled and thought of the deep, magical woods far, far in the north, the snow banks under the gray, low-hanging sky, and the impossibly long, deadly winters and the sometimes scorching, but so very brief summers filled with mosquitoes. Men warred there, it was true. Men warred everywhere, that was also true, but there the tribes were many, the available land few, and hunger gave the war an edge of ferociousness that was lacking elsewhere I had seen. You took the land, or you kept the land and damn the rest. The winners ate juicy cow and appetizing gruel and the losers ate each other. The Goths were sea-people of the islands of Gothonia, where the giants had once erected stones to guard the beach, and gods created Aaska and Esla, but the people grew many, too many and sailed to claim land in the east and the west and settled in. Svearna, the strange Germani occupying the lands in the north and west shores of Mare Gothonium were pushed back and god Woden be thanked they were as quarrelsome and feuding as we were, or we would have stayed sea-people. My tribe, the Suebi Goths were unwanted guests in the land I was born in. The Gothoni ruled the islands and the coasts, but the various tribes of the woods and hills envied them the sea they had once owned and so there was much strife as soon as the crops had been sown each year. Svearna were the strange people of the east, and the Semnones, the Langobardi, and the Saxones of the south raided them and us over the sea. And our tribes, the ones who left Gothonia? We had an enemy, our old relative, the Boat-Lord and thiuda of Gothonia, who envied our new land its trade. I smiled. Trade was good. Farming was not. Even the land itself was as harsh as the wine I drank. *Harsher.*

'Your lord,' the man said carefully, 'would know his enemy's past ... wyrd, and so please, tell me what you did, and why, and how you ended up with the Marcomanni, so far from the Gothoni. Would you consider telling this tale, lord? I have time as I told you. I can write it up. I know your hands hurt and I am happy to help. I will not change a word after we are done. Not one. I promise. This is for the Princeps, who—like you—is sick and dying. I think he is tying up loose knots, so to speak. He wishes to know who you were, one of the greatest allies to Rome, and one of its worst enemies.'

I snorted. 'They remember Armin, Arminius the Cherusci was its greatest Germani enemy. Both my service to Rome and animosity for it later have been long forgotten.'

'Then let us remedy that, my lord,' Marcus said with a smile. 'Even if it will end up in a closed archive. Let us tie it up, right here, right now.'

I stared at him and rubbed my feet together. They were bloated and pained and I decided against fetching more wine by myself. I also struggled against the insistent voice that kept telling me the water could wash down the aftertaste of the acrid, if good, wine. I addressed Marcus. 'Augustus killed my Roman son,' I said softly. 'The man who should have been the Princeps is dead at his hand. Perhaps it was Tiberius and not

Augustus who gave the order? It was, wasn't it? And I should do him favors? Tiberius was always out to kill me. He gave me the death sentence, didn't he? Will you promise to hold these words safe?'

'It is true much blood has flowed in this circle of yours, my lord,' said Marcus. 'But consider this your last word. Your legacy. I will guard it.'

'I would have my last words over Tiberius's corpse,' I snickered and rubbed my hand across the goblet and saw my face on its surface. Gods, help, but I was old. Once, I had been handsome, my hair red as fire, my body full of heavy muscle. I had been wily as a night-hunting fox, fearless as a cornered wolverine and I had–briefly–been a king of people who do not want kings. Is that not an accomplishment? I looked up to the roof. Now I was fat, sick, and gray and I lost the kingdom and I lost my sons and live as a prisoner. My one remaining son hates me. Hraban. He loathes me. He had me under his sword once, the father who abandoned him to death and ignominy, and I told him not to judge me for my Roman ways. He had no idea what life was like in Rome, for a man who had been in love and promised the stars.

'Lord, I—' Marcus began gently.

I lifted my hand and he went quiet. How easily that happened. A king should be able to lift his hand and people should heed him. Now, I usually could not command a slave to move out of the way. None would see my hand, and if they did, they would laugh at it. Perhaps that could be changed, by some miracle of the written word I grunted and nodded. Hraban. He might learn of the past of the family as well. 'You will make one copy for Tiberius. Then one that you guard.' He nodded warily. 'Make a copy for my son as well,' I told him softly. 'And bring more of this wine. Every day we do this, there will be wine.'

Marcus smiled and he bowed. 'I will, lord. Where shall we begin? And shall we begin today?'

I smiled. 'I'll begin from the beginning, of course. And you already started, didn't you?'

He frowned. 'I do not know if master wishes to hear of your youth. Your childhood, lord, might bore him.'

'How would you know it was boring?' I grinned. 'Fetch me more wine and I'll tell you of the Goth who lived west from the islands of Gothonia and what we suffered. I'll skip the childhood. I'll tell you of the time I was eighteen, and I'll start with how I killed my first man and fell in love. Her name was Saxa.'

I told him my story, and tried to figure out how to escape him while I did.

BOOK 1: The Gathering Storm

'Shall we burn and bury my great brother? And then we have things to decide. Important things, my friends. And changes to be made, I think.'

Hughnot to Hulderic and Bero

CHAPTER 1

The wind was terrible, its raging power awesome. While we were relatively safe from its worst brunt, the tops of the pine trees around the hillside were bent, swaying back and forth, and some had fallen already, snapping like twigs. The sea the Romans called Mare Gothonium was a brutal enemy, especially so during the winter, when it was iced over for much of its length. During the long springs and yellow-leaf falls, when such storms made it nearly impossible to navigate across it, you would have to endure snot and dampness, no matter if you holed up inside the best of halls or a crummy hut. This one was one of the early fall storms, and it was still daytime, but the heavy banks of spirit-borne clouds were racing across the sky, very low, nearly low enough for a good warrior to lob a spear into them. A pair of young vitka, wearing fox furs and strange feathers in their greasy hair were on their haunches, looking balefully at the clouds, and as the Germani gods live in the ground and the spirits of the air were our enemies, the vitka were not happy. Neither were the chiefs and the champions. The priests had spent an hour trying to dispel the worst of the clouds, but had failed utterly. They had demanded a horse as a sacrifice, but Grandfather had denied them that. 'We need them for the butchery, not to be butchered,' he had rumbled.

I suppose we were lucky our enemies were Germani like we were, and even the vitka finally agreed the gods would have no favorites in the coming battle. They scuttled up the hill again to Grandfather Friednot, where the old, nearly neckless, very thick warrior scratched under his greasy ring mail and nodded at the two men with bare civility. Instead, he gave more attention to a pair of men on lathered horses, who also whipped their beasts towards him. He leaned down from his shaggy horse to listen to the two, and spat in anger at their words while pointing the vitka away.

'They are delayed,' Aldbert said miserably. The scrawny poet held a shield and a spear, but nobody expected him to do more than observe. He had lived in our hall since he was a boy, and I had befriended him even if he could not defend himself. I don't know why. He was not ... brave? He was strange, and sang to himself, but he also had a great sense of humor and so I used to fight his fights for him. He *was* an odd sight amidst Father's grizzled men. *He had his role,* I thought. Timberscar and the surrounding villages had sent a good number of sturdy Goths to serve under Father's bear claws banner, but Aldbert would make a song of the battle later, and he would remember every man that was there. He would bring glory to all the standards on that hill, and the lords that owned them. He'd honor some, who weren't there, if they were influential enough.

'Delayed?' I asked him, eying Grandfather who was spitting new orders to some of his warlords, but especially to Ludovicus and Osgar, his champions and warlords. 'No shit? Did anyone tell them we are expecting them to be on time?'

Aldbert snickered dutifully, and so did many of the oaths men of Father's champions and the champions themselves. Dubbe, the rotund terror of a shieldwall quaffed and nearly choked on some watery mead, and Sigmundr and Harmod both rolled their eyes while they enjoyed the nervous, clumsy joke. I liked the champions, men who led Hulderic's war bands on raids and reprisals, and they liked me.

The Saxons were late, indeed. But that was better than early when it came to battle.

The chosen men of the three warlords shivered, draped in animal skins, double layers of tunics and trousers. The shields that were oblong and rectangular were glistening with water and some had paint running on the surface, creating strange looking puddles of red and yellow at their feet. Even the spears, mostly thin, iron tipped framae, that was a useful weapon for both throwing and melee, looked sad and slick in the brawny hands that clutched them. 'Do they move?' Dubbe asked, growling the question for eleventh time, and meant the half-hidden scouts below in the wooded valley.

'They are picking asses, still,' Sigmundr stated laconically.

'Each other's?' Harmod spat.

'Yes, of course, still,' Sigmundr said, as he had the best eyesight. 'They are using their spears.'

'I hope it's spears,' Hulderic, father and second son of Friednot stated. His wide shoulders heaved with silent laughter as his champions mocked the simple scouts deployed down in the shrubs and his eyes flashed at me from under a helmet of leather and chain that hung on his shoulders. 'Patience. We won't remember this misery when they bleed at our feet.'

'Shit terrible to fight in this damned weather,' I breathed to myself.

'They'll be fine, the men,' Father rumbled and winked me over. I sighed and picked my way to him, at the end of the line, not far. He was right. The men had an impatient, but deadly glint in their eyes as I reached Father, sitting on a sturdy warhorse with a shaggy mane. His beard was blond where mine was red, and I shaved my beard, but we resembled each other in face and mood. His bear hide armor stank and steamed as he ruffled it. 'The Saxons won't mind the weather. It's an opportunity for them. Always has been. They love this shit. But there is no need to mention that to the men. If you would lead them, always give them a good amount of hope.'

'We outnumber them,' I allowed. 'They'll bleed like pigs.'

'That's my boy,' he chortled. 'But stay close when it begins. You've never fought in a shieldwall. It's going to be different from hunting cow thieves in the woods. There will be widows, and let's hope most will weep across the straits this coming week.'

'Yes, Father,' I stated with a neutral voice. There was something about Father that always bothered me, the weighty mantle of a leader he carried, a trait that I hated, and that was the great care he always gave to decisions regarding feuds, war, life in general. He carefully weighed many ills against the good, and often left me desperate for action. I think I knew he was wise, but sometimes, I thought, such wisdom made us look weak. Especially since his brother Bero wore Draupnir's Spawn, the family's ancient ring, a golden, flower-etched treasure the god Woden had given to Aska and Esla when they were born, long before in the island shore of Green Gothonia, the island where the Boat-Lord held sway, always looking enviously our way, though they never told us why. He was old, terrible, a

36

relative, though I didn't know how, and he was rumored fearful of Draupnir's Spawn, as many Goth Thiuda would be. Friednot and Hughnot carried it away in their youth, and Friednot wore it, until Bero married. But the Boat-Lord had not given them his blessing to leave the land and he feared, despite his vast might. Should we so wish, we might call men of the old families to call us the lords and many would answer, having respect for the golden thing.

And yet, I was unhappy.

Bero held it, I cursed in my mind, *because he married a day before Hulderic.* It went to the boy who married first. And sometimes, often, I thought Father had wanted to dodge the great treasure Friednot had passed down to his first son. *It would have fitted Father's finger well,* I thought. Very well. *And ultimately,* I thought, *mine.*

Instead, it was held by an uncle, the strangely twisted, crooked-backed fool with jet-black hair and a scraggly beard. The champions, even Bero's own champions Danr and the dog-master Gasto especially, secretly thought him incapable of leading. I looked that way and saw Gasto's great blond halo of a hair in the fog, as the man was stroking one of his famed hounds, while one of his daughters tended another behind the line. They had told of their unhappiness to Aldbert once, drunk. I stood next to my father and could only frown at the thought. The ring, the fine, indeed hallowed thing was not ours, never would be, unless Bero died, but then the vermin son of Bero should die as well.

And speaking of the vermin, it spoke.

'Father says they slither like snakes and swim like damned seals,' Maino, my cousin said as he jumped over a jagged rock not far. Maino was a restless soul and was stalking the mossy boulders between all our men, as if the man but a year older than I was in charge of the coming battle, checking that everything is just right. Hulderic grunted, not really fond of Maino, either. The fool was red-faced from too much ale and bloated from hot air and arrogance. We had received our shields the same time, in the Yule feast Thing the year past, but he had a reputation for going berserk in battle, and men respected him, like they would anyone so loved by Woden. I was still the least of Hulderic's men, which was something I resented, but in my heart I knew I had not deserved a place like the others, or even Maino.

I had never killed.

I had never been in a true battle, ever. I had chased after cow thieves, rowed the boat when we went after men who burned a hall of Hulderic's oaths man, and did well enough, but I had never been shuddering with fear, guarding a man's side with my shield, pushing against a snarling visage of a killer who wanted to push his weapon inside my skull.

Maino had. He had killed four Svearna on a terrible raid to their closest village, one we had previously traded fox furs with, but who had cheated our traders and killed two men. Maino had danced before the spear wall, laughed at the vitka of the Svearna, challenged the biggest bastard to come out and fight and he had killed him with a single spear strike. And that feat was a song now, the poets and bards reciting it to my discomfort even in our hall. To hear them admire the idiot and then see Father reward them for the song? It left me gagging with rage. Grandmother would come to me, whisper words of calm in my ear, but I had a hard time calming myself when the gods seemed determined to keep my face under a pond, and deep inside I feared I'd be a disappointment to Hulderic. Father's fame was of his own making, a fierce fighter, a clever lord, a ring-giver and a gracious host, but what would our family be like, should he die?

I eyed Dubbe, Sigmundr, and Harmod. They would give back the weapons Hulderic gave them, and they would find new lords. They would not bow to me. They liked me, but I was a … nothing. That made me burn with rage, it did.

'Woden, give me a rich foe to kill today. Let them all see it, and let me send the cur into Valholl,' I breathed softly. I gazed at Maino, who seemed to read my nervous thoughts. His flat, meaty face had a look of disgust, and gods, I hated him. Maino stood with the champions of Bero, Eadwine, Gasto, Danr, and I would have to show humility before I equaled them. I should, at least. I gazed at the three men huddled around Bero, hearing advice. They were a sullen, silent lot around Bero's standard of horse jaws and wore steaming leather mail with metal links and rings, and thick spears. All had axes, clubs, and the best spears. Maino hefted a fine, tall

38

spear Bero had given him that summer, and wore a well-crafted, boiled leather armor that covered him to his knees. His shield was of the best make, and would stop a javelin easily.

I cursed Father for that as well.

For some reason he expected me to find my own gear. I had a thick spear, the sort the Romans call a hasta, a sturdy club and my shield, of which the paint had run off an hour ago, but they were not made by a master smith, or a leather worker of great repute. Granted, the metal of the spear was precious and I had worked hard for it, but the rest was what many regular warriors had. And I only wore a tunic, like such simplest of fighters. I was not being fair, I knew, as a simple peasant would have a shield and possibly only a simple framea spear, and often fought in nothing but pants on and a rock in hand. I had serviceable weapons, but not famed ones. 'Forget him,' Hulderic told me, apparently having heard parts of my whispering to the One-Eyed god. 'A weapon will look its best when dipped in blood and even best when looted from a wealthy foe. Yours are good enough for a battle and you might find a better onse you can truly be proud of, should you slay its master.' But my cousin didn't make it easy to forget him. He liked to seek me out and torment me.

He walked by Hulderic and slapped my shoulder hard. 'Anxious, cousin? Hoping for a good fight?'

'I am,' I said as steadily as I could, but I couldn't fool even a thick lump of muscle like Maino. I was nervous, and he knew it.

'You'll get your chance at glory, Maroboodus. And if you fall, I'll raise my mug to you while you watch in the afterworld. If you die, please take my greetings to your mother in the Hel's gray land. I liked her well.'

Hulderic shuffled in his saddle and stared at Maino coldly. The death of my mother had taken place two years before. She had died of fever, snot, coughs, and her spirit was with goddess Hel now, in her sad kingdom of those, who died without glory. And what Maino was really suggesting was that I had no future in Valholl, where the brave go, and Valkyries would not pick pick my sprit up and help me travel there.

'Shut your mouth, boy,' Hulderic growled. 'And make yourself useful.'

Maino looked up to the great warrior, and there was a twitch in his eye, and even he realized he had crossed a line. He nodded generously. 'Yes, lord. I'll just take a piss, then.' He sloshed his ale. 'This might be the nectar of the gods, but I bet they don't suffer the after effects like we do.' Maino had a sort of a mug in his hands, one made of well-crafted wood. Men around us hailed him with agreement, drinking as well. Maino set down the mug, and sighed. 'Damn them. The Saxons that is. Damn them to Hel. We should have taken after them.'

Hulderic shrugged at his nephew and spoke as if to an idiot. 'Sure. We should have. But we only discovered them last evening. We only had a hundred men at hand then and they have more. Now they are coming back, tired and probably hungry and well-bled from fights. Trust your grandfather.'

As if he heard it, there was a whistle from the top.

We all looked up at Grandfather Fridenot, the Thiuda of the two gaus, and he was staring down at us. His squat shoulders shook, the silver and gold beard dripped wetly and he carried a huge sword, the Head Taker, another treasure of our family. His banner of scalps and skins was swaying high up in the air behind him as his great warriors were readying for battle. Osgar, his warlord, a tall man with a scarred jaw and the beardless Ludovicus, a young terror of battle were readying the men. Grandfather nodded at us, and we knew Friednot could smell battle, always had, like a dog smells excrement, and so Maino and Hulderic nodded and even Bero's men began to get ready. 'Best piss now,' Hulderic said stiffly.

Maino looked down at the obscure path below us. 'About damned time. They have been raiding for days in the inlands, and sure, they are probably tired and starving. The Svea have killed some. I am certain of that. But still, we might have stopped them before—'

Hulderic nodded. 'Yes, they have lost some. And that's how we wanted it. We might have deals with the Svearna near our borders, but we don't mind seeing some humbled. And there is the rumor of the Thing.'

There was indeed. The Svearna had ever been divided like we were, but that spring they had called for a great many men to sit somewhere days away from us, and what followed was a virtual peace between Svearna.

There had been few burning villages, very few mounds being built for their fallen, and they had had an excellent harvest. 'They are making peace. Next spring they will attack us together,' I said, having heard Hulderic discussing it with Bero.

Maino snorted, readying a disgusted comment, but instead shrugged, as Hulderic's eyes were on him.

'We'll be ready,' he stated.

'Saxons today,' Hulderic agreed. 'Svearna tomorrow. Let's think about the scrawny sea-dogs now. This is where they will come and we need not look for them. They are coming. Father knows these things.'

'Maino!' Bero called from the side. He had thirty men, we had the same and Grandfather had the rest of the men we had had a chance to gather so fast in our gau, another thirty. It could be thousand and more, but we only had had a day to gather what we could. 'Get here and stop prowling.'

Maino set down his mug and spat. He was groping with his pants, trying to fish out his cock to take a piss and stopped to regard me. He was not ugly, nor handsome, just strangely beefy and powerful. He could not resist a final jab at me. 'You wish to hold if for me, Maroboodus? I must preserve my strength, and it is rather heavy.'

I glared at him as men laughed around us. 'My hands are frozen. Wouldn't want to make it even more insignificant, cousin.' Hulderic quaffed and looked ahead as his nephew glowered at the men around us.

'It's a fine thing,' he told me, 'and you should learn to respect a berserker. Gods love me, cousin, and you should not doubt them. They would not favor a man like they do, if I were armed with a small cock.' He turned away from me, unable to show his size after my insult and the men noticed that, and were laughing softly. I leaned over and slowly spat in his mug. The yellow snot fell true, though some of it landed on the rim and hung in there. He straightened, grabbed the mug and scowled at me. Then he walked back to Bero, drinking heartily. I felt very happy as Dubbe held his belly, chuckling like mad.

'You should not,' Hulderic said, hiding his mouth with his hand, trying not to laugh, 'antagonize him. He is not all well up there.' He tapped his

41

forehead. 'His brother Catualda is a saner specimen, but there is little Bero in Maino.'

'This was all Bero's idea,' I cursed. 'Standing here in the rain.'

Hulderic nodded. 'And Father agreed. We could have fought them in the cover of the woods, but we want to annihilate them. We have to hide here for a bit.' He glanced up the hill at the lord of the gau who nodded at Father. Hulderic was the steady spear in Friednot's hand, Bero a fair tactician. There were some six thousand people in our gaus, but most were responsible to defend their lands against the southern Goths, raiders from the sea, Svearna, and so the men we had would need to do. 'It's a good plan,' he added and nodded towards the great Saxon boats that could be seen jutting on a rocky beach. We saw their proud wooden noses over some woods and a stretch of the beach, beyond a palisade the Saxons had built to guard them. They had landed there, in a remote part of our land, but we had been lucky and a boy had seen them the evening before and their surprise was gone. There were men waking the area between the palisade and the boats and those men were not Saxons, but the men who had killed them. They were the men of the Black Goths, of Hughnot, Friednot's brother and the lord of north, the lesser of the two gaus. 'Hughnot was brave to send to many men to aid us with these dogs.'

'He happened to be in Marka,' I said. 'Of course he helps.'

Hulderic hummed. 'Friednot was worried about the Saxons, and there is something strange about them indeed. Its almost like he knew they were coming. The boy found them, but did he send the boys around looking for them? I think he did. Has been for a week or more,' Hulderic wondered and looked up at his father. 'He keeps secrets and holds spies and these Saxons made him very anxious. And that Hughnot is here, tells a story. They both have an interest in these Saxons and whatever they were doing here.'

I nodded. 'Hughnot fought well to take the stockade.'

He agreed. 'Uncle's men suffered ten losses in wounded, but they took it easy enough. Saxons were napping,' Hulderic said. Hughnot had some forty men and they would keep the ships and the palisade, and that would make things very interesting, when the Saxons arrived. 'Well, ours is to fight, and let your grandfather worry about the bigger issues. He will tell us in time.'

'It's a nice plan, I suppose,' I grumbled. 'But it should have been our plan.' I growled, as I looked Bero's way.

Hulderic eyed Bero. 'I've said it before. Respect Bero. He is not a warrior, son, but he is keen enough and close family. We will get our chance to shine,' he said with a smile. 'Just wait.'

'I'd shine sooner than later, Father,' I said.

'You *must* learn patience,' he said, and he said it with a tremble in his voice that led me to believe there was more to it than just trying to educate me. He was afraid. Of me? Surely not. He gave the horse away, to be led over the hill where Scald, my horse was and he did it just in time.

We did not need to wait any longer.

The scouts below twitched. We all saw it. They looked uncertain and then we saw a man rushing from the woods, waving his hands crazily. 'Kneel!' Hulderic commanded tersely. His men went on one knee, and then hid totally. Hulderic's standard of bear jaws was pulled down. Friednot's better-armed men above us followed suit as well and the standard-bearer was careful to hide the mighty artifact behind a tree. Bero's men were busy as they stumbled on their knees and elbows.

A crude laughter could be heard from the woods.

Then more. Men were talking and soon we saw three men wearing wolf skin coats walk the path. They were tall, lanky and blond men, obviously tired for the campaign they had been involved in. All had dark shields. Hulderic grunted. 'They didn't lie. It's Cuthbert, all right.' Cuthbert, a sea Saxon, a ruthless, battle-scarred chief of Bjarnheim, the islands of the southern lands, across the straits that separated Mare Gothonium and the sea to the west. *All* the men had huge, dark shields and that was the color of the enemy Thiuda, Cuthbert the Black. He had been raiding our coast from across the sea for years, every spring, summer and sometimes even fall. This time he had landed on the fringes of the Gothoni powerbase and had gone to sack the great hill forts and trading villages of the Svearna, but he would not leave.

A man pulled at Hulderic. Father turned to look at him, puzzled and I saw Bero was being similarly instructed. 'There will be a woman with them,' the warrior said simply. 'You must—'

'Of course there will be women with them,' Hulderic growled. 'They have been raiding. They are slave-taking.'

'This will be a *special* woman. A high-born Svea. She must not leave the field, if some escape.' Hulderic gazed up at Friednot.

'Is this important?' Hulderic asked the man thinly. 'I cannot vouch—'

'She must not leave the field. Dead or alive, she must not be allowed out,' the man told Hulderic and disappeared back up the hill.

Hulderic grunted and adjusted his helmet. 'So, this is about a woman? There is something Friednot's not telling us about this war, and Hughnot is on to it, no doubt. Well, its for us to fight, not to dwell on. For now.'

More men pushed out of the woods. They were a savage-looking lot. They were muddy, their shoes were stuck with leaves and covered in mud, and mostly ripped at seams and many were barefoot. They all carried javelins and spears, their shields made hollow sounds as they hit each other while the column of men stumbled on. There were at least a hundred and fifty of them.

And they had prisoners. Slaves. Miserable Svea slaves, though perhaps there were some Goths amongst them, because they Saxons had passed through our lands as well, no matter how thinly populated.

Most were women, many were children, though there were no men amongst them. Thirty of them were carrying great bags full of loot, but very likely their only interest were the human prizes they had captured. We usually raided for cows and horses, the true wealth of any man but it was hard to transport such loot across the narrow sea.

And then there was the dreadful lord of the enemy.

It was Cuthbert himself. He was famed as a raider, a lord of a Saxon gau, and a noble of old Saxon blood and we all knew him. His standard of dark wolf's pelt flapped up and down amidst the trees, and the great, bald lord of the Saxon islands nearest to our lands was unhappily conversing with a woman of exceptional beauty. She did not answer him, but looked forward as if there was an annoying wind rustling by her ear. Her face was smudged, but otherwise she wore strangely pristine doeskin cloak and a gray tunic of fine make. Her fibula—the brooches holding her tunic on each shoulder—were of silver and her shoes were made of sheepskin. It must have been the woman Friednot wanted. Dead or alive.

Her face was striking. I could not help staring at her.

Her skin was pale as the fresh snow and her long, braided hair was nearly black, as black as the ravens of the deeper woods. She was a high noble, that much was clear and the suffering slaves that were being pushed for the ships were likely her subjects. Cuthbert sat on his horse, talking to her harshly, and as she still did not acknowledge him, he finally toed her so that she stumbled, before leaving her to walk in peace. Her eyes glanced furiously at the high Saxon lord, and her eyebrows were raised in a rage that made men in the Saxon ranks close around the lord. There was a look of such goddess-like rage on her face, the lord should have fallen from his horse, dead, that very moment. Instead, Cuthbert just spat at her feet. There was angry rumbling amongst the men, even if the Svear were not exactly friends to the Gothoni. Many former Goth women lived in the Saxon lands now and we would not forgive the slavers our losses. Suebian knots, the elaborate hair braids bobbled in our hidden shieldwall and the men spoke to each other with subdued, harsh tones and I almost felt sorry for Cuthbert then.

The army below us was strong, though.

And I felt fear. Yes, Maroboodus who would become a legend later in his life, feared.

We were slightly outnumbered. Cuthbert had brought a sizable number of his men to the field. The outcome of the battle was anything but certain.

I glanced at Maino. He was joking with some of the warriors. Bero was whispering to his champions and Hulderic, Father was speaking with his three most accomplished fighters as well, all glad in leather and furs and holding heavy axes. We watched the enemy scouts wind their way for the coast, obviously drunk. The army followed them, shuffling along in the strange, thick column, bristling with spears, the prisoners in the middle.

'Try to spare her, if you can,' Hulderic said softly. 'She looks important.'

'She does, lord,' said Dubbe, and I was jealous as his lips were smacking lecherously. 'Important was not the first thing that came to my mind, though, lord.'

'Sultry,' Sigmundr suggested.

'Shapely,' Harmod grunted. 'Like my wife used to be, before she gave birth.'

'You are a bastard, Harmod,' Hulderic chortled. 'But spare her, no matter what she looks like.'

'She looked beautiful,' I said and bit my lip as the men gaped at me with astonishment. Then they jeered me softly, so as not to alert the men below. 'She did,' I added, after they had finally shut up.

Soon, the last of the Saxons walked away from under our hill. They would reach the beach in a bit and our scouts ran to see if there were stragglers. There would be. 'Doesn't matter now,' called out Friednot from behind us. He was leading his men to us. 'Let's get down there and close off the escape route.' We got up, and Friednot led his men to the middle of Bero's and ours and we walked down the muddy hill in ranks. The rain was coming down in a pour now and limited our visibility from bad to nearly zero. 'God's should weep for their souls,' Friednot laughed as he cursed the rain, 'but they are premature. The dogs live still. Let's enjoy this, and give the god's tears some bloody meaning.' We walked on, thick in the lines, pushing each other. Men fell, and so they took down some others and many cursed profusely. The warband didn't look very glorious during that decent, and perhaps the gods wept for our ineptness as we slid more than walked down that hillside. There were some yells in woods to our left and a ragged group of tardy Saxons came running out. Some were bleeding and I knew the local villagers had done their bit well enough.

'They are herding the dogs now,' Hulderic said, and he was right. Javelins flew after the stragglers and the vanguard of the Saxons. Most missed, some hit and three of the enemy went down, screaming. The rest, some eight men saw us and headed for us, and pointed their spears at the woods, yelling gutturally, thinking we were with Cuthbert.

'They think we are their kin,' Dubbe chortled. 'Oh, they will learn a hurtful truth in a bit.'

46

'Kill them. It's our job,' Hulderic said coolly to his men, as the enemy was close to us. We turned that way, thickened into a column—a cunus resembling a boar's tusk—with Hulderic as a deadly tip and I was at the rear. The enemy slowed down, cheering as they saw us coming but then some spotted our strange standard and one, cleverer than the others, noticed our hair knots.

They had no chance.

Javelins flew at them, several of the unlucky Saxons howled in pain and we spread to chase the last ones. Hulderic roared at one who turned to fight and spears flashed as the long-faced enemy tried to impale Father from under the shield. Father had none of it, but bowled the enemy over with his shield and then his spear flashed down at the kicking corpse, puncturing his belly. The man shuddered and prayed and wept and died, and we stopped after the small skirmish. 'One got away,' I hissed, ashamed, for I had not even gotten close to the enemy. 'One ran there to the woods.'

'Doesn't matter. The villagers will have him,' Hulderic said happily, his beard wet with blood as well as rainwater. 'Run after Friednot.' We jogged after the advancing column of the Gothoni and we were panting when we reached them at the woods' edge, the one separating the beach from the hills. We plunged in, our hearts racing and on the rain-beaten beach, there was chaos.

Some hundred and fifty Saxons were milling in confusion, as there was a block of Gothoni guarding the doorway to their ships. The three Saxon scouts were on their faces by the gate and a huge man, Hughnot, was making mocking dancing steps before his troops. His standard was behind him, one of dark, dead crows.

'You wish to live?' Cuthbert was screaming, sitting on his horse. 'You have come to the wrong place to have a dance! Are you lost, perhaps? Give me back my fucking ships, and perhaps you can go home and weep with your rancid women, Hughnot!'

'You, lord of tears,' Hughnot was laughing, 'will sleep under the stars this night. You'll be alone and afraid, and the crabs will have your

47

coward's heart! I'll shine your bald head, you filth, after you are dead. I'll take the skin and stretch it on my shield. I'll shit in the skull, too.'

Cuthbert turned his horse and his men rippled in anger. He was pointing his ax at Hughnot's forty Black Goths. The pirate was utterly enraged, spittle flying and the horse echoed his master's mood. It was dancing around madly, its eyes huge and ears flattened on the sides, perhaps sensing our presence, but it was wiser than its master. The Saxons yelled raucous encouragements to each other. There were few men with strange coats of feathers and they strutted forward. 'Damned vitka,' Hulderic said somberly. 'And ours died in the winter.'

'Friednot's will do,' I said.

'They are useless as a bent cock,' Dubbe spat.

'Theirs will die today,' Maino laughed from nearby. 'I'll slit their spines and lick at the marrow.'

'Spare them, if you see them,' Bero hissed at his son. 'They are holy men. We are Gothoni, the first men and will act like it.'

'Probably the only time I agree with the ham-faced bastard,' I muttered, meaning Maino. I hated and feared the priests. I glanced at Bero's hand. There was Draupnir's Spawn, the family ring, old as time and rumored to be given to the first humans by Woden, to Aska and Embla. The Gothoni, the Suebi tribes across the seas, revered it even. Our lost family in islands of Gothonia wanted it back. It was as magical as the spells of vitka, but I could at least understand its power. It was real. I would have used it, I thought, to stomp the Saxons into the cracks of the riverbed in *their* lands, not ours.

But that was not to be. It would be Maino's next, just like it had been Friednot's over Hughnot. Maino would always be above me. I could not stomach the thought and bile rose to my throat.

The enemy was chanting now. They were banging their spears on their shields and some were herding the prisoners to the side. Hughnot was laughing at the vitka, and showed them his hairy ass, before marching disdainfully to stand with his men. Some javelins flew after him, one shuddered in the palisade. The enemy shrieked, lifted their shields, slammed them together and walked forward with a tromp of heavy feet.

Some broke off to climb the palisade on the sides, but Cuthbert was taking his best men forward in a thick column and the Black Goths cheered them on, mocking their efforts, tightening across the palisade's opening, ferocious, shield over shield, spears ready, vastly outnumbered, but not by valor.

'Wish they'd hurry it up,' Friednot said as he was dismounting. 'I have not eaten since early morning. This is a bloody nuisance.' He looked calm, but there was something in his eyes that belied nervousness. The enemy was more numerous, but not by much. We had an advantage of surprise. All should have been well. Yet, the great man was nervous and then three ravens flew across our troops, and that made him serious and silent. The vitka looked away, avoiding Friednot's eyes. The Thiuda slapped Osgar, his champion on the back of his head. 'Bastards. Yellow damned bastards. We shall go and kill them. Fear nothing. We cannot get them in any better place than this.'

'Yes, Father,' Bero said, his voice thin as he stood twisted to the side a bit, as was his way. 'Straight in?'

'No need for a plan, son,' Grandfather said, assuring the men around him. 'Straight into their thin backs. Split the necks, spear the backs, and rout them to Hel and have them drink tears.'

The enemy cheered, as if to deny Friednot's brave words.

They charged.

Swift javelins and stones flew from Hughnot's troop to rip out the worst brunt of the charging Saxon mass. We didn't see them hit, but a chorus of pained shrieks told us many found their marks in the enemy ranks and here and there, a head disappeared to be trampled under the men behind. Most found shields, some flesh and there was a lot of confusion with the Saxon troops as wounded and dying men hampered the column. Spears and javelins flew back and forth as the troops closed and now Hughnot's Gothoni were also falling, gaps appearing on the shield ranks.

'Charge!' yelled Friednot with a thrilling voice, his standard of flayed skin flapped under the gray sky. He drew his sword, the Head Taker, and we went on, wild and mad and cheered ourselves hoarse.

The Saxons were near oblivious to our attack. Their Thiuda, Cuthbert had had a bad day, a serious lapse in his normal cunning, and that's what Bero had suggested would happen, when the enemy king saw his beloved ships taken. The ones guarding the prisoners turned to look at our wild troop, their mouths open, unable to respond, but that was all. The rest did not notice, as they were shouting like mad, concentrated on Hughnot. There was a thundering sound as shields met shields, spears thrust down and up and men fell. The Black Goths took a step back, another, under the terrible pressure, but then the men gritted their teeth, and pushed back at the Saxons, who had been marching for days, fighting and were half starved. Screams of pain drifted across the beach and I was sure I heard Hughnot's voice shout out a filthy challenge to Cuthbert.

We rushed to the back of the enemy. 'Ready javelins!' yelled Bero thinly as we ran.

'Pummel them! Then straight at them!' yelled Friednot. 'Throw javelins when in range, and then rip the bastards in half!'

'Follow me!' shrieked Hulderic, as his men tightened into a boar's tusk behind him.

We all stopped for just a moment, javelins were hoisted by those who held them, men drew them back and let go, cheering gleefully as the missiles flew like a flight of deadly sparrows, grabbed another and let them go as well, and we went on with our framea. The missiles hit the Saxon back, men mostly not ready for such a surprise. A dozen or so, then twenty or more went down in a rattle of shields, pushing on to the backs of their friends, causing terrible chaos. Friednot's and Bero's men also bunched into arrow-shaped columns and charged over the dead and dying, trampled over the wounded and crashed into the rapidly turning and readying, shocked to its core, but bigger enemy column. A haphazard shieldwall was facing us, led by a tall, scarred Saxon with a seax and a round shield. Hulderic bashed into the wall, his men followed him and the cunus penetrated deep, bowling over bleeding Saxons, gouging inside the ranks, reaching the men who didn't expect the battle from behind. Men were punching their framea over the backs of the first rank, then axes and clubs joined the fray and we slowly spent our rage on the enemy shields

50

and skulls. Friednot's and Bero's men did the same and soon, too soon we had flattened into a ragged shield wall facing another.

Saxons didn't die easily, not by far.

They knew the dead would be left unburied, the wounded would be sacrificed to Woden and Donor and the few lucky ones would end up prisoners and slaves. We stabbed at them with the ferocity of the jotuns, hacked madly in the terrible chaos, and pushed savagely and they did as well. I was in the third rank, and men left and right of me pushed into the holes that came to be as the wall lived, or when men died. I saw Dubbe and Sigmundr stand next to each other, guarding Hulderic's back, slashing axes at Saxon skulls, ripping them out, then repeating the deadly chops at the panting, scared enemy who were pushed to stop them by their friends. Somewhere Hughnot screamed in triumph, and his warlords, Ingo and Ingulf, and son Hrolf were probably doing terrible harm to Cuthbert's best men. I cursed and feared so hard I wanted to piss my pants, and begged Woden for mercy so I would not. I saw Maino raging with Bero's champions on the left. He pushed between two tall Saxons, and hacked left and right in berserker frenzy, his eyes wild and mouth foaming. He was bleeding from a shallow wound on his shoulder but otherwise he seemed unhurt. 'Donor! Smite them in between their shifty eyes!' he was hollering. 'Between their eyes!' he kept yelling, a ferocious, nearly hysterical note in his voice.

A Goth fell before me. His face was battered by a rock and he crawled away to moan in the mud next to me. Sigmundr pushed me from the side. 'Take the place in the second rank. Stab at anything armed and ugly! Except Dubbe!' The fat champion was near, grunting as two Saxons were trying to pull his shield away, unsuccessfully, and I knew he was laughing at Sigmundr's words.

Before me, in the exhausted and bleeding first rank stood a Goth who held on to his battered shield. He had no weapons, but kept blocking two young Saxons. They kept trying to hack and stab at the man with clubs and a stub of a spear, but he held his place stubbornly. I was hovering over his shoulder, trying to find an opening, despairing, but then, when one of the Saxons got frustrated and stepped too close, the Goth grabbed the man's

51

wrist expertly and pulled the Saxon to his shield. That was my chance and I used it. I rammed the heavy killing spear in the young face. His eyes grew huge as he saw me lunging, he tried to dodge, but could not as the Goth held on to him and so my spear slid into his throat. It was hard to understand how fast, how effortless it was. There was a gaping maw as he screamed; the tip was under the skin, blood came out of it. He was mortally wounded, his eyes red, full of despair and fear. He lived, hanging on to the spear, and then the living thing turned into a sack of rotting meat. He was a shuddering corpse at our feet, on his way to Valholl.

'Well done, boy!' the man before me yelled. At that point, a savage, tall Saxon killed a man who had been covering the Goth before me, and that spelled doom for us. The tall Saxon turned his spear to the unarmed Goth from his now uncovered right side, and the man who had fought so well for us gritted his teeth as he tried to step away, but bumped into me, and so the Saxon with a club struck him across face. His head flew back, teeth flying, and there was a strange look of confusion of a man dying as he fell at my feet. Another Goth to my right screamed as a seax cut to his knee. He fell and was hacked to pieces by a fat Saxon and his ax. And that left me a first ranker, as I was pushed to straddle the fallen man. The ax man raised his blood-spattered face to me and so did the club hoisting one. We all looked at each other, all bewildered, flushed in the throng of battle, spattered by blood, mud and reeling from the stench of sweat and piss. Then the ax man charged, hoping I'd be too terrified to react, and perhaps I looked like I was about to run. Instead, I braced the spear and he ran right into it. It did not go deep, but deep enough to make him scream like an animal. I shook in shock as he slid away from the weapon. I had killed again. I had *earned* my shield. The club Saxon had stepped away.

Something happened up ahead. Men screamed happily, others screamed hate and defiance. Either Hughnot had died, or perhaps Cuthbert, or some greater champion everyone knew.

Hulderic was near me, and his spear was all bloodied and so was his arm to the shoulder. He and the men of our villages were pushing, then hacking, pushing, and hacking and slowly, very slowly the enemy gave room. Men fell; the Saxons were being pushed from the sides and every direction now. I held my spear, wounding men, pushing them as they stood before me, some turning to push away through the braver Saxons. Dark shields were broken, weapons were spent, and then the Saxon chief, seeing the fear in his men's eyes, decided to turn the fates. He was a toothless man with a huge jaw, golden beard with silver rings and a brooding forehead, and he resembled a spirit-taken maniac as he danced away from the first rank near me and went hunting. He had lost his seax, but had found an ax. He was after important prey. He pushed into the second ranks of the Saxons, got stuck with his shield in the press of battle, abandoned it, jerking it off brutally from his arm. He was eyeing Friednot's skin banner, not far, jumping and reaching across his men's backs to see our lord. 'Look out! Dubbe!' I screamed, but the warrior was heaving with the enemy, so was Harmod next to him, strangling a man in the mud. *Osgar and Ludowig were there to protect Grandfather*, I decided, prayed, and fought a young Saxon whose shield had fallen apart and hung around his wrist. I kept glancing Grandfather's way, feeling something terrible was about to happen. I saw Friednot's horsehair helmet, not far in the line as he was pushing at Saxons, trying to slay a wounded man with the Head Taker, sawing it across the man's face. Then he was swinging the great sword in the limited space, but it was not taking heads as the enemy was so close, instead it was splintering shields, spear shafts and carving flesh. Then, a Saxon fell, and the tall chief appeared, as if by a miracle of galdr song magic of a mighty vitka. The Saxon prayed, I saw it. Osgar saw him, but hesitated, his shield down. The Saxon threw his ax. It spun in the air, missing men's heads, but it did not miss Friednot. Grandfather's battle ended midswing, and his thick, near neckless head jerked to the side as the ax hit true and he was badly hurt, we all could see that. Osgar's face was one of grim acceptance. There was a great wound in Friednot's cheek, running to his throat and bone could be seen glinting amidst bloody flesh.

He fell on his back, clutching his sword and disappeared from our sight.

Maino screamed a challenge. Ludovicus as well, stabbing at Saxons, who were jubilant at the fall of the great Goth. Osgar was bent over Friednot, finally guarding the fallen Thiuda. The enemy chief was laughing amidst the Saxon lines, mocking Friednot's valor and turned to move away. He was again passing the man fighting me. I shrieked in hate, and stabbed the man with a broken shield so hard the spear went through him. I pulled him away, saw the Saxon troops scattering. 'Maroboodus! Wait!' Hulderic yelled.

'You wait!' I screamed and rammed my spear thorough another man's shield, and kept it there, pushing him, and he was stuck with the blade. He pushed back, looked terrified, fought to discard the shield, but could not stop me from coming and the blade went to his belly. I stepped on the shield, ripped off the spear, danced over the wounded, screaming man. There was no longer a Saxon shieldwall there to stop me. It just fell apart. It happened so fast. Despite Friednot's fall, the enemy had suffered too much. There was chaos, and men were falling, rolling in mud and blood and guts, some were vomiting, others surrendering and then I saw the tall Saxon chief run across my vision. Maino was hot on his heels, his beefy face flushed red with anger and likely blood and he was reaching for the enemy chief. The man looked back to my cousin, scared.

And I stepped in front of him and placed the spear under his chest.

He ran straight into it, let out a small, child-like moan and fell like a sack of leeks on his side.

Maino looked at me incoherently as I stooped over the man, reaching for his furs and ring mail. 'His gear is mine,' he hissed.

I spat at his feet. 'Does the Sunna shine when it is night? Can you possibly understand what I'm asking? No? It is like talking with my ass. You did *nothing* to deserve anything of his.' I hissed and stepped on the corpse and stood there defiantly, feeling strangely brave and fey.

'He was afraid of *me*!' Maino roared. 'Me, not a pup of a lesser brother!'

I shook my head at him, the spear pointed his way and that was not lost on him as he gaped at me in disbelief. 'Probably thought you were an ugly troll out to hump him. *I* killed him. You can go and impale yourself.' He stood there, indecisive and then waves of men pushed into us, most Saxons bent on running. I slashed and stabbed around me and then, suddenly, there were none to kill and wound. The last of the Saxons streamed past us and ran along the coast for north and south. I contemplated on resuming my looting activity, but then I saw something more important.

Cuthbert was in the midst of the group going for north.

Dubbe ran after him. I saw Sigmundr struggling with fatigue as he tried to give chase. Black Goths pointed at the tall Saxon lord, standing still in the palisade, a heap of corpses before them and Hrolf, son of Hughnot was screaming harsh orders for a chase under his raven wing standard.

But we were the fastest, closest ones.

There was no cohesion in the rainy pursuit. Men ran after men, all tired, many wounded and rocks, spears, clubs, and axes hacked into men's backs. Warriors fell, theirs and ours. There were perhaps sixty of us chasing, thirty of them and then I saw Cuthbert dragging at the fine, incredibly beautiful woman. I ran his way without thinking about it twice. I dodged fighting men and unhappy prisoners, stumbled on the wounded, and saw Hughnot trying to catch the enemy king, perhaps unaware Friednot was hurt.

Cuthbert knew his danger, his best men milled around him and he pulled himself on the fine horse of his. He dragged the struggling woman before him, spat at us and hit the flanks of the fine beast. He turned to spit our way and screamed defiance. 'Friednot, son of a pig, a pig yourself, die, if not today, then soon!' Spears and rocks flew around them. A Saxon fell with a howl, holding his face, and a small shieldwall they had erected to cover their lord's escape was bowled over and ripped apart by enraged Goths.

I flipped my sticky spear in my hands, and saw how Cuthbert would have to cut left to avoid some fleet footed Black Goths. *He would have to turn*, I thought, *and I'd be ready*, I decided, and waited for the opportunity.

Cuthbert's horse steered to the left.

'Woden, let it miss her,' I breathed, and threw the missile.

My spear flew. It thrummed and spun in the air, rain touching it. It went over men's heads, nearly hit another flying spear and then went down.

It sunk in the lord's side, and he slapped at it, instinctively, breaking the shaft, his eyes huge with surprise.

Then Cuthbert shrieked and threw his hands to his sides. The woman fell heavily, the bald chief of the Saxons fell forward and clung to his horse's mane and then slid from the horse's back and landed with a splash and a muted, pained scream. I grabbed my sturdy club, raised my shield and charged.

Cuthbert cursed on the ground, he cried with terrible pain, and his bodyguards, his sworn men, his last surviving oaths men streamed for him. So did the Goths. Dubbe killed a man. Hrolf was near, stabbing repeatedly at a man's belly, and Ludovicus was ripping a shield off a thin Saxon. We tore into the enemy and most of them died around Cuthbert's writhing body. We swarmed them, the brave Saxons dying for their lord's honor as they had sworn to do, seeking to keep him company in Valholl. A Gothoni pushed between two such tall champions, pushed one at me and I swung my club on the back of his head, and he fell, forgotten. I wanted Cuthbert. I wanted him so bad, I could taste his blood in my mouth. We *all* wanted him, and perhaps I already had him with my spear, but I wanted the honor and the men watching as I, Maroboodus, the son of a *lesser* brother killed a king. I ran over a fallen Saxon and jumped. I landed on Cuthbert's back and hacked down with the weapon, seeing the man's eyes flicker over his shoulder with fear.

My soul sang with happiness. I'd kill the terrible enemy of our people. My fame would soar like a hawk in a morning sky, and if Aldbert survived, I'd have him sing my song until my ears bled. Then he would travel to Maino's hall in Marka, and sing it there until they wept for mercy.

Then I flew over his body, as someone had slammed me with a shield.

I landed heavily, lost all the air in my lungs and struggled to my fours, gasping. I groped for the club, ready to defend myself, but it was not a Saxon oaths man who had attacked me, but a Goth.

Maino was standing over my prey and before anyone could stop him, he axed Cuthbert in the throat. He grinned at me, his meaty face a mask of mocking victory as he hit the chief again, finally killing him. He growled like a wolf, yapped like a dog, kicked the enemy hard and then he turned to the beautiful woman, who was not afraid at all as she slowly climbed to her feet. He grabbed her roughly and held on to her hand like he would hold a chunk of ham. 'Mine! Mine brothers! Maino's, the slayer of Cuthbert.'

They cheered him wildly, and the lie poisoned my heart, filled my belly with acid and I didn't have to think at all on what I would do.

I got up, grabbed Cuthbert's ax and stepped forward. The woman's eyes followed me and Maino's eyes followed hers and enlarged with surprise, as I slammed the weapon hilt-first in his face. He fell like a log. There was blood on the sand and he was moaning, holding his forehead, his legs thrumming on the sand. There was a silence around me, save for the shrieks of the wounded, but the woman stepped closer to me and smiled. She was so beautiful, pale as a sunny winter morning, but her lips were red and full and I could not look away. It was as if she was trying to thank me, perhaps to make a plea, and I was not sure what it was, but I already knew I'd do almost anything for her.

A shadow fell across me. Hughnot was there, looking at the carnage. His eyes were relieved as he saw Cuthbert was dead and then he looked at me with an upraised eyebrow. I pointed a quivering finger at the body of the Saxon thiuda. 'I killed Cuthbert. I did. That's my spear point in his side. I threw it, I felled him. Like I did that other chief. I took his life, and Maino's a damned liar.' Some men who had seen it, rumbled agreement, but not all.

Bero hesitated, looked at Hulderic who shrugged. It was my fight, apparently. The twisted lord stepped forward. 'Maroboodus did *not* kill him. No matter who took Cuthbert down, Maino's strike took his life. Maino deserved the honor and took the life like a man, like my son. Maroboodus has to pay for the insult. I say he loses the loot he thinks is his. Then he will tell Maino how sorry he is. His attack was a coward's strike. Maino's honor demands humility from Maroboodus, not lies and insults.' He turned to Hulderic, his voice quaking. 'I am sorry, brother.' Hulderic looked resigned, and said nothing, his thoughts hidden under sweat, blood, and a frown.

'We will decide these things later. Friednot, Father is dead,' he said.

Hughnot nodded heavily. Bero rubbed his face, shocked.

But there was a small, though brief smile on Hughnot's face. And he also looked at the woman covetously.

CHAPTER 2

Father sat on his well-carved seat as Erse, his pretty slave and Ingild, Grandmother sowed his wounds. I sat and sampled mead as his men feasted in the hall next to us, their voices heard, though softly as Grandfather was dead and they had lost friends. Aldbert, his long hair brushing the table, hiding his face, was seated on the side, rubbing his temples as he tried to figure out a song to celebrate the great lord's life. 'How goes it, Aldbert?' Hulderic grunted and then hissed with pain as Ingild's old, but deft fingers stitched up his forearm.

The young man looked startled and grasped a horn and pushed away a plate full of bones, our recent meal. 'I am trembling to claim I know your father, lord. I am hesitant to say it will be good enough to honor his memory. Woden will blink, he will cry but not from pride, if I fail.'

'Let Woden cry, boy,' Hulderic said gruffly. 'Your poem will do just fine, and will do Friednot honor.' His eyes turned to me and he sighed heavily. I didn't budge. Since we returned home to Timberscar, carrying our fallen, he had avoided speaking with me. I fumed for a day, humiliated by what had happened. Maino, *Maino* had been given Cuthbert's weapons. And Hulderic had let go of the ring mail and fabulous seax of Ulbrect, the Saxon warlord who had killed Friednot. They would be burned with Grandfather, and the sooty lumps of iron would accompany him to the grave mound. I heard Maino suggest this, after they had argued who had earned the armor. I had, *I* had earned them, like they said Maino earned Cuthbert's gear. He got his, gods would get Ulbrect's. *Bastards.* The fine mail would be given to Woden, the god who surely had far too many dverg-crafted weapons to begin with and I'd wear a tunic to battle again.

Gods, curse even Hulderic, Father who had not budged a muscle when I was robbed. I sat and stared back at him, feeling the stirrings of a violent argument in the air and so did Grandmother who had stopped sewing the wound, and stared at her son. 'Let the boy be,' Ingild said softly.

Hulderic did not oblige her. 'I wonder, Aldbert, what song will you sing of my son Maroboodus? What grand poem of idiocy will you sing of him when Maino wants to get satisfaction? He'll not settle for a simple "I am sorry, my lord". He will want my boy on his knees.'

Aldbert shook his thin shoulders many times, stuttering. 'He fought well.'

'Short poem that,' Hulderic laughed bitterly, but gave an approving nod. 'But I guess better than some that were made that day.'

I got up and leaned on the table. 'I didn't even see Aldbert in the battle. Hiding behind a tree, no doubt. I—'

Hulderic slammed a hand on the seat and cursed, as Erse's fingers slipped during the final stiches. 'Stay still, you wool-smelling goat-brain,' she hissed.

Hulderic looked to the rafters of the hall. He mocked me. 'But *I* killed the chief. I killed *two* chiefs. *I* rescued her. It's so wrong! It's unjust! It's a damned shame!' he mimicked me, and I bit my tongue as he stole my words, nearly exactly as I had imagined uttering them.

'All of that is true, thank you, Father,' I said so coldly, he should have been a shuddering lump of blue-lipped meat. He was not and his face was red from anger, in fact. 'And why didn't you stand up for me? Dubbe would have. Harmod and Sigmundr as well—'

'Harmod,' he said icily, 'would *not* have. Dubbe and Sigmundr would have slammed their shields with their spears, calling out the lies like the messengers of Tiw, god of justice, but Harmod would have stroked his dammed beard, and he would have made so very sure we do not suffer needlessly. Patience would have served us well. A Thing should have decided this and it would have, perhaps, judged your claim just. He struck you from behind. Everyone saw it. You *were* the wronged party. You lost your temper. Then you were not the wronged party. You fool.'

'Why didn't you—'

'*My* father died, Maroboodus!' he yelled. My eyes went to Grandmother. Friednot had lived two days away to north with Bero, she lived with us, and there was no sign of sorrow on her face. What had happened between them years past was hard to say, and she never mentioned it. Some, evil tongues, wagged it was a split over another woman, but such a thing was unthinkable and would have resulted in a trial, though Friednot might have been powerful enough to dodge any repercussions for breaking the sensible rules and laws of the gods.

'*Grandfather* died, Father,' I agreed softly. He nodded, mollified and reprimanded as I had also lost family. 'And *I* avenged him. I did.'

'Maino was after him,' he sighed. 'You both had a part to play in the death of that man. Try not to be as damned stupid as your cousin, or you have no high horse to sit on.'

I sat there and shuffled my feet; staring at the burning shingles set on the pillars of old oak. There were some fires in the fire pit and a stallion was neighing in the stables, apparently unhappy about some rival of his for the attention of the mares. I let the sounds and sights calm me, and spoke only when my voice was steady. 'I wanted to kick his teeth in, Father. Why do we always bow out of confrontations with your brother? That is a very simple question, but one I never hear answered.'

Hulderic slapped his knee. 'Your valor was unquestioned. I saw you. They all saw you. It was well done, Maroboodus, smartly done, he ran right into your spear. It was not a raging battle of two stubborn bears going at each other, but a wise, immensely wise way to kill the bastard. You have to be careful, son, and think ahead when you choose battles.'

'How does that answer—'

Aldbert groaned, despairing, as I was unable to read what Hulderic was saying. The two women stared at me with some incredulity. 'So,' I breathed. 'You are saying you choose your battles.'

'I choose your battles as well,' he growled. 'I *have* to support Bero.'

'Why?'

'Why? Why?' he recited. 'Because, bone skull, Father loved Bero better. And we have enemies all over the place. The Boat-Lord is looking for any excuse to grab Draupnir's Spawn and our trade.'

'Why does he hate us? Who is he, even? I know he is a relative, but—'

He snapped his fingers. 'Matters not who he is. And he hates us, because Friendnot and Hughnot escaped his power. He resents that. He never wanted to see them go, especially with the ring. And he is not our only enemy, no. Svearna have been co-operating and might not trade with us soon. To our south, other Goths are no allies. Ketil of Moosegrave might one day find a need for our fields, women, and ships. If I had challenged Bero against Friednot's wishes these long years, Maroboodus, then Friednot would have been forced to hurt us. Because he would have had to keep us united. Puss and rot is removed before it kill you.'

'Bah,' I uttered, unwisely again.

He sighed. 'And there is more. Hughnot, my boy, might be happy to see us fight each other. Never, ever, put us in such a situation for simple yearning for fame and honor, and that stupid, damned ring.'

Grandmother grunted. 'It's a real treasure of the gods, boy.' She meant Hulderic by the word "boy", not me. 'Do not mock the ring, or you will put a curse on us.'

'I'll not,' he said with a sheepish voice and addressed me again. 'Now you were wronged. But Maino beat you to Cuthbert. He did. If you don't keep an eye out in battle, boy, you get stomped like a drunken fool. You got cocky.'

Aldbert chipped in. 'He wanted to save the princess.'

Hulderic rubbed his face. 'Poets. Always seeing women—'

'I did want to save her,' I stated bluntly.

He whistled. 'So, you liked her smile. Wait, she didn't smile.'

'She smiled to *me*,' I informed him smugly.

'The girl did not need such rescuing. Her fate is not to marry a man she loves. She is a high noble. And more, she is not of us. Svearna are no friends to the Goths, even if some trade fox furs with us. They do not love us, we do not love them, and I shall not ask what you planned to do with her.'

'She would have left the field, against Friednot's wishes,' I stated. 'I stopped them. But yes, I had a plan for her. A simple, selfish plan.'

He waved his hand. 'Fine. You stopped her from disappearing, and yes, well done. But what—'

'I planned to marry her, Father,' I said and looked up to avoid the eyes that stared at me in stupefied silence. I wasn't sure I had told them the truth, but I felt the need to shock them and perhaps it had been the truth? She was special, very special.

Hulderic was massaging his temples. 'So, Maino put his hands on the girl of your dreams. Gods above. He stripped of your honor *and* a wife, eh?'

'Perhaps?'

He roared. 'I'll find you a girl to marry! Like it is with her, you are a noble. And you will marry as I wish!' Grandmother was looking sternly at my father, and finally Hulderic growled, somewhat subdued. 'I'll pick a fine girl.' His eyes went to Erse, who smiled back and he actually blushed. I noticed Aldbert frowning at the exchange. Hulderic shook his shoulders, speaking dreamily. 'It shall be a girl that serves the family interests, perhaps from the Gothoni islands, and you shall marry that one. Why would you think otherwise? Marry a Svea? No!'

Aldbert chortled. 'She was a rare looking girl.' His smile froze as Hulderic's animal eyes turned to bore a hole in him. He stammered. 'So they say. I can't see very well. Probably very plain and boring looking doe, after all.'

'Shut up, poet,' Hulderic growled. 'Concentrate on your sad songs or you will sleep in the stables with the dogs. They'll teach you to yap.' Indeed, there were at least six large dogs in the hall, eyeing us curiously, hoping for something to gnaw on.

I shook my head at the young singer and sipped my mead. 'So, Father. What now? You expect me to dance before Maino like a trained bird, hopping from one foot to another to amuse his crude, evil little mind? And who will rule the gau?' Father had mentioned Hughnot.

Hulderic shook his arms to be rid of the probing fingers and Grandmother and the servant stood up and went to sit on the side. 'Who?' he asked, amused. 'Now you finally think like a leader. That is the question, is it not? That's why you will bow to Maino. Bero shall rule. And as I said before, now is not the time to be quarrelsome, boy.'

I slammed my hand on the table so hard a horn broke and fell to the dust in pieces, dripping the drink to the floorboards where a slinking, brown dog lapped at it while keeping a careful eye on me. I got up and pointed a quivering finger towards the north, where Bero ruled. 'Not time to be quarrelsome, Father? Bero? He holds Draupnir's Spawn. I bet he takes the Head Taker as well?' I saw it in his eyes. He would. I went on, my voice thin with rage. 'He has wealth, more than we do. If Grandfather is gone, why should it be Bero? Because it's just so? Who will get the Saxon ships? The slaves? Shall we even get a fair choice or shall they leave us with the sickly wounded and near floundering tubs?'

'We will get our share,' Hulderic said mildly, but there was fire burning in his eyes. 'Are you saying I am letting them fool myself? And yes, he has wealth, more than we do, but it's not because I am weak, but because Friednot favored *him*. It's not Bero's fault. Do you think I'm weak?'

I opened my mouth to say exactly that, but closed it instead with a clacking sound that echoed in the hall.

'He is,' Aldbert said, and had a terrified look on his face as he realized he had echoed his thoughts aloud. Maroboodus took his words as mine.

He growled. 'Fool. Utter and total fool. You disdain me for being wise enough to know what my own strength is? What is my uncle Hughnot thinking about?'

I hesitated, feeling like a trout swimming in very shallow waters and Hulderic, a bear, his hair knot adorned with long fangs of such a beast was hungry. 'I have no idea what the seedy, rotten bastard is thinking about,' I mumbled. 'Women, like I am? His thoughts are beyond my care.'

'They are *not* beyond your care, fool. Friednot was his brother—'

'I understand family connections, Father. I have not been living here, wondering who Friednot was and why Hughnot looked a lot like him. I'm not like the Young Cilarg, forever smiling and nodding after he fell to the river and bashed in his damned skull on a bloody rock.'

He cursed and threw a mug my way. It spun in the light of the crackling shingles and the fires in the fire pit and hit me squarely in the forehead. I stumbled back into my seat. 'A fine aim, my lord,' Aldbert said happily, and Hulderic nodded in thanks. I bit my lip, for that had hurt, but I refused to give him the satisfaction of reacting.

'Boy,' he rumbled. 'Shut up or I'll have your rear whipped before Erse here.'

That got my attention. Erse was my age, pretty and lithe and I blushed at the thought of the indignity. She gave me a wicked grin under her bushy braided hair and I was sure she hoped I'd keep fighting Father. No, I wasn't prepared for that. 'I'm listening now.'

'Good,' Hulderic said and flexed his massive arms. 'Hughnot was always the *second* man in the alliance. He rules his gau, but it's not as strong as ours. Ever since they left the islands as young men, he had to follow, because Friednot had the ring and he had the men, and Hughnot had to be patient. He and Friednot were like Bero and I. Friednot was more powerful, and had the favor of *their* father, for a while at least. He was given the ring as he married first. He was allowed to carry the Head Taker. He had more cows, better ships, richer pastures, back in Gothonia islands and then also here. Friednot, Father, ruled this gau as nearly a king would, and Hughnot gave him his support, shared his ideas and guided our fortunes from the shadows. Hughnot grew his lands strong, but as the northernmost Goth he is weaker than we are. They have many problems with Svearna up there, enemy that is strong in ships and men. He grew sons, lost two, attracted champions, made sure he was always there to have a say in the matters and the Black Goths are nearly as strong as we are now. He was careful, he grew wisely and well and prospered and waited.'

He was silent and eyed me curiously, trying to see if I had any understanding of what he was saying. I did. *The Black Goths might be our enemy now?* There had always been something aloof about Hughnot, and his terribly powerful son Hrolf the Ax. In our feasts they sat separately, to the side, enjoyed their own jokes, applauded the performances a bit later than we did, and didn't complain. Was Hulderic truly right? 'I see,' I said sullenly.

He saw I finally understood. He walked away and slumped back to his seat. 'Now is not the time to start quarreling. I agree, son, that Bero has grown spoiled like a runt with a fresh honeycomb, licking it greedily and he is loath to share, but we are in this together, tethered on the same plow. We will go to the funeral and Hughnot will demand something in the Thing that follows. He will demand the rulership of *our* gau. He has waited long enough and his beard is not a young man's bushy brush any longer. He has bigger plans and he will damned well see them come to fruition. He will come to the feast, and he will sit there, gloating. He will look at his dead brother, spit in the funeral fumes and give gods thanks Friednot died. Then he will turn his eyes on us. In Bero, he sees weakness. In me? He doesn't know me. He knows I hanged fifteen Svearna last year, and left them in the woods to rot. He knows I am silent, second to Bero, and he, I hope, sees me as a nonentity, a fine sword but not the brains. Someone to ignore, perhaps? Gods, we are fucked if he thinks I'm a danger. He will do something and Bero and I? We have to be *one.* Hughnot is dangerous. And there are other things brewing.' He hesitated, but spoke on.

'The Boat-Lord, he is trying to ally with the Svearna.'

'What?' I blurted. 'Our enemy trying to ally with—'

'Our other enemy.'

'Yes,' I said, shaking my head, 'but how? What would—'

'Bero told me. He knew. Friednot knew about the Saxons from a spy in the court of the Boat-Lord. He also heard about the Thing of the Svea last year. The Boat-Loard has proposed an alliance, a marriage and this Svea was to marry him or someone he chose, since he is ancient and unable to bed a woman. The Saxons heard of it as well, since they spy like anyone, probably pay the same spies even, and Cuthbert likely wanted the girl so he might sell her to the Boat-Lord. Friednot saw the opportunity and wanted the woman to break up the alliance. This is why we went after the Saxons. They did not attack us, but it was a grand opportunity. And so, you will not marry her.'

'Who will?'

'Who?' he asked with a raised eyebrow.

'Yes, who?' I growled. 'I guess she stays with us, since she is so important?'

'Shut up. It wasn't really a question,' Hulderic growled back. 'Someone important. Someone with the stature of a warrior.'

'Not the so-called Cuthbert's Bane?' I asked, near hysteric with rage.

He ignored me. 'And now Hughnot sees the girl. He know the plans Friednot had for her. He will want to dictate everything as we hope to break this blossoming alliance between our enemy Goths and the Svea. Hughnot is not an idle ruler of his gau, and if we fight—'

'But—'

'Silence!'

'Let him speak,' Grandmother sighed. 'He is a big boy and—'

Hulderic ignored her. 'Maroboodus. It is simply stupid to start quarreling with Bero on how many of the Saxon ships comes to us, or what prisoners we took, or whose men were more valorous in the battle. Even over your honor. That is the way for Hughnot to start luring away our allies now that our enemies threaten. Bero and I will not bow to him. Many would, because they think we will do badly in this dire situation. That is the way Hughnot will slither into our halls. He will have reached out to Bero's lords, the old families already.'

'Why not join *him* and let Bero be the least of the family?' I snarled.

He smiled. 'You mean Maino.'

'I mean Maino, yes,' I agreed and Erse laughed softly. 'Be rid of him. Send him to the woods to eat old berries. Let me find joy as I think how many wolves are out there for him to worry about.'

He sighed. 'Listen. Just listen. I don't trust him. Hughnot. Never did. Friednot insisted we stop the Saxons and we would have, even if we had to do it with the men of our gau. Hughnot helped, but he had a lot of men available. Far more than he needed as he visited Marka, and was it a coincidence he was there at all? Did he know about he Saxons as well? How did he know? Does he pay for spies as well? At the very least he wanted a stake in the woman. Hughnot *was* very useful in the battle, yes, but now, finally, he is the eldest chief within our gaus. Maroboodus, I doubt Hughnot is the sort that shares power.'

'He might,' I growled.

Hulderic scowled. 'Now we make our own plans, Maroboodus. It's best one of us leads, Bero more naturally for he has the ring. And yes, the sword. We know each other, truly know. He listens to counsel, Bero does, if delivered in such a way to make him think he came up with the idea. We will keep *our* people intact, Hraban. Hughnot is family, but not as close as Bero and I. We shall not want a war. We need each other. We will strive to keep our two gaus allied, but if we cannot, we might have to wage a war. If I think I should *now* inherit Father's role in the gau, it will push Bero over the edge. We will be broken. Perhaps for real.' He seemed breathless after the rant.

'Do it fast,' I insisted.

'Do what fast?' he asked with a frown.

'Take Bero fast. Take his hall and his men and then plant your flag over the gau. Take him with surprise and then Hughnot has no time and no way to get our lands. The families will flock to you. Hughnot will deal with us carefully. You.'

'Us, you,' Hulderic smirked. 'You mean I should murder my brother.'

'I …'

'He does,' the poet whispered.

'Make it look like Hughnot did it,' I went on, gnashing my teeth and kicked Aldbert rather hard. 'Then take *his* gau.'

Hulderic shook his head sadly. 'Make it seem … you don't honestly think this would be a good idea?'

'I don't know, Father,' I said miserably. 'I'm just unhappy you don't seek power. Your goal in life is to hold Bero's cock when he pisses.' I blanched as I remembered Erse and what Hulderic had threatened me with, but he seemed saddened by my words rather than angered.

'I am heartbroken to see you have no more wisdom. Woden curses liars, Tiw hates lawbreakers, Freyr would call you dishonorable, should you kill a relative with no true cause but your soiled honor.'

'The gods have done worse,' I retorted. 'They murder, betray, deceive, even take women against their—'

'True,' the poet said.

Hulderic got up again. He walked over and leaned over me. My eyes followed him as he stared into my face, as if trying to find a familiar man he had known, but didn't see now. 'Tell your grandmother you wish to see Bero dead.'

Grandmother got up and I did not look at her, trying to force the words out. She walked to me and put a hand on my shoulder. 'You hate your cousin Maino. Not Bero. You hate and you fear him and you are so very impatient.'

'I loathe him,' I corrected her. 'I'd not hesitate to push him over a cliff and I'd shit over his body after. He humiliated me in front of the whole damned army. And in the Thing, he will demand more humiliation.'

'I'll talk to Bero about it,' Hulderic rumbled. 'He cannot alienate me. He knows Hughnot is dangerous now.'

I looked up at them. First Father, then Grandmother. 'I respect the gods, the family. Our honor. But I also think our family would be better if it were smaller. If Maino wishes to smear my face in wet mud, if he is no more prudent than I am—and he is not—then I'll not bow my head. If he wants to bend me over a table and make me, son of Hulderic, adeling of a noble house, humble, I'll slit his cock off. And he will try. He won't take cows and horses as wergild, he'll not listen to Bero, but he will call me a coward. I will not have it.'

'I'll talk to Bero, I said. Maino will keep his loud, rotten mouth shut and serve his family,' Hulderic growled.

'He will not,' I insisted. 'And I want that girl. I want to court her.'

'She is Maino's prisoner,' he said with a scowl. 'And I will not have you marry her. I told you this already. Now answer this. Will you obey your father?' I hesitated, trembling with the rage. He leaned very close to me. 'Eat shit, Maroboodus, for all of us. Forget Maino, forget the girl. Be patient as Hughnot has been all these years. We need no foolish bucks now, their antlers tearing at our house's timbers as they fight, and while the black wolf is sitting in the shadows, licking its lips.'

I slammed my hand on the table in unbridled fury, startling even Father. I had not meant to, as Father's words should have been respected, he had delivered them with reason, and Grandmother was already teary-eyed. Aldbert put a hand on my shoulder, but I didn't care. I was so mad, so angry at Maino, and the girl's face haunted me. The inglorious Thing, my humiliation and coming shame left me unable to see reason. I could not let Maino spit on me, not at all, nor for all the silver of the short folk. I got up, pushing the table. The plate full of bones scattered on the floor. I kicked them, they landed in a heap and I stormed for the living quarters. I turned to look back and saw Grandmother on her knees. I hesitated, feeling terrible as the old lady was bent to clean up after a mess I made, and though it was not a man's lot to clean, she was too old for the chore. Yet, Erse was not moving, but looked on reverently and I frowned as even Hulderic was uncomfortable at the way his mother was mumbling. She was muttering under her breath, strangely and sibilantly, hunched over the pile of bones and then she looked up at me. I took a step back. There was fear in her face. Her old, wrinkled face was strangely smooth, so stretched her mouth was with horror, and then sorrow replaced the look and the wrinkles returned on the pale face. She spoke softly, very softly, but I heard her. 'It is him. *The Bear.*'

Hulderic also looked at me in shock and there was a frown on his face. We stood in place for a long time, until Grandmother got up and walked off, Erse following her. Aldbert was sitting still, his eyes cocked strangely as he regarded the bones.

Father wiped his hand across his face. I nodded at the pile of trash. 'What? What did she read in them? Was the animal naughty? Did it also misbehave? She read the bones, didn't she?'

'She read the bones, Maroboodus. And we didn't need this trouble.' He looked at me darkly and I noticed he had a hand on a long seax. He saw my look and took the hand away, though reluctantly. 'We shall ride in the morning, Maroboodus. When we have buried our great relative, we will sit down. We will have a Thing, and your feud with Maino will be settled. You shall not marry the girl and we will be wise, we will serve the family, and you might have to endure insults for it. Do so, and give me a reason to think you might not break all our dreams. And I will speak with you later on the matter of the bones.'

'They are bones,' I hissed.

He laughed harshly. He pointed at them, and how the dogs slunk away from the pile of trash. They would not hesitate, normally, but they did now. That was odd indeed. Aldbert eyed me carefully, and left with Hulderic.

69

I cursed and went to my quarters to sleep. 'Donor help me,' I prayed to the god of hammers and the guardian of men, for I felt something terrible was going to take place.

And it would be my own doing.

In the morning, the bones were still there, and the dogs slept around them.

CHAPTER 3

The month, *wīndume-mānod* had been very wet. Men curse the damp weather, the sickness that follows, and the general mood-killing gloom, and they fear freezing nights and frosty mornings and so it was that the fall months didn't cheer many people, unless they hoped to die in the winter and knew their time was near. The land was steaming with misty vapors as the cold breath of Ymir spread across the land from the north, where nights were already long. Father and his champions were dressed in rich furs. Their shields were covered with wet rime, and hands with mittens held the cold shafts of the framea and javelins. The moss and grass crackled under the hooves of our horses. It was the sort of weather that left you itching and unhappy, and you would try to remember what the splendid summer looked and felt like, and it was a very hard thing to do. Aldbert, the poet was bringing up the rear with some slaves who guided spare mounts and heavily-laden work horses and I was somewhere in the middle, certainly behind the champions and a step away from servants. I was a man, yes, and Father's adeling, a lord of his house by blood right. And now, I had killed in battle. I had fought well enough, that was true. No. In fact, I had killed *two* very famous men and that was a feat few achieved in a lifetime. *I was a clever fighter,* I decided, lucky, favored by the gods, and while I had no rage of the gods making my spear faster, I was no weakling. More, I had what Hulderic had. I had wits. *In war, if not with Maino,* I added in my head.

I could be anything, if I chose to be.

But didn't I disdain the gods, the vitka, and all the magic of the woods? Now I saw their favor in my recent victory and so I was a hypocrite.

I brooded and kept riding and thinking.

Despite the gods, it was true I could change my life. *Choose to be something else than a son of Hulderic and a foolish slave to their schemes,* I thought, and looked to the sky, cursing the many obstacles in the way to my glory. To living my own life, indeed.

Yet, Hulderic disagreed. I had no life, no plans as far as he was concerned. He took it for granted I'd obey. He knew I had no real power and powerless men could not choose to be anything, because they would starve or turn into a maniac in the woods, bereft of friends, food, and shelter. A simple warrior might just leave, having nothing to lose and brave those things, but Hulderic also saw my greed for what Bero had, and he knew I hated the thought of the gau in the wrong hands, and to leave it so would gnaw at my soul forever.

He was a fool.

All of it was wrong. Father, or ... I? Yes, I might rule it well, in time. The three ravens flying the battlefield *had* been heralds. Perhaps of the death of Friednot, but perhaps also a nudge for an overlooked warrior to step forward and had not the gods given me favor in the battle? *I'd start believing in the bastards, if they gave me what I wanted,* I decided. Was Maino my test? Were the gods seeing how far I'd go to right a wrong? Did they not speak with more authority than Father?

I frowned at Hulderic's back. Father's words still echoed in my mind, and his warnings had had a sinister edge. He truly believed we would face a challenge from Hughnot. And there was the strange business with the bones, as well. He had not even greeted me that morning, and more, Grandmother had not appeared. I clapped Scald's back. '"She is feeling very sick, Maroboodus",' I mimicked Erse's voice as she had lied to me, while she served me some cold vegetables with gruel.

I asked her if she had said anything that evening, but she had shaken her head, looking very troubled and she had gone away, and she had not even winked at me, as she usually did.

Yes, there was something strange going on with all of them, and as I gazed at Aldbert, he looked like he was hoping I'd not greet him. His eyes also sought Hulderic's back, and he was frowning to himself, tugging at his weak beard. I hated that. He had been the one man I was able to speak with, to share my sorrows and thoughts with, the one I felt at ease with. Sure, there were plenty of high Goth families in and out of Timberscar, with lots of men my age, but I had not made close friends with them, had I? Instead, my weak, foolish poet of a friend was looking terrified and I cursed Hulderic softly, but loudly enough to have Dubbe smack his lips with disapproval.

We would ride on, Hulderic would brood, I'd sulk, and we would be miserable all the way to Bero's hall in Marka. And there I'd have to let Maino piss all over me, while smiling thankfully like a child given a horn of mead. Was that better than braving the woods alone?

No. *No, I'd bold myself a man. A man like I wished to be, and not become Father's vision of a subservient fool,* I thought and realized I meant it. I'd rather leave the Goths, our lands, family, than suffer that, but only after showing Maino what I thought of him.

But was there a third way? A better way?

Something growled in the woods, as if to answer the question. None of the others turned that way to see what it was, but I had heard it. Was that too, a sign? I kept staring at the thickets, but nothing moved and unsteadily I settled into looking at the passing land.

I looked away to the far woods. There were thick oaks, tall pines, birch forests, all gleaming wetly, and rolling hills as far as the eye could carry. Tens of thousands Goths and Svearna lived in the harsh land, and I supposed it was a land worth fighting for. It was our home, no matter the misery of the winter and harshness of the soil. The sea was our own. Few foes arrived to the shores, save for the Saxons and occasionally the Langobardi, and some mighty Svea lords from the north. The sea made it all worth it. It was rich, led to lands far, far away, and we would exploit it to grow richer. Surely we should? To toil the same land, year after year was not a plan worth spitting on. Would Bero make such plans? Had Friednot?

Would *Father?*

Svearna detested our presence in the land that had once belonged to them, of course, and we had fought well with Friednot to keep what is ours.

Father had said Hughnot had strange plans, wide-reaching plans, perhaps.

Our real enemies were the Goths themselves, I decided. We were too tied to keeping what we had. We risked little. Father was cautious. A thinker. He wanted me to be as deep, devious, patient, but it's hard to think when you hate someone like Maino. And when you honestly think life would be better with your family … or perhaps you? Yes, you, in charge. I looked away, ashamed of my treasonous thoughts and afraid Father could read them, somewhere in his closed, devious mind.

I could leave. Be destitute.

And then Woden whispered to me and I nearly laughed aloud.

There was the woman.

She was a Svea. She was a rich one, an important one, a toy in the games of power, but she had smiled at me.

At me. Not at anyone else. *That I knew of*, I thought with a frown, but shook the unsettling thought away.

I had said I'd marry her.

I smiled as I thought about it. It had been nothing more than a barb at Father, but what if I did? I'd not be a lost soul in the woods, and I would have, perhaps, a life out there? My home would not be a cave in a hill, where I'd fight with the bears, but a place of warm fires, riches, and most of all, power. I felt like a bastard for pushing such thoughts of power and riches before her smile, but why could not my plan be for both power *and* love? It could, it would make sense if it were, in fact. And my feelings were real. I had dreamt of her the night before. I had seen her walking through pristine, brilliantly golden wheat fields in my torturous dreams, looking like a spirit of the flower stalks, a beguiling, benevolent thing and she had approved of me, smiling at me, holding out her hand and if that was not a sign of the gods, then what was? The memory of her smile filled me with lingering, deep warmth. There was longing and lust and gods be cursed, I had not looked at a woman like her before. It was the sort of feeling to make you press your palms to your face, leaving you bewildered, feeling reborn, desperate, on the brink of something new, not knowing if you might reach happiness. The memory of the curve of her lips caressed my nerves, and then made them taut as a bowstring, as I thought Maino was putting a claim on her.

Did he have one? A claim?

Perhaps in the eyes of the men of the villages. And if she were a tool for Boat-Lord to destroy us, she would marry one of us.

I could take her, and leave?

And there it was. My plan. I'd take her home.

Home? Did she have a home left, after the Saxons raided the land? She might. She was rich, well to do, it was clear by her haughty disdain, brave loathing of Cuthbert. Her dress spoke of it, even. Such riches don't go away if a hall burned and slaves died. She was beautiful as the Sunna riding the sky. She was powerful in the lands of the Svea, perhaps, with connections that would be useful. My mind was whirling, as I straightened on the saddle. She—

A hand startled me, slapping on my shoulder. Hulderic had swerved around, waited for me and I had not noticed him. He nodded at me, his fur dripping with dew and there was some snow falling. 'You looked starry-eyed, Maroboodus. You dreaming of a better place to be? Somewhere far from me?'

I shook my head. 'No, not far from you. But a better place, perhaps.'

'You are still a pup, boy,' he rumbled. 'Pups should accept their fathers are wise and the pups can barely walk straight. The Pups should pretend even when fathers are fools. We will stay the night at Birmhelm's hall, and next evening we are at Marka.'

'I know the way, Father,' I told him. 'But thank you for making sure the pup's not lost.' He chuckled softly.

Marka. The Boundry, it was Friednot who built it, and now it was Bero's village by the lands of the Svea and Hughnot, separated by the Long-Lake, a cold swath of sea reaching far to the lands of the Svearna, where salt and sweet water mixed. 'You do know the way, son, but you should practice the art of civility towards the rest of us while we have to trek so miserably.'

Dubbe grunted in agreement, and if Dubbe agreed with Father so readily, then I had displeased them indeed. I shrugged and straightened my shoulders. 'I'll try,' I said loudly and they said nothing, but I sensed they had accepted my apology. We rode in silence for a while, until a raven flew over, croaking forlornly. Hulderic looked at it and mumbled something about Woden.

I smiled. 'The god is not watching, Father.' I cursed myself, for a slayer of two high warriors I now wanted to believe the ancients were hovering above me and begged they didn't take offence as I dismissed the bird.

He did not smile back, but stroked his braided beard and adjusted the tunic under his pelt. 'Your grandmother seems to think he is. And you saw the damned birds skimming the shieldwall, didn't you?'

'Hugin and Munin are two ravens, Grandfather, what was the third?' I asked carefully, hoping he'd tell me about the bones. 'They do look fateful, the birds but Grandfather died because his face caught an ax, not because a bird shat on him. And he died because Osgar was too slow.'

Dubbe chuckled, Sigmundr slapped him and Harmod straightened in his saddle, but Hulderic kept his silence, brooding as he looked at the raven that was circling something in the woods, a carcass, a rabbit or a moose the wolves had killed. 'You just hate the unknown, boy.'

I nodded with agreement. 'Sure I do. Who wouldn't? You practically shat yourself yesterday, when Grandmother went dog-like over the remains of our dinner. What was that all about?' I asked him. 'All that unknown nonsense nobody seems willing to speak to me about?'

'The bones?' he said softly. 'Bad omen. But you don't think it was strange, no?'

'The dogs?'

'That, and your grandmother's vision.'

'She looked like she saw Grandfather or some dead, old vaettir of the stony, deep holes in the woods. Or perhaps an alf in the bones? What is this bear? He mentioned a bear.'

He shook his head and spoke very softly. 'She saw *the* Bear,' Hulderic said and looked saddened. 'It's an old family, Maroboodus, ours. We are the first people, the Gothoni who were born in Midgard before all the others and from our blood, stem all the creatures that drag their feet across the misery of this world. Woden crafted Aska and Esla from dry logs to fill the silence of the world, his brother Hodur and Lok helped him and here, in Midgard, and the great god set his table and feasted for the birth of his own race. Us. He sees himself in us, perhaps? Raw, raucous, violent, moral, and then immoral.' He glanced at me suspiciously. 'No dry, sarcastic comments on how you already knew this?'

'I resisted the urge. What has that got to do with bones and grandmothers?' I asked him.

He grasped my shoulder and pulled me to him so hard I nearly lost my grip on the shield. 'There is a *curse* in this family. One the gods, jealous of Woden's power and Midgard cast on us the moment we were born of driftwood. It's not clear what the curse is, but it involves members of our family and they say the danger is greatest when such men fail to be *noble*. When they are selfish, violent, out of control, the Norns stir, and gods rumble. Your grandmother is a seidr-maddened woman, a völva. She was one, at least. She has sacrificed for the gods for decades and quit after a bout of near deadly fever. Her family is related to ours, she met Friednot and fell in love and then she had us, Bero and me, played a dutiful mother, a good wife—and yes, Father had another woman—but she has dreaded the day she would see the Bear roaring. Being a mother doesn't shut down the gods in her head, and—'

'She saw bones,' I said stiffly and pulled myself from his grasp. 'Bones. Not even bear bones. Damned cow, I think.'

'Horse,' Aldbert whispered near, 'Saxon horse,' but we ignored him.

'You threw the bones, and there was a terrible warning in them,' Hulderic continued sternly. 'One you should heed. Your grandmother thinks you are the Bear, and the Bear is the herald of evil times, my son. She thinks you might be the weak pebble that will cause the boulder to shudder, to move, and finally to roll. She thinks that men Woden created were cursed so that this world, Midgard, the gods, their Nine Worlds will be swallowed should they fail to be as noble as Woden is, and the evil of the vile gods who hated Woden—still do hate him—will come to pass. We shall be no more. And the Bear, it will be there, at the beginning, and that is why she fears. And why I do, as well.'

I stared at him aghast. I swirled to look at Aldbert, who looked sheepish. He had told the poet. Why? I decided it didn't matter and tried to think about what Hulderic had said. The end? *Ragnarok*, I thought. End of the

Nine Worlds. It would be the final battle, the bane of the gods and their lands. There would be horrible destruction of the Aesir and the Vanir and even the wily Jotuns, and finally, the birth of a new, lesser world.

I quaffed. I had promised myself to believe, but this?

Then I laughed and everyone turned to look at me with astonishment, and then frowns of deep disapproval. I could not stop, and tears ran down my cheeks, until I managed to stifle the roaring, shaking laughter into barely controlled chuckles, now anticipating a slap from Father, which never came. He was shaking his head.

'You damned fool,' he said sternly. 'I don't see anything funny about that. You live amongst the miracles of the gods, and seek to outdo them in arrogance. You really don't believe in them, do you?'

I got a full hold of myself and sighed. 'I'm sorry. I want to. I killed two men in the battle, and perhaps they do occasionally help us. But not everything is magic, Father. I was sitting on the hillside the day before yesterday, looking at Maino strutting in his gear, and the dolts,' I nodded at Dubbe who chortled, knowing somehow I had meant him, 'and I was thinking how I'd never amount to anything. Now I am "The Bear", terror of the shaking gods and the Bane of Midgard! And that's because I kicked a plate of horse bones to the dust and the dogs didn't want them? Perhaps they were sated. Even dogs can be full.'

He did not see the humor. 'Well, think about this, then. You are not the first one.'

'There are other fierce bears in the family, ready to gnaw on the old Midgard's bones?'

'Yes,' he said darkly. 'There are. Were. Have been. In this cursed damned family, when a völva or a vitka of the blood sees such terrible signs it is no small matter to be ignored and made fun of. Ask Hughnot, if you wish. They had a brother like that, wild, unruly, and he, Maroboodus, was given to Donor and the god took him and now he is dead. Boat-Lord condemned him. There are boys and girls who have been sacrifices all through the ages.' He frowned at that and waved his hand weakly. 'Or sent far, far away. And let me say this again. Understand. Listen. Some have been sacrificed to the gods. Laugh at that, Maroboodus.'

'You ... ' I began and sputtered. 'You mean Grandmother wants to kill me? Because of some gnawed gristle?'

'She loves you,' he said thinly. 'I ... we do. But there is no denying it. She had a terrible vision in the bones, a terrible one, be they horse bones and greasy gristle or indeed god's fine lots. She saw Draupnir's Spawn, she saw you reaching for the ring, and she saw battle and death and you trying to slay kin for power, against my wishes. She saw you roaring in rage, and she thought she saw a Bear roaring in your voice, it's evil vision over your shoulders. She said if this comes to be, she wanted me to make the ... decision. If you will not bow to my wish for obedience—'

I glowered at him. 'And all of this damned threatening because I hate Maino more than I'd hate the worst enemy of the Goths and like the girl he stole? And if I decide my honor is more important than giving Maino a humble, girly smile, you'll listen to Grandmother's raving mad—'

'Kingdoms have toppled for less than unruly adelings,' he said with a pale grin. 'Remember what I said. Endure. Be patient and heed me. You have been warned.' Hulderic whipped his horse's flank and the beast surged ahead with a snort. 'Pray and obey,' he called out.

Aldbert rode next to me, his eyes never leaving Father. 'You should take care, Maroboodus. He is not joking. I know he can *laugh* at jokes, but he rarely tells them. Keep that in mind, my friend.'

'I'm his son, I know he is a dour block of ice,' I said.

'He is a good father,' Aldbert said. 'Wish I had one. Even to warn me of a prophecy that seems very real to me.'

'Did he tell you about this thing yesterday, when he dragged your skinny ass with him? Did he scheme with you, hoping you would make a lamb out of me?'

He smiled slyly, pulling at his beard. 'I'd not make a lamb out of you, lord. Who would fight my fights then? And as for him, your father, anyone can see he is utterly serious about this. Do not threaten their plans, Maroboodus. I also think your grandmother is not addled, or an idiot. She really had a vision.'

'Have *you* had a vision?' I asked him, pulling my horse away from his as they tried to nibble each other. 'Ever? How would you know she had one?'

He smiled wistfully. 'I've had some when I'm too drunk. It's usually all very confusing, and not very informative to be honest. Your grandmother wasn't drunk.' He looked startled. 'Or was she? No, I don't think so. She is very sensible. Hulderic would let you go to your death if he thought you a risk.'

'I'm his only son. I doubt he would,' I told Aldbert darkly, ignoring his attempts to guide me to calmer, more sensible waters. No, I wanted the storm. 'The Bear! It's just a ruse they are trying to use to hammer the girl out of my head.' *And my other plans*, I thought, though I was not sure what they were, yet. Rescue the girl? Find a home? What more? Could she be trusted? If not, what could I do to survive both my relatives and her people, if they would not have me?

Aldbert shook his head over dramatically, his thin beard swaying. 'The three spinners are holding your strings tight, I feel it. I have sense in these matters. Poems and songs do not come to those who do not think deep and listen to omens. I saw her. Your grandmother is a seer. She truly sees these things. And I see them in her. I ...' He hesitated.

'Yes?' I asked, amused.

'I have, sometimes, a glimpse of truth when I sing, do galdr, spell-songs of the higher worlds, my friend. Perhaps I'll approach the gods for you. I'll speak to them and sing a spell. I'll—'

I cursed him. 'I have but one friend, and it's you. You should be on my side and now you pretend to be a vitka. You know I hate them. Perhaps I'll make new friends,' I grumbled and he patted my back happily.

'*I'm* your friend. Ever since you gave me your last mead when we were six, I've been on your side, or at least behind your back, even when you are mulish and stupid. I've not been happy these last years, but you have been my friend. I'll always help you. So I swear.'

I smiled at him thinly and nodded in thanks. I was selfish. 'Not happy?'

He sighed. 'I've endured Erse's smiles at—'

'You like Erse?' I asked with a surprised laugh. 'Does she like you?'

'She liked my voice,' he said stiffly. 'But thinks I'm not really a prospect.' He looked very unhappy and I clapped a hand on his shoulder.

'She will,' I said weakly, not sure she would.

80

'She won't,' he whispered. 'I'm no fool. They gave me a shield and a spear, but she is after something else. Perhaps someone high? But I will try.'

I shook my head. 'I've thought about her, but now—'

'I know! You're not that high! She liked them older.'

'Father?' I said.

'Shut up!' he hissed, too loud and looked down as the others glanced at him. He looked stricken and I felt sorry for him. Perhaps he was right. Erse was a great mystery, but she *did* like Father.

I decided to humor my miserable friend. 'So, you know the spell-songs of the gods, then? What galdr do you know, Aldbert?'

'Woden knows songs against biting—'

'Biting? I'm not going to fight a horse. Or a woman,' I told him with a laugh.

'Fight?' he said with worry. 'So, you will make trouble.'

'Only if trouble finds me,' I said darkly. 'I heard Father, but I'll not budge. I will not kiss his ass. Maino's. Father's.'

'If you need galdr to fight Maino, best not fight at all. I have no guards against spears and swords, though yes, perhaps one against biting. I only know one useful that is not meant for battle, really. Perhaps it's only good to avoid battle?'

'What's that?'

'I can speak with the dead,' he said with a pale face.

'Damned liar,' I said. 'You cannot walk straight and you can speak with the dead?' I laughed, but still felt cold claws of terror rake my back. 'You shouldn't speak like that.'

He was silent, then humming uncertainly and I wondered if he was to try to do his galdr-song right there, but then he spoke. 'Meet me in the woods this night. There is a copse of oak near the hall, holy and ancient, said to be devoted to Freya, the Red Lady, goddess of wisdom and war and from her, I shall find guidance.'

'On what, exactly?'

He nodded at Hulderic. 'On if he is right. Let the dead tell you what you should do, friend, and I'll help you endure.'

I didn't agree. But I knew I'd not be able to resist.

CHAPTER 4

Hulderic and his men enjoyed a small, intimate feast. There was convivial chatter in the smoky, dark wooded hall of Birmhelm, where a near deaf Goth with two pretty daughters, served us smoked bass with greasy gruel, and famous ale brewed by some secret old recipe, something the old man had been perfecting since he was beardless. It was an excellent drink, with a thick wheat taste, and always left you yearning for more, and Birmhelm was not a rapacious host and shared the drink willingly. The man's hair was white and long, and it brushed his plate as he leaned forward to hear what Father was telling him in a low voice, apparently scheming and gathering allies for possibility of war as Birmhelm sent a man out with a message. Another man, perhaps Birmhelm's son, a large, fat man with a savagely scarred face kept nodding at Father's words. Dubbe was dozing on a bench, Sigmundr and Harmod were sharpening their axes by a small workspace in the corner and mostly it was a very homelike place and strangely comforting.

The shingles sputtered angrily set in some trunks by the fireplace and I waited for Aldbert to get up. Mostly, he just slurped on the ale, and seemed to be muttering to himself, and I realized he expected to perform his poem for Friednot, or a song and it would be requested during the Thing, or before the funeral, after the blessing and sacrifices of the coming day. It left him listless with worry. I chuckled as he slapped his forehead, berating himself mercilessly, and left a red welt as he had forgotten to put down his drinking horn. I sat there, admired the two pretty girls, and waited, though my patience was growing thin. Talking to the dead? Gods above, but he was crazy. After an hour of looking on as he kept suffering, I saw his face tighten, and he drank down his mead. 'It's time,' he said like a wounded hero of old and got up, looking grave as a stern father about to berate a boy for having let the cows escape, and I hoped he was not too drunk to amuse me. He burped and smiled sheepishly, caught my eyes, and nodded for the door. I nodded back at him and pushed back the bench, which drew an inquisitive smile from our host. I bowed to him and indicated a need to piss, and went out under Hulderic's long, speculative gaze.

The night was windy, and some specks of snow were coming down, riding the breeze forlornly and I saw Aldbert marching resolutely for the darkness, carrying something. 'The bastard doesn't even know this place,' I murmured and cursed I had left without a spear. Had he not gotten lost in Timberscar just last month? And there were wolves about, no doubt. They smelled the feast, and they were always hungry. And perhaps there was something else, something on two legs as well? I walked after him, nonetheless. We went on, until he stopped to look back at me, clutching a huge sack and nodded with reverence for a dark wood, not far. *Damn him*, I thought. We had vitka, and völva to perform such magic during the high rituals, and sometimes they took a life to give to the gods in return for the wisdom. These woods looked just like something that had been dedicated to the Aesir or the Vanir. While I had mocked ravens just that day to Father, it was a different matter to do so in the depth of a night. No Germani was a disbeliever when walking dark, lightless woods. Woden's ravens would be skulking around indeed, eyeing our progress, the boar Lord Freyr and his bloody-handed sister Freya, they would stir as the fool made a mockery of everything our people considered holy, and Donor and Woden would probably send down a plague or a lightning bolt before Aldbert would understand to stop the charade.

He scuttled for the thickest part of the woods, took a wrong way, one that was hopelessly entangled with branches and had to come back a ways before finding the right path, looking flushed, but still I followed. I felt danger lurking in the shadows, saw gleaming, small eyes, and some larger ones. A night bird, probably an owl fluttered ahead, its shadow splitting the few specs of light from the settlement, and despite the foolish company of Aldbert, I felt alone and afraid in the wood. It was the sort of child-like fear you remember from your past, a terror lurking on the edges of your memories, a fear of creatures in a dark room with you, things you have been told are not actually there, but you are absolutely sure they are, nonetheless. My belly twitched with the fear, and I was cold, strangely cold, and resisted the urge to rub my arms. Were there vaettir there? The sprits of evil men, destined for the dark lands, but still lost, having been abandoned by the Valkyries, or perhaps just not welcome in Helheim at all? It was night, it was a very holy month, and the vitka said the spirits were close to our world during the weeks that led to the Yule feast. *Then again, they seemed to think every month was like that,* I thought. I walked past stumps of trees and dodged low hanging boughs that wetted my face.

Then, a skull swung in the air and slapped into my chest.

I squawked, then changed the terrified noise into a cough and heard Aldbert chucking somewhere in front of me and I bit my tongue, and slapped the clammy, brittle thing away, as I stepped away from it. I hung from a rope and looked oddly alive. I kept staring at it, still unreasonably suspicious it might jump at me as I moved away, ready to latch into my neck for a late evening snack. It was brown, stretched skin hung from it in tatters, and it looked sinister as Hel's dead eye. 'Are you going far? Isn't *this* creepy enough? Does it have to be a certain bit of this crappy wood or can we just sit down here?'

'They were sacrificed to Woden a year ago,' he laughed hollowly. 'Svear. They cannot hurt you now. Later, perhaps, but not now. Slap them out of your way and they will not hurt you.'

Hurt me later? I thought and cursed him, this time aloud and clear and crudely. 'You salt-faced charlatan. I'll slap *you* if I have to wet my shoes in some damned stretch of swamp,' I growled and then found him. He was slouching over a stool, trying to make it stand in the wet, half-frozen moss. 'Seriously, you brought a seat? In that sack?'

'Yes. A self-respecting poet does not squat in shit,' he sniffled as he finally managed to find a proper position that held promise not to topple him to the perfectly good grass. 'This is rickety, so don't mope. Not comfortable. And you might have brought one yourself. Not my fault if you have fewer tools inside your bony skull than I do.'

'Last time I'll fight your fights, poet. Seriously, you didn't bring me one?'

'You won't need one. I'm supposed to sit higher than you, Maroboodus. I'm the respectable medium between you and the gods, and you are the humble, if ugly warrior whom they might or might not hear out.'

I poked a finger in his chest. 'Hear me out? Aldbert, I don't know *why* we are here. I wanted to see *you* speak to the dead, but you seem to think the dead can do something for me. What, exactly, should I wish from the things? Will they tell me how to kill Maino? And I won't sit below you. I'll stand.'

He shook his head, as if trying to find an answer. 'I don't know. With everything that's happened these past days, I think it might be a good idea to ask for their guidance. You need it. And no, not on how to kill Maino. Just ask them what you should do. Obey your father? Rebel like an idiot? Ask them! The dead can be very helpful, if they feel so inclined. They have helped make me a better poet.'

'In that case,' I told him maliciously, 'they have enjoyed a grand joke. And I don't want to join that herd of fools who think they are special enough to have the ear of the dead and the gods—'

'Can you please give them a chance, Maroboodus?' he breathed. 'Here,' he said, and showed me a horn full of mead, stoppered with a leather cover. 'It's a very good sacrifice. Hold it!' He handed it to me as if it was the blood of the highest king in Midgard.

'I think they might enjoy a drink, but perhaps also a human sacrifice?' I asked with a growl, holding the horn.

'Don't be tedious,' he answered. 'I spared that bit when you guzzled everything down, little thinking you might have to sacrifice something for the answers. And you mope after a stool, when I go thirsty?'

'Damn liar. My heart breaks. I'll just laugh over here, by the tree,' I told him with a wry grin. 'And you ask the spirits on what the future holds for me? Ask them that, eh? That's what I want to know.' And then I waited, as he sat there. I did so for a few minutes, and realized he was trying to figure out what to do. 'So,' I said, eyeing the woods where I saw many skulls hanging from the boughs. 'What now? You have no clue what your galdr-song is like, no? You've never spoken with the dead, only a mug of ale where you saw spirits and tits. Admit it.'

But he didn't and I bit away the rest of the mockery. I saw he was actually afraid, shaking as he gathered courage and I looked away, feeling sorry. 'Now, be ready,' he said, breathing heavily. 'I'll risk much for you, you ungrateful lout. I'll ask the hidden spirits to help you. To guide you in your way. Us, in fact, as I am stuck with you, a damned fool that I am. They will aid us. Both of us. Pour the mead on the ground. Do it respectfully, slowly.'

I did. I rued the waste, but I let it trickle down to the frosty dirt, and Aldbert looked on with a critical eye, until I was done, making sure I saved not a drop for myself.

'Go ahead then, sing them a merry song,' I told him, though I tried to avoid looking at the skulls that were now hung with small icicles. Had they been there just now? No, only regular skulls, and no ice. The air was chilly, and the leaves and pine needles were icy, but I was sure the skulls hadn't been so afflicted with the rime and ice before. I put my back against a heavy pine trunk. If the dead answered, they'd be creepy and deadly shadows, resentful of the warm blood in our veins and I'd make sure they could not sneak up on us. And if Aldbert's head was not full of cow turds, and actually spoke the truth about his galdr singing, his ability, I'd be sure to knock him out if he lost control of it. I clutched a sturdy branch to be used as a cudgel and tried to concentrate on thoughts of a happy, warm hall's fire, a pleasant summer morning, but instead, I had to focus on Aldbert. I couldn't help it. His act looked very genuine indeed. Far too much so.

He was speaking gutturally, spitting words between his teeth, his weak beard swaying as he shook with an aggressive spell-song's casting. And that was not all. He was rubbing a strange-looking wand with pale green leaves. It was a rough bit of wood, and I shook my head in wonder as it was truly a magical wand, like the vitka used, being wand carriers, and even the female völva, when they practiced their dark magic in places much like this, carried such things. I had not seen the latter take place, of course, as the völva would be truly dangerous, but the vitka carried their wands brazenly to the sacrifices and used them for their spells and for sprinkling blood, of course. Aldbert's was made of dried oak and he took ridiculous, meticulous care to make sure he rubbed every inch of it with the leaf. He even rubbed the stubs and the shoulders of the tiniest branches as well as he could, his eyes crossed, but all that time, he was speaking the spell-words with a rhythmic voice. When one leaf predictably developed a hole, he grabbed another from the pouch with such practiced movement, I was beginning to believe he was actually onto something. Then he was humming, looking relieved, as if after a good shit and his voice grew in power and determination slowly, hypnotically. His voice changed, slowly, resolutely, until it didn't resemble his own anymore. It was thrumming in the woods and across the ferns, carrying a strong tune and he stared away from the wand towards a pile of tinder. I gawked at it.

Had it been there before? Surely it had. If it had, who put it there? If it hadn't, then there were beings there I could not see. Alfs? Dead? Something that never lived? I grasped the club and felt my hand shake with anxiety, and sweat trickled down my forehead.

Then I cursed myself for a fool.

Of course, he had brought it there to begin with, earlier, when we had arrived. Or had someone bring it. Or perhaps the real vitka left it there, whenever they were done with their strange spells.

But it was dry.

I saw it. The pile was not wet or frosty in the least bit. Surely it would be, if we had been—

It burst into flames. Blue and red licks of heat grew up from it like aggressive lizards and Aldbert's eyes were large with wonder and fear. An act? He was mumbling again, almost apologetically, swaying like a boat in a tide, and praying to the great spirits, the old gods that live deep in the earth. He called for Woden, the All-Father, for hammer god Donor, for Tiw the just, and finally, with great fear and reverence, to Freya, the Red Lady, goddess of wisdom and war *both*, the odd duality of the goddesses' nature evident in her titles. He tapped his wand in the blazing twigs, hurling fire around, causing a small storm of angry sparks to sputter across the near woods, like mad flaming flies out and lost and then he slumped into a sack-like shape, his hands lax on his sides.

His voice sang, and it was weird, guttural, and then suddenly clear, bright as rain with an oddly mocking note.

'*Yea, you mortals,*
hear the gods chortle.

Twigs and skull,
and an old, rotten hull.

The Bear shall choose,
between a woman and a noose.

A surprise for the murderous lord,
and death at the end of the sword.

Victory for the beast,
but there shall be no feast.'

He sat still for a while and I tried to focus on his words. His eyes fluttered, the whites showing strangely, and I fought the temptation to shake him awake. Instead, I let the words flit through my head. Was this my future? 'Nonsense,' I whispered, but could not shake the gloomy terror away. It was Aldbert, for Hel's sakes, he could not act worth a damn. But *this* was an act worth the old skalds, I had to admit.

He sat there for a long time, until his wand fell from his nerveless fingers, and I decided there would be no more words forthcoming. 'Aldbert,' I whispered, and cured my timidity and spoke louder. 'Lout?'

It had an immediate effect on him. He twitched like a tired fish on a hook and shuddered as if an old man waking up from a long, pleasant nap. His eyes kept staring at the fire. Then his voice took on a mysterious, ridiculous tone.

'*Your father is right,*

89

you're a blight.

The Bear should obey and pray,
and his father he should always hear.'

I stared at him with a frown. That was it. No more was coming. Now that was the Aldbert I knew and occasionally liked well. I stepped closer and bent to eye him close. He did not move, his eyes fixed on the flames, which still burned brightly and I stared down at him until my back ached. And then I kicked the stool from under him. He fell on his rear and still did not move, though there was a brief look of disgust on his features as the wetness of the grass and the icy water of the sodden moss infiltrated his ass. I crouched before him, and smiled like a clever wolf would to a wounded rabbit, measuring its bravery. Finally, I shook his hand. 'Drop it. Father put you up to this?'

He said nothing.

I smirked at his blank face. 'He put you up to this, sure he did. And you came up with something like that. Pray and obey? I've enjoyed this, but I'm not convinced. How much did he pay you? Some of his better ale?'

He twitched. 'Erse.'

I stared at him with stupefaction. 'Erse? He gave you the right to ask Erse to marry you?'

'He did,' my friend said, still staring ahead. 'He was looking at me carefully, smiled as I named my price, and finally shrugged, and told me of course I am free to ask her. I know he likes her, and it was a struggle for him to agree, but—'

I laughed with mockery. 'This was what you were discussing with him that evening? A girl?'

'*The* girl,' he moped. There was a disgusted look on his face and I stretched my neck to see his fine moose leather pants were soaked through.

'Pissed yourself in your god-like bliss? Freya gave you a fright instead of a sight?'

He smiled sheepishly as he picked himself up from the ground. He fingered his wetted pants with despair and shrugged. 'He didn't pay me

90

anything else. Just that. Didn't make me any promises. He asked for help, and help I tried to deliver and he did give me permission to ask Erse's hand, though he warned me it was not likely to had.'

'You know you are right. He will probably marry her himself,' I said with mirth. 'Probably told her to say no just after giving you the promise.'

He looked shocked. 'He wouldn't. He is fair.'

'He is about to have me lick Maino's balls,' I reminded him and he frowned. 'He might not be as fair as you think,' I said, surprised by the hurt look on his face. 'He likes Erse well enough, even if she is very young and would probably kill him in a week.' Anger played on Aldbert's face, but then he rubbed his temples and waved his hand tiredly.

He sighed. 'Doesn't matter. He is almost like a father to me as well. Granted, it was not a very inspired performance—'

'It was just fine until you dropped those stupid, terrible lines. Should *obey* indeed. A blight, pray, and obey? You took Father's own words, even. Didn't you?'

He smiled and rubbed his face. 'Yes. It would have been a *lot* better if I hadn't spent all my considerable skills and creativity on the song they want to hear of the mighty Friednot. This was really a seat-of-the-pants kind of thing. Your father worries about you, so be happy about that. He asked me to make sure you find your respect for the gods. That you will heed his words of wisdom when it comes to Maino.' He was silent for a moment. 'For your own sake.'

'He should have sent a real vitka to frighten me, I think. You are far too fond of the simple drinking songs, far more so than holy messages and galdr-songs. That was terrible. Absolutely horrible. And no, I am not convinced. I'll do what I must do, friend. Gods or not.'

'I'll try to help you, Maroboodus,' he said sadly, and picked up his piss-ridden seat. 'We have been friends for a long time. Almost like brothers. Don't tell Hulderic I failed. It's the mead, as well as momentary lack of inspiration. Strong drink, it addles my brain. Some say you should make songs and poems when totally, utterly hammered, but I lose all sense of drama that way and begin to spew silly crap that sounds as terrifying as a sparrow in love. Erse told me I am far too happy to be a good poet.'

'She is right,' I grinned. 'I hope she surprises us all and says yes to you and then you might find inspiration for drama after she makes life terrible for you. She'll force you to become a warrior, she will.'

'She would make me chirp like a bird should she marry me, she would, out of happiness, and I'd be anything she wanted me to be,' he said, entirely in love.

'Well, when she marries Father, you will find many poems from that sorrow,' I said and clapped his back and walked back for the hall, disturbed by the thought of Father taking another woman, though of course he should. Then he would not have the energy to worry about me. 'What a waste this was,' I stated. 'But perhaps a bit fun, as well. Thank you, you charlatan.'

'Just listen to your father, for my sake,' he laughed and nearly fell over a root.

'How did you make the fire?' I asked.

'I didn't!' he breathed. 'You lit it?'

'Gods above,' I cursed him as he nearly fell again. I grabbed his flailing arm and he nodded at me gratefully. 'So what were the other lines about, eh?'

'Which ones?' he asked, confused as a blind man trying to find his cock in the dark.

'The bit about gods chortling, beasts roaring, the lack of a feast, twigs, skull, and a rotten hull? And that bit about a girl and a noose, and a surprise and a murderous lord?'

He stared at me as if I was mad. He lifted my furs and even my tunic, and I pushed him away. 'What the—'

'You have more drink with you? You must be roaring drunk, friend. I only had that silly line about the blight, prayers, and obedience. And I lit no fires.'

'The game is over,' I told him tiredly as we walked to the hall's main entrance. 'You should know when to quit an act, friend. Let's go and throw dice and see how lucky I will be.'

'Maroboodus,' he told me, standing in the dark. 'I didn't say those lines. Tell me exactly what they were.'

I looked at him hard, and shook my head. 'No, I won't. It doesn't matter. Either you are desperately trying to make me look like a fool, or you fear my father. Suffice it to say that the beast shall rear and scream, and people will probably die. That's how it went, it's just what Father feared, and you did well until you went on from that line. But you won't tell him. What comes, comes, Aldbert.'

'What comes, comes,' he agreed. He shook his head with resignation and pointed a finger at me, no longer the fool. 'But I think it's really important you won't let Maino annoy you to violence. I'll help you, as best I can as I love you and owe you, but believe me; perhaps a father's advice is good. It is so, sometimes. Don't go the the Thing, at least. Stay away. Let Hulderic deal with Maino and don't be rash.'

'You never knew your father, so how would you know? But I have plans and yes, perhaps I'll miss the Thing. I'll deal with Maino later,' I said. 'Unless he challenges me publicly. Then I'll piss on him. Come?' He did not come in, but stayed out, sat on a bench by the hall's door and wondered.

I went inside and bowed to my father, who smiled at me, relieved, unaware of Aldbert's failure.

CHAPTER 5

W e rode to Bero's village the next day. My friend had stayed silent most of the day, worried and brooding, in a mood very unlike him, but Hulderic and his champions were in a merry mood. The reason was the bright, autumn weather and the bright Sunna, and the brief warmth that graced the party. The bright light played on slightly yellowed leaves, on the lake surface and the small rivers, and moose and deer were gazing at us from the depths of the moss-filled woods and recently abandoned fields. Most of the men drank ale and mead, Hulderic as well and while the business at the end of the road was the burial of my grandfather and a perilous Thing of utmost importance, men were as relaxed as I had seen them. Fat Dubbe was singing lustily and Sigmundr, his tall frame swaying in his saddle was doing his best to ruin the tune, and his best was really good. Harmod looked like a spooked hare, his eyes crossed, as he had a horrible hangover, the gods' punishment for men who didn't appreciate the commands of their wives and lords to drink modestly, but he still chortled at the antics of his fellow champions. The trails were easy, and I had time to think. While Maino and the funeral were both depressing specters on my horizon, I let the merry weather calm my nerves into a pragmatic state of mind, one that tried to accept what was unalterable.

I'd risk my life soon.

While they all expected me to be calm and subservient when Maino strutted before me in the Thing, perhaps there would be a way to turn this all around. He told me Grandmother wanted to sacrifice me? To take me away? And I should just accept it and be like the meekest man in the warband for the rest of my life? No.

He'd have to choose, I thought, as I gazed at Father.

And I'd make him.

I'd act that night, and it all depended on what happened that day. If they held the Thing, could I do as Father suggested? Could I wait for my revenge and submit myself to their damned, demeaning wishes and get my vengeance later? If he claimed *her*? Maino? I shuddered. *Married* her? *That very night?* I would have to see her at his side in every feast from then on. I'd see her herding his ugly children, no doubt unhappy and broken, for who would find Maino a pleasant company? I'd see him smile snidely at me, knowing I would suffer like a glutton deprived of food when he took her away to his hall. I'd weep with rage, cringe with fire as though burning shingles had been stuffed down my pants. I looked away, darkness conquering my brief joy over the bright rays of Sunna and only forced a smile on my face when I saw Hulderic looking back at me. He nodded to himself as he turned away and then we saw the smokes of Marka, Bero's village. Hulderic waved in that direction and the champions were speaking about the place.

He'd have to choose.

I'd take her away.

I'd rescue her, marry her, and then, if she had any power at all with the Svearna, I'd marry into that power and have a force to decide the matters of the Goths. Father would take my side. Of course he would. Meek and silent, obedient? No, let them be those things. I chortled and shook my head. Hump their bones, if they think I would be that sort of an adeling. I'd try to dodge away from the Thing so I'd not get maimed by Maino, and one day, even much later, I'd punish Maino.

My thoughts were treasonous and I sneaked a glance at Aldbert, who was looking at me steadily. He gave me a small, dry smile but I didn't let him read my thoughts, and gave him—like I had Father—a small smile and added a nod. He had promised to help me. He had, and he had claimed to be my brother. So he would help me, as I could not do it alone. And I also had an idea on what I might do to survive, if the girl turned out to be tricky.

I saw the rooftops of Marka.

Like most of our villages, Friednot's former, glorious village was spread over a large area, cut into thick woods, riddled with fenced fields, vegetable gardens, and animal pens. There were craftsmen's houses by a small pond, and smoke rose from the leather-maker's shed and that of the blacksmiths, who probably were working on the bog iron, hoping one day to find a better quality ore, like our cousins over the sea occasionally enjoyed, trading it from the Celts.

Like Timberscar, this village was nestled on the shore of the sea, by a small bay and several ponds, guarded by islands filled with even more woods and rough, stony beaches. Gulls were shrieking high in the air, probably hunting after herring, some seals were slinking between waves on the same business as the gulls, and fishermen were drawing nets to the bay, fired up as their competitors were out to claim the known spots for great catches. It was the same thing in Timberscar, and indeed elsewhere. We needed the fish to survive.

Bero's lords, like Danr and Eadwine, had halls near the beach. Gasto's was further inland. He trained hounds there. Each hall was long, tall and well-built, and the rich ones had slaves aplenty to deal with the domestic issues. Fields of wheat and barley also separated them from each other, though they had been all reaped. Friednot's and now, Bero's oddly-built hall was settled right next to the beach and the boats. There were bits of old ships built into the walls, ship heads, sterns of old boats, and it looked strangely like a nest of an old hunting bear, one that had dragged the bones of its victims for its bed. Indeed, men said these were the ships of Friednot's old foes from Gothonia, and some were indeed elaborately carved and decorated, clearly boats of great lords, from times before we had even been born. The hall's doors were chalked white and gray and they said the structure had been there always, though that was of course a lie, but it had been there at least since the brothers arrived in the shores of the land. It had been Grandfather's war-hall and what was before, was probably a Svea village they had razed. It was called Bone-Home, or Bone-Hall, and inside was littered with elk and moose antlers as well as the weapons of those who had stood against the Goths in the past. Men were fixing the thatch of all the halls, preparing for the winter. The finer, larger

MAROBOODUS – ALARIC LONGWARD
halls had the healthiest looking roofs, made of hay, and thick, well cared for timbers, some of which leaked smoke from the seams. Some had an elaborate door, carved with symbols of vaettir, spirits and those of the gods. Small cows were herded around and some were separated and taken away as both sacrifice and for the coming funeral feast.

Aldbert pulled at my arm, and pointed a finger before Bero's hall, between the beach and the doors to the Bone-Hall, where there was a field meant for meetings. The center of the clearing was filled with wood.

What had looked like a half-finished heap of a hall was actually something else. On the beach, a large bonfire had been built. It was tall as three men, and slaves pulling draft-horses were still bringing more wood to it.

I also saw Bero and my hands twitched with hate.

We could all see him, standing by the door of the Bone-Hall. He was tilted in his usual pose, leaning strangely to the side; his dark hair hanging behind his back and no doubt there was the customary frown on his long, sad, and uncertain face as well. He was staring at his father's funeral preparations, deep in his thoughts and whether or not he mourned, or hated the terrible weight on his shoulders, I don't know. Hulderic grunted as we guided the horses down wooded trails where Goths now greeted us, sitting on their horses in the deeper shadows, guarding the land. There was a large clearing we had to cross and after this, we were much closer, and then I noticed Bero was actually frowning as he was looking at Hughnot. That would do it, if Father was right about the northern threat. The Black Goths were arriving in boats. There were many boats, at least five, and all had twenty men. Father turned to look at me and lifted his eyebrows. I nodded and spoke, knowing I knew there was something odd about Hughnot's arrival. 'I don't think he needs all those men to grieve his brother, does he? And where did the extra men come from? He visited his home over the Long-Lake just briefly, and now brings this many men? Were they actually somewhere else, already coming this way? Ready in case he needed them?'

Hulderic looked at me with a relieved smile, hoping I'd see the danger he had been talking about. 'Or perhaps he was just really fast and happened to have the men available. But not likely. I'm happy to see you find some sense in the jumble of confusion inside that bony skull of yours, son. They are here to guard him, at the very least. But also to give credence to his claim for power. He is not here to bow his head. He is here to make a point, we won't like the point, and he wishes to be sure no spear finds his heart if discussion gets heated in the Thing. So do you see why we don't need issues with my brother's lords and son now?'

'I see Hughnot is growing bold,' I told him sullenly, 'but I don't like anything about my lot, Father.'

'Just endure it,' he said with a wry smile. 'For all of us. Be patient in the Thing.'

I'd avoid it, I thought. I'd have to.

The Saxon ships were in the harbor, pulled up to the beach. A hall was heavily guarded by the the ships, a bit to the side, and no doubt that is where the poor prisoners, the captured Saxons were waiting for their fate which would not likely be a kind one. I felt sorry for them; at least briefly, men as much doomed as I was, I thought, and then shook my head, as I knew many of them would actually be sacrificed, not just unhappy. Some would be given the hanging man's death, what Woden once endured to give men wisdom, or speared and nailed to a tree, and vitka would read signs from the gods from their suffering.

But perhaps they'd all live, after all, I thought and smiled wickedly.

Hulderic was keeping a careful eye on the man who was perched on the bow of the best boat, a red-hued one with a high prow. The large lord was there, looking at Marka with keen eyes. 'He is going to challenge us. He wants the ring,' he told me, though it sounded more like he was just stating a fact he had hoped would turn out false, but could no longer deny after having read the man's intentions from the number of men accompanying him. 'He'll want the girl.'

'How many men does Bero have in the village?' I asked softly, counting the terrible many men that would soon disgorge to the beach. 'He might, you know, just kill Bero there and let him join Grandfather in the pyre? It would be convenient. Or make a pyre out of the Bone-Hall?'

Father smiled smugly. 'He has two hundred.'

'Bero? That many?' I asked, shocked. 'How?'

'They cajoled all the men nearby to join the Thing. All. Many more than we had in the battle. Danr, Eadwine, Gasto are there with *all* their warbands and they dragged everyone they could find here. Hughnot will be surprised.'

'We brought none,' I growled and then frowned. 'Wait, why didn't we take the boat here?'

He roared with laughter. 'We didn't want to be obvious. Our oaths men will be here as well. Are almost here, indeed. They follow a few hours behind us,' Hulderic said steadily. 'Eighty of my men will be near and so Hughnot will not make hall-burning nor try to voice too harsh demands on us and if he does, he won't be able to force the issue. We'll keep the men in cover but close and hidden. No need to make it obvious that we are expecting trouble. If he makes a sudden, early move, Maroboodus, if he has surprises of his own, we will have men available as well and he might fail utterly, fall heavily enough that he will not be a problem for us in the damned future. If he moves and tries something, boy, then we will surprise him. It is our right to do so then, but not before he commits a crime against his host. And then we will kill him. If he is content, preferably even happy with the current deal, where Bero shall rule the gaus, then we shall feast and mourn Friednot and he will leave his legacy of discontent to Hrolf to chew on. And one day you and Maino will have to deal with him.' He looked hard at me. 'You hate Maino, Maroboodus, but be very afraid of Hrolf the Ax. He is his father's son. Only younger. And less wise. That's what young men are. Less wise and get caught up in wars.'

'What if,' Aldbert whispered, 'he will not use spears and won't submit to your ideas? What if he—'

'Poisons us?' Hulderic asked, bemused. 'We will be careful. And if he goes to war? We still have the ring. If he finally loses his patience, and breaks off the alliance, the ring will matter. His warlords will be unhappy if he shatters them from our ancient blood and the ring's legacy. Poisoning is a threat, Aldbert, so you shall taste our food and drinks.'

'Why, thank you,' Aldbert said and hawked a half-fist sized chunk of yellowish spit, that ended up tangling from a low-hanging branch of a tree.

'Hard to eat, been having fever and snot keeps flying, lord. But I'll gladly sample your food. I only hope I shall not sneeze, my lord.'

Hulderic looked warily at the nasty display hanging from the branch, and apparently, decided Aldbert would not taste their food. 'He will have many plans,' Hulderic said and flashed us a dark look. 'He'll juggle them all while searching for the best one. Dubbe and Sigmundr will keep an eye on things. Bero's Gasto and Eadwine will as well. Danr rides around and makes sure nothing strange marches out of the woods and we will keep an eye out for treachery and schemes. Grandfather's champions joined us. Ludovicus and Osgar are ours, though the latter is shamed by his failure.'

'They joined *Bero*,' I corrected him sullenly and ignored Hulderic's long look.

Aldbert nodded uncertainly. 'Yes, lord. But I was wondering if they might be simply buying the supporters from under lord Bero's nose?'

Hulderic nodded. 'He will surely try that as well. The Thing will decide these matters, and we will stall, if we must, to make sure the families see the right path clearly. If they don't, we will risk a few feuds and hang those who would serve him.'

'It's an interesting time in our lands,' I said.

'We will be changing the gau a bit,' he said with agreement, 'so listen carefully in the Thing and stay calm.' He looked at us, but mostly Aldbert. 'Keep an eye out as well, Maroboodus and Aldbert.' Hulderic stiffened as he saw his father's corpse being carried out of his hall. 'They should have waited for me,' he whispered hoarsely. The body was wrapped in furs, and looked surprisingly small, but that's what death does to a person. There was more than flesh and bone to man's stature, and death robbed all of their former glory and dignity. We rode to a route that led through two rich fields and passed a crumbling well, and we reached the Bone-Hall when the men of Bero were lifting Friednot on top of the pile of wood with many soft curses as they were slipping. Bero glanced at Hulderic with relief and then at Hughnot, who had jumped down from his ship and was wading for the pyre, his long black hair whipping wildly in a brief, cold wind and he looked like a raven fighting currents as he made his way forward. He was like a bad omen, and both Father and Bero looked at each other, having agreed to stand united, but perhaps even Father had doubts about Bero's toughness. I noticed the twisted lord tapping his finger on his belt nervously and there was Draupnir's Spawn, something that was not lost on Hughnot. As the lord closed to the Bone-Hall, his men began to disembark from the suddenly crowded beach, and Hughnot's eyes enlarged, as Bero's plentiful followers began to emerge from fields and halls, over a hundred men. Hughnot was nodding to himself, as he glanced back to his men and when he turned, he clearly understood the subtle message and there was a thin-lipped smile on his wolf's face.

'So long any surprise Hulderic was hoping for,' Aldbert whispered to me. 'Bero showed their game. Hughnot won't make a mistake of trying to kill the lords now.'

'Bero's a damned coward fool,' I agreed.

'Well met,' said the huge lord of the Black Goths to Hulderic and Bero. He ignored the armed men surrounding the area and looked up at the body of his brother, his face unreadable. His men were pulling the last of the sleek rowing ships to the beach as Ingulf and Ingo; the red-haired champions stepped closer to him.

'Our hall? You have one set up for us?' Hrolf the Ax asked brusquely as he followed them to Hughnot. Son of Hughnot was not in a patient mood, his square beard quivering, and his strong, savage face was twisted with impatience as he eyed the army Bero had summoned. Bero scowled at him, but nodded at his own hall.

'Bone-Hall has space for you, lord, but not your ...friends. You get to sleep in our father's old rooms. Your men are numerous,' he stated unkindly as he stared at the disgorging men. 'We were ... not prepared for a full warband. You were quick to fetch them, though why? I wonder.' There was no answer and Bero pointed a finger towards his village. 'Space is sparse. But something will be arranged, of course.'

'Thank you, my fine nephew,' Hughnot said and thumbed the warparty. 'They came along to give me honor, and my brother.' I noticed the villagers collecting near the Bone-Hall, many of whom were Friednot's former men, and many of them, older families seemed to pick up the tension between the relatives as they were whispering.

101

And then I saw Maino.

He walked up from a large group of Bero's men and Hrolf spat at the sight of him, subtly, to the side, his eyes never leaving Maino and while I didn't exactly like or know Hrolf, and Hulderic had warned me about him, that gesture made me smile like the very best of jokes had been told by the wittiest man in all the lands under Sunna. I noticed Hughnot's eyes on me as I smiled and I straightened my face as fast as I could, but my joy had not gone unnoticed to the lord of the north gau. There was a strange moment where the gathered champions, men and lords looked awkward, as there were no laws and rules at to the behavior at funerals. Many fingered their weapons, as if ready to fight, in order to skip the bothersome demands of good manners. 'Frigg's milky tits, but why isn't Bero taking control?' I whispered.

Aldbert shrugged. 'He's afraid.'

He *was* out of his depth. Perhaps he was just learning, and would know what to do when given some time to grasp the oars in the storm he would be in, but he didn't have time, and was doing poorly. Even Maino looked dubious as the silence reigned.

'Shall we prepare?' Hulderic asked finally.

Men relaxed and were nodding. Hughnot waved his hand at the lot of us. 'Yes, indeed. Shall we burn and bury my great brother and your father and our lord? And then we have things to decide. Important things, my friends. And changes to be made, I think.'

BOOK 2: Third Choices

'You will die sad and reviled one day, Maino. It is evident as an eye in a head.'
Hulderic to Maino.

CHAPTER 6

The hlaut vessel would be filled to the brim from the open, gushing wound in the horse's throat, but it takes time for the sacrifice to calm down enough to do so, and so we waited, eyeing the bloody ritual take its course. Bero stood on the side, holding a seax, which was dripping dark blood to the sandy, partly stony beach. It was supremely hard to keep the dying beast still, but the men struggled, wrestling the beast down while whispering words of comfort to its ear, and Friednot's horse slowly calmed down to accept its fate. Its eyes were like pools of cold, lifeless water, though it still twitched when two old vitka strode purposefully forward and finally managed to fill the stone urns to the brim with the lifeblood of the mighty animal. The other holy man was a scarred, ancient creature, and had previously blessed the site with pleas to Donor the Thunderer and the other one, a bald man with very light blue eyes was now begging Woden to receive Grandfather in his halls. Then, a high woman, Bero's wife Sigurd walked around, about to offer the very best of mead to the highest ranking warriors standing around the bonfire and the sacrifice, while the first volva used an evergreen sprig to sprinkle the blood on the watching villagers. The people received the blessing stoically, while anticipating the boasts and oaths made by men who would be draining the fine mead either arrogantly, or reverently, depending on their fame and stature.

Sigurd's dark braids shook as she strode to the middle, and then turned to measure the fame and wealth of the men around her. Where she had normally walked to Friednot, she now had to determine where to turn first. Her tight, hard face twitched as her eyes passed Hughnot, and then she walked forward and stopped before Bero first. It was a direct message to Hughnot, who said nothing, his eyes glinting. Sigurd's husband and the lord of Friednot's former village grasped the horn from her hands and raised it. His voice was surprisingly strong and he hailed the many gods, who might or might not be listening, as they were fickle and expected men to help themselves before giving aid to those who asked for it. *We should help ourselves*, I thought. *I would, at least.* My eyes flickered to Maino, and I felt the darkness creep inside and my fist balled. I didn't see the girl anywhere, but she would be close and I knew Maino was keeping an eye on her. I shuddered as I thought of Hulderic's request, nay, an order to bow to the sack of shit, of Aldbert's words and then I embraced the darkness fully. *Gods might help me, but I'd help myself,* I chanted inside my skull, gathering resolve. Draupnir's Spawn glittered on Bero's finger. 'All-Father, Woden, Donor the Smiter, and Freyr, God of Growth! I, Bero, son of Friednot beg you. Take our father into the wealthy halls of the Aesir and the Vanir! Let him sit on the right hand of the high heroes of old, and let him fight well for you gods, for his and your amusement, for honor, for fame. He is a shield-breaker, a gut-splitter, a law-giver, and a great father, and we shall miss him and his strength and wisdom.' He went silent at that and I saw Hulderic look down, and Hughnot whispering with his son and champions, while eyeing and measuring Bero, who had claimed he needed his father's strength, and so perhaps he had none himself? Bero finally raised the horn and drank from it, as men around him softly banged their shields with their weapons. So did I. Then Sigurd took the horn back. Bero nodded at her.

She turned to Hulderic.

I saw Hughnot's jaw tighten at that, the insult echoing clear and loud in the clearing and few men missed it. The old nobles of Friednot's were nodding sagely at each other, and it became clear to them what the Thing would truly decide. Hughnot had always drunk the mead after Friednot, being the second most important man present, and now he, the lord of a gau, was pushed out of the position of power, further down the rankings of honor and I saw how Father took the stage, and there, that day, despite his often tedious carefulness, was not a shred of weakness in him. Hulderic flipped his helmet off and dropped it to the dust, his strong face staring straight at Hughnot, who, I think, flinched at the sight of the crow's eyes, as Father looked like a man about to commit his life to a battle. Hrolf leaned on his lord father and whispered balefully in his ear and Hughnot nodded briefly in answer to his son, knowing now who would be the sword of the southern gau, if any. Hulderic bowed to Sigurd and thanked her kindly and took the horn. He raised it high. 'To Freya, the Red Lady, Goddess of War, I give thanks, as Father often thanked her in his prayers. Let her warm amber tears make Father rich in afterlife, let him fight ferociously for his honor, and let Freya give my brother Bero her wisdom in the rulership of the Bear and Black Goths.' He drank and gave the horn away.

Bear Goths? I wondered.

Our gau had never born any name of the sort, but apparently Bero and Hulderic had decided to bind the gau together by naming us, and it suited us well, since the bear claws and jaws were hanging in the standards of the two brothers and you could not easily challenge or split a nation that stood under one name. Men's chests puffed out, they recited the words to their neighbors as they thrummed their shields with spears at Hulderic's words, and I felt immensely proud to be his son, for once.

But I'd still crawl in shit for Maino.

No.

Sigurd hesitated. Her eyes went over the multitude of warriors and that also was a clear message from Bero and Hulderic to Hughnot, something that again was not lost on anyone. Bero told Hughnot it would or would not be his turn, that Bero decided the pecking order, and that's the way it would be from then on. With practiced grace, slowly, and with some reluctance, Sigurd finally turned to the great man whose eyes burned in the night, impatiently, resentfully, nearly overcome by his anxiety to show everyone who he was, what he was made of, finally. He grasped the horn so forcefully that some of the holy liquid sloshed on his hand. It made Hulderic smile coldly at him, and Hrolf looked embarrassed for his father. Hughnot visibly calmed himself as he raised the great horn. 'I'll not toast Woden,' he stated bluntly and the silence was almost something you might cut with a fine spear-blade. The people looked on, clearly surprised by the vehemence in the voice of the disgraced lord. 'Nor shall I toast the Smiter, Donor, Freyr, or Freya,' he said with a strong, spiteful voice. 'I shall,' he raised the horn high, 'toast Tiw instead, the old lord, the forgotten brother, the god whom Woden pushed aside, the silent one, the patient one, sitting in the last rowbench of the pantheon of the gods.' He let the hidden meanings sink in to the keener ones in the crowd and went on with a sad, hurt voice. 'He is less rash, less wordy than the younger ones. He's the one who boasts the least, but when he is needed, he is the one whose mighty spear puts down those who would threaten the Nine Worlds,' he said and grimaced with hate as he looked at Bero, 'and those who would deny the old one his place. Let us not forget Tiw, *my* people,' he yelled and drank deep.

Then he thrust the horn high up in the air. 'Tiw the Just, the patient lord, you have been hailed, and yea, I'll also hail Friednot, my brother, my co-ruler, and the one man I'd bow my head to. But I'll not do so again, since he is gone.'

That also, was a clear message. None clearer. Then he saluted Friednot's corpse. 'Let my brother find favor with Tiw, if the younger gods bore him.' He poured the mead on the ground and let the fine horn fall, to Sigurd's shock. It clattered on the stones and rolled to mud as Hughnot walked forward where the horse was being butchered. Some of its meat would be sacrificed to the gods, some would follow Friednot into Valholl, and the rest we would eat. He passed the carcass to where Friednot's standard was, still tall and imposing, and yanked it off the ground, the skins flapping. He looked at us all, thrust the standard into the cooking flames and then tossed the flaming thing with all his might on top of the pyre.

Bero twitched, apparently having hoped to preserve the mighty artifact, but it was gone. There it burned, until fire caught Grandfather's furs and slowly, then with increasing gusto, the fire spread and the bonfire was alight. The men who had torches looked surprised and awkward but Hulderic nodded at them, and they too lobbed theirs into the spots where the fire had been meant to spread from. Bero and Hulderic stared at Hughnot and the dead father, all silent as a grave mount. Grandfather burned, his shield crackled, his face turned to look at us, skull visible under the flaming flesh and the vitka looked at the spectacle unhappily, muttering charms to ward against evil of the dead who would not go to the

108

next worlds. Men were banging their shields with their weapons, and we hoped the omens were good, as the other vitka cast lots and smiled coldly at Bero, nodding. There we stood for an hour, conversing gently, giving thanks silently, walking and stretching, heating ourselves with the blazing inferno's warmth, and after the pyre had burned and collapsed into a red-orange heap and only a skeletal hand could be seen amidst the embers, we turned away from Friednot. A mound would be raised in the harbor, though usually we burned and buried our dead in the woods and by the beautiful streams, but he would be there, a place where the children played, a testament to our glory, and a memory of our might to those who will never know his name, should we one day fall.

Bero led us away to the middle of the village where hundreds of the village's men gathered, as well as the hundred of Hughnot's men. The lords and champions sat on benches that were set in a circle and torches flared. The stars were bright in the sky for a while and Aldbert pulled me to stand behind Hulderic, as I stayed behind to stare at the twinkling, bright things. Aldbert frowned as he saw me standing there. I held my belly, and shook my head. 'I'll have to come there later,' I told him. 'Something I ate yesterday. Have to find a place to void myself, brother,' I said. 'I will talk to you later.'

He shook his head with bewilderment. 'Really? Pretending to be sick? Your father won't like it.' Then he understood. 'Oh! You are taking my advice. Good!'

Father looked back at me, a question in his eyes, and I ignored him, determined to slink away. My eyes went over to where Bero sat and met Maino's eyes. They were hard pools of glittering hate, his beefy face twitching with resentment, and I saw Bero look at Hulderic with worry. Apparently, Maino had heard words of calm from the lips of Bero, wise words considering the Thing's main purpose, but the frowning thing looking back at me seemed too consumed by his stubbornness and perhaps a bit of madness. I'd do something rash that night, I should have avoided the Thing like I had intended to, but Maino's eyes pulled me in. He was a stubborn, mad bastard.

And so was I.

Unity. We had to be united, Father's voice echoed. I should step away. I'd get him later.

He spat as he looked at me. He got up and made an obscene movement with his hips.

And so I decided to take part in the Thing.

Yes, I'd risk even my plans to spit in his face, I decided and walked after Aldbert, and Father's eyes glinted worry as he saw me approaching. I stood near him, as he sat down. Maino did as well, smiling spitefully.

We waited as the people gathered, and in the end everyone was ready. Finally, one of the vitka arrived. He pulled out a wand, a rod that was white and smeared with old bloodstains. He looked at Bero. 'Will we sacrifice a Saxon here today?'

Bero nodded. 'One of the wounded ones. I thought you already fetched him?' The vitka shook his head sheepishly and Bero sighed. 'Take the bleeding ones. They would die soon anyway.' The vitka turned to nod at some men who were to fetch one of the poor souls, but Hughnot sat on his bench and grunted.

'No, we won't,' he said. The vitka froze, surprised by the vehement expression of displeasure on the Black Goth's face. Hughnot's words cut through the air like a knife strike, severing us from the traditions, the excitement of the sacrifice. Hughnot was clearly angry, like a much wronged man seeking repayment for a sick cow and was about to use an ax rather than taking his issues to the Thing. He was high enough, in truth, to care little for the proper ways of doing things and he disdained the whole meeting now. I supposed that was a just sentiment, since he had been delegated to the lesser rank than Hulderic in the eyes of the gau. 'Sacrifice later, if you will,' he added darkly.

'It is the proper way to do things,' the vitka complained, a law-speaker in his own right, but even he dared not question the mind of the Black Goth over hard. 'Lord, if you would—'

'I said no,' Hughnot said darkly and the vitka nodded slowly. The great man went on. 'Bear … gau. Bears indeed. Mighty sons of a mighty lord should not be called the Sons of a Weasel, but a Bear. So be it. I like it. My brother never named you, his gau, his people, but it's proper you do. And enough of longwinded blessings and mumbled prayers, friends. Enough. The gods grow bored if we bless each and every word, stone, blade of grass in this yard. Let us move on. We are blessed, I am sure, already.'

Hulderic shrugged and bowed to the vitka. 'Very well. With no insult offered to the vitka, I think we have had quite enough of their wands. We desire for spears and shields to deal with many important issues we need to solve.' Men nodded with approval, and though Father meant our way of showing approval by banging the weapon on the shield, the words suggested a more nefarious possibility as well and Hughnot grinned at Hulderic as he acknowledged the dual meaning of his words. Hulderic nodded at the vitka. 'Spare the fool Saxon for some other purpose,' he said and then there was a glint in Hughnot's eye.

He pointed a finger towards the hall near the beach. 'And we don't even know if some of the Saxons are worth something, eh? How many are there?'

'Twenty are alive,' Bero said unhappily, unwilling to hand over the proceedings to the Black Goth, 'and two won't walk out of the hall.'

'Spare them all. We shall find a proper use for them later on,' Hrolf announced easily as he sat next to his father. It made the lot of us gasp with wonder. Where Bero and Hulderic sat a bit apart from their nobles and commoners, the two Black Goths sat right next to each other, as if they were equal in rank.

Hughnot put a hand on his son's shoulder and confirmed the rights of his son with a toothy smile. 'Hrolf here is the co-ruler in our family. Hail him as your equals, nephews.'

Hulderic smiled wryly, nodding at Hrolf disdainfully, an act of dismissal if any and certainly in no way a gesture of equality. Bero squinted, having not nodded at all. 'Surely his … rulership is something the men decide in your gau? Did they agree?' the twisted lord asked, puzzled. 'You have a fine son, but he is young, very young, and probably should *learn* rulership, law, and perhaps, if I might say so, war?' Hrolf got up angrily, but Hughnot pulled him down.

'I know war, uncle,' Hrolf hissed, and went silent as Hughnot's hands pressed his shoulders painfully.

'And what does co-rulership mean in your … family?' Hulderic asked softly, weighing the two dangerous men sitting across from us. 'You are not too old, lord. At least you are not crippled. You could lead for a decade still. And why would we treat him equally? This gau is ours, yours is yours and this is the stronger gau, the one that leads, as has been agreed.'

Hughnot shook his head heavily, leaning forward. He had a seax in his hands, and he was playing with it deftly. He pointed it at Father. 'As has been agreed? Such agreements have changed now. I said "in our family",' Hughnot stated. 'Yours and mine. We are that, never forget. A family. You have the same blood running in your veins as I do, only thinner like a muddy river that has run too far from its roots. Hrolf here grew up to be much like his father. You two are very unlike your father, very much so. One,' he said and pointed at Hulderic, 'is meek, and silent. Soft I thought you to be, but you are not, but you disdain power.' The silence was terrible, the insult enough for a feud. But Hulderic said nothing, his back tense and I wanted to kick him into action. 'The other,' Hughnot said, 'lacks something else.' *Bravery.* That was his lost word, but he didn't utter it. He slammed the blade into the bench. 'There are no two families here anymore, like we agreed with Friednot. That is done with. Now we have only one. Our roots are in Gothonia, my friends, and while we rule two gaus, in truth we are but one. Always were. Hrolf is your equal because I rule Hrolf. Hrolf is not equal to me. But he is to you.'

And there it was. He considered himself our lords. It made Bero cringe, Maino sputter, the champions of the Bear's shift in their feet and many crumbled angrily at the insults. Hughnot said nothing back, but stared at the lot, anticipating the mood. There were many who shook their heads at his words, but others looked down, thinking deeply

Hulderic, gathering his calm, grunted. 'Thinner blood, eh? Perhaps the river that runs far from its roots is clear rather than muddy? No, we are free, powerful as forged Celt steel sword. Hughnot eyed the Head Taker, held by Bero. 'I say,' Hulderic growled, 'that we are not less than our father, Hughnot. Do not assume so. That is an insult and insults do not lead to smiles and happiness. Especially if one has fewer men than the other.'

'I agree,' Bero said nervously. 'Hrolf is your adeling, but our adelings are equal to him.'

'Truly?' Hughnot said softly, his jaw tight. He slapped his knee. 'I apologize, Hulderic,' Hughnot said, with a cruel smile on his face, 'but I understand *Bero* here should rule us. I say I should. I have earnt the right. I am old, wily, wise, and my brother's right hand. I made him great, and well you know it. What say you, Bero the lord of the Bears?' The voice was mocking, and not lost on Bero. 'Do you think you equal me in stature? Truly?'

'I—' Hulderic began, but Hughnot shook his head.

'I asked *him*,' he roared and pointed his finger at the twisted lord.

Bero tried. He lifted his chin and eyed Hughnot with disdain. 'The family is one. I agree. The rulership is not. Marka is the capital of our alliance. The ring is here, with me. The issue was decided when I married and so it shall be, no matter my age. We decide the rulership of this gau amongst our people, you yours, and you shall follow my banner in the future. You and Hrolf. Things will not change,' Bero stated with a nervous stutter. The shields on our side were thrumming from being struck by the spear shafts, which emboldened Bero. 'Family we are, but this is not land where you, or your son have a say on matters of its free men. In this Thing, we decide on common issues, but not on who is equal to whom. Aye,' Bero said, gathering strength from some cheering nobles, 'Things decide many things, and we sit here now, and in the future, but what Friednot once was, I am now.'

'But you are not,' Hrolf said darkly. 'You are not the Thiuda. We elect war-kings for wars, and since we are always at war, Friednot was one for decades. But he is dead now and the spot is not something you inherit because of a band of gold, Bero.'

'I say it is, because this band of gold, this ring was Friednot's and gave him his authority,' Bero told the boy, who sneered.

Hughnot grunted. 'To the business at hand then. The Black Goths have agreed I and Hrolf shall be Thiuda, the war kings of *our* confederation,' Hughnot said darkly. 'We are changing the old ways.'

'Well,' Hulderic stated. 'Bero will be ours. And yours. Did you truly ask your men to lift you over the rightful wearer of Draupnir?' Hulderic's eyes went over the men of the northern gau. Some were steady, many were not, looking down and away. The faces of the Black Goths gave little away, but many eyed Bero's ring.

Hughnot's eyes also went to the ring on Bero's finger. *That* made our Thiuda the leader of the two gaus and that was the truth. The two Black Goths stared at us, until Hughnot sighed. He waved his hand. 'Here it is, nephews. The fact remains that the ... Bear Goths are more numerous than the Black ones. Your battles with the Svearna are not as frequent as ours. Svearna, and raiders from the coasts find us easier prey since we are the northernmost Goths, live across the Long-Lake, isolated, and so we must suffer more than you do, who have other Goths to the south. Even the Saxons find our land alluring, often rowing their ships past your land, and the Boat-Lord, our relative and a fellow Goth might soon attack us. Guess where he shall begin? He will burn our halls first, and you will help us, of course, but we will be the ones to suffer.'

'Powerful case,' Aldbert whispered. 'Well practiced.'

'Perhaps true,' I retorted.

Hughnot went on. 'With Friednot we had ties of blood. Yes, with you as well, but not as thick and strong as they were before and I mean no insult, this time. He was a strong leader. He anticipated trouble like a bloodhound would. We worked well together. With him in the rudder of this confederacy, we did well enough. My people suffered fewer losses when Friednot ruled. Svearna will raid harder now. Very hard, as they seem to be up to no good. They will bring thousands and they will do so in the winter as well. We need something new for our future. Something better.' Hughnot's men thrummed their shields briefly. 'We need to take war to them. And we have to drive them out, far away. And that means we have to risk what Friednot didn't wish to risk. Our lands. We have to risk war, and accept the need to conquer in order to grow. We have to risk our lives and crops. I can lead that effort. Hrolf will learn.' His eyes went to Bero. 'Our northern people do not trust you, though. Ring. Or no ring. Will the ring change Bero into a savage warlord as he leads us west? Or east? I doubt it.'

Bero grunted and there was an awkward silence. He said nothing, but stared forward and I saw there was a film of sweat on his forehead. Aldbert was frowning and Hulderic was fidgeting, and cursing Bero's silence softly. 'Lord uncle,' Hulderic said respectfully after a while. 'I say it is hard for a man to decide if a coming winter will be deadly beforehand. You have to endure it and see what happens. Perhaps the Svearna will not come? Perhaps they will see us still strongly united as they have always seen us. Yea, you suffer more than we do, but never have they tried to dislodge you. What we need is unity. But to go to war? Perhaps we should find out more about the threat, lord? More about the girl that was to be married to the Boat-Lord? Your brother stopped that, and perhaps that gives us time to act. Many things need clarity. Where would we strike? Against our brethren, the Boat-Lord's men? Against those Svearna who trade with us, still? Or beyond? We don't know who leads them.'

'I know who leads the ones who plan to destroy us,' Hrolf said and Hughnot slapped a hand on his shoulder.

'Oh?' Hulderic asked, cocking his head. 'Tell us.'

Hughnot looked like he was munching on a rock, grinding it to bits. Then he answered. 'One Gislin. Lord of Snowlake, a wealthy hill fort some days away, beyond Long-Lake, further than the Three Forks, the rivers of the west. I learnt it from a trader. I'll say no more of it.' And there was more, as Hulderic and Bero eyed each other with confusion.

'Did Friednot know?' Bero asked him.

'Yes,' Hughnot said. 'He did.'

'Is the girl related to him?' Hulderic insisted. 'This Gislin?'

'Might be,' Hughnot answered, glowering darkly. 'But we are not here to discuss strategy. We are here to discuss who will make it. I'm not inclined to wait until they butcher us.'

Hulderic nodded as he thought about it and waved his hand. 'I say sit tight on your throne, lord, in the north and trust we will prove to be careful protectors of all our interests. We will be hounds now, Hughnot. Keen, bloodthirsty and loyal to our family, to our ancient agreements. And perhaps we shall go to war together, but under the Bear banner. Does this please you?' Hulderic asked his brother and Bero nodded stiffly and Hrolf my father like he would a corpse. The twisted Bero cringed as Hughnot straightened his back slowly, and stood up. He pointed a finger at Bero.

'I want,' Hughnot said softly, his eyes glowing and voice crackling with impatience, 'Hrolf to live in the Bone-Hall. I want you to respect him like you did Friednot. And *then* we shall plan for war and for peace and that is the way of it. I'll not discuss this further.'

The silence that followed was so heavy you could hear a horse farting in the halls nearby. Danr and Eadwine, Bero's warlords were stroking their beards. Ingulf and Ingo were staring resolutely at every champion present and I noticed they held hands on their ax hilts. Aldbert leaned on me. 'That is why he didn't want the gods blessing on the Thing. If he is rejected, there was no real Thing, was there? Just a group of idiots refusing to see his wisdom.'

Aldbert's whispered words didn't carry to anyone's ears, but they did release everyone else to whisper as well. The Bear Goths were muttering angrily, though not everyone looked upset at the threat Hughnot was making. Eyes were glinting in the ranks of nobles on our side and the fact was not lost on Bero. Hulderic saw it as well and flashed a look at Bero. The twisted lord swallowed and shook his head. 'This is not a decision for today.'

'Not for today?' Hughnot asked softly. 'Why not?'

'I will have to consult a vitka,' Bero said slowly. 'And I will decide this only after my son's issues have been dealt with.'

'What issues are those?' Hrolf sneered. 'What issues might Maino have that are more important than the rulership of our people? I would think he can speak for himself? Or has he fallen over his ax and swallowed his tongue? Gotten lost in a mug of ale?'

Maino growled. 'I—'

'Come, stand up, I cannot hear you!' Hrolf yelled.

Maino did and it did take away the smile from Hrolf's lips, because Maino had a reputation and it was no less than Hrolf's. He spoke surprisingly strongly. 'I will not have you lot spoil the night of my marriage to the Svea girl.' Hughnot frowned at the news. If the girl was the one that had been planned on to cement the alliance between the Boat-Lord and the Svearna, this Gislin, then it would not suit Hughnot Maino married her. The angry reaction on his face told us that.

But someone else reacted more strongly.

'Marriage?' the question was growled so loudly it reverberated across the meeting. Hundreds of people turned to look at the source. Aldbert, and Father as well, their eyes scouring me feverishly, as I had uttered the word.

'To Snow-Flower,' Maino said with a sneer, turning to me. 'Happy you spoke up. You see, I need to pay her father a dowry. And you, Maroboodus shall provide it. You'll do it for the insult, the cowardly attack on me during the battle. Your father has agreed to this. Six cows and a horse. And you shall bring them to me, drag them to their new master and ask for pardon, cousin.'

'You want me to pay for *your* dowry?' I growled. 'You wish me to apologize to *you?*'

'Yes, cousin. You will bless my marriage with your gifts,' he grinned. 'I'll tell her it was the red-haired dolt who thinks he saved her, that paid so handsomely for our bliss.'

Bero raised his hand. 'We will speak again tomorrow, Hughnot. The Bear clan needs to sit down with its family heads. In the meantime, let us deal with these unpleasant matters, and pleasant ones as well.' In that meeting of the families that would take place in a moment's time, I decided, they would threaten the lords of the houses, bribe others and Hughnot would be left powerless. The wily Goth knew they would risk much if they chose young Hrolf as the new lord, but they had listened to the northern lord even then and would reap some rewards from Bero.

Hughnot nodded tiredly, and wiped his hand across his eyes. 'By all means, discuss the matter. But we are not changing our point of view. And we deserve better from you. And,' he said with a strong voice that brooked no argument, 'none shall marry the girl. None, before our issues are settled.'

Bero and Hulderic stared at him and the twisted lord gathered some of his pride, as he ignored the threat. 'We shall decide on that, Hughnot. And now,' Bero said, visibly relieved by not having to decide anything right at that moment, turned to us, 'we have to discuss the apology.'

Hulderic squared his shoulders and got up. 'We had an unfortunate fight between the boys, that is all. He will—'

And that is when Maino could not keep his mouth shut. 'He attacked me like a true coward,' Maino sneered and I reddened as men's faces turned my way.

'A coward who killed both chiefs,' I said icily.

'I killed Cuthbert, and chased the other one to your limp spear,' he retorted. 'I will want two boats in addition to what your agreement was. Two. After all,' he laughed, 'I'll have to feed my future wife. And our many beautiful children.'

I felt sweat trickle down my face and cursed him profusely, and felt Aldbert tug at my thumb for some reason. I glanced at him, and saw him trying to calm me down, but he was also terrified.

Hulderic looked at Bero, who was supremely bothered, his eyes drifting to Hughnot. Finally, he agreed with his boy's claim. 'The cows will be paid. The horses. And one of the two boats you were promised, Hulderic.'

Hulderic shuddered with anger, but nodded and spoke coldly. 'Four cows.'

'He said—' Maino began, but Hulderic got up.

'I said four cows, whelp,' Hulderic said slowly and with a clipped threat in his voice. 'It will be four cows and a boat and not a single horse. If you wish for Maroboodus to bring them to you, this is the price. You pay the rest of the dowry by yourself, boy, and that is your duty, not ours. You are stretching your luck, Maino, and I think *I* will be insulted very soon.' It was a clear challenge, but not one Maino wanted to take. His beady eyes glittered angrily and then he bowed stiffly.

'Four,' Bero said with a cold smile. 'One boat.'

They were speaking of it as if I was not there, and I felt rage tearing me apart inside. My fingers thrummed the hilt of my cudgel.

'And your boy will bend a knee before me,' Maino added with a throaty, thick voice full of malice. 'And he will give Snow-Flower to my hand in the wedding. He will bring her to me and stand and smile while we are wed.'

Bero covered his face with his hand, and cursed softly, unable to control the idiot.

Hulderic gave a guttural laugh and regarded him. 'Deal. May she bring you misery, Maino. You are not a gracious winner and she does not care for you. Who would? You are not worthy of her and one can only hope Bero will have more sons, and the wise gods will give them more blessings. You will die sad and reviled one day, Maino. It is evident as an eye in a head.'

Bero touched his shield's wooden frame at the terrible words and Maino's lips quivered as he tried his best to ignore Hulderic. He pointed his finger my way. 'Get the apology over with now, Maroboodus.'

Hundreds of mocking eyes turned to look at me, enjoying the humiliation, no matter what they thought of Maino. I stood up, and took a faltering step forward, ignoring the stern look Hulderic gave me, the eyes of Bero, begging I would behave and the calming whisperings of Aldbert. I hefted my shield, held my back straight and walked to Maino, who came to stand before me. I was tall as a tree, but Maino was taller and I resented the fact I had to look up in order to gaze into his brutish eyes. He pursed his lips and kicked the dust before him. 'On your knees. And you will tell me you are so sorry, with such a miserable, sad voice that even I am convinced of your sincerity. And I do not get convinced easily, cousin.'

My knees felt like they were made of hammered iron, as if they were tough spear points and would not bend. To kneel and go before Maino? *Impossible.* My lips moved, but only barely. And what came out was not an apology. 'Your ale.'

'My what?' he asked with incredulity. 'He is addled!' Maino yelled. 'Frightened beyond his wits.' Men laughed, women tittered.

'The day of the battle, cousin,' I said surprisingly steadily. 'I spat in your ale that day, when you took your piss. And you drank it down like the very best of drinks. You enjoyed my snot, you filth, and let my vomit travel your throat as if it was brewed by the handmaidens of Frigg themselves. You grinned like a child, Maino. You gobbled down my phlegm, dear cousin. It was like this.' And I spat on his face.

He stared at me. Hrolf laughed with a surprised, high voice.

119

In a few minutes' time, a dozen men had managed to wrestle Maino off me. I had bruises on my neck, some on my sides, but Maino's nose was bleeding. He had a feral, dog-like look on his face. His lips were drawn back, his teeth bared and yellow and his eyes were bloodshot as Danr and Eadwine held him. Dubbe and Sigmundr were sitting on me and I smiled at Maino. 'Girl,' I called him. 'Ugly, useless bit of lard. You go and hump your cows, idiot cousin. That's all you are good for.'

'I'll show you who I shall—'

'Silence!' Hughnot yelled.

Bero growled and slammed his shield down on a bench, silencing everyone. He got up and stood before me. 'Will you agree to his terms? Do it, Maroboodus, and save us this trouble. You've had your fun, now obey!'

'I'll fight him, and then I'll kneel next to him. I'll beat him senseless and tell him how sorry I am when he is weeping sadly!'

'Yes, fight!' Maino growled. 'Now!'

'No!' Hulderic said.

'Yes,' I hissed. 'Let him prepare first. Get the ax, get the mail you likely robbed from my kills.'

Bero rushed to my side and kneeled. He leaned closer and growled at the men to step away. They did and he whispered to me. 'We don't need this,' he hissed at me, trying to avoid looking at Hughnot. 'You know this. You must know this. He benefits from that.' He nodded towards the Black Goths.

'You will benefit from the absence of Maino,' I told him with a sweet smile. 'When your damned boy is gone, you will spawn wiser children, just like Father said.'

His eyes were so furious I was afraid for my life for a moment. 'Maino, despite his many faults hears Woden's call, Maroboodus,' Bero said softly. 'My brother will be left to attend another funeral, or to take care of a sad little cripple for the rest of his days. You will be sorry, Hulderic will be broken and I shall have to bear his resentment, your father's, my brother's for eternity. And if you win, I will hate you. And you will not submit?'

'Why won't *he* submit?' I asked him.

'He is twisted inside, Maroboodus,' Bero said desperately. 'Broken. He is touched by the gods. There is little kindness in him, boy. You—'

'After a while, by the funeral pyre!' I yelled at his face, and struggled against the men holding me down. They let me go after Bero nodded at them heavily, and Dubbe was cursing me softly.

Bero got up and nodded at the champions. They let Maino go. I saw Hulderic's feverish eyes staring at me, disappointed beyond words, afraid and what he was thinking, I didn't know. I was thinking hard. My thoughts were chaotic, desperate. I knew I was in trouble, and should hide like a mouse in a hole. And then Woden helped me and I froze. I walked to Aldbert who was gawking at me and I pulled him to the side. 'Here is what you will do.'

'I will bury you? Or start thinking about a funeral song for you as well? I'll not—'

'You will not bury or make songs about me, but you will be my friend. As I have always helped you, so shall you help me now and in the future,' I said and saw how he twitched at that and I told him what I needed. He smiled wryly and nodded, very unhappy with the chore, but still gleefully happy to do it. Then he left. I grabbed a mug of ale and sat down to stare at Maino's ferocious eyes. I met Hughnot's instead. And they were interested, too interested.

He smiled at me and toasted. I looked away, but only for a while before I answered his toast with a nod.

121

CHAPTER 7

You can do it, I thought, sitting there, glowering at men who came to wish me luck, or to tell me goodbye. I was lying to myself, of course, because if my small ruse didn't work, fighting Maino might very well leave me dead or a cripple, as Bero's chilling words had predicted. 'Gods, I should have stayed away from the Thing,' I cursed under my breath. Most men present flocked to Maino, clapping his shoulders, honeying his ears with their support, pouring praise and encouragements over him, words he didn't need. Many were young men, fawning on the man they saw as the champion to rival the fame of the greatest men in the tribe and many would, no doubt, hope to serve under Maino's banner.

And I had nobody on my side, save for some polite clients of Hulderic, giving me a sympathetic eye.

It had ever been thus.

I was *no* less promising a warrior in a shieldwall, a slayer of *two* chiefs, in truth probably a better leader, or at least I wanted to think so, but the thick-faced bastard Maino always charmed the lesser creatures with his confident boasts, arrogant blustering and outright threats. Few men cared to read hidden messages in men's eyes, and few looked at mine twice.

It would change.

Like a hunter scraping a layer of rich fat from a fallen beast, the fools would soon glimpse what sturdy muscle lay beneath the surface of Maroboodus. They expected me to fight and to fall, and Woden's prowess was expected of Maino. I heard them advise him. 'Give him not one moment of peace,' one drunk told him. 'Drive him around like a two-legged dog,' he added. I grinned. They expected him to be a brute and I would be the one he mauled.

But I'd give them a feat worthy of Woden's other side, his tricky side. Yes, great god's trickery would prevail there instead of his rage and prowess.

Unless, of course, Aldbert failed.

Then I'd be kicked around like a dog, indeed.

I prayed to Frigg, goddess of mercy that Aldbert would indeed help me with what I had asked for, instead of getting lost in his poems, or caught by a mug of ale and a smile from a pretty girl. It would be a perilous fight, dangerous, even if my friend managed what I wanted him to do because Bero had been right. He had surprised me with his accurate description of his son, the one claiming Maino was not all right in the head. He would possibly kill me. I'd use that very madness against the fool, but it would be dangerous.

Time was spent on more flattery and I waited as Maino got ready. He was wearing chain-mail now, Cuthbert's, a well-made, sturdy, strong, fitting armor that looked splendid on him. It had been the Saxon's great treasure, and I could, somewhere deep inside, understand why Maino would do anything to gain it, even kick me out of his way. He wore a helmet of leather, with ring metal neck guard. That also was new and much like Hulderic's. His shield was dark, glistening with grease, and had a fresh bear paw painted on it. In fact, so did Hulderic's and Bero's. And the champion's, I realized to my rage.

Not mine.

They hadn't bothered telling me about our new name and tribal symbol. Even after calling me *the* Bear, Hulderic had not told me anything about this Thing.

So be it.

I drank down mead, and eyed my cousin, trying to reason with the fear that was attempting to tear my composure apart. He was a *champion*. A berserker, a servant of Woden's darker side and now even the vitka doted over him, hissing spells in his favor, though did not his father pay the vitka to do so? He would, to spare him.

I looked like a peasant in comparison.

I pulled off my tunic and cursed when I felt there was a hole in the sole of my simple shoe. I looked at my shield. The frame was sturdy. I had fixed the holes and slashes on the hide from the battle and my hasta was of a good quality, the iron blade sharpened after the battle. It had killed men. That's all that mattered. No back-clapping, no spells by vitka, no—

Hulderic pulled me around.

I looked into his feverish eyes and he rubbed a hand across his sweaty face. 'Father,' I acknowledged his presence coolly.

'Son,' he whispered huskily.

'I would—'

He interrupted me. 'I'll not ask *why*, boy. I'll not try to reason with a simple mule. You did what you did, and I sense you meant to, all along. I hope you will understand one day why a father's lot is the worst lot under the Sunna, and the Mani. To be a father to an ox-brained idiot like Maino must be a test of endurance most gods would fail to pass, and I never thought I'd be measured like Bero is, daily, but here I am, struggling not to whip your rear. I won't because it will bleed soon, anyway.'

'You asked for too much, Father,' I told him honestly. 'And thank you for not joining the crowd of Maino's well-wishers. But maybe you should? For the alliance, eh? You go over there, Father, and tell him he shall win.'

'I'm not his well-wisher, son,' he told me miserably. 'I'm sorry.' He said it with a truly desperate voice, and I nodded before I could catch myself.

'Think nothing of it. And I'm sorry I'm a mule, rather than a slave.'

He poked me with a strong finger, and I noticed how men around us were now wagering on the outcome, some, the old hands at betting were eyeing me carefully, trying to hear what Father might be advising me with. Hulderic opened his mouth to give me some, but saw how people were leaning closer and whispered instead. 'I've trained you. Tire him out. But do not kill him.' He gave me a brave smile, but there was also sorrow in his eyes.

He did not think I could win.

'I'll spare his life, but not his hide, Father,' I told him after a moment's consideration. 'He'll live. But he won't enjoy his life after this night is over.'

'At least you have spirit,' he said. 'Fight. And then we shall speak. You know of what,' he growled.

'Of Aldbert's silly songs?'

He froze. 'He made a mockery of it?'

'He isn't much of a liar, Father,' I told Hulderic with a small grin, as Maino yelled a challenge to the gods, showing his spear to the people around him, who roared in support of him. Even Dubbe, the bastard, I noticed, who gave me a sheepish grin to indicate he was not serious.

Hulderic hesitated and wiped his face as Maino's friends exhorted their champion. 'He is your only friend, is he not? Aldbert.'

'He is, and do not ask him to lie to me again,' I said and tried not to look at Maino, who was flexing his shoulders, now glancing at me like a dog would gaze at an unwary fox cub lost in the woods.

'Here,' Hulderic said heavily and handed me a weapon. It was wrapped in seal skin and I felt its weight. Inside, there was an ax. It had a sharp half-moon edge, a sturdy haft and a deadly iron spike on the end of the shaft. The grip was made of thick cow leather and it had been painted red. 'I was going to give it to you after the battle. You can use a club, if you don't want anything from me. Works just as well, I'm sure, but this is better. It belonged to a man who died defending Cuthbert.' His eyes measured the chain mail of Maino disdainfully. 'Not as good as that thing on him, but a very good weapon, son. Worthy of you.'

'Thank you, Father,' I told him uneasily. 'You asked me not to kill him, and then you give me a butcher's weapon?'

There was a brief smile on his face and he shrugged. 'It's not a simple matter, is it? You will need it, whether you win or lose,' he said sadly. 'If you win, I will have to send you away and you shall need a good weapon. If you lose, use it with honor this night. May Woden walk with you.'

Send me away? I'd do it myself, I thought. But there were tears in the corners of his eyes, and so I sighed, and drove away the resentment and anger and nodded at him gratefully. 'Make more boys, Father. You are not too old yet. Erse might be a good one for you, no? Perhaps you should finally have her? Even if you promised Aldbert he could ask her as well.'

He looked for Aldbert, who wasn't there. 'He wants her, did you know?'

125

'I do know,' I told him, 'but Erse wants you. Make her a wife, and enjoy your life a bit.'

'Now *you* are thinking of marrying *me*?' he said and smiled and then sobered, nodding his head. 'I'll think about it.'

'Good,' I told him and got up. I embraced him briefly and pushed him away. *Gods, let him understand what I will do, if I survive.* I held the magnificent ax and stood there, alone. Maino's eyes went to the weapon, and measured its worth. *The beastlike, dull-looking creature was not entirely stupid,* I reminded myself, but had a cunning of a hunting wolf as well as the brawn of a bear, but none of it mattered then. Men, even women were still making wagers. Only some shrewd older men or total fools were betting on me, so it was a one-sided affair. I saw how Ingo jogged to Hughnot's side, and whispered something with a grin. Hughnot roared with laughter and gave me a vicious grin.

'I'll bet four fox furs on young Maroboodus there,' he yelled and that got Maino's full and undivided attention.

'I take that bet,' Bero said stiff with pride, though he avoided looking at me. I stared at Hughnot, and tried to push away the burst of gratitude for the great man who had quieted a sizable number of people in the crowd, though surely most thought he was just mad.

'Are you ready?' Hrolf yelled and I noticed he was looking at me. 'We have no time to spare from the feasting. It will be a busy day tomorrow, anyways, with so many great things being decided. Like we think Maroboodus is the better man in this contest, tomorrow our reign shall begin, a sign for the better future of our people.' And that silenced the crowd entirely.

Bero was glowering and Hulderic stepped forward. 'It is not a sign of the gods they support your claims, Hrolf, if my boy wins,' he said.

And Bero ruined it. 'But he will not.'

'We shall see!' Hrolf laughed and pointed a finger at me. 'Are you ready?'

'I am,' I said sternly, hoping my voice would not break. I tucked the ax to my belt and grabbed my spear and shield.

'He's not,' Maino snorted. 'He's like a spent arrow, no flight left in him. Let us go and I'll break his sorry neck.'

I nodded at them arrogantly and turned away and stomped to the darkness. 'Let's do this under the gaze of Friednot, eh?'

'Why not here, pup?' Maino yelled after me, but took steps to follow, anyway.

'Because I want the dead and the Saxons, no doubt staring through the cracks in the walls, see how Maino gets his pride stripped like a maiden loses her virginity on her wedding night,' I laughed and went on, and people agreed it was the best place for the fight, since most cheered wildly. I cursed myself for mentioning a virgin and a wedding night, since our fight would also decide the fate of the girl.

I would not steal her away if I lost a limb. Or my life.

I walked first, headed for the harbor. The villagers followed, muttering, laughing and the air was practically rippling with excitement. If anything, the fight had driven out the worry from their minds, made them forget the strife between the Black Goths and us, but Hrolf had made it a prophetic event, Bero had agreed with his pride at stake, and so it was as if the gods would decide the outcome of the battle, and that would also affect the Thing's decision. It would be harsh work for Bero and Father to make sure the nobles of Marka and the surrounding villages of wavering loyalties would support Bero's claim to be the Thiuda without me beating Maino.

I clutched my spear and shield so hard I was afraid they might break. We passed halls and their vegetable gardens, a small patch of oaks, walked down well-trodden paths and saw the Bone-Hall very soon and some excited dogs chased after us, yapping hysterically. Maino was walking close now, and I heard him whispering. I resisted the urge to make sure he was not close enough to attack me from behind again, and kept looking ahead. He was likely praying to the gods, begging to receive a vicious rage, a killer's state of mind as the battle began, and he probably prayed Hel would make a toothpick of my bones. 'Will you ignore me, Maroboodus?' he finally snickered. 'Will you not grace me with your pretty eyes. Star-Flower will. She will look at my face for years to come, above her in the bed.'

'Star-Flower?' I spat. 'Surely she has a proper woman's name?'

'She might,' Maino allowed. 'I—'

'She will not share it with you,' I said spitefully, 'because she will not have the vitka bless your marriage and have her real name soiled by such a travesty. She reserves it for me.'

'She might blurt it out, though,' Maino said spitefully, with spittle flying, 'when I bed her. It will be exciting for her, won't it?'

And with that, I was not afraid any longer. I looked his way, felt a call, a savage need, a bloody craving to fight him and wished for the gods to give him some luck so it would not end quickly. I didn't need any. He would.

I had made mine.

I arrived before the Bone-Hall. The funeral pyre was still flaming gently, the heat from the furnace of glowing coals nearly overwhelming if you ventured too close, and some did, to glimpse the remains of Grandfather. But I was not interested in Grandfather's blackened bones. My eyes sought out Aldbert and I spied him by the doorway to Grandfather's former hall. He stood to the side, behind some confused slaves and nearly jumped up and down as he tried to catch my eye, until he hit his head on the prow of a former ship. He massaged a painful lump and pointed at a muddy mattock and winked at me. I turned to look at the battlefield and walked over to stand with my back to the pyre, and felt my clothes warm against my skin. I welcomed it as my eyes sought the battle ground. The villagers slowly filled the area and Aldbert helpfully began pushing them so they would form a tight circle around us. Maino pushed through to stand before me, ten paces away. It all took time, as the people filtered to find places, the warriors in the fore, the best shields blocking our way out and I admit it was a strangely honorable, exhilarating feeling as they stared at us over the rims of their shields, painted with devices they had carried to the battle. While many of them had previously been betting against me and had been vocally supporting Maino, now they were quiet. Bero was there, frowning and nervous, Hulderic appeared as well and Hughnot came to stand opposite them, pushing some of the lesser men back so he and Hrolf would find a place to stand.

I turned my eyes to Maino. He stared back at me, and I was gratified to see he was not brimming with confidence. His eyes glowed and danced with the fire that reflected from the former pyre behind me. He sweated, he trembled, and he looked anxious as a small girl. Even the bravest fear, no matter if they face a worm or a real man and Maino was not certain what I was, despite his arrogant posturing. He remembered me from the battle, and I had not been a weakling then, and he knew it.

The baldheaded vitka appeared and danced between us, and I cursed profusely under my breath as his feet stomped the ground. He was whooping, praying and cursing and he squinted at the sky, as if trying to fathom if the wolves chasing Mani across the sky would give the fight their gracious attention. A bank of clouds filled the sky and I chuckled as the vitka's face turned into a confused frown. He stopped dancing, standing over a tall tuft of grass in the otherwise pristine field, and called out. 'Gods will see, gods will hear and let them judge the unworthy one fairly. Donor bless this fight, may Woden give your spears speed and Freya, the Red Lady fill your hearts with savagery. Fight, fight!'

'Father?' Maino asked gutturally.

'Try not to kill your cousin,' Bero said softly. 'But beat him to mud for your honor.' His voice betrayed his fear Maino would not oblige and try to kill me. Or that he would fail.

'I wish the same,' Hulderic said, even if most of the villagers quaffed. Dubbe, and Sigmundr swelled at the indignity and disrespect they gave me, but I did not care. Harmod, the wisest of Father's men, shook his head at me, and his eyes scourged the battlefield, and a small smile lit up his face. I looked away from him, but I was sure he had figured out what surprise I had planned to make Maino's evening painful and shameful.

I pointed my spear at Maino. 'The loser will forget the Svea girl for good. That one shall marry the winner of this fight.'

'That,' Bero called out heavily, 'is a bigger issue than the animosity between two idiots. It concerns *all* the Goths.'

'At least,' I said darkly, 'the loser shall not marry her.'

'Say yes, Father,' Maino growled, hefting his shield. He had a brutal-looking club with iron studs on his belt. I was sure it had been especially designed to be used on my back and ribs after he had me down.

'Fine,' Bero said suspiciously, eyeing me and wondering at my request. 'Begin.'

'Begin,' Hrolf yelled, stealing Bero's authority, but it worked.

People thrummed their spears on the shields, and a terrible noise filled the night. It was a blood curdling, exhilarating, dreadful, and savage sound. I felt Friednot, Grandfather standing in the former pyre behind me, looking at me with approval, though he had loved Bero and Maino best, but he would not spit on a brave man and I was just that. I begged for his help and then Maino roared. His eyes stood in his head, whites shining. He was raging, spitting and dancing back and forth, the framea held high, overhand. Some berserkers get their rage from such rituals, like awakening hunger with the smell of roasted meat, the rage can be forced. Some come to it naturally, when threatened, and yet others, only pretend. Maino was one who could enrage himself into it. Despite the fearful display, I snorted. *He makes even himself mad,* I thought and laughed aloud, which infuriated him even more. He squatted behind his shield, his eyes glinting at me with feral intensity, like a bull boar getting ready to charge from the underbrush against a weak, wounded intruder. I saw him snort, snot flying and I braced myself, aiming my hasta his way, bending my knees and lifting the shield I took a step forward. 'Come, Maino, and let me piss on your yellow teeth as you gasp for breath.'

He bellowed. He charged. He was fast as **only a berserker** can be, his legs stomping the ground with anger. In his expression, I read a resolute wish to plant a foot on my face. He pounded across and his spear came at me with terrible speed. I whirled out of the way, threw up the shield and cursed, as he had thrust down deceitfully fast and I felt his framea's tip tear a shallow wound on my thigh. I yelped and he laughed like a spirit made of hate, a dark shadow creature of the fogs of Helheim. He roared and yapped like a dog, and I gritted my teeth as his shield slammed so fast into mine, so powerfully I had to take a hasty step back. I kept glancing at the dust and the mud, and tried to draw the beast after me. He came willingly, the spear stabbing again and again, reaping ribbons from my shield, and my hasta had not made a single strike against him yet as I staggered away from his relentless attacks. Then he charged low, his shield high and the spear rushed from under the rim for my gut. I heard Hulderic draw in a terrified breath, a scream of horror from the people around me as the spear entangled in my pants. I kicked back, ripping the pants and cursed him. He was not trying to spare me, not at all. He laughed gutturally, and slammed the shield at me again, then again and I decided I'd have to play on his overconfidence. He came at me, not expecting me to do anything more than wither away, but instead I pushed back with all I had and staggered him and he fell on his knee. My spear stabbed from high, I spat my defiance at his shocked face and the spear scraped his helmet, but he was ferociously pushing up and I fell away, taking hasty steps back. He jumped after me like a ferocious evil squirrel and I again pushed back and punched my spear to meet him. I was lucky. While the weapon went through his shield near the upper rim and trapped it, it was like it had been in the battle. I could push through the leather and score a hit. I had a moment and I roared and pushed forward amidst screams of surprise and Maino screamed in pain as his shoulder took a wound and not even the chain mail could stop the blade from bleeding him. Dubbe was bellowing encouragements to me, Danr and Eadwine were hollering like madmen and only Hughnot's evil looking group stayed quiet, frowning at the terrible battle.

He trapped my spear under his armpit and slapped his spear-clutching fist at my head and I saw darkness, as I tottered back, reeled and cursed, as I lost my spear.

'Eat mud, cousin! I'll leave you a weeping girl, I'll geld you and your father will watch,' he screamed, enraged as he eyed the blood on his shoulder and indeed he almost did geld me as he slapped my shield aside and stabbed his swift framea between my legs. I rolled away. I rolled again, feeling the spear slash the air above me, felt a heavy kick in my rear and fell on my face. I twisted to face him, and grabbed at the figure of hate above me, and clutched his balls before the shield that was coming down could beat my face into a shape I'd not recognize. I squeezed as hard as I could and he meowed like a kitten.

'Not much use with the girl, eh? I'll make breakfast out of them. Good with lentils, no?' I hollered angrily, and pulled so hard he fell over me, his eyes pools of pain. He did not let go of his shield and it came down hard on my chest and part slid to my throat. I gagged, cursed and bit my tongue and struck the leering face above me. His spear was hovering, the tip inching for my face, far too close now and I yanked him over and under me, his framea breaking. I slammed my fist in his face, splitting his lip totally, and he slapped me off like a bear would, an overhanded swipe of pure ferociousness. He was getting on his feet, and there was no sign of human kindness in his furious face and I staggered to the side. I pulled the ax and he pulled his club and walked for me, like a buck moose out to trample a weak competitor. Then he ran and I prayed for gods as I maneuvered to put the lonely tuft of grass between him and me.

'Cousin! I'll have none in a bit!' he screamed, rushed shield first and got to me. He stepped on the tuft of grass as his hand went up and I readied my shield.

The ground gave away, revealing the hole Aldbert had hastily dug up and camouflaged.

Maino's eyes betrayed his shock as he dropped knee-deep into the hole and fell forward while trying instinctively to stop the fall from breaking his legs. He yelled from pain as he twisted, mud was flying and my ax came down. I saw Bero's face, shocked, people shrieking, Father's relief, and then a frown as he considered the hole. The ax hacked down from high, and a bit of leather helmet flew to the side, along with a piece of my cousin's ear. He screamed, let go of his shield and while the whole village was yelling encouragements with shocked, terrified and elated voices, I kicked the squirming mass of Maino. I kicked and kicked it until I hit his jaw and those once so terrifying eyes rolled in his head, the whites showing as he fell to his back. I stood over him, breathing hard, aching all over, and Bero took a hesitant step forward and then another. He walked to me, with a pleading look on his face, and began to pull Maino away.

I growled like an animal and pushed him so he fell back. Silence reigned, and even Hughnot's all-knowing eyes were incredulous at what I had done. 'He is still mine,' I hissed. 'Still mine! You'll not touch him until I say so, you rot-tit bastard. I'll release him when I'm done gnawing at his bones.'

'Do *not* make an enemy out of me, nephew,' Bero hissed. 'Do not!'

I laughed and bent down. I grasped Maino's braided beard and put the ax blade against his throat. 'Maroboodus!' Hulderic said sternly. 'Do not.'

I looked up at Bero, grinned, and cut. In silence, I pulled away the cut beard of Maino. I placed it on my smooth cut chin, and pranced around like a mad man, mimicking my foe and finally threw the beard away to the pyre, where it sizzled and burned. I grasped his shield and broken spear, threw them after it and stood there, breathing heavily, staring at the hundreds of people.

Bero was trembling with rage. He pointed a finger my way. 'For that, Maroboodus, you are not welcome in this village. There was no honor in that.'

'There is no honor in that pig-husk of a lord,' I laughed and pointed my ax at the beaten man. 'None.'

'He *shall* marry Snow-Flower,' Bero said viciously as his men came to carry Maino away. 'The promise not to marry her to the loser was given in good faith. Such holes do not appear out of the dark.'

'That one did,' I hissed. 'I begged it from the gods, I asked them to eat the villain, to hurt him as he deserved, for me. And they listened.' I'm not sure what went over me. I felt invincible, and my chest was heaving with a joy I had never felt before. 'Such dogs should not champion the Goths. I will. I'll give this land such war it has never imagined.' People were whispering now, hissing and giving me long looks. Hulderic's face was grave. He was not relieved by my victory, but apparently he was thinking hard on the words I had uttered.

Bero stood forward and eyed Hughnot. 'And no. Your son will not rule here. There will be no discussions tomorrow, no decisions. I'll make sure we will remain as one here in the south gau, Hughnot. Join us or fight alone. Take your men in the morning and leave, if you will break our alliance. Go over the Long-Lake and rot. And if someone,' he said, for once showing vicious strength, 'would join you, there will be a hall-burning here.'

Hughnot nodded heavily. 'I will give it thought this evening.'

His eyes sought mine.

CHAPTER 8

I sat on the beach that night. I bled from the wounds that had been stitched by a slave in Bero's household, a man with deft fingers, and no doubt sent by Hulderic. Finally, Hulderic came to sit next to me. He sighed and looked over the lapping waves as the celebration in the village reached the stage where most men were roaring drunk. He put a hand on my shoulder. 'Congratulations.'

'I did well, didn't I?' I asked him, sure I had failed after all.

'Aldbert isn't one to dig holes, is he?' he asked. 'But he did well at it. Harmod spotted the—'

'Aldbert was on *my* side,' I told him simply. 'And here I am, alive. And Maino's ugly. Or more so.' I laughed.

'And some of the people respect you for the trickery,' he agreed, not saying whether he did or not. 'Though not all. Not by far.'

Respect. The stuff of songs. Fame. 'Bero's accusations—'

'Ring true. And now we have to deal with Hughnot. My brother has made blunders one after another, and we have to tough it out now. Hughnot will be very unhappy this night.'

'I can understand him,' I said sullenly.

Hulderic glanced at me with an amused grin. 'Just because he supported you, doesn't make him your friend. Yes, you think we should, we could actually find our own roads, better ones, those that suit our family better than this arrangement I have stubbornly been so damned keen on upholding. You think we should start looking at other Goths to ally with. And yes, you think my brother will not make a good enough leader to see us through a war with Hughnot.'

'You might, Father—'

'Might?' he mused with a smile. 'No.'

'No what?'

135

'I know he is a terrible leader, Maroboodus. He does well, if someone else is at the rudder, he is a good warlord, but a bad Thiuda. But I cannot break—'

'He will see us in gravemounds,' I insisted.

He turned my face to him. 'I *promised* Mother I would not fight my own brother,' he said sadly. 'And I also promised her I would not ally with Hughnot. If that is what you want? He did take your side, didn't he?'

'Hrolf seems like a coming man,' I told him softly. 'He has bullsized balls where Bero's are in his mouth.'

'Bull's balls will not make a Black Goth our leader, but tempered intelligence,' he laughed and sobered. 'We have spoken on this before, and will not again. You will travel, boy. What you spoke in front of everyone, that shit pompous speech about brining war to the land made it damn clear that you are one of the few cursed men in our family who would risk anything to get what he desires. So you will travel. Far. As far as you can. I will have men take you south, over the sea, beyond the glittering southern rivers and then further where the mountains split the land and a rolling river runs from east to west. There you will make your own life, if not further. Make a life, build a kingdom there, boy, if you can, and be happy. And this is a favor to you, a curse for me, as I will miss you.'

I sat there, chewing his words as if he had stuffed a fistful of rocks into my mouth. 'I'll miss you.'

He grunted affectionately and squeezed my shoulder. 'And still I don't know if I'm doing Midgard an ill favor by sparing your rebellious hide.'

I nodded and tried to ignore the fear and pain of his words. 'So be it.'

'You'll leave when we go back to Timberscar,' he told me with a subdued voice. 'Best not see your grandmother. She might disagree with my mercy.'

'I am your son,' I told him. 'And all I wanted was to stand strong when a pig-looking bully tried to take my honor and more. Yes, I wanted the girl. Still do. And I think you should break your promise to Grandmother, as it will never work out with Bero. Hughnot's way sounds far saner, a better one for all of us. He makes sensible plans, Bero is a weakling. But I will obey you, Father, and wish you luck with them. Hughnot won't back down any less than I did.'

He measured me with his eyes. 'If he does not, then he will have to fall.' He looked to the cold bay, and somewhere, a gull shrieked in the night, forlornly. 'It will be a terrible war, if he won't bend his knee. And I agree. He won't. He might not do anything now, or this winter, or this night. He'll go home and seethe like an insulted woman.' He ruffled my hair. 'And Bero is not hopeless, it takes him time to make his plans, but they are sound ones. Trust me. And I will miss you, you will miss me and that cannot be helped,' Hulderic said. 'You try to learn patience, to respect the gods, our family burden. And to amuse you, I'll marry again, as you suggested, and have other sons, but you will always be my precious boy. You will not go away poor.'

'Tomorrow then?'

'Tomorrow,' he said sadly and got up. Dubbe nodded at me respectfully from the shadows and Hulderic walked away with him.

So I sat there, eyeing my ax and felt the unjust decisions gnaw at me. It didn't matter, I would leave one way or the other, but I gnashed my teeth and cursed loudly, bitterly and in the end, to my surprise, wept like a fool. I turned to look at the charred skeleton, lying amidst the ruins of the fire, waiting to be covered with a mound. The skull was there, plain to see, blackened and it was smoldering. Then, suddenly, under it some twigs burned brightly, and the thing looked deadly, uncanny, unnatural, and the burning twigs curled around the skull. It looked like a fiery crown. I felt cold shivers go up an down my back. Aldbert's words had spoken of twigs and a skull, and was this it? Yes, perhaps. Was this a special moment, holy and dangerous? Related to the Bear, somehow? Was I to choose or do something that might change the course of our history?

No, of course not, I thought and wiped away my tears.

I spoke to it. 'Well, since you are there, oh spirit, tell me this. Am I to accept his decision? Father's?' I knew the answer already, as I would go and attempt my dangerous plan, but I was still startled when I got an answer.

'No,' said a voice and I scuttled back in breathless panic and sat in pool of seawater. I squinted at the bones, but Friednot was dead indeed and there was nobody there, no sorrowful spirit, no husk of lifeless flesh staring down at me in the night. But there was a large shadow walking for me from the side.

Hughnot.

I gathered myself and got up to stand to face him. He had been listening in the shadows, observing me, and so, he had heard me praise him to Father. He looked dark and menacing and his wise eyes looked at the ax on my belt, as if wondering if he was in any danger. Hrolf and the twins were not far in the night, I was sure and also felt unsafe as I knew their eyes looked at me, and perhaps they had bows and javelins. Hughnot stopped before me. He hesitated and spoke. 'You should not accept it. I know you won't, but there it is. I agree with you, Maroboodus.'

'You do?' I asked with a nervous smile. 'And you are thinking about my best interests, with no bone in this dog fight eh? Why do you care?'

'Oh, I do have a bone in this fight and I have fewer dogs on my side, Maroboodus. Don't be sarcastic,' he said with a scowl. 'Perhaps I'm like you. Perhaps I do think you shouldn't suffer for the damned prophecy and the old gods and their squabbles. I hate the stupid old beliefs of our family, all tied to the ring and mysterious Bears and perilous Ravens and such. Your grandmother was bred on such stories, and when she married to this family, she always worried about giving birth to an ill-omened one. Our grandfather infected us with such nonsense. The Boat-Lord, he believes in it, and now your father, who did surprise me with his words today, by the way, is a fool to let go of a son like you because of our old oaths to gods and vitka who somehow see visions of the danger. You are a hardheaded bastard, but also a keen-seeing, sane man, because you see Bero as a fool and I have no idea why your father would do this to you.' He smiled and bowed. 'And I thank you for your kind words, even if I did eavesdrop. But I must, since Bero and your father would deny me the right to lead. I regret your father isn't going to see the good sense of letting our family work together as it was meant to. If he were on my side, Bero would be made a housekeeper of Bone-Hall. Hope Woden is merciful to Bero, my boy, because I won't be. He is kin, but not kin enough in spirit.'

'Father is merciful. He is not giving me to be sacrificed, after all,' I said with a wry smile.

He laughed and nodded. 'Generous of him.' Hughnot stopped speaking for a moment and leaned forward. 'But I know you care for him. Your father.'

I hesitated and then spoke the truth. 'All I wanted for our family, his and mine, was to take our rightful place. Friednot should not have given the ring to Bero.'

Hughnot nodded. 'I agree. He shouldn't have. He should have made sure it came to me.'

I felt uncomfortable speaking with the great man. Wasn't he dangerous, after all, and unpredictable, and were we not speaking of matters I really knew nothing of? 'Doesn't it always go to the son who marries first? The son of the one who holds it?'

He smiled. 'That's the story. But perhaps it should go to the brother who rules the best?'

'Perhaps, lord,' I said and eyed him carefully, hoping for some sign on what he desired.

He gave it. He turned to me and placed a heavy hand on my shoulder, less gentle than Father's had been, but more respectful. 'I will spare him. Him, and your mother.'

I blinked and felt the discussion had taken a dangerous turn. 'Spare him, my lord? And my mother?'

His eyes twinkled in the dark with mirth. 'Come now, Maroboodus. You know what I mean. Hulderic thought I'd not keel over. And I won't. And that means someone else has to. But it need not be your father. And no, I won't sulk in my lands over the winter. I'll make some moves now.'

I didn't say anything for a moment. I had planned on breaking away from the tribe with … Star-Flower, or whatever her real name was and I had felt there was something very sensible about Hughnot, not to mention him supporting me in the duel, but this was all too real. 'I think I do know what you mean. And you won't spare Bero?'

'Would you care if I didn't?' he growled.

'I'll not betray Father,' I said, without even thinking about it and I realized that's where I drew the line, indeed. I looked at him and licked my lips. He was offering an easier way to do what I wanted to do. To be rid of Bero, to gather glory for the family, Father and I.

He smiled and agreed. 'I respect your father. He surprised me today, having been the second son in your grandfather's family, though I knew he was a fine warrior. He finally stood up, a formerly silent, thinking man, and he spoke loudly, brazenly, and he has his men near, doesn't he? I bet he didn't want to give away the fact Bero had so many men here in Marka, and perhaps I might have been tempted at trying to take the ring. And the sword.'

'You want the Head Taker as well?' I asked him. 'Surely it's a fine blade.'

'It's the very best of blades, and it too, has a history,' he said. 'It takes lives, but it also enjoys taking the lives of the men in the family. The Boat-Lord fears it. He hates us and our small land here. But Hulderic. He is Bero's sword. Yet, if you remove the head the sword may yet be of use. Wouldn't you enjoy seeing him reach the clouds, your father?'

'I'd like to see Father serve a higher purpose than Bero's, indeed, lord.'

He shrugged, and seemed happy I agreed. 'In that case, call me lord, if you like, but my champions call me brother,' he said steadily, his eyes flickering into the darkness, when the twins, Ingo and Ingulf were probably standing ready. 'You call me brother as well.' He opened up his fibula, a silver bear raging amidst flowers, an exquisite thing and took off his heavy bearskin cloak. He then draped it around me. Then he pulled out a short sword from his belt and showed it to me. It was heavy and fat in the hilts, a sturdy and serviceable killing weapon that would be deadly in a shieldwall. 'I am not going to buy you. But I am giving you respect. Such respect you didn't receive when you beat Maino into pulp. You are due some. Your father gave you an ax, because you deserved it. Let this join it, as a show of love for a fine warrior from his relative.'

I stared at the sword feverishly. It was a kingly gift. Few warriors had such a weapon and my eyes went to the ax of my father. I felt like a fat bear

140

tromping on the thin ice of a spring lake, about to plunge in. All I had wanted was to take the girl to the Svearna, marry her and then, if she had any powerful relatives, help Father rid himself of Bero and this man. And now the man was offering me another way. He said he would spare Hulderic, he'd give him respect. He did give respect to me. I eyed him and begged Woden to help me make a decision. I took a deep breath and spoke. 'It is true I would like to be thanked when I deserve it. I would be married, I would have received the fine treasure I fought for in the battle, Cuthbert's gear. I fought well and bravely. All I ask for is my lot, and when I deserve it. And I am not getting it while serving my family.'

He nodded, sympathetic. 'As I said, I will spare your father and grandmother,' he stated like a kind grandfather speaking of a misplaced prank, except he was asking me to betray Father. 'If you'll help me overcome the lords and those in the family that would defy me, you will never lack thanks. This place of rulership, the silver bracelet and iron sword of a Thiuda is mine, Maroboodus. The ring and the sword belong to me. Marka? I helped build it, with my ax and strong arm and I bled for it. I was here when no Goth yet looked upon these woods, the long valleys and the glittering lakes, and I fought to free this land from them. I made the Long-Lake and its northern shores Goth land. Friednot had the ring, and that was fine, back then. And I don't care about the family's rules on how it gets inherited. It's ours to change such rules. I've waited for it for such a long time.' His eyes had lost focus and his cloak began to feel like the suffocating wings of a great raven as he spoke, almost to himself. 'I looked at it, glimmering in his hand for twenty years, patiently, upkeeping our tribe's honor and fame when he could, *would* have failed to do so for many times. That he heard of the Saxons and the girl and Boat-Lord scheming from a spy. It was a rare show of brilliance from him to capture her before the Saxons bartered her to the Svearna or the Boat-Lord, but mostly he was slow and dull. He always was. Did I not sit in our father's hall, looking at the ring when I was but a boy, sitting in dirty hay and shit, thinking how one day, the first to marry would get it? Then I saw our father ruffling Friednot's hair, never mine and so it was like it was with your father. Friednot was the loved son, and he had no love left for me. He married

Friednot first, because Father willed it. I married later, and knew I'd never see it unless, one day, I changed the rules. Friednot was strong, I was wise and now I am strong and wise both, and your uncle, *and* your father would say I have no right to rulership?' His compelling, terrible eyes turned to regard me, and I could not turn mine away. He pressed his hand on my shoulder, and if felt like a ton of rocks. 'What say you? Should I have the ring? And the rulership?'

I struggled. I wanted to say it was his, should be his and would it not be just to think so, as he had waited for it for such a long time? Yes, it would. He had kept the two gaus alive, held our Goths strong in battles I knew nothing at all about, helped guard the lands, to expand them, to make us rich and independent.

It should have been easy to say yes.

But still, I hesitated.

I also had sat in dirt and cobwebs of our halls during feasts, wondering at the fine, golden thing Esla and Aska once carried. I had done what he had, and like Hughnot said, why would such a decision, the ownership of a mighty relic be dictated by fairness? Did gods endorse fairness? Was life fair? No, it was not. It was cruel as winter's blow, merciless like freezing water, and then I hardened my heart to his promises. I began to deny his right to rule. I wanted to. I would not bow to him anymore than I'd bow to Father's wishes.

I had planned to be a lord, none above me.

And that's what I would be.

I opened my mouth to deny him.

But then a spirit of a wily nightfox whispered to me in the darkness. It spoke of caution. It had no words, but I felt it tugging at my hem. Hughnot was wily and clever, and also ruthless. I felt cold fingers hold my heart as I knew there were men in the dark, ready to kill me.

I had to say yes.

I would be careful and despite the many dangers, I still had my plan. It was supremely hard to abandon a less dangerous road, to give away promised support and honor and companionship, and exchange it all for fear and uncertainty, but I was willing to bet few old Germani heroes, sitting ancient, smelling of ale and farts and scarred in their smoky halls, rich and affluent and famed, ever took the easy road.

I'd lie.

I nodded. 'I think you should have the ring and the rulership, indeed. And I should help you.' The words were surprisingly easy to utter, and I had a hunch lying was not hard for Hughnot either.

'I should, Maroboodus, yes I should have them. And I do thank you for your words.'

'I'll help you, if Hulderic retains his honor and fame, not to mention his *life.* 'His eyes lit up. 'What would you have me do?' I heard myself asking, terrified of his answer. He might, after all, set guards on me for whatever he planned for me to do. And it might take place that very night.

His eyes twinkled and he regarded me, deep in his thoughts. I began to wonder if he had any real plan, but was making it all up as he went along.

But no, he had a plan all right.

Mine.

'I will want you to be married.'

'All men marry, lord,' I said carefully. 'Though I'd not be tied to some terrible, if noble old broomstick.'

He laughed hugely and happily and clapped a hand over his mouth as he glanced furtively around the dark, and turned to look at me with a wink. 'That is the thing with you young men. All you think about is the bliss, but in the end you will start to go hunting, join a war band of some ferocious boat-lord and hope to endure the winters when the children crawl over your legs and back, and your wife cannot stop jabbering. But it is the mistake every man must endure, and serving me,' he said with a smile that made him look like he was thirsty for blood, 'you will at least get to go and make war when home becomes a burden. You will marry this Svea girl. You will marry her tomorrow.'

'How will I marry her tomorrow?' I asked in wonderment. 'I'm to be banished tomorrow, not married. There will be a boat's bench, and I'll be hugging a thick oar, and hear words of Harmod, no doubt, not the willowy voice of that wonderful girl.'

He chuckled. 'If I had not seen you fight so well, I'd think you are more suited for that Aldbert's job, singing of birds, and love.'

'He sings of spears, meat parting, and death as well as kisses of fair maidens,' I told him sullenly.

He nodded. 'He is a fine one for the art, I know. But you need to forget such thoughts of cozy love for now, and concentrate on the issue at hand. We will need you to fetch her. She has to be freed, and you might do it, now that Maino is not constantly hovering nearby. They carried him to the vitka's hut and there he will stay for a while. You fetch the girl. She is important. Like the Boat-Lord intended to use her, so can we. She will give us peace, at least from some Svea clans. She might give us warriors.' He looked at me and I was terrified he had read my mind and was only torturing me. My hair was standing on my neck, but he went on. 'Then you will drape her over a horse, make sure she won't scream—'

'Why would she—'

'She might, if she has fallen in love with some finer, or at least a more handsome warrior than Maino, and she might not wish to go back. I've had that happen to me once. There was a girl who asked me to free her from her father, but when I got there, and sneaked to her bedside, she had married that very day and I had to clobber the husband in order to get away. Terrible mess, boy. Father had to pay a high wergild.' He poked a finger at my chest. 'You know nothing of her, really, Maroboodus. It's going to be an adventure for later times when you get to know her, but now, we need her for our alliance.' My heart fluttered and I felt blush conquer my cheeks. He was right. I was premature. He smiled and sighed, amused by my struggles. 'You will fetch her to a cove not far from here.' He pointed a finger over the hilly shadows of the night. 'There are crags on the beach there. Take her there this night. Hide. Hide well. They should be busy here in Marka, but they might be more determined to find her than I think they would. And we shall row by later in the morning to pick you lot up.'

'And if I marry her and serve you, you will make war on our family,' I stated. 'You will want Draupnir's Spawn, and Head Taker. But what then?'

144

That was the big question. So far, he had only been rewarding me with the sword and the girl.

He smiled wistfully. 'Oh, I will want more than your service. It will not suffice to topple those… Bear Goths. You see, the Svearna tie us down, and keep us looking over our shoulders, when our distant cousin, the man they call Boat-Lord, rules rich parts of the Gothonia Islands. He has been busy in the south, and has been fighting with some savages across the eastern sea for a decade, but sooner or later he will come and land on these shores, as this failed marriage proves. He will have ten thousand men, and thousands he will send here to Marka, to split our lands up. He will still try to ally with the Svearna. Our spies in Hogholm, his capital told Friednot so. And if he wanted the girl,' he nodded towards Bone-Hall, 'then he is getting ready to make a move. That is why I am doing this, Maroboodus. For all of us. We will stop him.'

I stared across the dark sea for the old enemy of our family, and family in truth. The man was rich, his hall called the Silver Anvil, and while the reasons for the split in the family were never discussed, there was something sinister about it. Hughnot followed my gaze, and nodded appreciatively at my hidden thoughts. 'I'll tell you more about our ancient home one day. For now, I will make alliances. I will build our two gaus into ten stronger ones. I'll use you and the girl to pacify, nay, to find allies from amidst the Svearna, and build hill-forts all across this land. I'll build boats as well, hold Draupnir and call for Boat-Lord's oath men to join us. Some will. I shall take our men over the sea to our Gothoni islands, and conquer there without mercy. I'll piss on his hall's fireplace while he quakes in terror.'

I saw his vision, and a part of me ached with disappointment, my decision hard pressed to be kept. His words echoed with wisdom, with strength, with unwavering confidence. I could see him, in the fore of hundred long boats, holding an ax, guiding his men to Hogholm's harbor, and I could taste the mead of the fine feast he would set in the hall. And I could be there, standing next to Ingo, Ingulf, Hrolf? I could, I surely could. He saw me licking my lips, my hands trembling with his vision. 'Then, to the south. We shall row there. We shall pacify the treacherous Langobardi and carve ourselves a piece of rich land worth being proud of. We can rule the coasts, and who knows, you serve Hrolf and see far greater glories. The Goths are not meant to ride the waves of this gray, frigid sea forever, no. It might be the gods holy water, the sea of their tears, and yea, Freya's golden ones litter its beaches. But gold flows elsewhere and there are old and famed, warm lands in the south. I am tired, Maroboodus, of being the Black Goth. What is that? A lord of lamb-herders? A king of a hamlet? I wish to be the Red Goth, and the forefather of a dynasty that will echo across lands and time itself. And Bero? He would hold the ring and till the land in peace? Bah!'

It sounded ridiculous. Bero, and Father had erred.

'And you will be one of the dozens of great men with a high hall in lands that once nourished our enemies. You will sit on a throne, give gifts of stolen gold to lords like my champions, you will lead men into battles of shieldwalls. Not dozens, but thousands. You see, I am old, Maroboodus, and Hrolf will need you and other young men like you when he matures into a high man. When my pyre burns, somewhere far one day, make sure you will make Hrolf a king, a Thiuda of note. And for this, you will be rich and married to a dream.' He smiled. 'Though, I will warn you again, nightmares often have such nice hips and sultry lips.'

'I will risk it,' I said softly, struggling mightily with my conflict, but I was also grateful to him.

I'd not make Hrolf my king. I'd take his dreams and make them mine.

'Kneel, son of Hulderic,' he said harshly, blushed by his own dreams.

I nodded and kneeled. 'I will. Lord. My father …'

'Will live. He will fight us, Maroboodus, but will he fight his son? I know him. He blusters and is the fighter of the Bear Goths, but when his son faces him across a shield rim? He will not fight. Not well, at least. He will live. We will capture him and give him honor. Serve me, serve Hrolf, Maroboodus. And he will join us. I know he will.'

I thought of his fanatical belief in the prophecy, and frowned. I was not sure Hughnot was right, not at all. 'You wish an oath? I give it,' I said, feeling twangs of regret over the whole situation.

'You are mine, then,' he said happily.

146

'And how will I take the Svea to the cove? She is in the Bone-Hall?'

He leaned on me. 'Ask your Aldbert to guide you. She is guarded by a woman in the Bone-Hall and he is a poet. He will go and make a song about the princess, or even the hag, and when he charms them, you will follow. You will lead her out, while the crone swoons over Aldbert's charm. Or just tie her up. Use your imagination. Or the sword.' He nodded at the weapon and I felt uneasy over such a terrible suggestion. 'You will lead her out. The woman guarding her is old. Feeble.'

'The Bone-Hall will have guards,' I stated. 'She might scream and warn them, and then it will go terribly wrong, and we shall be captured—'

'No. Nobody will hear her as she struggles.' He smiled like an evil spirit, his mouth half open, tongue flicking in the maw.

'Why not?' I asked him, boding ill.

'There will be a fire in the hall just to the north of here. Everyone will rush to help them,' Hrolf said from the dark, probably too loudly and even Hughnot frowned. He shrugged at me and my shocked face.

'He has a thing or two to learn of subtlety,' he said with a grin. 'A thing or two that he will learn, I know.'

'When?' I asked, afraid. 'The fire, I mean.'

'An hour from now,' Hughnot said, squinting to the sky. 'Talk to Aldbert and nod at Ingulf. He will be keeping an eye on you for a time. If Aldbert refuses, you will wear this cloak tight around you and do the deed anyway. This is the night for brave deeds and yours shall be just one of them. You have already started, oh wily lord of holes.'

I didn't deny having dug the hole, and I didn't have to. They had probably seen it. 'It shall be the first of many such deeds all through your lifetime under the family banner, and when I'm the Red Goth, you will hear them sung in your hall. Say "yes".'

'Yes lord,' I told him. 'Brother,' I added, as he frowned, and the frown turned into a smile of a honey-stealing child.

'See you tomorrow, my boy,' he laughed and got up with a groan, smiled and pulled our foreheads together and squeezed hard. 'Do not fail me,' he said, his eyes cold and I knew he was not a man to tolerate failure.

He left and I sat down to mull it over for a while. I turned to look at the darkness, wondering where Father was. I felt the unkind eyes of Ingulf somewhere in the shadows and hesitated as I got up. I walked for the Bone-Hall and found Aldbert near the doorway, where I expected him to be, waiting for me to appear, patiently, probably happy to prepare to travel in exile with me, if Father would let him. He should, if Father would marry Erse. He likely knew all about my exile already. I walked up to him, and his eyes enlarged as he looked deep into my eyes. 'So,' he said, without expecting an answer. 'We are in trouble?'

'I am in trouble, poet,' I told him brusquely. 'I'm being exiled.'

He was nodding sagely in a way that annoyed me. 'You *knew* you would if you decided to be the idiot of the Thing. You fought him.' He leaned closer to me and put a hand over his mouth. 'And that speech! You will bring war to the land. You will—' He breathed deep with admiration. 'I wish I could come up with such nonsense when some chief dies, but that was exactly what your father didn't wish to hear.'

'I'm not surprised, Aldbert, not trying to make excuses—'

He poked me. 'You should be happy you are not being hung as we speak, like a grouse to make it ripe. Pissing your pants. Your face might be uglier than Maino's, your broken skull nailed to a tree. I'd probably sing your death lament and then write my own before I joined you, stuffed and bound at your feet in a gravemound.' He looked inspired by the vision and I knew he was adding them to some poem he had been making.

'Stop being so dammed gloomy,' I told him and poked him back. 'I'm going to be an exile all right. But not the way they think. None of them.' And saying that hurt painfully. How would Hulderic, Father ever think I was doing him any favor by running away, but I was. I fondled the sword hilt, and felt the hand of doom press down on my chest.

'Really?' he asked, looking suspiciously at the weapon. 'Where did you get that? It's a sword? How did you get it? Did you steal it? You didn't?'

'Shut up, no, not yet. I didn't steal it yet. I was given it as a sign of …respect, and I suppose as a payment for an alliance. But I'm not taking that offer, either.'

'Hughnot?' he asked, suddenly very serious. 'You telling your father?'

'No,' I said sternly and looked at him. 'I'm not listening to him, either.'

Aldbert began to look very worried. 'And you are telling me because I have another hole to dig for you?'

'So to speak,' I told him. 'I need you to get me to the girl.'

'*The* girl?'

His eyes thinned and he didn't look like the usual fool. He was thinking hard, trying to decide how to get on with the discussion. He reminded me of a sneaking lynx. He smiled and waved towards the Bone-Hall. 'So, you wish to speak with her?'

'Not now, later,' I said.

And you need a poet to get you to her and to win her heart for you. I am not well-liked with girls, my friend, as you know with Erse who doesn't even look my way. You would do better to get your own lure, and I think she liked you already. I'd make her confused,' he said. 'And the guards—'

'The thing is I wish to take her for a ride,' I told him.

His eyes went large as a boar's balls and he gawked at me. 'A *ride*?'

'Yes, I'll need her to take a ride with me,' I told him bluntly, so bluntly he began rubbing his face as if physically struck.

He stared at me as if he had not heard what I said. In his eyes there was a look of bottomless sorrow. 'So. You want me to steal a woman from Maino? Or help you do that. I will sing a song to her and she will doze off, and you will just haul her over your shoulder, place a meaty, greedy hand on her rump, and carry her off into the night. And where are *we* going with this woman? You realize I cannot stay behind. They'll feed my guts to the seals while I watch from the beach. And, if I may ask, why her? There are a host of far better looking women out there. I know this, because I talk to traders. They wouldn't lie. You would find a woman in the south, one that doesn't smell of reindeer fat, and likely a woman that would make Woden touch himself. Please be patient. I knew a trader—'

'Traders can take them for all I care. I want the one that smells of reindeer fat and looks beautiful as a winter storm.'

He was shaking his head. 'This one looks like a snowflake, but I doubt she will melt in your palm. Just—'

'She will be warm enough in my lap,' I told him. 'I don't want her to melt. I like the thought of a woman with spirit, not some simpering, foolish thing that would nod away when I do something that would make an idiot cringe. And I will be a good man for her.'

He sneered. 'Coming from a man who has never had a woman sit on his lap.'

'You have sat in my lap,' I told him helpfully. 'Soft and good smelling you were, though drunk and insensible. And I never put a hand on your rump, though no doubt you would like me to.'

'Now wait a moment!'

I put my hand across his mouth. I looked around and thought I saw Ingulf's shadow flitting in the darkness, keeping an eye on me, and the man must have been worried Aldbert was reluctant to help me. 'There will be no guards, only the old woman who looks after her. There will be a *fire*. That means a hall will burn, somewhere in Marka.'

'You will burn a hall,' he mumbled under my hand. 'A hall. They will have a dozen feuds against you. You will ride away a fugitive. You'll eat raw meat in some wooden hole in the woods. You'll live in a cave, a hunted criminal and your father will be amongst those who send men to find you. I will be there, cooking squirrels for you, bearded, starving for mead, and smelling of shit.'

I ignored his babbling. 'A hall will burn, or two, and all the women and men will rush to save it. Marka will stop at nothing to put out a hall-fire. Winter is coming and I bet it's going to be an important hall.'

'You bet? So you won't burn it, but who?'

I pushed him to keep him quiet. 'People will go that way to gawk at least, as they love chaos and bad news, love to gossip and no doubt they will think the master of the hall was a drunk deserving such a calamity, and that is our chance. You and I will fetch her. I'll tell her she will be free and she'll not scream, will she? Who would, if the alternative is a marriage to Maino? Anyone would rather choke on their tongue than risk that.'

He agreed. 'A marriage to *any* Goth is not freedom, but slavery to a smelly damned animal. You are betraying our lord, are you not? Your Hulderic? Father? My lord? And now you are asking me to …' He shook his head. 'Maino and Bero think I dug that pit. The slaves saw me doing it. Of course they did.'

'Have they spoken?' I asked, not really caring if they had. I was committed. I'd have to commit Aldbert as well.

'I loaned the mattock from Bero's slave,' he said with a very small, apologetic voice. 'I didn't have a choice.'

'You—'

He sighed. 'Yes. See what I do for you?'

'You did well,' I told him heavily. 'Yes, I am changing loyalties. My father is my lord, lord of my heart, but he's not the lord that respects me. If a lord is dishonorable and treats you like moose dung on the sole of their boot, who would not leave? I am joining—'

'Hughnot,' he stated.

'Hughnot,' I said softly. 'I should join him. He has vision and he is hungry to change things, to make a name for himself. He has lived in the backwoods of the Svea lands all his life, when he should be a boat lord, a Thiuda, and only because he was second to Friednot. I'll not suffer that fate. I'll not be second to Bero's whelp. Nor shall I be second to Hughnot's. And I do not trust him. I don't. So here is what we will do after she is free—'

'If she is free. We will do what?'

Wind was blowing and I lifted the cloak higher. I breathed and told him. 'I'll take her home. Then I'll marry her and raise Svearna to help me. I'll be a ring giver who shall decide which Goths will live, which shall die. And then I'll do whatever I want.'

He listened and looked horrified. 'You will … what?'

'Just what I told you, friend. Are you with me? Lots of songs for you?'

'Songs of lament! You will betray your people. Not only shall you run, but you plan to kill them. You will be reviled---'

'Yes,' I said. 'And I won't be reviled, if my enemies are under grass. They will be very silent while rotting there.'

'She *is* the daughter of Snowlake, is she not? This Gislin's daughter?' he asked, and the fact seemed to bother him.

151

'She is. Why is that a problem? She has power. The Boat-Lord would not marry a lesser noble.' He opened his mouth, but shut it so hard he winced. He looked supremely bothered, blushing, as he did when he was at a loss of words. He looked at me with begging eyes, but I didn't let him look away when he tried. 'Will you help me?'

He shook his head in terror, swallowing. 'I suppose it will make a great song, or something to amuse men.'

'Thank you. We will get her, then you shall take her to safety, while I do something.'

'Where shall I take her?'

'Saddle our horses. Take father's horse as well, for her,' I told him steadily. 'We shall meet at the north end of the beach, under the trees. We will go fast, running and riding as fast as we can.'

He got up unsteadily. 'Despite the friendship we share, this is terribly a lot to ask. Too much. You have no idea.'

'Because of the friendship,' I told him, 'I trust you. Things will go very wrong for all of us under Bero's rulership.'

He shook his head. 'Yes, I'll follow you. But one day you will learn patience, at a great price. Let's hope your sons will have less prickly natures.'

'They will be like I am,' I said steadily, not knowing how right I'd be. 'Get ready. Go in, and ask questions. Make sure there are no warriors guarding her. If so, tell me. Find rope, and an old tunic, and we will gag the woman guarding her. Or you will. You will take her to some empty room, where I'll be waiting, and it will be easy, no? Before this, prepare the horses, pack up food, drink. Enough for many.'

'Many?'

'Yes,' I said. 'Many.'

He fidgeted. 'You think this guard, this woman will let me bind her?' he growled. 'Have you ever tried to gag anyone unwilling—'

'I just fought Maino,' I told him steadily. 'We will defeat one old lady, I am sure of it and I can be licked in the ass by Freya's dogs for eternity if we fail. Later you will take her to cover, not the old one, but the prisoner. We will be in the cover of the woods, but you must be careful.'

'I will be very careful. Where will you be?'

'I have something to do after. Remember. When the fire starts, we shall meet here,' I told him, and hoped things would go well. I left him and he disappeared inside the hall, where he spoke with someone, a slave, a warrior, trying to find out more about the girl and her imprisonment.

We would flee the land. I'd take her, but I'd not do it alone.

The Saxons would help us get away from the nation that would be my enemy.

They would be grateful and had they not visited her village before? And if things went to shit, they would give me a new home amongst my enemies. If she proved treacherous, they would help me.

Perhaps.

CHAPTER 9

T he fire started so suddenly I half wondered if I'd imagined it. I was lounging near the Bone-Hall, impatiently walking back and forth, and then people were yelling. There were panicked screams, animals were making a terrible racket and a yellow glow lit up the woods and fields. It was a sizable inferno, a hideously hot storm of fire that was devouring something precious and it interrupted the feast and the merrymaking, sucking in people from every hall. I waited under the shadows of the wall, and tried to see what would happen, but I had no reason to worry.

Hughnot's plan was perfect.

People were rushing about in utter panic, until there were screams by chiefs to organize a rescue of the horses in the stables of the unlucky hall, and others would bravely try to haul water to douse the flames. Men were rushing out of the halls nearby, women and children as well, some with their asses bare. The men and slaves of Bone-Hall followed suit. 'The bastards really know how to torch a hall,' I muttered to myself. 'Probably had a lot experience up north.'

Aldbert appeared, uncertain, licking his lips. He looked pale as milk, and ashamed. I raised an eyebrow at him in an unaired question. 'Yes, you are right. I wasn't going to come. But you are my friend. And—'

I frowned 'Your only damned friend. You didn't scout the place?'

'I did.'

'Did you go and prepare what I asked—'

He rubbed his face and nodded. 'I did everything you asked. Reluctantly, but I did. Maroboodus. Listen. If Hughnot gets caught, and speaks of our involvement—'

I pushed him, partly to feel braver. 'They won't catch them. They are old rogues, well versed in mischief. How many halls have they burnt?

154

Hundreds? They are long gone, and there is no such thing as *our* involvement with the fire.' He raised an eyebrow at me and I waved him down. 'Yet,' I added. 'But there will be. We will do this.'

'Gods,' he whispered.

I held his arm and looked at the Bone-Hall's door. It was silent. Men were nearby, some leaving their halls still, but most were gone. The ones we saw were rushing with buckets of sloshing water and people we saw were mostly far, running, and some were trying to find gourds and water skins in huts and craftshops, and even drinking horns and mugs would be useful. I felt a stab of guilt at the chaos that was unfolding, but I was determined and breathed a prayer to the gods, like Aldbert had. I eyed the darkness, uncertain and raised my hand.

A shadow moved. I spotted Ingulf. The sturdy twin. He was frowning as he stared at us, trying to make sure Aldbert was going into the Bone-Hall and would help me, and not hinder. He had a hand on a huge two-handed ax. I waved at him and nodded vigorously and he stopped frowning as I gave him a small bow and an encouraging smile, hoping he would understand it was all going well. He hesitated, grinned savagely, and thumbed towards the conflagration, apparently going to help put out what they had started, waved at me and rushed to find Hughnot. 'Ready?' I asked Aldbert.

'They saw me!' he said, shaking so hard his teeth clattered. 'They can—'

'Shut up,' I said, grasped the sword hilt and considered the ax. I hesitated, and handed Hulderic's weapon to Aldbert, who took it, wonder in his eyes. 'I'll hold it one day again, friend. You use it for now. I don't wish to sully its fame. Father will have to understand what I'm doing before I'll use it again.'

He raised a hurt eyebrow. 'But it is fine if *I* sully its fame? A high opinion you have of me!' He looked grateful, nonetheless. 'I'll use it well. I'll defend your life with it. So I swear.'

I chuckled. 'I doubt you will kill anyone with it. Just look menacing. It will do the job, often.'

'I'm not happy with any of this,' he said, holding the ax as if he was afraid of it. He pulled me around, looking at the darkness, as if to make sure no more of Hughnot's dangerous men were lurking there, but of course he saw nothing and then pressed me to the wall with surprising strength. 'Please *don't* enter this hall. We cannot change anything after. We have a good life here. There are things about the Svea you don't know.'

'I *will* enter the hall, find out everything about the Svea, and so will *you*. In we go,' I told him and pushed him heavily. 'Let's do this.'

We walked through the door. The acrid smell of smoke filled our nostrils. It was dark, though some fires were burning in the fire pit to keep the warmth in the hall. The walls were filled with antlers of many kinds, including great ones from a gigantic moose and there were wolf and bear jaws aplenty. Their shadows made the whole feast hall look very ominous, and if it had not been for the stable side of the hall and the whinnying of horses to our right, it would have been damned scary in the room. I pulled at Aldbert. 'She somewhere in here?'

'I asked the servant who guards the girl. She spoke with me in the main hall,' he said. 'She said she's in the room down the hallway, but didn't let me in.'

'See, I told you you can charm a woman,' I grinned.

He wasn't convinced, and still white as milk. 'She's supposed to be through those doors,' he answered, sounding resigned, and pointed a finger where a corridor led to shadows. 'She called me a useless little sparrow. Don't like poets, she told me. I charmed no one.' His hands were shaking but I ignored his fear and sneaked to the end of the main hall, where the living and sleeping quarters began. I avoided benches, chairs, and a cat meowing in the corner under the shadow of some reindeer antlers. A massive barrel blocked the view to the door, and I sneaked a look past it to the dark corridor. Nothing, the door was clear, so was the corridor, with not a soul in sight. I pulled Aldbert with me.

'But that woman stays with her?' I asked him. 'Did you ask her?'

'No, I didn't ask if she stays with the girl,' he answered but raised his hands as I glowered at him. 'She probably is, but I don't know. I think the girl is living in an alcove to the right, beyond Maino's room. Third? Yes, I think so. That's where she went, at least, before they ushered me out.'

'Maino is not there, is he?' I asked, suddenly terrified.

He gave me a cold smile. 'Gods, what skillful planning this must have taken. But you are lucky. He is with his father and a vitka. His ear is half missing and they are making a poultice for it, and the two vitka fuss over him while he drinks to his sorrow.'

'I hope he chokes on a bone,' I said, relieved. 'Right. Let's forget plots,' I whispered. 'We go in to the room, and gag and tie the servant there. If the girl screams, I'll gag her, and we hurry up. Then we run like whipped hounds with the girl.'

'Right,' he answered, his voice dripping with terror and doubt. 'Whipped hounds.'

I entered the hallway, and it was nearly dark. There were no shingles or fires at all in the empty rooms, and I frowned at the lack of light. Surely, the high Svea woman didn't sit in the dark on a feast night? The flickering of light behind us in the main hall threw our shadows to the corridor and I noticed Aldbert was still standing in the doorway. I turned to look at him, gesturing with my sword. I whispered frantically. 'Come, now.'

'I'm sorry—' he began to say, his voice shaky and sorry indeed.

A shadow moved out of Maino's room and a hand grabbed me and for a moment I thought the servant lady had unleashed an attack on me.

Then I realized it was not a hand of an old, frail servant, but the iron-hard hand of a warrior, and that hand pushed me to a wall, and for a moment I saw the snarling visage of Friednot's champion, Ludovicus, his hair flying as he kept me still. 'And here we are, master Maroboodus, a woman-stealing bastard, caught like a rat. You will not—'

He had not seen the sword. And I didn't think, but acted.

Despite its cumbersome make, the weapon pushed easily into his exposed throat. His eyes enlarged with pain and surprise, his hands clutched me, then his throat, and he gurgled, and spat blood and fell on his back with a clatter, inside Maino's room and his feet thrummed the floorboards so hard hay and dust made a thick cloud in the air. I stared at the man, and I knew he was gone. He might have breathed still, terribly afraid and very much fighting for his life, but he was a dead one. I held my face with one hand, the sword with another and fought to get my thoughts under control.

Murderer, a voice told me without pity.

Another fought it. *No, a warrior.* I tried to listen to the second one, but also knew I had done something that would haunt me forever. I kept reasoning with myself, though panic crept in. *Isn't this what I had planned to do with the Svea? To cull Goths who would stand against my father and me?* However, it was all much more real now.

I had killed a hero. A good man.

I turned to look at Aldbert, at his shocked face. 'Aldbert?' I said unsteadily. 'What is this?'

He shook his head and took a hesitant step forward. 'I didn't know ...' he began, but then kept his mouth shut as he tried to gauge my mood, which I didn't know myself.

It took time, but I forced myself to move my feet. *Evil or necessary,* I thought, *it was now past time to hesitate.* I had killed a man in the Bone-Hall, and while I could be judged by the law-speakers, elders and condemned by the vitka and the völva for my schemes, a murder would be a hard matter to overcome in the minds of the people. Ludovicus had family. There would be a feud, no matter if Hulderic paid a hefty wergild and that wergild could be so high we could very well starve during the winter. He had been a great, famous man, no peasant, no slave, and I was in trouble. 'You didn't know?' I asked Aldbert. 'He said I'm woman-stealing—'

He shook his head and waved his hands and I wanted to slap the truth out of him. He might be lying, but I had no time to force the issue. If I did, I felt I might murder him as well. He spoke so fast I could barely make out the words. 'I ... you should have guessed they'd have a guard here, one who doesn't dash off to douse fires. I warned you. I knew this would go sour, and—' he said, his voice rising to a pitch close to panic as he looked behind me.

There was light in the corridor.

The Svea woman, her thin eyebrows, smooth, pale skin, and well-proportioned face all betrayed shock at the sight of the twitching legs. She looked at me, then at my sword and I was sure she'd scream. She considered it, I saw it. She took a long breath, but let it go after all and took a step forward.

158

'You are Maroboodus?' she asked steadily.

'Yes,' I said huskily. 'I came—'

'I know,' she answered huskily, considering me. 'You didn't expect him?'

'It was an accident. The dark, he lunged for me. I didn't mean to—'

She said nothing but I saw her face relaxing. 'I can understand it. But it's done. It's his wyrd, and behind you. You must run. And I'll go with you.'

'Was there a woman guarding you?' I asked her nervously, eyeing the dark rooms for a sign of danger.

'Was,' she said softly, and I noticed her fist was bruised. 'I wasn't going to get married to that ox of a relative of yours so I would have tried an escape on my own. She lives. I tied her down. I'm not sure I needed rescuing, but a generous heart should be rewarded. I can take you with me.'

'Take me with you?' I asked her, astonished. She had more balls than some men. 'You are kind.'

'Yes, I'll save you,' she said with a hint of humor, smiling like a wicked spirit and perhaps there was some truth to the stories of Svea and spirits mating in the night. Then her eyes turned to Aldbert.

She went still, silent, unsure.

It was an awkward silence, but she finally pointed a finger at Aldbert. 'And him?' she asked me. 'There's something seedy about him. Something familiar, but also hidden.'

I considered my friend. 'He can stay if he wants to,' I told her, and shrugged at Ludovicus. 'This was an accident. He can explain it, when they come to ask about me.' I said it harshly, for I didn't believe it was an accident. He had tried to make me stay, had spoken to Father, perhaps to Bero and they had left the champion there to wait for me. I didn't look at Aldbert, but I knew he was so rattled, he likely shook in his shoes.

'They'll geld him, Maroboodus,' she said with a smirk. 'It will be messy since he quakes so much.'

I felt disappointed and worried for him, but decided she could be right. 'Are you coming?' I asked him harshly. 'Or shall you stay and explain why he died?'

MAROBOODUS – ALARIC LONGWARD

'I am coming,' Aldbert answered softly. 'You should come with me. I'll take you to Timberscar—'

'*She* is taking *me* with her, Aldbert,' I told him sarcastically. 'We shall travel with her, and she's not going to Timberscar.'

'Very well, friend,' Aldbert said and pointed at the man who had now stopped twitching. 'I swear I didn't know … I couldn't have known—'

'Where are we going?' the girl interrupted his futile explanations. 'Since we travel together now.'

'I'll take you home,' I told her, tearing my eyes off Aldbert, suspicious, angry, and guilty for the death of the great man. He had been there, hiding in Maino's room. And Aldbert had hung back.

'I know you will,' she said with a strange, cold smile. 'But now? Horses? What's the plan?'

I stared at her for a moment, wondering at how confident she was. Her eyes were clear as the stars, and she nodded to coax an answer out of me. 'I'm in a proper fix. I'm fleeing my father and the … Bear Goths. But the Black Goths expect me to come with them. I'm not. It's just you and me, and him.' I nodded at Aldbert and she frowned at the thought. 'I think we need some men.'

'They would slow us down,' she said. 'Best just rush. I know the woods.'

'But if there will be fighting, wouldn't it be best to rush with a band of men?'

She considered this and her face screwed with suspicion. 'You have such men? You don't look like a lord with oaths men. And adeling, and powerless one?'

'I killed your captor and his chief. And … him.' I nodded at Ludovicus.

'Power, experience, and wealth are a different issue. Ability in battle is not the same as power and fame,' she said with asperity. 'You have no men, right?'

'I know some desperate ones who would probably help us get you there safe. Though you might not like them.'

She blinked and her head cocked, and then she understood what I had been planning. 'You don't mean the Saxons?' she whispered.

'They would help, I'm sure, if we help them get home,' I said. 'I'll fetch them and meet you.'

She chuckled and shook her head. 'They are *Saxons*.'

'They must appreciate the fact they won't hang, no?' We could use men,' I said forcefully and she gave in.

'Fine, you bull-headed fool. Your Aldbert and I shall meet you wherever it was you had agreed on and you get these …men. But I don't want him armed.' She was looking at the ax on Aldbert's belt. I grunted with agreement, turned to Aldbert, and walked to him.

I poked a finger on his chest and he flinched as he saw my hand was bloody. 'If she is not safely taken to the end of the beach, under the woods, I'll not be happy, Aldbert. You be there, waiting.'

His eyes looked at me long and hard, and he was biting his lip, his eyes venturing to the girl. 'She'll be there. So will I.'

'And I'll have that,' I told him, and grabbed the ax from his belt, and he looked away in shame. I hesitated, gave the ax to the girl and she took it, with wonder in her eyes. The weapon suited her. 'He will still have a spear,' I told her with some concern, but she shrugged.

'As he said, I'll be there,' she told me forcefully. 'And so will he. And if he tries something with his spear, I'll cut off his balls.'

Aldbert opened his mouth to protest the sudden reversal of roles, but I was still suspicious of his role at all, so I didn't care. I moved to the hall, eyed the shadows, and nodded at them. 'Horses, and I'll be there soon. Right?'

'Right,' Aldbert said and pointed to the door. She passed us, eyed the shadows like a fox looking for dangers, and looked back.

'Be careful,' she said with a smile and disappeared into the darkness, Aldbert in tow. I gave a last glance to the bloody hallway where all my doors had closed.

CHAPTER 10

I crossed a vegetable garden, slipping on something cold and rotten, pushed away a docile dog that was too nosy for its own good, young as it was, jumped over a well-concealed cellar and finally saw the hall. It was on the south edge of the village, near the harbor, like most of the important buildings. It would be half filled with poor Saxons formerly oath-bound to Cuthbert. I navigated shrubs, flitted from tree to tree like a cattle-thief, and then I spied the doorway to the hall. There was a man guarding it, though he too looked restless. He was fidgeting, clearly worried and wondering, and he walked to the corner of the hall every now and then to gawk at the white smoke that filled the night sky and he cursed audibly at the screams of men, who were trying to save the hall. Happily, it had been a wet month, so the sparks would not easily light the roofs, but Hughnot's rogues would have done a good job and it was not likely to be put out anytime soon, if at all. I walked in the deepest shadows, praying the gods to heed my needs that night, positioning myself so I could see the man better, and the door.

It was latched. There was a heavy bar blocking it, but nothing else. The warrior came back to the doorway, then walked to the other side of the hall, gazed at the sea, then stopped to stare at the boats, trying to decide if we were under attack.

I would have to kill him.

I had just killed, but the thought made my belly churn with despair. He was a young man, his blond beard long and the Suebian knot was haphazardly tied. He walked back to the door, took a swig from a horn that had been set by the wall and put his spear away. Then he walked to the woods, towards me. I crouched as the man came forth and for a terrified moment, I thought he had seen me.

'Donor's lathered balls,' I cursed under my breath. The man came to stand very near. I trembled with anticipation as he untied his pants and bent down to sit amidst the shrubs. He was taking a jotun-sized shit, judging by the smell that permeated the air. I wrinkled my nose as he voided himself and felt bad for the fact I was about to interrupt his happy moment, but perhaps he would live, if he didn't fight. I sneaked forward, saw him there, holding his head with both hands, and then I kicked his back as hard as I could. His lungs emptied of air with a wheezing sound, he farted loudly and flew forward with a hoarse yell of surprise, and I was over him in an instant. He struggled briefly, writhing in pain, but then he saw the blade twinkling in the light next to his eye, resting on his throat. 'What—'

'Move, and you take your next shit into a silver bucket in Asgaard,' I hissed. 'Do not move, and you will live to take another one later here in our world. Remember how fine it felt? You can have that again. Shout, and me and my friend here,' I said, and decided to name the sword there, thinking it looked as dangerous as the beasts of the goddess Hel, 'Hel's Delight, will take your guts and trail them behind us as we run away, and that will not feel as pleasant as a good shit, my friend. Can't fix ripped guts, no.' I pressed the cold iron on his neck and he stiffened. 'Hands behind your back.' He obeyed and I took his rope belt, and spent too much time as I tied him tightly. While I did, I endured the stench, and begged I had not stepped in any of his excrement. 'Gods, man, what have you eaten?' I cursed as I bound his knees and ankles together.

'Soup,' he whispered. 'It was something with lentils and it was somewhat rancid. I'm not rich.' I patted his head and then gagged him with his tunic and made sure he could not easily hop away.

I got up, and knew I was trembling with fear as I eyed the door. I approached it and hesitated, and then I lifted the bar, which was a bit stuck, and threw it aside after a small struggle.

I stepped in.

Inside there were shingles burning in the fire pit. There was a smell of farts and sour ale drifting on the air, as well as the stench of unwashed bodies. There was also the stink of rotten wounds and I looked carefully around as eighteen men, shadows really, got up and two remained lying down. They were a gangly, savage lot, unkempt and perhaps afraid, but like a wolf might fear, ready to claw and savage the one trying to hurt it. Most were strong from their time in oars, calloused and callous Germani, and formerly covered with riches and fame. The beastlike crew stared at me with uncertain frowns, most looking over my shoulder expecting to see armed men come in after me, but none came and it puzzled them. They must have thought about this scene a dozen times an hour, waiting to be taken out to be judged, sacrificed, sold, and generally dealt with. Few would go home. I briefly bit my lip as I stepped forward, trying to hold my composure and the sword, Hel's Delight, was on my side. One, a Saxon with curly, long hair stepped forward, glancing at the blade greedily. *Thieves, the lot of them*, I thought. Perhaps the girl had been right. 'Are you,' the Saxon asked with a spiteful voice, 'here to find sacrifices for your feast? We are oar-bound men, tough as iron. Saxons, boy, that's what we are and well should you know we don't bend down for rutting. None shall volunteer, so you will have to—'

'Who is the leader amongst you?' I asked and cursed as I spoke too quickly. Our accents were close, we could speak, but I didn't want to sound like a fool to them. I needed their respect. *They might find Ludovicus at any moment*, I thought frantically, and so I slapped my blade on my thigh. 'Well?' I demanded.

They whispered amongst themselves. Finally, the curly-haired man stepped forward and thumbed his chest. 'Ceadda. That is I. I lead them, for now. I fought for a champion of the dead lord and I am the best of them.' His eyes crossed and he looked like a dog as he sniffed the air, smelling my sweat, but perhaps also my fear and hesitation. 'You are a Marcomanni. A pup?'

I balled my fist and he grinned in the dark. He had a thick beard, I noticed, and a rich belt, that had not been taken from him and that meant he was likely a brave man indeed, one who was given some measure of respect and dignity, even in a hall turned prison. 'Yes, I'm young. But if you wish to insult me, at least call me *the* Pup.'

He thumbed the north wall. 'We saw you. No disrespect meant. We were looking from the cracks as you fought. You downed that ugly berserker, right?'

Another lanky and gaunt man pointed at my torn pant that had a smear of some crusted blood. 'Yes, it's the redheaded, baby-faced one. The hole-digger.'

'It was a good hole,' I growled and they all laughed like a pack of demented spirits, and none judged me for the hole. They were raiders, and even if honor and fame were as important to them as they were to our people, these men had fewer scruples than ours and accepted that many ways lead to glory.

'That is Njord,' Ceadda said. 'My brother. I think he is, and Father claimed it is so, despite the way he looks, misshapen and ugly. Gods piss on some of us, and bless others.'

Njord spat on the floor, and he did look strange, with large white teeth and thick lips and he certainly didn't look like Ceadda, though they clearly loved each other well. 'What do you want, pup?' Njord asked, his eyes large. 'Got lost?'

'I am not lost,' I said steadily, trying to keep the situation under my control, which was of course as likely as stopping the tide with a prayer and a wish. 'I am the son of Hulderic the Goth, lord of the … Bear Goths and I killed your chief in the battle, perhaps two. I threw a spear at Cuthbert, and while I didn't finish him, he was grievously wounded. I—'

'Floundered in mud as that Maino killed our lord. Being a fool, pup, is what you were,' Ceadda said. 'Not sure why you come here to tell us you are the one who took our future? Come to clear your conscience?'

I fumed for a moment and then went on. 'I have none. I also slew a chief who killed Friednot. I killed him when he ran into my spear.'

'Did he see the spear?' Njord asked with amusement, chuckling and I didn't bother answering and turned to Ceadda instead.

I nodded to the north wall. 'And yea, I fought Maino. I tell you these things, because I want you to know who stands before you. I'm young, but I have done well. Woden wouldn't spit on my face, should I proclaim my deeds to him—'

'*We* might,' Ceadda said cheerfully. 'We don't care who you are, pup. Don't care for your glory. Yeah, you fought well, but we won't sing your praises to the gods and Valkyries when they come. You'll see bravery soon enough. We do not go easily to our deaths, and if you think we'd be sacrificed to the gods like lambs, even to celebrate your ... glory, you have a thing or two coming. Saxons are not soft people afraid of taking some Goths with them to the afterlife. We shall row together, merrily across the dead seas.'

'Neither are the Goths soft fools,' I growled. I turned the sword in my hand, so the blade flickered, and it was not lost on them, as their eyes hardened. I breathed steadily, and relaxed. 'I am not here to take you to Woden's stone, or to be hanged for some fool vitka's pleasure, no. Not yet, at least, and should something like that take place, at some point, it will happen somewhere else. And I might join you in such a fate.'

Ceadda eyed me and stepped forward until I could see him properly. His hand was clutching his side, as if trying to find a weapon he had been accustomed to holding there, but there was nothing on his belt and his hand was clutching air, repeatedly. I stepped out, grabbed the hasta, the heavy spear of the guard, and came back in. The Saxon looked at me and shrugged. 'You are here for yourself, yes? Where is the guard? He pissed in our food, you know.'

'He has paid for it,' I told him with simple bravado and he snickered nastily. It was like dealing with a snarling beast, but his mirth had a hopeful note, and the rest of the Saxons were looking at each other, surprised. 'Yes, I am here for myself and for causes of my family, but first I have to do a very hard thing. Already have, in fact.'

'What do you really want from us?' Njord asked with openmouthed curiosity.

'I'm in need of a guard and perhaps a crew. I'm leaving this place. I'm an adeling without a home and would find a new one. In the end,' I said with a ferocious smile, 'if you lot survive, you can go home and join some other crew of raiders next year. And if my plans for a new home fail, I'll row with you.' I had not told that to the girl or Aldbert. I needed the Saxons to give me a chance for an escape, should everything go wrong.

Ceadda nodded as if what I was offering was the most natural thing in the world and tugged at his long beard. 'So, you tell us we will give you oaths of service until you are happy and settled in your new home. Where is that, if I may ask?'

I nodded towards the west. 'The girl.'

'A girl? That's not a home,' he snickered. 'We cannot find you a girl, boy. Do we look like ones to hide girls in here? You came to the last place in Marka to find a—'

Njord grunted angrily. 'The girl, you damn fool. He's talking about the Svea princess. He wants to elope with the *damned* girl.'

'Oh!' Ceadda said with sudden, horrified understanding. 'That sort of a tragedy, eh? *That* girl,' he said emphatically, 'was the bane of our lord. She will be yours, perhaps.'

'She's a girl, you brave Saxon,' I mocked him. 'What's there to fear?'

He waved his hand towards the Svea lands. 'You've not been out there, have you? We only went there for her, and a fine promise in treasure. I—'

'The Boat-Lord would have offered you cows, boats, slaves, even gold and silver for her, no? You went there to steal her away, because you knew she had been promised to the great Goth by the Svea.'

'Oh, ho! You know a lot for a pup with wet ears, don't you? Yes, perhaps. I don't know how exactly Cuthbert heard of the deal the Svea and your Goth enemy made, but your Friednot did as well, and also heard of our plans. Probably had spies where we have them. He surprised us, didn't he? But her village is a strange place, the people are queer and I will not say more about it.' His words left me uneasy, and I faltered and wondered if I should take her across the sea instead, and build a life there, after all. Then I shrugged, and knew I could not. She didn't seem like the sort of a woman who would appreciate a man who steered away from rushing, raging torrents for the comfort of the calmer waters. She'd expect I keep my word, indeed.

'I'm taking your captive back to her home. I don't really know a lot about the west, you are right, but I will tap into your well of hard-won wisdom.'

'Shit,' Njord said softly, rubbing his temple. 'Not again. This had been a terrible week, hasn't it? Cuthbert's mother always told him not to seek out trouble with the wicked Svearna, but he did, and his curse is ours.'

I ignored his ominous words. 'And you will guard us as we travel where she would go. I will—'

'You will marry into power, eh?' Ceadda said with almost fatherly desperation. He leaned closer. 'I like you, lad. You would probably do well in the shieldwall and pulling at our oars, you would, and I smell determination born of desperation in you, you know? You are a man who tries to make things better, no matter the obstacle.' He pointed towards the village and withdrew his hand as if it was terrible luck to invoke her name. 'But this obstacle? That terrible kitten? She caused our lord to go mad. Utterly crazy. Marching through your Goth lands to capture the future wife of the Boat-Lord? Mad. We had men, but never enough to pull it off, and he should have known it. He didn't and went ahead anyway, and every moment from the minute he saw her, to the minute he died holding her, our lord was as desperate as you. His face was gray, his voice weak, he was feverish, and stared at her like a faithful, stupid dog would stare at a cruel mistress who never feeds it. Now you would take eighteen men to the west on her behalf? Mad, mad. Here we are, all men you have been told are like animals. We are Germani like you, Suebi all, but still pirates and raiders. You think we fear nothing? We do. You want us to go back there, but perhaps we are not so desperate? There is nothing there, Goth, that promises a better end than we might get here. We would die less tired here, to be honest. Won't have to run from a nation of Goths, and Svearna both.'

'Coward,' I said with spite. 'Too lazy to grasp at a branch offered in good faith, one that might see you to your homes.'

Ceadda's eyes flashed and his fingers twitched aggressively. 'Perhaps so. But why should we go with you? What could you do, boy, if we just helped ourselves now?' They took a step forward, all of them and even the two wounded tried to sit up.

I pushed the spear in Ceadda's chest, the tip breaking skin. His eyes widened, but he clearly contemplated walking on, anyway. I shook my head at him, begging him not to. 'If you have no honor, you do have sense,

I am sure. You will help me, or die here. I have never seen a Saxon die happily in a cage, fed, rested. Think of the songs they shall sing of Ceadda and Njord, the fat, lazy sacrifice. They will, you know.'

'Wait a minute, I—' Ceadda began but I didn't let him finish.

'They shall laugh in your halls. Except for your sons. They will weep as they are mocked.' His face went slack and he looked away and I knew I had won. I went on, brave as a young god. 'You could kill me, but you know it's a bad idea, because you would be running around the Goth lands until my people catch you again and they will string you up like wingless sparrows, a feast for the crows.'

'We'll row out,' Njord said stubbornly.

I snorted. 'The oars have been taken from the boats. Paddle with your hands and feet?'

'We can make oars,' he insisted.

'They will find you,' I said with a bored voice, hoping they would listen. 'The horses are guarded, most of them, despite the fire. Come with me. This way you will help a high lady of your enemies, and those enemies can and will help you in return.'

'Interesting thing, that fire,' Ceadda said darkly, 'but I'm sure we don't have to know what's going on there.'

I had nothing to hide. 'You will know everything, or most if you come with me. We are in the same floundering shitty tub together, my friend, I admit that much, and it won't be easy. You can, if you wish, stay here, and wait for one of the damned vitka to sober up, and start to ponder how to fulfill some fools request. There will be a chief, who is wondering which cow he should buy from his neighbor. Then he will need mighty magic to find an answer, and perhaps your blood will decide which one it shall be? Soon they will sacrifice some of you to Woden. The rest will be split up and sold as slaves, nonetheless, and you won't be Saxons any longer. Some few might go home if a ransom is paid, and that could take years. Your wives will take new husbands and your children will call them Father, and forget you, and just think of the mockery they'd endure. Imagine, slain by Bero, the least of the Goths.' That didn't go down well with them. They all twitched with anger. 'Or,' I said, 'have an adventure with me. Free as birds,

169

or dead.' I leaned closer. 'And I doubt you are honorless men, no matter if you raid, rob, and murder. We do as well, don't we? I'm here to offer you freedom. You can go and try to figure out a way to get some oars together, but you won't get far. Help me,' I said proudly and bowed to them.

Ceadda laughed softly as I straightened, and shook his head. 'My, but you are a wordy one. Bowing to a Saxon? Should be happy you don't have an ax in your skull. You are leaving the Goths? All the Goths? And really wish to travel to the west, boy?'

I nodded. 'I was offered a place with the Black Goths. My father told me never to trust Hughnot and I agree with him. I don't love Bero. I even hate him. I know I hate Maino. And now I don't trust my father, either. Moreover, there was an incident in the hall, as well. In the Bone-Hall.'

'I thought the sword had a red tint,' Njord said. 'I smell guts and shit on it, pup.'

I shifted the weapon, but didn't smell a thing on it. 'No shit, but blood. It visited a throat. But you have a good nose. Look, we don't have all—'

As if to make my point, a man was screaming nearby, apparently chasing a horse spooked by the fire that still seemed to be ongoing.

I took the spear away from Ceadda's chest. 'You will make oaths to me. Your brothers, fathers, and relatives will hear, across the oaken floors of Valholl, and hold you to them. I need you to help us get there. Take it or leave it because I have to run, nonetheless.'

'Gods above and below,' Ceadda said, looking desperate as he tugged at his beard. 'What say you, boys?'

They said nothing, but somehow Ceadda read an answer in their weather-beaten faces and the sullen silence and turned to me. 'When she is home, we go free. We won't come to the Svea village, though. They'd roast us.'

'Get us there,' I smiled. 'And you go free. We will try to get you a boat and you can take the Long-Lake back to the sea, if it is feasible.'

'The wounded,' Njord whispered. 'We must leave—'

'No,' Ceadda said sadly. 'We help them to Woden's care.' He eyed the two men, who shuddered with fear, but did their best to look brave, clutching their wounds. He leaned on me. 'They have heard us speak, as well.' I flinched as they approached their brothers. They seemed half dead, horribly wounded anyway, but the deaths were brutal, neck-breaking affairs in the dark, and I realized I was in league with *real* killers. After the deed was done, Ceadda nodded at me and came to stand before me. 'Oath?'

'Give them,' I told him. Outside, yells were getting more desperate. I heard pained whinnying of horses as the hall was probably a terrible inferno and likely, the fire had indeed spread, perhaps elsewhere, further away, helped by Hughnot's seedy men. Ceadda kneeled and so did the shadowy, murderous Saxon crew. 'We shall honor you as our lord ...'

'Maroboodus,' I said.

'Lord, Maroboodus,' he went on, 'the Pup, and shall fight to the death to get you to the safety of the Svea village. Then, we are free to go. Moreover, we would appreciate some help in the form of a boat, when we get there. Long-Lake is Goth and Svea waters, dangerous, but better than walking.'

'And you shall honor the girl,' I told him. 'She must be safe, no matter how much you fear her and her village.'

'Yes,' he stated simply. 'Of course. Do we have to spell everything out? You wish to have a Thing here and settle terms? Trust our word.'

I had one more point. 'And you will take me with you, if this is a terrible idea,' I added.

He cursed, for he had probably thought about leaving that option open still. 'And that, lord Pup. An oath on that as well, damn you, though I don't know where we shall go, if it is that desperate and there is no boat.'

I shrugged and wiped my stubbled chin. I hesitated for a moment and then handed him the spear, which he took after a moment of stunned silence. I felt like I had given a wolverine claws, but it was a tamed beast for a moment as he grabbed the weapon gratefully. For a few moments, I wondered if he would be ramming it in my belly and by the look on Njord's face, he was as well. Ceadda did not, but set about speaking to his men in a way that left me confused. They rushed about, picking up their few personal items. 'Shall we?' I asked him.

'Lead on,' Njord said, eyeing the spear unhappily and enviously. 'I'm better with a hasta, brother.'

'You'd confuse it with your cock,' Ceadda said and pushed me on. 'I'll keep it.'

We rushed out. I ran in the shadows of the village's halls and sheds, the Saxons followed me nearly soundlessly, but most everyone was fighting the fires and indeed, there was more than one hall on fire. We flitted from shadow to shadow, hall to hall until Ceadda stopped us near a ship. He hesitated, his eyes glinting and I felt rage creeping into my heart. 'You renegading already? I told you they don't have oars. You cannot seriously think you will get away—'

He shook his head and grinned like a naughty child. 'No. Let's release one of them. Push it off, perhaps it will drift away through the islands with the currents, going far to the sea, and they shall look for us there? Or it will just look silly, stuck on some branches over there in the bay. But first, we need weapons.' He nodded at me, I nodded back, and they climbed the boats. Some came back with spare spears, some had bows, none had shields, but they also found axes and seaxes, long, thick daggers. It was Hughnot's ship they found most in and I grinned at the thought of the lord's fury, and then felt cold claws of fear dance on my back as I remembered his face when he had told me not to fail. I was failing, spectacularly. Finally, the Saxons let the ship go after pushing it mightily and we ran for the end of the beach, a line of fugitives, and nobody cared to stop us, not even the few dogs that came near to sniffle and wonder at us. I scuttled to the woods and turned to look back at the village. I eyed the ferns and thick woods, hoping to see a glimpse of Aldbert. Ceadda pulled me around, nervously looking at the burning hall, where hundred men were trying to put it out. 'Are we going?'

'We need her, first,' I said. 'And my friend.'

'Oh, they are here,' he nodded towards a pair of shadows and I saw it was so indeed. There were horses and I saw their faces in the pale light of the conflagration. I walked forward, cursing as I struck my toe on a root, and felt sudden reluctance, as I was afraid the woman would reject me in the end. 'Do not tarry, lord Pup, and let us get on with this,' Ceadda said darkly as he eyed the woman he so feared. Aldbert rode forward and looked sheepish as the beautiful woman rode next to him. Her eyes were cold as the north as she eyed the killers of her kin, blue and icy and her lips full and without emotion, drawn in silent rage. Her long, dark hair was braided thickly and her animal skins clung on her round hips. My eyes did not leave hers and I felt the Saxons making some signs to ward off evil spirits and bad luck. She had been unlucky for them indeed. I bowed to her stiffly but she did nothing in return.

'Boat over the Long-Lake, across it to the Svea lands?' I asked. There was a long stretch of water, and while it was called the lake, it was a sea and lake combined, and ran for days to the west, separating Hughnot's and our lands, leading deep to the lands of the Svea, past our gaus.

'Yes,' she answered. 'That would be good. That or a smaller boat down one of the rivers leading west. There are some this side of the Long-Lake.'

'No,' Ceadda said and rubbed his face, as his eyes gauged us, anticipating an argument and it was easy to see the girl was about to give him one, because a furious storm gathered behind her eyes. Ceadda lifted a hand before she unleashed her spit on him. 'You don't know shit about boats and being hunted in one. We would be visible to everyone. We don't have the time to go slowly, to avoid villages, and wait for the night. We'd have to row fast. They would come after us, send messages ahead, and if there's a lord out there with some boats, they will find us. All they would have to do is ask the first fisher they meet, and they would happily tell them when and where we are. No. We, my crew will escape carefully with a boat, taking our time, but we take you two where you want to go through the woods and hills and hope they think we are *stupid* enough to try the lake. Even the Saxons rowing about with great many boats try to avoid that bit of cold water. It's a death trap. Though it seems we must brave it to get home later, as you know.' He gave me a resentful look, knowing I might be with them then.

The girl sighed. 'You promised them a boat?'

I nodded. 'Yes. And we might wish to listen to them. We should.'

There was still rage on the face of the girl as she looked at the Saxons, but she finally nodded. 'Do so,' she said coldly. 'Over the land, then.'

'Lord Pup,' Ceadda said and I nearly shouted for him to remain silent, but the girl bent down and put her cool hand on my cheek.

'When we get where I wish to go to, I will marry you, mighty Maroboodus. I see power in your future. I also see and smell blood and death, I see unhappy sons, dying lords, betrayed tribes and many riches for you, and I see you will be both happy and unhappy. You'll ride to war a king, with an old sword and a ring. I will marry a man the Red Lady so richly loves. Freya approves of you.'

I let her keep her hand on my face, and braved a question. 'Do you see us together, sharing such riches and happiness?'

She hesitated and shrugged, straightening in the saddle. 'I don't know. It is possible. Anything is. But I see we will have happiness, though as for the future and how far that happiness lasts, it depends on our choices.'

All the Saxons shifted in their feet, unnerved by her intensity, and I knew Ceadda had a look on his face that was directed at me, and was saying, "I told you so, Pup."

I took a deep breath and so began our flight. 'Let us leave.'

We rushed up the hill, spears clanking on trees in the darkness and the night seemed to disapprove of our haste as we all stumbled along, save the horses, which were wiser. Then we took to the west over some harvested fields, and crossed a ball-freezing river and rushed for a village that was days away, in the land of the Gislin, lord of Svearna. Behind us, horns blared.

I was a Goth no longer. I was not sure what I was.

But I knew I was in love.

BOOK 3: The Hunt

'Gravemound is warm.'
Njord

CHAPTER 11

W
e trekked swiftly and quietly through the woods and over the hills, and there were plenty of rich valleys and hillsides filled with Goth homesteads. Dogs were barking lazily, the sound eerie in the night, echoing everywhere, and often leaving one confused of the direction of such possibly dangerous signs of pursuit. The four-legged guards sensed our presence, despite our attempt at stealth and when we did see a smoky hall half hidden by the woods and night-fog, men would often stand at the doors of the halls, squinting into the darkness, expecting beasts on two or four legs. We would wait, and then move, keeping close together.

'We are lucky so many are in Marka,' Aldbert noted and he was right. Many warriors had indeed traveled there for the funeral and the Thing. We moved like young hares, carefully, expecting to be pounced upon, but determined to find safety. The horizon and the clouds in the sky were light behind us, likely with the fires in Marka, but soon that too ebbed, and I swallowed in terror at the thought of them finding Ludovicus's corpse in Maino's room. There would be a thorough search. I looked at the Saxons guiltily, for even if I hoped for their protection on our journey, it was true we might have moved more stealthily and quicker with fewer people. No battle would end well, when there were only eighteen of them, and while I also thought they might buy me a way to escape the land altogether should the girl prove to be a liar, I had half hoped they might be blamed for stealing her, and for taking me as well.

But Hughnot would know.

Bero would guess.

No matter what conclusion Father reached, it would be safe to assume most thought I had reconsidered my allegiance and changed sides, and not even Father could spare my rear. Though, of course, they would be right to do condemn me. I *had* changed sides. It felt terrifyingly invigorating, everything was new and at the same time also rotten. I was a traitor. Savage men were there with me, a woman worth dying for, but I still felt terrible for my choices.

And it might all go to waste. They could catch us.

I just wish we had more time to escape, but we didn't, I thought. They would know I had done it. They would know soon. I thought about the guard I had let live, and cursed myself for not taking his life, but in the end, I decided I couldn't have performed such a murderous deed, and I knew it well enough.

I gazed at Ceadda. The man's face was looking right and left, his head swinging, his grip on the spear strong, tense, as he passed from shadows to lighter spots, ever ready. He had been a warrior for a decade, at least. They would have had no issue with slitting the guard's throat, but they had missed him in the dark.

We might have to fight. *Perhaps we could do well in a battle,* I thought.

The Saxons had no shields, but the raiders were a hardy bunch, their beards long and limbs strong, and they would not play fair, should something be thrown at them. They would be brave. They were also wise. One could see it in their eyes; concern. We were walking on very thin ice, and the ice was cracking under our weight, but we had no chance to be cautious. We had to risk much. They had been promised a boat, and for that, they had given oaths, but not a man amongst them could be sure to see their wives and children again.

A wolf howled somewhere near, startling me from my contemplations.

Ahead, the girl guided her horse with her shapely thighs and looked over the vast woods as if she owned them. Her eyes didn't tell me anything like those of the Saxons, but she must have known how desperate our escape would be, no matter our trickery with the boat and not taking a one across the lake.

'What will we be eating?' Ceadda asked me as if this was the most pressing concern on the muddy track to freedom. He eyed his men running ahead in the woods, scouting, sniffling the air. Others were bringing the rear and he was right. We would need to eat. I eyed Aldbert, who patted a bag on his horse, a bulging thing, and I hoped he had not failed me there. I needed time with him to fully understand the level of his treachery. He had been my friend since our childhood, but while I wanted to understand him, to give him many chances to redeem himself, I was reluctant, and perhaps the Maroboodus that would later be the dread of his enemies was already rearing his bloody Bear's head.

I wanted to hurt him for his deed.

I did.

I couldn't help myself, but there was some petty, and also practical part of me that looked at him and found him a distraction, a potentially dangerous one and I was ashamed as well, because he had a hurt dog's look on his face, and I had forced him on a very dangerous road. I regretted taking him, I regretted asking him to help me, but for some reason he was still here, trying to stay with us, so I'd have to give him a chance.

'Bark,' I told Ceadda and rapped at a passing trunk. 'We can eat that, if nothing else. No time to eat now.'

'I ate some of my oar once,' Njord noted. 'It was salty with my sweat and tasted all right. Kind of squishy after I let it settle under my tongue a bit. We had lost our munitions.'

I chuckled and pointed a finger at the bags on Aldbert's horse. 'But I came prepared.'

He noticed everyone was staring at him and startled, he tapped the bags. 'We have bread, lentils, and meat. It won't last, though. We forage as we go. There are cowberries, mushrooms.'

'We don't have our womenfolk with us,' Ceadda whispered and nodded at the girl. 'Can she help pick the food, so we won't eat something deadly? She knows the woods, no? We are sea people, and don't farm or forage. Do I look like a bear?'

'Smell like one. You ask her,' I told him, eyeing the pretty creature on the horse with awe and respect, and the same part that doubted Aldbert also gnawed at my thoughts concerning her.

Surely, she would betray me.

She had made me so happy with but few words, but it was like a dream, wasn't it? Words were nothing. I'd have to speak with her soon about her

179

life, my plans, and what I hoped I might accomplish with her and the Svea, and if the gods were kind, the doubts would fly away like sparrows. They would, if only she smiled. She was the key to my happiness, and to power both. 'I wish I knew her name.'

Ceadda quaffed and shook his head. 'Ask her, fool, and while you do, you ask if she could aid us so we won't have to starve more than we did while enjoying your Bero's hospitality,' he chuckled.

'And to drink?' Njord asked with an eager grin. He poked at Aldbert's bags. 'Did you pack any? Some Goth ale? It's weak piss, yea, but still I'd rather have that than nothing. Imagine that's the only thing we never, ever looted when we raided a Goth hall and now I'd kiss a hairy Goth ass for a sip of some of it, even if it were served in a filthy pigsty from a slop bucket. It's good for dousing fires or bathing in, and does nothing to quench a man's thirst, but I'd still love some.'

'Saxon ale,' I said. 'We have loads of Saxon drink.'

'Oh?' he asked, and smiled with happy anticipation, eyeing the bags with such hope my heart nearly broke.

'Tears. Eat your tears,' I told him as I looked at Aldbert whose face wore a disapproving frown. He looked like an old woman who was eating dinner with her husband's young lover. He hated our Saxon company. Perhaps he hated the girl as well.

'Very funny, Goth,' Njord said, chortling. 'Tears. Saxon ale. I like your humor, Goth. It's the sort of stuff you hear them meowing at you over their shields before they weep and shit themselves at the end of a spear.'

'We drink *water*,' Ceadda said simply. 'Plenty of springs around, and rivers as well. Now, the Svea village is two days that way.' He pointed to the west and a small river that ran that way below us lazily. It was glinting in the darkness and I heard it's gurgling voice. 'That river will combine with two larger ones a day away and that's where we're going.'

'Three Forks,' the girl stated.

'Right, forks,' Ceadda allowed. 'We won't go to the Long-Lake as we agreed,' he nodded to some hills to the north with a hint of longing in his look. 'We raided there three years ago, went past Long-Lake and I know there are some steep hills between the river to our south and the lake and that's where we will hike, if the lady approves. We'll avoid all the valleys,' he said and bowed towards her back, 'and that way we should avoid the villages and the heavily used hunt-trails. We will find some smaller game trails, and jog all the way and worry about drink and food as we go. Let's hope they thought we took a ship away south, but if not, then we will have to be really resourceful. Let us lead, and it shall be well, eh?'

I looked behind to the east, for the coast that was not too far yet, but I was surprised I could already make out its gray surface. Then I noticed Sunna was rising. The morning had arrived. The celestial horses were dragging up their beautiful burden in the bright chariot and Hughnot would be roving to the cove, only to eventually find that I had betrayed him. I nodded at Ceadda. 'Lead on.'

The girl turned to us. 'It's a good plan. But we won't go to my village.'

'What?' Ceadda asked, alarmed. 'Not going home? Where are you going?'

'And why?' I asked, horrified. 'Surely we would be safe there?'

Njord groaned. 'I know what she'll say. She forgot something. We have to go back—'

She slapped her palms together. 'Shut up, Saxon. We won't go back. In fact, we won't go as far as you thought.'

'Good news, finally,' Ceadda grumbled.

She pointed a finger to the horizon in the west. 'We will go that way, a day or a bit more away, and go over those three rivers, certainly, but we won't trek much further from them,' she said. 'There is another village we will visit and that is near the river's so you Saxons should be happy. It's by the Long-Lake, very near the end of it.'

'Why won't we go to your home?' I insisted. 'Why—'

She leaned closer to me. 'I'll tell you a bit later.'

I opened my mouth but growled agreement and turned to Ceadda. 'Lead on. And make sure we leave no tracks.'

'Impossible,' said the woman with a smile.

'Why?' Njord frowned. 'You think we don't know how to lift our feet?'

She shrugged. 'There are twenty men rumbling along in a wood filled with twigs, shrubs, and some of you drag your feet, Saxon, indeed they do.

Any half-blind Svea could track this party and the tracker could be very drunk and probably crippled in addition to being blind and still have no problems finding this lot. You will have to hope and beg the Goths are not as skilled running the trails as are our hunters.'

'They are Goth trails, aren't they?' Aldbert said unhelpfully.

She glanced at Aldbert with curiosity, but went on and spoke to Ceadda. 'They'll not be stupid, Saxon, the Goths. They will check the hills as well. They will herd us. They'll come by the Lake, the rivers, and send men to look at the hills. They'll make good time and go past and hope to catch us in a net. We will have to beg the spirits for help, for rain to pour down like a giant's hammer, flattening all tracks, and even then we might walk right into them. Now we don't have rain and will be careful and meticulous. When we stop, bury your shit. Dark gods of the rocky Jotunheim only knows why you brought horses along, as they will lumber along like a blind bear and will leave tracks a child might spot.'

'You seem to enjoy the beast's back just fine,' Ceadda said with a mocking smile. 'And I didn't bring the horses. He did.' He thumbed me and my red hair matched my face as I sputtered, and bit my tongue as I decided there was nothing I could say that wouldn't sound like I was making excuses.

She glanced at me and smiled. 'Yes, I enjoy it, Saxon. It's best I won't slow you down, at least, so let's give my young, handsome Goth adeling some credit. In any case, you will make no fires. Don't break branches, and tear out moss, if you can avoid it. Less you do, the better. Do drag your feet, and spears, and try to pretend you belong here.'

'We have lived in these lands for a long time,' I said with some pride. 'We have hunted through these lands for both moose and for your war-parties—'

'Your kind,' she said with amusement, 'sailed to these shores a hundred years past from the islands. Your family, Friednot and Hughnot, only twenty years past. Your family is not the first who tries to take the lands from us. You know, my tribe lived in the coast then. Father often tells how his father grew up not far from your Marka. Now we have the woods and the lakes, but this is *not* your land. We made these trails, and we know them, Maroboodus.'

'Well, while some others *tried*, we *took* the land. And kept it.' It was a bluntly delivered statement, and I felt immensely proud for airing it.

She went quiet, her face smooth and there was no sign of anger. It was a curious, calm look, and while I wondered what that meant, Ceadda was trying to pull my sleeve. As a married man, he probably knew I was rowing into shoals, but he was too late. The girl took a long breath. She rode close to me and leaned near. 'You, while handsome and foolishly brave,' she said with a small smile, which made the men groan and me blush, 'are ignorant as a babe. You and the dirty Saxons know nothing about this land. You don't really know its smell, its beauty, the weakness and the power of the men who inhabit it, and you have never heard the voices of the spirits who occupy it, because they don't speak to you. And you,' she smiled very close to me, 'would marry me? You need to know the land better, I think. Taste the turf, boy.'

She pushed me and I toppled from the horse and fell amidst brambles, mud, and dirt. The Saxons were chuckling and Ceadda grabbed the horse, but she smiled sweetly at me and I could only frown in return. 'I will lead us to the trails. Your Saxons don't know them.'

'Wait a minute,' Ceadda said. 'Please! No woman—'

She spat and Ceadda went quiet 'I shall. I have better judgement than you do. You don't even know your friends. That one,' she said and nodded at Aldbert, 'the one I don't trust, but who feels strangely familiar, has been twisting twigs all the time. With his hands. Deliberately. Perhaps he left a sign back in Marka that we took no boat? That we are here?'

We turned to look at Aldbert, who looked terrified as he still held a fresh branch of a rowan in his hand. He looked down at it and then at us. 'I'm sorry. I've not done this before. I need something to hold. This is all—'

'Hold your cock like a proper man,' Ceadda growled. 'What's the matter with you? You some kind of a coward? Or a woman?' He looked startled and bowed to the wonderfully composed and brave girl on the horse. 'No offence, lady.'

183

'Some taken,' she said coldly, but I pushed to Aldbert and grabbed the twig from his hands.

'You trying to get us killed?' I asked him, dreading the answer.

'No, I was just deep in my thoughts, and I often need something in my hands. You've seen me making poems.'

'Poems, by Donor's gangly nose,' Njord moaned. 'He is a damn poet. Can't even eat him, probably tastes like lies.'

Aldbert went on. 'I'm nervous. I won't deny it.'

'Shh,' Njord said, exasperated. 'Best be quiet now or they'll throw you in swamp. Break no more twigs, or the next twig might be your neck.'

I slapped my thigh with the twig and stuck it under my belt. I hesitated, wondering what to do with Aldbert.

'She is right,' Ceadda said and smiled like a wolf at our long looks. 'We will be careful.' He meant also Aldbert, as well as the way we traveled, and I agreed with him.

'Is she?' Njord asked, his thick lips pursed. 'You called her a rancid witch when Cuthbert died. Thought she was ugly too. A spirit.'

Ceadda slapped his brother and didn't look at the girl. 'She knows her woods. Svearna might be … ' he stammered and gave her a small bow, 'less noble and more akin to the vaettir and spirit animals of the deep, but they did live here first.'

'Akin to animals?' the girl asked him, aghast. 'You are really trying to get that boat from my people, aren't you? Perhaps they'll cook thin broth from your bones, instead?' They smiled at each other and I guessed they were not as opposed to each other than they had been. Goths made great common enemies. Or at least Aldbert.

'She leads us,' Ceadda allowed with some incredulity in his voice and the girl smiled and nodded in thanks.

'What about him?' she asked and pointed a finger at Aldbert. 'I don't like him. Not one bit.'

'I will keep an eye on him,' I told her but noticed she was not convinced. 'Let me look after him.'

'He is dangerous,' she said softly. 'Maroboodus—'

'I'm a poet!' Aldbert said. 'I've done nothing to—'

'A liar by nature, as the Saxon said,' she said as if she had just proved a point, and perhaps she had.

'I say he comes,' I insisted and her jaw tightened. 'I'm the leader here.'

'Listen to the Pup,' Njord laughed and the way his head swung from her to me, perhaps he hoped she would tear my head off.

She opened her mouth, but clearly counted trees as she sought to hold her temper again. She waved her hand in my direction. 'I'll teach you how to treat a princess,' she said sweetly as if offering me honey and ale. 'And in the end you will see every great leader has a goddess they must follow. My mother was like this to my father. You will see.'

'You are done for, Goth,' Njord chuckled as I glowered at him, having lost my authority, if I ever had any to begin with. He pushed me playfully. 'There was no oath against speaking our minds, lord Pup, and I don't remember making any to take your side in an argument.'

'To you, I am Maroboodus,' I said and was rewarded by snickering Saxons.

'You two will have some interesting chats, I'm sure,' Njord said happily. 'So, we shall take to the hills then?'

She glared at the man, but he didn't die as she probably hoped. 'We go that way, yes,' she said with determination. 'I'll show you some trails Father once showed me near here. It's dark, but I think I'll find them. Then we go over the hills, follow the Long-Lake, skirt that river, and then when we reach the Three Forks, the three rivers I'll tell you where to go.'

'So, let us move,' Ceadda said and we traveled. We ran softly and rode carefully for the north, for the Lake, then turned northeast as a scout found trails that the Svea princess approved of. She would frown, squint along the tracks, and like a goddess of the hunt, her dark hair blowing in the wind, she pushed us forward. We made good time, avoiding people's dwellings and the Saxon scouts were very good, wily, careful, and stealthy, especially with the girl's help. We would stop, and crouch when we saw a local hunter and then another, trailing some deer, and wait patiently until they passed. We trekked through a deep, mossy wood that was steaming in the moist air and then took to the high ground of the hills Ceadda had mentioned, where it was dryer and heather fields were red and white in a late fall glory. They were very tall hills, though easily navigable, even on horses, and when we'd made our way across a few, it was afternoon. I gazed at the Long-Lake to our north, stretching from the coast far to inland, swallowing rivers as it went deeper to the misty lands, and to the south, where Goth settlements still showed by trails of smoke and well-tended fields. The wider river was making its lazy way to the west through the Goth settlements to our south. Ceadda was talking with the girl and she gave him some words, and the savage Saxon nodded. He walked to me and nodded at a patch of stony land where tall boulders stood on the side of a hill. 'We stop here and rest for some hours. Then we shall run with the wolves of the night and make our way as far as we can.'

'The horses need rest,' Aldbert said softly.

'We will eat them, if they do,' one burly Saxon said happily and I saw by the shocked look on Aldbert's face he had decided the horses were fine. He probably thought he might escape with the help of a horse, should there be any trouble and he clearly regretted having said anything at all. I'd have to talk to him, and despite the promise I had made to keep him in my sight at all times, I couldn't be sure he wasn't giving us away.

The Saxons were sitting down, few were running to the woods to scout and Njord came to Aldbert and grabbed the bags of food from him, opened them up with a practiced yank and went on sniffing at the contents, like a pampered rat as he poked inside. I groomed Scald, checked its hooves and tied it to a tree, and noticed Ceadda standing on top of a tall, mossy boulder, gazing back the way he had come. Sol was getting lower in the sky and the peculiar, drowsy, and somewhat depressed mood you often suffer when everything is murky and night is falling, took over the camp. I went to Ceadda and he nodded at me and gave me his hand. I grasped it, he pulled me up to stand next to him.

'You ok? Thighs not too sore?' he teased me for riding.

'My ass is sore,' I agreed.

He laughed and clapped me so hard I nearly fell and he grabbed me. 'Look, Red,' he said and pointed a finger to southeast. I couldn't see anything special and squinted. He noticed my hesitation and grunted, casing a nervous eye to the girl. 'Pretend you noticed it, or she will probably not respect you. You did well to argue with her and not look like a spineless maggot, but just pretend to know what you are doing now, as well.'

'I saved her ass, she should respect me,' I told him, feeling like I was lost in the mists. 'What am I seeing?' I saw only trees and that made me anxious.

'Not yet you haven't,' he told me darkly and nodded for the horizon. 'Her ass is far from safe,' he said and kept nodding towards southeast. 'Especially if that Maino gets her. She'll not like that.' There, the endless hills, valleys, pine and birch woods as far you could see, dotted with some fields and even villages that were hard to spot. I nodded sagely, made him snort with amusement. 'You are blind as a drunk rat. And I've seen some. They don't see a cat if they run over its tail.'

I cursed him and turned to look west, the way we were going. The river snaked that way and then I saw it combine with others far away. 'At least I see that.'

Ceadda sighed. 'Three Forks, as she called them. Beyond that, is where our scouts placed Snowlake. There is a small body of water, lake or a swamp, nestled by the two forbidden looking hills,' he said and shuddered. 'Her tribe, they live by it. It was a large settlement of a hundred Svear, and they were well armed. But we surprised them. I'm happy we save a day's hike.'

'Your lord went all that way for a woman,' I stated. 'That he would have given our enemies in return for silver.'

Ceadda laughed. 'Can you blame him? I think he forgot his greed the moment he saw her staring up at him furiously, her guards dead around her. She didn't fear, not one bit,' he whispered and turned to look at the girl, who had produced a comb and was looking up at us as we stood there on the rock. 'He tried to have her the first night we made camp, but she refused.'

'Refused?' I said with a cold smile. 'Tried to have her?'

He waved his hand, bothered. 'Cuthbert the Black wasn't a good man. What can I say? But she raked his face and kicked him in the balls so hard we all heard the chain mail jingle and him yelp. I doubt he has ever been more hurt. Well, except the day he was killed. He was grimacing when he tried to sit in the saddle, I tell you that, so his balls were probably swollen. He decided to wait,' Ceadda said and smiled. 'He planned to give her over to the high Goth for silver, but I'm not sure he would have. I didn't always like our lord but he gave us plenty of loot, fine homes and our families what they needed to survive. Our land is no less harsh than yours. We get droughts, and sickness and fight Chauci in the south every year and I tell you now, those bastards have many men. Each year we bury a dozen of their warriors, but they seem to seed more and more just to spite us. Cuthbert was a famous lord, but there are others and someone else will take our oaths and we fight again. With you lot, even.'

'He fought well,' I stated reluctantly. 'But if he tried to hurt her, I'll kill him again in Valholl, the rotten bastard.' I looked back to where we came from, thinking about Bero, Hughnot, and even Father. And Maino. Him above all others. 'But then, so are many others. Rotten bastards.'

'Now that you have her,' he chuckled, 'I thought I wanted to give you a fair warning. Keep your legs together when she hugs you.'

I chortled and nodded, wiping my nose that was dripping. 'Gods, give us a hall and mead. So, what was I supposed to see out there? No more games.'

He shook his head. 'Blind bastard, but I suppose it's good you know it and don't pretend. No good at sea, you wouldn't be, but perhaps you could just sit at the oars, eh?' His eyes were dreamy as he gazed down the hillside. 'I bet your lazy Goth ass would love a hall at the end of the road and some well-brewed ale or sweet mead to invigorate your weary bones, but I'd love to have our ship,' he said wistfully. 'We do love our ships. They are almost better than a hall and a field of wheat or barley, and a warm wife. It's a man's life, that.'

'Forget the damned boat,' I growled. 'What did you see?'

He nodded and pointed a finger down the hill. 'Now look there,' he said, pointing southeast. 'See?'

And I finally did. There was a glint by a winding river, not very far. Then another. 'I see it.'

'Them,' he corrected.

188

'I see …them. Hunters? Locals?'

'Manhunters,' Ceadda said sternly. 'I bet there are dozens. I just feel it in my bones. And if you ask Njord, they are a hundred or more. And they will have dogs. God Saxenot spare us if they find our trail. It's a miracle they have not already. Perhaps the girl knows her business, after all, but I dare say I chose well to take the hillside.' He stammered and blushed. 'Though perhaps I would have stumbled on some of those halls she avoided.'

'We could have taken a boat after all,' I said and turned to look at the stretching body of water in the north and froze. There were specs gliding over the waves, ships rowing up and down the coast.

'They have been there since morning,' he smiled with a cold smile. 'Goths. Most local, having been warned to look for us. They are careful Goths since Svearna will not like them this deep in these waters.' He turned back to the valleys and spoke hesitantly. 'I think you might have done better by leaving us behind and just riding off with her.'

'But what if she would have left me in the woods?' I asked him with a smile. 'Or gave me to her people as a sacrifice?'

His eyes brightened and he chuckled. 'Yes, I know we were to guard you more than her.'

'We might still need that route,' I reminded him and he didn't seem to mind either way. Perhaps there would be an escape with them, should things go terribly wrong, but the Goths were guarding the waters now. He shrugged, eyeing the glinting metal not too far in the woods. 'Too bad it wasn't easy. Can't be helped, I suppose. Looked good for a moment there, but now it can end up like a badly built hull that never sees water. Forgotten bones on some sad meadow,' he said, eyeing the girl. 'Why don't you just go and talk to her, lout,' Ceadda said. 'Might want to know her name before things turn ugly.'

They did.

'More men,' said Njord below us. I had not noticed him coming forth, but he pointed a finger where the glints had been apparent.

Indeed, I saw men, but not that many. I hesitated as I stood on the ledge of the rock, and wondered at the Saxons and their firm belief there was something more than a few hunters. Perhaps it was some Goth lord out to hunt the regular Svea raiders, or to pay back for some insult that had been given earlier in the year, a feud solving in the process. 'Shit and Donor's balls,' Ceadda cursed crudely and pulled me to my belly. Dozens of men appeared, tiny specs at the edge of the river. There were too many men, well-armed and dangerous to be a local party and indeed, I could now see slinking shadows of dogs as they loped to the edge of the water to lap up some of the clear water. Gasto bred dogs, I remembered, were often silent in the hunt. They were infamous all across the land for being disciplined, uncannily obedient, and terrible in battle. The ones I saw were like just such slavering, nasty beasts they used in the hunt and battle both.

'You have great eyes,' I stated after a while 'But why are they by the river? Pausing for a camp?'

'Look now,' he said softly. 'To the *water*. Forget the bastards dragging their feet across shit in the woods. Look at those other bastards.'

And I saw them as well.

I had been looking at the woods, but there were large boats rowing on the river and the boats were filled with rowers. They were not the seagoing ships we used to travel the stormy coasts, heavy and clinker-built, but lighter, longer ones with high prows. I noticed many of the men sitting on the benches were glinting dully as the chain mail on their torso gleamed. I shuddered with fear.

'Is it possible it's your father?' Njord asked, having placed his spear in the grass to avoid it shining in the light.

I shook my head reluctantly. 'Not likely. Those must be Bero's champions. Maino, certainly, shall be there, slavering for my head.'

'You shouldn't have cut off his beard,' Ceadda said. 'But it was amusing, I give you that.'

'He'll be there, hoping to shear off my fingers, toes, nose—'

'Cock,' Njord added unhelpfully.

'That too,' I said softly. 'Unfortunately. Yea, he shall be there if he wasn't crippled. Danr, Eadwine. And Gasto. Perhaps Friednot's former men. But Gasto, yes.' I said the last name with dread, as he was a great tracker and the dogs were his, no doubt.

190

'The dog lord?' Ceadda said. 'Yes, we once had a shieldwall broken by those slavering bitches from Hel. His dogs, not his daughters.'

'His girls feed the dogs, I hear, and train them with Gasto,' I said sullenly.

'Perhaps your lord Bero is out there as well,' said the Saxon with almost perverse happiness at being hunted by so many. 'There is a man with long black hair and a brooding, dastardly face. Tilted to his side he is, like a man with only one useless ball.'

'You cannot see that far!'

'No, I cannot,' he grinned. 'But I bet he is there nonetheless. Let's hope your father is there as well. Though that might not make any difference to how things will end, right?'

I nodded. 'He wanted to exile me. My grandmother thinks I should be sacrificed,' I stated. 'Let's try to make it out of this without my father, in any case. He might be tempted to knock my head off, and not just knock sense into it.'

He gave me a long look and then at the girl. 'Go now. Speak with her and then we leave. You two make a great, if strangely ill-omened couple. Let's hope they stay down there for the night indeed, and the dogs are in a lazy mood, but they will get to the river's end before us. They can use those smaller rivers to get before us and those dogs will make life miserable for us. They'll swing north, they'll swing south and will always have dozens of men near. We will have to rush west and hope we cross those hills and fields,' he nodded to the land directly north of the three rivers crossing each other in the west. 'We have to get to that village before they cut us off.'

'Gasto will pick up the trail,' I said with dread. 'No matter what. They are sure to have something of ours that the dogs can smell, and—'

'We will deal with him if he gets close,' the Saxon said with a grim grin. 'We are not easy pickings, even without our shields.' He gave me a long look. 'Go and speak with her.'

'Why?' I said, feeling reluctant and scared suddenly, and that made me smile, since she was scarier than the hounds.

'Because,' the Saxon explained, 'you're a young man and could use a kiss. Go and charm the girl, my lord. Do so for all of us. Make sure she is really into you. She is the key to our boat, isn't she?'

'Yes, of course,' I said, much more terrified than I had been when I fought Maino, I made my way down the boulder. It was mossy, and some gave away from under me and I fell and rolled down with a shriek. I bumped to the muddy ground, bit my lip, and tasted blood.

'Not like that,' Ceadda said, and then roared with laughter, which he subdued into chuckles as I picked myself up. Aldbert scowled at the Saxons that were all laughing like damned bastards, walked over, and pulled me up. I also found the girl hovering near, her eyes hard, but mouth twisted with mirth.

'Maroboodus ...' Aldbert began, but I shook my head at him.

'Later, over a mug of ale,' I said, not looking at him. 'Many mugs. I need to be drunk to have a discussion with you.'

'Later, yes. And drunk,' he agreed and I made my way to the girl. She squinted as she looked up to me and got up and brushed off her furs and tunic from brambles and mud. It made me feel somewhat better to think it was important for her to look presentable before me.

She scowled as she saw the relieved smile on my face. 'I'd brush myself off for the meanest peasant. I don't like to look untidy. I'm a—'

'Princess,' I said.

'A woman,' she corrected and smiled to take off the bite. 'You're clumsy as a newborn horse when I'm around, but you know I'm relieved it is you who saved me,' she said with a small bow and nodded towards the woods. 'Come, walk with me. Didn't your Saxon dog tell you to have a chat and make sure I won't have you lot stretched nude on an altar to one of our gods? We do have some gods we don't share with you, cousins, and their vitka would make your belly churn. Literally. With a knife.'

'He did ask me to make sure that will not take place,' I told him and looked away from Aldbert who had begun to say something, but went quiet. 'You stay here.' He nodded and obeyed.

She pulled me higher up the hill, and we navigated the heather bushes under the steady eyes of the Saxon sea wolves and Aldbert, who was frowning after us. I followed her willingly, happy she had brought up the subject of our future, and after some time, she found a log, where she sat me down. I pulled the sword out and put it on my side and she adjusted the ax as well and we both smiled at that. She gazed at the weapons and put her weapon aside. She looked at my lip with a small frown, kneeled before me, and touched it. Her finger came off bloody and she sucked it clean. I started to speak, but she waved me down. She stared at me steadily for a moment and then finally took a deep breath, as if awakened from a dream. 'Your father is Hulderic the Goth, no?'

'Yes,' I said. 'He is my father, and Bero is his brother.'

She nodded steadily and smiled. 'My father speaks of your family quite often. You are of the old blood, very old indeed. The oldest, he says. He is Gislin, of Snowlake, and we are of ancient blood as well. Father claims we are as old and holy as you.'

'Everyone thinks they are old and holy,' I smiled.

'Yes,' she said with a small laugh. 'People think themselves special. Why live otherwise?'

'Do *you* have a name?' I asked.

'Yes, one very much like your Saxon friends,' she said mischievously. 'I'm so happy you finally got around to ask it.'

I frowned. 'Saxon name? They have names, yes, but—'

'My name is Saxa,' she said incredulously. 'Princess of Snowlake. But call me Saxa.'

'Not of Snowlake?' I asked her, watching her eyes as I did. There was a brief stab of pain in her eyes, but she shook her head and hid the emotion.

'No. As I said, I won't go back there. And should I one day go that way, my father must be dead and I won't stay. I'll spit on the land, and leave it.'

'Why? Why are we going to some other village?' I asked her and she looked confused for a moment.

She smiled sadly. 'Like it is with you, Father and I don't see eye to eye on many things. Our village is not large, but our family commands great respect across the Svea lands, as we have a special ... role to fill.' I could see she hoped I'd not ask for more information, but I had to, and she saw I would and put a finger over my mouth, while fingering my long, red hair with her other hand. 'He is a very … holy man, Maroboodus. A man devoted to the gods, one god especially. We live in the villages around the Twin Prisoners, the hills where we live, and sometimes … under them. Our homes were in the coast, but that was the place of worship, where they would travel few times a year. Now it's home, a cold, sullen home. I hate it. As for me? I'd wed a cousin, eventually, I'm well past the age, but I was lucky and the first such cousins died in Goth wars these past years, but the last one didn't and so I'd have wed him, and I wasn't very happy with the thought of being forced to live with the mongrel. He can barely speak, little less be gentle. Then Father held a Thing, and the marriage was canceled.'

'You were to marry a Goth instead. Our enemy,' I stated.

'That's right,' she said unhappily. 'I was to marry so many times, but it felt I never would. Then the Saxons came. I didn't like Cuthbert, of course, but for a moment there, when they had slaughtered many men in the village, I hoped I'd come to enjoy life elsewhere, eventually and so when they chained me and dragged me off to marry someone, not likely Cuthbert, I didn't drag my feet.'

'I think most young people feel like that,' I said with a smile. 'Rather live in misery elsewhere, than in the misery they know.'

She tugged at my hair playfully and nodded. 'Yes. Most people might be like us and hate the choices thrust on them by the darkness of this world, our duties, the needs of our families, but my reasons were deeper. Our lives in Snowlake were …are driven. People there are mad, perhaps? Yes, definitely.' She had a haunted look on her face.

'What do you mean?' I asked her, fighting an impulse to take her hand, though for some reason I thought she wanted me to. She looked at my hand, and grabbed it and I wondered if she read minds.

'Father is always waiting for a sign.'

'A sign?'

She nodded vigorously. 'A sign indeed. Our god might one day awaken from his slumber, escape his prison, and that is what our village waits for. We wait. Wait and wait. We live by the old, ancient temples, listen to the spells and bitter, long-dead words, and sometimes, if feels just utterly mad to spend one's life like that, waiting, wondering, hoping, cursing, suffering, and just breeding more fools to start the cycle again. All for a god, who keeps sleeping. And should this god awaken? Well, we'd die. The whole world.'

I remembered Father's words about Ragnarok and felt my blood turn to ice. 'Indeed?'

'Yes,' she said. 'As I said, people there are mad. Then I was freed from them. The Saxons,' she said with a smile and gestured down the hill where two such pirates were looking up at us, making sure we were safe and not running away, 'were different. Driven by hunger and thirst, they make plans for the next year. They live, love, murder, and I loved to listen to them speaking about the future. I was exhilarated. I was to be taken to some Goth across the sea, I heard, and that thought didn't please me, but for some reason I thought it would all be well, soon enough. And then I saw you.' She smiled at me, her eyes glittering like stars and my breath nearly stopped.

I stammered on. 'That is crazy.'

'What?' she laughed, though there was a hurt look on her face and I half hoped Ceadda would be there, pulling my sleeve or slapping my mouth shut, but I was on my own.

I struck my head. 'No, I mean it's not crazy. It's ...unexpected. And I have nothing against you being mad.'

'I am mad?' she asked softly, which I had learnt meant I was in danger, while squeezing my hand.

'Gods, help me,' I cursed and slammed a fist on my thigh to focus. 'Not mad, but different, outspoken. So fine.'

'That's better,' she said and relaxed her grip. 'Much better. You should beat yourself more. I can, if you want?'

I ignored her teasing and went on, stubbornly, hoping I'd not ruin the moment. 'But I'm a man, and a man needs to understand everything and so I have to know why do you act like you have ... feelings for me? You don't have to. I'm committed anyway. You say you saw me there, that day, fighting and it makes me feel warm like the fires of Muspelheim were coursing inside my veins, but I guess I need to know—'

'If I really mean it?' she asked and tilted her head at me, and grasped another lock of my red hair. 'Tell me, my boy, what do you feel?'

I stammered and swallowed like a fool with a bone in his throat, until I managed to calm myself and stroked her hand, still holding my hair. 'I felt like all the other maidens I have ever seen were smoke and mist and you are the Sunna, chasing them all away, across the horizons, to the cracks of the Midgard, and they never were more than a dream.'

'Have you many such girls you no longer think about?' she chuckled.

'No, but you know what I—'

She laughed softly and stroked my face, her cheeks blushed. 'You are the first *hero* I have ever seen, Maroboodus. The first one. There are champions aplenty, fine warriors, but a hero is a man who risks all for love, just like the poets sing. You are mine and I need no other hero. I see a great man in you. I told you. I saw you shall be great. I didn't lie. It was a dream, but dreams are reality sometimes and I knew when you threw the spear that took Cuthbert out of the saddle. I saw your face. You were jubilant like a warring god, covered in blood, and while there were high champions and old, famous, and some fat, warlords aplenty, there was something different about you. Your eyes betray ... love? Pure love. You don't hide it. You love. You feel freely, deny yourself nothing, and you react when you want something. You defied them all to get me, because you wanted me.'

'Yes,' I said huskily.

She smiled crookedly. 'And I am no fool. I think you make high plans while you love. You are a hero of love, and a lord of wits. You have ambitions?'

'I do—'

'And you love your father?' she asked, tilting her head, as if prodding me to be brave and answer truthfully.

'Sometimes!' I answered. 'Look—'

'You would have him rule the Goths. You want me for love, and for power. And I can indeed help you.'

I felt my heart soar. I felt dizzy, so happy and I believed her with all my heart. I understood her. She knew what I wanted. It felt like the gods had prodded her to me, and she was part of me, I was part of her. 'Yes,' I told her as steadily as I could, holding her hands and she came closer.

'I will help you. Us. But not if we go to Father's village, where I will have no freedom and my lot will be to seed children for a mongrel. We will find other relatives, others who hate my father. It should be no surprise he has enemies even in our family, and he does. There is one. Agin. He is a great man, nearly greater than Father and he will summon men to your banner. He will share power with us and take our plans as his own. We have an old dream, Goth, one to claim back our lands.' She hesitated and shook her head, letting her love for me bury such dreams. 'But he will see times have changed, and we have to stand together. Goth and Svea. We shall herald such a change. We will work together, share lands and some will resist. They will have to die. Others will join us, and we shall be anything we wish to be. You will indeed be able to help your father against all your enemies and the Svea will be united. We can succeed, but we must start with Agin.'

'I'm not sure—'

She put her hand on my shoulder. 'In my dread I saw just a glimpse through the gray mists of secrets that such a fine future is what the gods wish, that it might be possible to attain if we succeed. Should we choose well and be brave, we could indeed reach unprecedented heights in glory. Our children could rule vast, rich lands and the Saxons,' she said with a smile, 'would not raid us. We would raid them.'

I lifted my hand and she didn't flinch as I stroked her fair face, but instead pressed it against my palm like a cat would. She closed her eyes for a moment, and I felt like a fool, because I'd never again think she would be trying to betray us. Ceadda would soon probe me for how our chat went, and I knew I'd tell him she is as honest as goddess Frigg, and I'd risk them and myself for her. I already had, but after her speech, I would always trust her, even onto my death. I spoke strongly. 'I dream of something similar, though I wasn't sure what that would be. I only wanted to restore our family honor, to carry the ring of Draupnir's Spawn, hold our family sword, and be high. You gave my thoughts form.'

She nodded resolutely. 'Svearna will not go anywhere. We won't disappear. If you wish to stay here on these shores, you will need the clans, at least some of them to join with the Goths. The northern Svearna are powerful, with fleets and fine warriors, but there is strength in the wilder, animal-like Svea, like Ceadda called us, and with patience, we could form a grand land that can shake the coasts.'

'I've never heard a woman speak like this,' I said with a smile. 'I wonder if this is what Father had with Mother. They often sat by the fire, whispering for hours on end, speaking, laughing, and sometimes, weeping.'

'We shall have the same,' she said. 'And more. We shall sit like that when none stand against us.' She had strength of mind that could turn battles and I loved to look at her fair, fierce face. I could imagine her on the prow of a boat, seeking to put a relentless enemy to sword, and I, her husband next to her.

'This Agin is someone you trust, then?' I asked.

'It's not a new idea, love, combining our tribes. Some Goths live with us, some Svea with you already,' she said. 'Agin will see the light. Apparently your relatives in the east wanted to use Father's influence to help us wipe you out, after I've been taken and married to that one and perhaps Father saw an opportunity to end Goth wars. It was put before the tribes, and many agreed, though not all. Enough did and so I was to be married off. Father is all about our gods, thinking about ancient prophecies, but he is also a keen lord of the land, a ruler of a gau, and does not spit on alliances that make sense to get Goth loot. He will,' she said with some trepidation, but I smoothed her face and she calmed and went on, 'give us trouble, but in the end, if we stay true to each other and summon men to fight for us, we will overcome him. We shall, love. Yes, I trust Agin, though he opposed Father's plans, he opposed Father more than the plan.'

'I agree to everything you said,' I smiled and hesitated. 'We spoke of it already and I would wed you,' I told her. 'As soon as possible.'

'My words won't change. You need not worry like that Maino did. He was jealously guarding my doorway, haunting his father for my hand, suspicious even when I was promised to him. He was stalking the hallway where I was held, sighing beyond the wall, whispering to me like a ghost of some sad, lost idiot. He thought I was but a prize of war, a sack of loot, to be shown around, bedded and mistreated. We shall marry, Maroboodus, as soon as we arrive where I am taking us. You can tell that Ceadda that as well.'

'I'd not mistreat you,' I told her. 'And I would rather see you prosper with another man than see you suffer marriage you do not desire,' I said, and I knew I had lied, as I would not handle such a scenario well at all, and my hand went to my sword's hilt and she laughed at me. I shook my head clear of the unreasonable and misplaced rage. 'At least I would not see you in a marriage you do not desire,' I corrected myself and she giggled, and put a hand before her mouth.

She smiled for a long while, her eyes lit with happiness, and finally leaned forward to put her forehead on mine. I was startled, but decided it was nice, in fact very seducing, as her nose brushed mine and her eyes, deep as summer pools of light blue waters were gazing at mine. 'This is a village near a red hill and the Long-Lake, and I'll take us there, near the Three Forks. They will give us food and shelter, there is a völva there who will marry us, and we shall live there, and grow powerful. This I can do, and we will be happy and careless, if we are lucky. We shall have much to do.'

'Much indeed,' I agreed, gazing at her eyes.

She lifted her head and looked at the woods and frowned. 'That friend of yours.'

'Aldbert,' I said.

'Keep an eye on him all the time. There is something very familiar about him, as I said. I smell lies in him. I'll try to like him for you, but—'

'He is a coward, a fool, but my friend,' I said, 'and I shall keep a close eye on him. I already have.'

She nodded, and came even closer. She pulled out a ring. It was made of tiny branches, sturdy, simple, beautiful. She pulled out my finger and put it there and my heart sang. 'It's not golden, but it's made of love. Smile, Maroboodus and kiss me.' And I did. I kissed her, and held her to me. I was drunk on the kiss, forgetting time and place and the embrace was better than the beadiest of ale, sweetest of wine, and better than my honor, that I had forfeited for her and for my plans. It all made sense to me then. We stayed there by that log for a long time, entwined in each other's arms, until Aldbert sneaked up on us, blushed and retreated.

'They are leaving,' he called from the bushes as he went, disapproval thick in his voice.

'We didn't really do anything,' I told her. 'He—'

'He doesn't like girls, because girls don't like him,' she said. 'If he gets insulted by your happiness, he should leave with the Saxons.'

I nodded, seriously. 'If he does, I will miss him. I have no idea why he tried to betray me.'

'For love, Maroboodus,' she said with a sad smile. 'Love or power. It always goes like that.' She pulled me up and pulled me along. We walked down, and she stopped by some bushes. She frowned and looked in my eyes. They were twisted. 'Keep an eye on him,' she said again. 'For our sakes.' I looked after Aldbert and went to speak with Ceadda, heavyhearted.

Ceadda clapped my back and arched his eyebrows. I smiled and he took that to be a good sign and didn't ask more. 'So, let us travel the night. We go as fast as we can. They won't dare to row those boats in the river when it's dark. We'll make it.'

We marched through the night and reached a large area full of fields very early in the morning.

Dogs were barking. Just briefly and I was sure they were Gasto's hounds. The problem was that they were barking ahead of us.

They had rowed through the night.

CHAPTER 12

'I'd rather just try to dodge them,' Ceadda growled, shading his eyes with his hand as he checked for any sign of the dogs, and clutched his spear tightly. The Goths had rowed on, passed us by, fast like wild spirits, but not all, because there were bound to be parties behind us. They had risked the river at night, and we had had to navigate boulders and trees and the harder trails and so we were slow. We had moved all day and afternoon and knew the enemy was ahead of us. The Saxon leader fidgeted as he looked north to the Long-Lake. 'We could swing further north? Sneak by the lake, just out of sight? It will take time, but it's better than getting caught here. We could wait for the night and try to find something that floats and cross to the other side.'

Saxa sighed. 'While the north shore belongs to Svearna, they do not particularly like Goths or even my tribe. Feuds are many between our clans, just like yours, and there is no safety there. And we don't know where Hughnot's lands begin and end. We might row into a Goth ambush.'

'I hate his land. I do,' Ceadda cursed as he brooded, thinking about our predicament. 'It will be so euphoric to be home,' he added. 'Nice and flat there, like Njord's wife.'

'Shut up,' Njord said dryly. 'Won't turn hilly and fat like yours.'

Saxa slapped his head, and he went silent with astonishment, though he smiled mischievously at her. She spoke vehemently. 'No crossing. No waiting. We should press on. It's a risk if they're ahead of us—' she began, but Njord interrupted her.

'They are,' he said gloomily. 'Didn't you notice? They are gone. There will be men behind here, looking for us, but most passed us in the night.'

'Since they are ahead of us,' she went on after another slap, 'and perhaps they hope we just hunker down while they make the net around us tighter and tighter. Best go now while they are still rushing.'

'She is right,' I said. 'We shall have to risk it. We'll rush on, cross the Three Forks rivers somewhere, hope there are no Goths sneaking and skulking nearby. It's simple. No time to take longer routes. We'll go where it's likely we would go, and hope they think we are trying to be clever and do otherwise. We'll brazenly hack our way to this village of Agin's if we must. Then we will be as safe as we can be, and think how to get rid of the lot of Goths rowing about the land.' Njord was opening his mouth. 'Except for me, of course. I'll stay here.' He looked mildly disappointed at the lost opportunity to mock me, but it probably saved him from yet another slap.

Ceadda was cursing, and then he nodded. 'So let's hope we find the village before they find our trail, then. And I want a beautiful boat after this miserable trip. The very best, I say.'

'You get what Agin gives you,' Saxa stated, making the Saxons unhappy. She smiled at the lean, morose faces. 'But there will be a bed, and food first.'

'Didn't want to enter a village,' Ceadda grumbled. 'Now we have no choice.'

'There's mead in there,' Aldbert murmured. 'Warmth.'

'Gravemound is warm, our vitka always says,' Njord said while staring at the hills. 'Under all that dirt, grass, mud, your bones don't get cold and—'

'Shut up,' Ceadda said and fidgeted as he gazed across the land. We were again on a small hill and silvery, glistening streams ran around the hillside, providing us with cold water. We had waded in them for a long time, leaving our legs and feet numb and white, near frostbitten. Despite the fact, and no matter how tired we were, we packed up and moved on. We walked for an hour, and the Sunna was getting lower in the sky. We traveled between some hills, until we climbed one to see where we were when Ceadda stopped us on the summit, and we froze and dismounted.

The reason was a pack of feral-looking hounds led by well-armed Goths not too far to the west. All eyes were drawn to the moving column of men trekking another hillside we would have passed soon. I was sure I saw Gasto, his strong, red shield, and long blond hair evident even from so far, and I thought I saw his thick braided beard swinging as he stroked a sleek beast, and I felt shivers of fear running down my spine. The man and his companions weren't too near; but I also saw his men were spreading the dogs on the hillside, all across it, and slowly they were making their way toward the north and Long-Lake, hoping the beasts would catch our scent. The rest of the war party we could not see, but they wouldn't be too far. They were fishing for clues, not sure where the school of fish was, drawing nets across murky waters and then tightening the noose, and if they caught us, it would be our end.

'Why aren't the Svea here to chase them off?' Njord said bitterly. 'It's their land, no? Screw them. Humping their cows, no doubt.'

Saxa sighed. 'Not many Svea live here. Most live over the Three Forks rivers and west of it. This is contested land. And some Svea hump their Saxon slaves, so you should be careful with what you say.'

'The dogs will be the end of us,' Ceadda growled and turned to look at Saxa. 'Can your Agin chase them off? How many men does he have?'

She shrugged. 'Yes, he can, I think. We have to warn him as well as save our hides. The Goths won't dare to come to a Svea village. They should avoid Svearna just like we try to avoid them, because there are thousands of our people living over there in the west, even if it takes days to gather our spears.'

'There are a hundred of the Goths. Perhaps more,' Njord said, and looked like he enjoyed sharing bad news. 'Sure they dare to attack a village. We marched across both Goth and Svea lands to do that. Of course, we are braver than most Goths, but—'

'They can try, then,' Saxa said stubbornly. 'We are not cowards. And we won't be surprised as the day when your shit-footed Cuthbert attacked us.'

'I'll feel better with a deck under my feet,' Ceadda said and nodded, taking a ragged breath. 'Let's see what happens, then,' he mumbled. 'And we are not Saxons if anyone asks. We are just fools serving Maroboodus, destitute and stupid, hoping to gain a ship for a way home, the islands of the East. We won't speak much, and Njord especially will keep his dumb mouth shut, preferably for good.'

'Will you let me open it for a meal?' Njord answered. 'Surely the Svearna feed us before they kill us?'

Ceadda ignored him. 'You do the speaking bit, lady. Do it well. We'll wait until they move on.' He nodded at the hill where Goths were now crossing to the valley below us, and some began moving north. 'Hope they don't leave anyone behind.'

'They will, but we will go quickly,' I said, sure we would get caught. 'We'll be safe in a bit, hours from now. When we get to the rivers, it shall be all right. You will be rewarded. You might be a pack of ugly men, but loyal, like mangy dogs, and they'll love you for it.'

'Not all dogs are loyal,' Njord said. 'One bit my son a month ago. Had a bad day, probably. There was this bitch—'

Saxa slapped him, and we waited.

It took an hour, more, and then they had moved off.

'Let's go, then,' Ceadda said and off we went. We guided the horses down the hillside, taking care not to leave tracks, but it was impossible to avoid them, of course. 'They seem bent on catching you, boy,' he whispered to me. 'They'll not rest before they do. I do wonder if this Agin's up to the task. They'll be back as soon as you push the Goths out.'

'There will be winter. Let them stay. Hope they enjoy it,' I smiled. 'All we need is some time. Spring will be full of hope.'

'Full of mud, usually. We will row out in the night, but you are fucked. They will come in one night, come back and find you. It will not end well at all, no.' He gazed at me and seemed to have made up his mind on something he had been pondering. 'You are welcome to come with us. And her. I'm starting to like her. Unless we get killed, of course. Then I don't like her at all. But she'll be all right. She'll live through nearly anything that will take place in the village, no doubt. Valuable she is.' He blushed as he said it, and said nothing more of the matter, but I clapped my hand on his shoulder in gratitude.

We passed the hills, saw the track of the Goths and not one man looked calm and composed. We walked on under shadows, the horses kept quiet for the most part, and we didn't see anyone. If they had guards on the hill, they were asleep.

Except for one man.

While we trekked on a trail, with tall ferns hiding the woods around us, something moved in the dark. It could have been a wolf, or a fox, or any night animal for that matter, but I saw shadows move, and Mani's light revealed a figure for just a moment, a man on a horse, and he whipped the beast hard as he noticed he had been seen. A Saxon yelled a warning, but the Goth rode wildly in the dark, passing the scout. I turned my horse and rode after him. My hair was flying, I couldn't see branches and several whipped my face painfully, but somewhere, up ahead a Goth was going fast. He was probably trying to find his camp, where they waited for news, and I had to catch him fast. Scald was clearly happy for the hunt, his ears twisted back as we rushed on, and I hoped I'd find my way back. The shadowy rider had to veer to the side, and then his horse crashed into a stream, and he was encouraging it to go faster. I went after him, nearly yelled as the freezing cold water splashed all over me, but rammed my calves to the sides of Scald.

There was a dark lump of something ahead, twisted, like frozen snakes in the middle of the river. The man before me eased his speed, and I knew why when another Goth appeared, his Suebian knot bouncing as he rode up to the shallow river's edge. 'What is it?' he yelled.

The man I had been chasing was out of breath. He pointed his spear at me. 'He ... Maroboodus!'

And so I had to charge.

Scald went in fast. I felt Hel's Delight in my fist, and it was sturdy and trustworthy, even if the ride was rough. The Goth I had been chasing cursed and pushed his horse amidst the strange, snake-like things growing out of the river, and I realized it was an old, rotten hull.

Rotten hull? Another warning? Warning of a path to misery, as Aldbert had said, I thought, but then had no time to think any more, as the other Goth charged at me from the side. I saw his face, lean face, long beard, and his fear as well, but in he came, reaching for Scald with his spear. I instinctively slapped the weapon with my sword, and it went down and lunged at the mass of the man. He screamed and fell, but his horse crashed into mine, and I fell as well.

I flailed in the water under the hooves of the horse until eventually I got up, wiping water from my face, and saw a man sitting on the shore, his breath billowing in a thin mist.

That was not the other Goth, however.

That man was behind me.

A spear shaft crushed me to his chest as he pulled it under my chin. He fell back, held on tight, and I saw dark spots. Water got into my mouth as we dropped deeper, and he didn't let go. He was strong, young, and I tried to flail behind with Hel's Delight, but couldn't hit him, and I knew I was in trouble.

Something splashed nearby. I felt the man holding me relax his grip, probably because he was surprised, and then he screamed as something hit him. I could feel the strength of the strike. I pulled out from his grasp, held on to my throat, and got to my knees, pushing at Scald to move, and found Saxa, her hair wet, removing an ax from the Goth's skull. She was grunting as she heaved, and managed to extract it, and then she gave me a long look, one of concern, as her eyes took in the surroundings, looking for more trouble.

We were silent. Nothing moved. I turned to see if the man who had been sitting on a horse on the bank was still there, and he was. I growled and moved for him, and saw it was Aldbert. He was staring at the hull. He pointed a finger at it. 'Another one. It was in my lines, no?'

'Maybe?' I said and leaned on the rotten, skeletal timber jutting from the river. 'You didn't help me.'

'I'm no fighter,' he said weakly. 'I froze.'

'She is, though,' I nodded at Saxa. The Saxons were running near now, calling to each other, and some were in the river, not far.

Saxa was looking at us, careful, perhaps shocked, as she eyed the dead Goth. She shrugged. 'Your friend wanted you captured. We will have to deal with him when we get where we are going.'

'I suppose that is right,' I said, feeling numb for my friend who kept letting me down. He didn't meet my eyes.

The Saxons were there, their eyes gleaming as they took in the dead, and quickly they relieved the Goths of their weapons. Ceadda looked up and down the river and then at us, sensing not all was well but said nothing about that. Instead, he pointed his spear to what I thought was west. 'Let's go. They will miss these men soon enough.'

I turned away, wondering at the signs. There had been twigs, the skull, and now a rotten hull. I felt I had passed a point of no return after I turned west, but Saxa rode there next to me, and I looked at her and knew I'd risk any curse and spell to get her. 'Thank you.'

She smiled. 'I used to chop wood. Wasn't much different, really.'

We pushed on. A startled moose raised its head, and a squirrel was complaining high in the woods, making our men jumpy. Saxa was on her horse, looking back and forth, like a warrior queen with her ax, and the Saxons approved with a smacking of their lips as she kicked Njord out of the way as she rode back a bit. 'Seen anything? Anyone after us? They probably should have found they have some Goths missing.'

I began to answer, but Ceadda gave a wry smile and nudged me. 'She wasn't talking to you.' He turned to Saxa. 'He's blind as a bat. Never seen anything.'

'He's my Goth, nonetheless,' she smiled. 'He fought well. Like I did.'

'Yeah, you suit each other. A murderous pair of lovers, eh?' Ceadda said.

'Tell us about the village,' I asked. 'Is it fortified?'

She nodded. 'No, not that sort of a village. Spears and shields are the walls. The village is called the "Wolf Hole" and the leader is indeed a huge man, Agin. They trade black fox furs there. Most Svear are welcome there, but not Father and his men. My brother didn't go to him this year for the Thing of the clans but fought his ideas. Instead of marrying me to the Goths, he would have wanted to keep—'

'Killing Goths?' Ceadda snickered. 'This is a man who will join in your plan to unify the two nations?'

She smiled and lifted an apologetic eyebrow at me. 'Yes. He didn't agree because he hates Father and loves me. He'd do anything to see me happy. He hates most Goths, but we do trade with some.'

We made our way across a dark valley, and rode and ran in thick pine woods, took routes over vast cliffs and heather fields, and before the Sunna was dragged to the sky, Saxa informed we were close to the Three Forks and the lake. We smelled smoke, saw an occasional fur-garbed hunter who stopped to stare at the unusual procession. Then, in an hour, we spotted a party of fur-clad Svea that had apparently been looking for us. Saxa waved her hand at the group of white and gray fur-draped warriors on well-built horses, and they galloped off after scrutiny of our numbers and weapons. 'Soon,' Aldbert said. 'We will find out if she is true.'

'Or if her brother loves to kill Goths for the fun of it,' I said and looked at Ceadda. 'And Saxons, of course.' Njord spat in disgust, but we went on.

We closed in on one of the Three Forks, a river that streamed south, and crossed it at a shallow spot Saxa knew well, and then, as soon as the last horse rose from the river, we heard the Goths.

There was the barking of the dogs.

The terrifying baying came from the south and then the east. Ceadda turned and whistled, and a Saxon scout ran to us, looking terrified. Ceadda cursed. 'No more than half an hour away. They doubled back and picked up the scent. They have us now, and won't tarry.'

'Run,' Saxa said and nodded towards the lake shore and hopefully, the village soon after.

And then Agin appeared.

They appeared out of the woods like trouble follows a lie. They seemed to belong amidst the stones and leaves and a man riding deep in his thoughts might have considered them part of the scenery. There were fifty men holding shields of sturdy make, most fur covered, with crude talismans hanging from the rims and their spears were long and thick, well made and the spearpoints broad and deadly-looking. They had a wild, barely man-like look about them as they loped from the woods and the man leading them could have passed for a young bear. His beard was long and unruly, thick and curly and his chest was as wide as Scald. He carried a wicked, one-edged ax over his shoulder and had a frown on his face that would have stopped a charging boar and sent it scurrying away.

Then he spied his sister.

The frown disappeared like fog in the morning.

His face lit up with surprise, relief, and happiness, and he took uncertain steps forward until his men stopped him. Saxa whipped her horse, and it surged for them, and she left us standing like men taking a leak, unable to move. 'Grab her!' Ceadda said softly, but Njord couldn't get to the horse and fell on his face as he tried. We stared at her back and huddled together instinctively and finally stood in an unimpressive rank, eyeing the woman warily as she whooped, rode into the group of men and jumped down to bury herself in Agin's hug.

'I bet that is her husband,' Aldbert complained.

'If that is the case, they will roast lord Pup for his plans to whelp babies on her,' Ceadda said with a nervous smile. 'He will put that ax in our friend's rear and pull it out through his mouth. Will be a sight to remember. Though I'm sure, it's not the only rear that will see that blade. How big is that man?'

'Big all around,' Njord said with a twisted smile. 'I hope he is not into Saxon.'

Saxa was released from the hug, and she was now gesturing at us, and I would have given my left nut to hear what she was telling the huge man. If she told them to kill us, I'd die a fool, and we would not escape, no matter if I brought the Saxons to make sure I'd survive. If she were what she claimed to be, in love, I'd be married to a powerful Svea woman in a very short time, and that would certainly change things for all of us. The baying dogs didn't help the anxiety. Agin was listening to her with a tilted head, and his eyes instinctively sought me out. I straightened my back and gave him a small bow, but not a deep one. Then his face melted into a ferocious scowl, and I feared Ceadda's estimation of our demise might be right, and I cursed myself for not giving a deeper bow. She pointed beyond us where the dogs bayed, and finally, the large man nodded and gave orders to some of his men, who looked at him with open mouths and then ran off. Agin gestured us closer, and we looked at each other until Njord

MAROBOODUS – ALARIC LONGWARD

pushed Ceadda on, Ceadda pulled him with him and so we all went forward, looking at Saxa and Agin like a pack of scared puppies, hoping for kind cuddles and loving attention, and we all gave Agin's ax long glances. The Saxons were rumbling something, and I was about to warn them to keep their warlike prayers in check when I realized they were just praying for deliverance. Had they not raided the people not so long ago? Perhaps Agin's villages as well. It was not so far to where Saxa had lived, was it?

My fears turned out to be unfounded.

Saxa bowed at me. 'This is the man I was telling you about.'

'Indeed?' Agin said dubiously. 'Red-headed, sturdy, and has a look on his face that suggests the head is not just a decoration? Where is his beard?'

'He shaves it,' she said apologetically. 'He'll learn. He has cunning,' she said with a fond smile at me. 'He is brave. And he—'

'Yes, yes. The others, though. Thick like mules. The lot look like they use their skulls to grind barley, no?'

Njord opened his mouth, Ceadda slapped him, and the Saxons stayed quiet.

Saxa was glowering at her brother who smiled and leaned over her to whisper, except he didn't, and I could hear every word. 'You sure? Cunning and brave aside, he doesn't look any different from any of the Goth bastards we string up like pinecones every year.'

'Can't help being a thieving Goth, can he?' Saxa beamed at the large man, happy and strangely wild and I found she was much different amongst the people she trusted than with the Goths. 'And I'll have him, nonetheless.'

'You don't have to, you know. You don't need to, now that you are here and—'

'It's what I want,' Saxa said, blushing. 'I will have that one.' Her words made me blush in my turn, and Agin groaned and rolled his eyes.

'Father might have a thing or two to say about that, though,' Agin said darkly, and then brightened. 'But if he is upset, then I'm jubilant to help you marry into a robbing Goth family. Father failed to marry you to one, but if you chose one for yourself, then I'll forgive you and help you.'

'There will be things we need from you, other than shelter,' Saxa said.

'Oh?' He frowned at her. 'What else?'

She rubbed his cheek and made the Svea warriors chuckle as the big man seemed to melt like an ice cone. 'We won't be fugitives for all our lives, living in the corners of halls, hiding under the beds. We have plans. Father will be supremely unhappy I am doing this, brother,' Saxa said with a broad smile. 'This will kill him, perhaps. Finally. If you help, especially. And then we shall see how to build something that's good for us all, not forced on us. We can spit on his god. We will be strong together, and none of the northern tribes can threaten us, if we—'

'Work with some of the Goths, you mean?' he said with horror, began to shake his head and stopped himself as Saxa's hand took a painful hold of his shaggy beard.

'Yes,' she said resolutely. 'Don't be as stubborn as Father.'

He let her hang on to the beard and nearly lifted her off her feet. 'He wanted to work with the Goths. He did. I just said "no". Our supporters will think I can't make up my mind.'

She shrugged. 'But you saw how many of Father's supporters agreed. And if you take over the plan, imagine what you can accomplish. The Goths won't go away, brother. We must begin to think past our old grudges. I'll start.' She eyed me warmly, and I'd sold all our lands back to the Svea right then because of her beauty.

He gave her a long look, and I decided Agin was far from a fool. He had a thoughtful look on his face, and clearly there was hidden ambition inside that thick skull. They had likely spent a lot of time together when growing up, running through the meadows of Snowlake, resenting their father's intensity, and when Agin had grown into a man and a lord on his own, the resentment had only grown. Every son knows better than the father, I thought and smiled. Agin would go on a shared quest for his sister. He was rubbing his chin and nodded sagely. 'It might. And we shall discuss how that might take place later. I agree it has possibilities. Goths fighting for us for once?' I stiffened because I had planned to use the

Svearna to fight Bero and Hughnot. Nonetheless, I smiled at Agin, he gave me a grim smile in return, and he seemed to approve of me, for he clapped his hands together. 'I'll call the völva for the evening, and we shall have a small, discreet feast. Just us. The few of us. Not many. And they are ...' he pointed a thick, dirt-crusted finger at Ceadda. 'They are not Goths.'

'They are thin mercenaries from the south,' she said with a hint of worry in her voice. 'Don't know where they come from. Cannot speak what we speak, I think, or only barely. They'll need a boat, and that's what we promised them for their help. Savages they are.' Ceadda smiled wryly at the payback for calling the Svea animals.

'You promised them one of my boats?' Agin said with horror, his fingers twitching.

'Yes,' she said and saw the big man was still trying to find clues to the origin of the men. 'Doesn't matter, trust me. Come brother. Let's do what I said. As I asked?'

'Sure,' he said, his beady eyes never leaving Ceadda, who was fingering his spear with worry. 'Strip.'

'Strip?' Njord asked, horrified. 'What? Out of our clothes? Totally?'

'Not out of your skins, for now,' Agin growled and nodded for us. 'Can't speak what we speak, eh?' Agin said with a scowl. 'Sister—'

'Some can,' she said with fury and turned to the Saxons. 'Strip.' The word snapped with finality.

'Why do they need to strip?' Aldbert asked, puzzled.

'You shall all strip,' she said with some satisfaction as Aldbert's mouth shot open. 'You, them, him.' She pointed at me. 'We will take the horses, the clothes—'

'This is my horse,' I said, for I loved Scald dearly, but saw her face and she was adamant. 'But there will be others,' I amended.

'Many horses,' she agreed. 'We are a horse people, Maroboodus. Ships and horses, and perhaps we are not animals at all. They,' she pointed at some ten Svear, who stepped up. 'will take your horses and cross the Long-Lake, leaving the horses behind. They will rush to the north. They will take your shabby clothes, and the dogs will follow, bay at the banks of the lake, and the Goths will have to give chase. Our men will travel that way for some days, visiting villages of our northern tribes, going at a great pace to keep the Goths confused and that might leave the Goths in boiling water should they dare to go there—'

'Dog-humping Goths,' Agin agreed, and I decided to agree with a ferocious nod, which pleased the massive man immensely.

'Keep the dog-humping Goths confused,' she continued with asperity, 'and perhaps they shall go home. They would be far from home and hall, and they won't have the men to fight in the north. We will keep an eye on them from now on. We will hide in Agin's village for a time.'

'We will keep our weapons,' Ceadda said more than asked.

'Yes, you will,' Agin said tiredly. He eyed his sister, and she nodded, to his chagrin. 'We will arm you with shields as well since you Saxons will help us defend the village if the Goths don't trust their dogs. You will fit in. Saxa wants this, not I.' He nodded at Saxa, who grinned up at the giant. 'Strip. And yea, I know you are Saxons. Do it.'

We stripped. I got down and pulled off my heavy cloak. I placed my sword and belt on the side and gazed at Agin, trying to gauge the mood of the great man. He was silent, not the huge buffoon he had seemed, but a shrewd man who let no detail escape him. He didn't judge me, and I shrugged at him as I stripped, hoping the man would be a great ally. Whether or not I'd honestly rule with Saxa, depended on men like him, and I sensed there was as much honor in him as there was in Hulderic. We were all the same blood, divided into tribes and clans and feuds ages old, but men like Agin could mend old feuds. The Saxons had few scruples as they stripped, used to little privacy in their ships, and were soon standing over heaps of their clothing, holding clubs and spears as if they were all they needed and didn't even mind Saxa, who was looking discreetly away from them. Aldbert was blushing fiercely, and held his hand before his genitals, as Agin was smiling at us lecherously, whispering to Saxa, who turned to look at me. I cursed the cheeky grin on her face and pulled off my pants and shoes and frowned at her as she arched an eyebrow, hopefully as a sign of approval. I pointed a daring finger her way 'And her horse and clothes?'

Agin's face brightened with shock and realization. 'He is right.'

'What?' she asked furiously. 'I'll not strip before you mongrels.'

'Take my cloak,' he said, 'and do it in the bushes. Discreetly. If they try to peek, I'll play dice with their eyeballs.'

'You—'

'Do it,' I chirped and the Saxons laughed gutturally. 'We are in a hurry.'

'Fine,' she whispered, and Agin gave his cloak to her. She ran off to the bushes, and after some time had passed, she came out, swathed in the woolen thing and she gestured in the direction of the village. Our simple band ran that way while the Svea gathered our clothes, horses, and took off for the north. They were fast, so fast, much faster than we were and they knew the land as they galloped with our well-wishes, hoping they would drag Bero's hounds after them like a bloody haunch of a cow would attract wolves. They were rubbing our clothes on trees as they went, and the dogs would know.

Agin snorted as he saw my lingering look. 'Don't worry, my adeling. They will lead the Goths on a merry chase. I'll start gathering men from the villages, and we will see them off for good if they come this way. I should be able to collect hundreds, given a few days. For now, this is good.'

'I thank you, Agin,' I told him with respect and bowed.

He shook his head. 'So, you and Saxa.'

'It seems so,' I said, looking at her back, wishing to see her face.

'You are Hulderic's son, no?' he asked wryly.

'I am—'

'You are,' he said. 'Never thought his son would rescue my sister from Saxons,' he eyed Ceadda like a fox would look at an unwary mouse, 'and then come here with some Saxons, hoping to marry her, and more.'

'More?' I said dreamily. 'I came this way because I grew tired of being the plaything for my relatives. I wanted to make my fortune, to become a ring-giver, a warlord, and help my father overcome those relatives who would harm him. And perhaps also—'

'To rule over your father,' Agin smiled.

That bothered me, but I didn't deny it. 'Perhaps in the future?'

214

'Or sooner,' he chortled. 'I know Saxa told you it is so with me as well.'

'It is true,' I admitted. 'Partly so.'

He chuckled. 'She is a Svea princess. You, a Goth adeling. Rarely have there been two people more tied into plays of power. You have been sitting in the back row, seeing how things will unfold but never quite able to affect the future to their liking. She has sat on her father's counsels, our father's counsel, that is,' he said, looking miserable with the fact, 'for a decade. He considers her precious; all his family has a role to play in his games. But more, he is a Thiuda of our clans. Father's been plotting with a Goth to kill your father and Bero the Crow.'

'And to kill Hughnot, as well,' I said.

He agreed. 'Him. Others, later. There are many Goths to the south of us. This Boat-Lord hates you rogues as much as we do.'

'The Crow?' I smiled. 'Bero? He does look like a crippled little bird.'

'He does,' Agin smiled wolfishly, proud to have named my uncle, but sobered and went on. 'I'm curious where the Saxons were taking her. Father had agreed to marry her.'

'To the Boat-Lord,' I said. 'Our enemy.'

'Likely so,' he agreed. 'But the Saxons came and took her.'

'Cuthbert would have sold her to the Lord. He smelled coin and riches,' I said. 'Learnt of the deal from his spies.'

'Yes, perhaps,' he said though he wasn't convinced. 'Yes, we all have spies all over the place. Mine died in Marka this past year. Snot. Shitting disease. But I thank you. You saved her from a Saxon, then from a Goth and I think, my Lord, that as an adeling of the least loved son of formerly great Friednot and not a very famous young Goth, you saw in her more than a lovely smile. You saw your future in the bosom of her love, and a way out of your dilemmas. Make an enemy an ally, marry high, defy your relatives, and raise yourself above all of them.' He was nodding. 'You saw love and power, and I salute you. No, worry not. I doubt you not. I see you have real feelings for her. And if you don't,' he said and leaned close to me. 'I'll cave your skull in.'

215

I gave him a wry smile. 'Is it true,' I asked, 'that marriage to her can give me the power to decide on the matters of the Goths? I love her like people love summer.'

He gazed at me, shrugged, and finally, after a long moment of contemplation, 'You sound like a moonstruck calf, an utter fool, but I'll allow it since you are a fool for her. And yes, she can give you spears. If I allow it. It's time to change things, though, she is right in that. The northern clans care little for our troubles here in the south, but there are perhaps ten Svea lords who decide on things around here, and Father's been trying to subvert the four highest ones to his side. He has promised them Goth lands, to be shared with Goths, as I told you. He has been dealing with the Boat-Lord. Three chiefs follow me. The rest change their mind as often as the wind changes, and if we can topple Father, then we can indeed have a profitable alliance and settle these lands for the benefit of all.' He smiled as he gazed at me. 'And you will know that we will want to have a piece of the coast again. It's not negotiable. Long-Lake is where we dip our toes into the sea, but we want access to the trade, and that means the coast.'

I smiled. There we were, dividing lands. It was intoxicating, making plans like that. It was better than the beadiest of wines.

'Boat-Lord,' I said, 'wants the land as well. We will have a war on our hands, even after we settle the scores with my family.'

He shrugged. 'I've no doubt you are right. This Boat-Lord sent men here last year. I never saw any Goths of this Boat-Lord in Snowlake, because I didn't go, and Father, Gislin merely informed the absent chiefs this marriage would take place. He told me like that, probably happy I'd suffer because I love my sister well. Then the Saxons came,' he said and eyed the men with hostility, 'and took her. Now she is to marry a Goth. You see why I'm feeling an itch for my ax, but I'm happy to see you are much like us. And that you Goths squabble like the Svea do. Of course, you do, but it's fine to see it in the form of an exiled Goth adeling, chasing after my sister,' he told me, amused. 'We have been losing far too many times in battle to your people.'

I braved a question. 'Since Saxa and I plan to rule—'

'You are children,' he reminded. 'Dreaming of war. Not all dreams come true, just remember that. We shall try, but gods will decide.'

I went silent, dragging my feet, hoping to refute him, but he was right. We were children in the art of rulership, but he was also wrong. 'The heroes the poets sing of?' I said, and he cocked an eye at me. 'The ones who sit by the gods in their golden halls? Were they old when they decided to change things? They carved vast lands for themselves with war. They were young when they began. Those songs began from dreams like ours.'

He gave me an uncertain eye and smiled. 'I almost went to my knees before you, mighty Maroboodus, since you dream so high the gods would tremble at your greed. And I give you a hint. The songs and poems are mostly paid for by men who did terrible things to reach that far. They sit in their seats, listen to liars like him,' he thumbed Aldbert's way, 'and smile benevolently at the flattery, but some part of their minds will always reel under the weight of betrayed men, foully slain enemies, burnt halls with babies and women, and broken oaths. I've never become so high as I wanted, just one of the warlords around these woods, because I am honorable.' He looked at me uncertainly and brooded as he looked away. 'I have a hunch you and Saxa will rule us all, but will you ever be truly happy? I know not.'

'Aldbert,' I said, 'how many times do you lie when you make a song of a hero?'

He walked on behind us, uncomfortable in his nakedness, reacting ridiculously to the stinging twigs under his bared feet, but finally shrugged. 'Mostly.'

'If you made a song about me, would you lie?' I asked.

He frowned. 'Would you like people to know how I dug that hole?'

Agin didn't know about the hole, but he did chuckle, and I frowned. Then I shook my head stubbornly. 'I'd not feel bad about the lies, if the purpose serves greater good.'

Agin chortled. 'You should, no matter what you build. But yes, I'll help you two. I have power. Father and I split up, but as I said, at least three chiefs follow me, some others will come to our side. It will be an even struggle. And while father has a great following, he has been a ruler for a

217

long time, many of the smaller Chiefs hate him. Father has enemies, and men often look at me to solve an issue he has caused. Should there be a high Goth on our side, be that a youngster like you, married to a grand lady like Saxa? It will probably ruin Father's plans. It will bring us followers. It will mean men will die here, instead of in the lands of the Goths,' he said and frowned, 'but next year we might solve the issue between Father and me, and then we shall solve our issues with the Goths, and men will die there as well until everyone is sated, eh? Hope you can stomach seeing a shieldwall of Goths falling under our attack. It will cost you a lot, though. The coast, parts of it. Perhaps Marka.'

'I'll stomach it. There will be Goths in our shieldwall as well,' I said dubiously. 'We will change things.' Back then, I believed it was possible, to build a nation of Svea and Goths, and Agin looked severe as he stared at me.

'You are surprisingly steady and dedicated, Maroboodus. I think we will try to build something out of this mess, indeed. And Father did lose many men of his warbands. Fifty splendid men are gone thanks to the Saxons. He was well weakened this past summer by that lot.' He nodded at Ceadda and leaned on me. 'Do I *have* to give the murderous bastards a ship?'

I chortled at his outraged tone. 'Give them a fair boat, but do give them one. A fast one. They have kept faith with us, and they only followed Cuthbert as oaths men do. We could have made it here on our own, probably, but they helped us along like oath-bound men should.'

He chortled. 'They were your hope of escape if I turned out to be less than amicable? Yes?'

'Yes,' I agreed.

'In that case,' he said, 'I'll marry you tonight and send them on their way when the Goths are gone, with weapons and a boat fast enough to make them cry with joy. Tomorrow, we shall send the Goth bastards on their merry way, chase off your Crow Bero and begin to plan for the Spring, and we will decide on many things during this winter.' He eyed me and asked a question. 'Will Hulderic, your father, help us?'

'I don't know,' I said glumly. 'But perhaps he shall not stop us, at least. Perhaps he will not fight us. And if Bero and Hughnot are weak and divided and fight each other, then we can see where we shall turn when things have been settled with your father and the Svea lords.'

'We have the winter to plan, if you can manage to tear yourself from my sister, you Goth mongrel,' he said and slapped my back with what I took as a friendly gesture, even if I bit my tongue by the force of it.

We marched on, cursing the lack of shoes, and Svea scouts ran back and forth, reporting on Goth movements and finally, as evening arrived and the lazy wolf Hati chased the glowing Mani to the sky, we were rewarded by a chorus of dog barks going far to the north, for the Long-Lake. The sound was ominous, dangerous, and close, but at least the enemy was going the wrong way.

I looked at Aldbert, who nodded, visibly relieved and Saxa and Ceadda gave each other grins. Nothing like the common fear of death to make true enemies the best of friends, I thought.

We hiked the final stretch to the northwest, passed homesteads hidden in small valleys and fields of barley, and arrived at the village.

It was dark, but Mani revealed the shore of the Long-Lake, the surface of the dark water rippling with cold wind, and our teeth were chattering because we had no clothes. There were many fishing boats, some made for war, and Ceadda and Njord were admiring them, the clinker-built things giving them hope to reach their homes one say soon. We were led forward through trails that meandered past tall oaks and thick pines, and earthy, moldy halls nestled in the trees. The village had a name, Wolf Hole, and it felt home-like as we were led to a tall and long building with a yellowed doorway, from which poured the smell of fish and meat and the unmistakable aroma of good ale, and Njord grinned like a wolf indeed, hoping to hole up inside.

There would be a feast.

A wedding feast.

CHAPTER 13

We were given woolen tunics and trousers and well-made leather shoes with furry, out-turned insides, and everyone got leather belts that were simple and practical, and the generous Agin waved away our thanks and gave us more. Cloaks of fur were placed in our quarters, and I could tell the Saxons were well impressed by the Svea lord. Ceadda bowed, and when he had done so, Njord leaned on him. 'Maybe we should ask for some fat cows and even pigs and perhaps precious treasure as well, and swords,' Njord wondered, but Ceadda pushed him away in disgust.

We were led to the dim main hall of the Svea lord. There, the host of the trading village sat, beaming like a robber god at each of us, happy to have made us respectable. He snapped his fingers and pointed the Saxons and Aldbert to the seats by sturdy oak tables, set around the fire-pit, and the Saxons happily took their places, the fears for their lives gone for a moment. The feast was indeed a small one, and silent; sturdy guards stood or sat in the shadows of the hall, and no local warriors took part in it, which was probably for the best considering the Saxons had not so long ago trekked through the land with less than friendly intentions. Some shaggy hounds were lounging by the fire, their snouts high in the air as they smelled roasting meat, and the Saxons and even Aldbert looked like they did as well, as we were all starving for something cooked. We flinched as a maid snapped her fingers after a cursory glance at the hall, and then slaves carried in food on wooden platters which they expertly left within reach of every man. 'Eat,' Agin said dreamily, apparently drowsy and tired by the excitement. 'There is more. Enough for all, even with the winter coming.'

'Thank you,' I said, and he nodded me closer. I ambled to sit on a bench near him.

He smiled and probably thought I was timid. 'Do I stink, Goth? Or have vomit on my beard? Come closer.' I got up and walked to stand near him. He went on. 'I've sent out a call to my villages. We will have two hundred men here by the day after tomorrow, and we go and hunt the Goths. It will be glorious, and brief.' He smiled. 'Hope you won't find you love your relatives after all?'

'I can love them dead just as well as alive,' I said and nodded, not sure why the words bothered me. I cared little for Bero and Maino, but there were Bero's men out there as well, and some had treated me well, and while they were enemies whom I had just feared and loathed, not hours ago, they were also mostly good men. I shook my head to clear it of such thoughts, growled away the shame and indecision and nodded at the great Lord gratefully. I looked at Aldbert, who was fidgeting at the end of the table, afraid, as Agin was looking at him. 'Lord, this is Aldbert, a poet—'

Aldbert surged up and bowed deeply. 'At your service.'

'I know he is one. A poet, a Goth poet, used to making songs and poems about Goths killing Svea. Tomorrow you shall make one for our small war with Bero,' Agin said confidently. I frowned because I knew the Goths were no pushovers, and we didn't know how many there were out there.

'I am not sure it will be that easy—'

He waved me silent 'Oh, don't give me advice on war yet, Maroboodus. Let us see how you do, first. Sit down here,' he said and slapped his heavy hand on the bench next to him so hard splinters and dust flew. Aldbert slid back to silence, his eyes full of fear and indecision, but I had to ignore my friend's strange mood, and I nodded gratefully and sat my rear down.

'Thank you, Lord,' I said gravely.

'No, thank you, young Goth,' he chuckled and rolled his eyes as the Saxons tore into the meat and gulped down horns filled with ale. 'Look at them. Murdering scum, but still men I fill with the best food this night. They should be sacrificed to Boar-Lord Freyr, of course, but let them feast here in thanks for their protection of my Saxa.'

I decided to advise him, nonetheless. 'The Goths you will chase. There will be famous champions, wily warriors, and—'

He chuckled. 'I know, I have met them in battle, but I know my land as well,' he said with relish. 'The Goths will be ready, Maroboodus, I know it. They will have surprises of their own. But we know where they are, and we know what they will do, and there will be powerful warlords on our side, the favor of the gods we know, the spirits and the vaettir speak as we do, and we will have more spears, and that's what counts. They are like a magnificent auroch, lumbering along, thinking it the master of the woods, but in truth it is not, and the Goths? They are the prey, and we are the hunters, and we will nip their balls. Nothing can change that. I'll look forward to fighting with your Danr, Eadwine, and Gasto. They have killed many a brother of ours in the past. And this Maino. Your cousin?' He glanced my way.

'I wish you success in killing that bastard,' I said sullenly and showed him the recent wound on my leg from our fight in Marka. It was healing well, thankfully.

'Oh, his handiwork? Well, that explains what pushed you here, eh?'

'I beat him, they didn't reward me,' I said with a growl and gripped my sword hilt.

Agin slammed his hand on my back while laughing. 'To imagine, they wouldn't be here in our woods, hoping to find an errant Goth adeling, had they been fair as gods expected them to be! You will find it hard to see Goths getting hung by our priests for the glory of the boar god, but you will endure it. Saxa is worth it. And so is the future you hope to build. You will be a great Lord and will see even the ones you love die one day.' His words made me shiver with premonition, but he went on. 'I said few dreams come true, but let us try to make them real, indeed. We will conquer left and right and grow fat and rich and share blood, Goths, and Svea, and it will do us all good. But we will change, mind you that, Maroboodus.'

'She is worth it all,' I said, trying to chase away his words and he saw I needed cheering.

He gave me his mead, his brew, and I drank it down gratefully. Agin smiled. 'Be happy, rather than a damned soul that worries about tomorrow. I'm sorry if I made you gloomy. Yes, yours is a possible union of two similar minds, but falling in love is a mystery even the Aesir and the Vanir do not understand. Didn't Freyr give away his sword for his giantess? Yes, he did. Love is as good as the secret of mead, and you shall sample it this night.' He hesitated. 'At least young mead. Let it fester for too long and it turns into bad brew indeed, but you'll see what I mean, if you are unlucky,' Agin beamed a smile my way. 'Saxa will not be an easy woman to live with. I've known her for a while, you see.'

'I agree,' I told him, nervous now as I realized I'd be married in a bit and so I drank down another horn, this time of ale brought to me to steel my nerves. It was instantly filled by a plump woman who chuckled to herself as she eyed me with appreciation.

'I like a man who can drink,' she chirped. 'Have another and forget what Lord Agin is blathering about. He loves despite his fear of marriage.' I drank the ale down and had it refilled.

Agin chortled. 'I do fall in love, at least a dozen times a day. Just looking at some young girl can make me sigh with love. It's terrible, for I'd like to marry one of them one of these days, but then I couldn't admire the daughters of my warriors. I have time, yet. Now—'

The door opened. A figure entered.

The guards stepped away from it as if it was a harbinger of Hel and it stopped to stare at me. At first, I was not sure if it was a human at all, because some fog entered the hall with it, casting an ethereal blanket around the figure, and even the dogs were on their feet, their tails between their legs. I noticed there was a hank of golden hair pouring from under its hood, and then the hood was pulled back. It had a face, and the head was turned my way, but the eyes looked strangely to the sides. It was looking at me nonetheless, I was sure, and I realized it was a woman. The nose had been broken, some teeth were missing but the skin was smooth, and I decided it was the village völva, seidr-seer, holy woman of Freya, mistress of magic. 'I was summoned,' she said, her voice smooth though it was impossible to decide if she was old or young. She wore a seamless tunic of good make, though bloodstains dotted her ample chest and the brooches on her shoulders were glinting redly as well, for some reason. I thought better than to ask, though.

223

Agin leaned on me. 'Hild,' he whispered, 'was caught by a rival chief in a battle once and left on the field for dead. Father exiled her, because she had told him they would win the battle, and she was wrong. Father hates being wrong. She is crazy, my age, thirty or so, but her face is as broken as her mind. Her eyes don't function very well, and yet she seems to know where she is going. She will marry you.'

'No, I was to marry Saxa,' I said nervously, and Agin and the Saxons laughed hugely while Hild seemed to give me a wry smile. I shook my head and bowed to the great woman. 'Yes, I see what you meant, I am sorry. I—'

'Shut up, Goth,' Agin murmured. 'Lift your rear up and bow to her, or she will put something uncanny inside your belly, and it will gnaw its way out of there while you weep and wither.'

'Lady Hild,' I said, getting up. I bowed her way, and she tilted her head in acknowledgment as she made her way around the Saxons, who were all making near unseen warding signs at her approach. She came to stand before me, grasped my hand with her left hand and put her right on my face. She was cold, and her skin was dry. Aldbert was looking on, clearly distraught, but he didn't move.

Finally, she stepped back. 'You are a strange one. An odd one.' She tilted her head at me. Aldbert was trying to get up.

'He is just a Goth,' he said quickly. 'Nothing to worry about. Really.'

'I'm a Goth,' I said, waving Aldbert down. 'An Adeling. Just a—'

'Traitor,' she finished but didn't judge, as the word was delivered matter-of-factly. 'A vagabond out for a new world.' She hesitated and tilted her head. 'Like a … young bear out in the spring, finding fresh horizons.'

I shook my head, but Agin roared with laughter. Hild looked around the tables. 'And they are … from the south. I smell it. Salt. Blood. Vermin.'

'He is a traitor, and they are very loyal vermin, and worthy men at the same time,' Agin said and gave the Saxons a warning sign they all took quick note of. They relaxed, despite the fact they had been found out.

'You will not go to Snowlake, then?' Hild asked softly. 'To meet Gislin, her father?'

'They should stay here,' Agin said. 'But Saxa knows her duty to Gislin, so perhaps we shall visit it one day soon, eh?' The threat was not lost on Hild, who cocked her head quizzically and hummed as if seeking answers somewhere none of us could see. Then she leaned forward, and her guttural voice silenced the hall.

'He will wish to see this man,' she told me. 'Gislin. The man who breaks his plans.'

'He means to court Saxa, not Gislin,' Njord said mischievously, but went reticent, chomping on his bit of meat as the Svear glanced his way with a clear message that suggested the Saxon was wading in treacherous waters.

'He will wish it,' she told me again. 'But the Spinners shall decide how it goes, eh?' She looked at Aldbert, who tried not to be noticed, fidgeting with his horn of ale. Finally, Hild looked away from my friend and sighed. 'Tonight you shall enjoy, yes? You will be married, under the rays of Mani, blessed by Freya, the goddess of love. Where is she?' Njord bit his tongue before hazarding a guess as to where Freya might be, but Saxa was not far.

She entered. She was wearing a simple white tunic, with bared arms, and bronze fibulae on each shoulder and on her feet there were doeskin shoes. Her hair was glimmering in the light of the shingles, and I cursed my state, as I should have bathed at least. Agin seemed to agree, as he leaned towards me and sniffed experimentally. 'Pigs are a cleaner lot,' he said happily, 'but this pig will marry well tonight.' Then Saxa saw me, and smiled, her full lips and eyes joining in a look of love, and I nearly fell to my seat, breath caught in my throat. Agin muttered something and gulped down a full horn of mead. 'She is too good for you.'

'She is too good for every man,' I stated confidently. 'Gods included.'

'True, probably right,' Ceadda said from the side with wonder, his previous apprehensions about Saxa gone as he admired the wondrous girl.

The völva's crooked mouth turned into a smile, and she turned to Saxa. 'Let's not tarry, then. The goddess hears, and she will be here only for a short while,' Hild said reverently. 'Come here,' she said sadly and pulled me after her. I stumbled like a man in a daze and Saxa beamed me a smile that would have melted an icy lake and woken up frozen butterflies. I nearly fell over a bench, tried to regain my composure, but I felt entirely detached from the holy ritual about to take place. I noticed my hand was draped over Hild's shoulders, then she removed my hand and placed it in Saxa's hand, who was chuckling at me. She held on to me fiercely, and I remember Freya was mentioned many times. I was vaguely aware I was being asked questions about my bravery, my honor, and my fame, some of which I no doubt lied about, but I did not care if it won me the girl next to me, and finally Hild pressed her hands on our cheeks. 'Is there anyone here who would deny them their happiness?'

A bird flew in.

Everyone saw it, a delicate thing trapped in the hall, but this one stopped to sit on a beam, and stared down at us with near intelligence. It was brown, delicate, but beautiful, and should have been sleeping with others like it, but there it was.

'I take that as a good sign,' I murmured to Saxa.

'It is a spirit,' she said with a smile. 'And it approves.'

Oblivious to the holiness of the bird, Agin smirked. 'What will you give her as dowry?' he asked darkly, though there was a glint of humor in his eyes.

'I have nothing,' I said. 'Nothing, my lord. Only my sword, but that, I suppose can make her a dozen dowries.'

'Her father will ask this question,' Agin said. 'Just give him the sword when we meet him. At least the pointy bit.'

'He gave me my freedom, brother,' Saxa told him. 'That is the greatest dowry Saxa of Snowlake can ever ask for.'

'That is a great gift indeed,' Agin said softly, though his bear-like voice still thrummed through the hall. 'Though it might be an ill deed to chain him for his bravery this way. Be good to him, nag little, and if he mistreats you, bring him to me, and I'll sit him on an anthill until he is a woman. Maroboodus. Kiss her! Eat well, drink too much, and retire, with my blessings.' He nodded for the sleeping quarters. 'Then, tomorrow, we shall begin to plan, eh?'

'Yes, Lord,' I told him.

Hild nodded at us. 'You are one.' There was intensity in her eyes as she clutched our forearms. 'Enjoy your night.'

We were married.

I kissed Saxa. It was a clumsy kiss where our noses got in the way. After that problem was solved, the kiss went awry in a show of sloppy lips that sought each other unsuccessfully, and we broke it off, chuckling, and what followed were tilted heads, a perfect kiss, a long, happy union of lips and she pressed her lithe body against mine with a force and warmth born of love. The Saxons murmured appreciatively, and Aldbert frowned, but that's all I remember as I kissed her. Thus, we stayed until Hild poked us. Apparently everyone was standing up and reluctant to stop cheering us until we quit the embrace, and we did. I guided Saxa to the table, and spent a supremely happy evening with the merry, drunk party of relatively friendly Saxons, my former enemies the Svear, and my Goth friend Aldbert, and a völva Hild who ate and drank more than the rest of us, though she kept casting her crooked eyes around the party, and shaking her head. Aldbert was careful, silent, worried, and would not sing when asked to. He kept staring at Hild, who stared back and then, at some stage I saw him gesturing for me, and he was pulling at my sleeve.

The look on his face. I shall never forget it. There were tears in his eyes, and his face was haggard with the massive knowledge he wanted to share, reluctant, like someone who had lied all their lives and were making a supreme effort to salvage their soul, but I denied him that relief, cursing him for his timing. 'Not now, Aldbert.'

'And I don't want it to be now,' he whispered. 'I just wanted you to know you are right. I did it all on purpose.'

I stopped and rubbed my forehead, pushing away the anger his words made me feel. 'I said not today. I don't want to have this discussion today.'

'Leave the village with me. Leave her with them. Go back to the Goths,' he begged. I pushed him away from me and turned my back to him.

I was happy. I was married. I had no time for him.

He disappeared.

Finally, when it was late, we retired. I dragged Saxa to my alcove, and she pushed me as I did. I tried to take my time, but she wanted passion rather than care and opened her brooches deftly, the tunic peeling from her, and I held my breath as she pulled at my belt. My hands were touching her shoulders, my lips devoured her neck and face, and lips, and what followed was bliss, full of the loving energy of the gods themselves, full of Freya's blessings and that night, it was good to be a man.

It was the best night of my life until then, and probably one of the best I ever had. But as happiness must eventually be balanced by sorrow, as the Norns weave it, so also was our happiness to be tested by spears.

That next morning, we awoke to the voice of battle.

The Goths had not been fooled, after all.

Someone had betrayed us.

CHAPTER 14

I had been dreaming of a red bear, standing majestically above a herd of black wolves. There was a white fox sprawled on the hillside, and dead bears littered the land. Wolves approached the red bear with reverence, their heads bowed, and the great creature smiled. It did, like a man would and that puzzled me. Then the majestic thing made a high-pitched sound, and that was even stranger, because it was like a distant scream of death.

A crow croaked, and my eyes shot open as I sat up, breathless.

My hand sought out Saxa, who shot up to a seated position next to me, her eyes drowsy, but clutching at my hand. The hall was smoky, as they often were in the mornings when men kept heating the place and burning wood in the fireplace, and I curbed a cough in order to hear.

Another scream, a longer one. Not far, even. 'What's that?' Saxa asked breathlessly. 'Was that—'

'A man dying,' I said with worry. It wasn't hard to understand what the noises meant, and Saxa nodded as she came to accept there was something more sinister going on than a simple fight between some men of the village. Something was out there in the woods, or even in the village.

Then, there were horns being blown. The noises were brazen, rough, and spoke of war. They were our horns. *No, Goth horns,* I thought.

'We must get up, immediately,' I said and pulled Saxa up. 'Dress up, grab everything you need to survive.'

'I don't need much,' she said resolutely, and stopped, pulled me to her, and I saw fear in her eyes, as she embraced me furiously. She was reluctant to go, and so was I, and I felt like cursing the unfair gods for their callous act of spite, and felt they were throwing dice while playing some very unbalanced game where my happiness was at stake. I pushed her from me, and looked into her eyes.

'We will survive, whatever it is,' I said. 'But it sounds like a battle and perhaps it's lost already and then we have to make other plans than staying here.' Now I could hear the blood-curdling barritus yell, where men put their shields before their mouths and made an ominous sound by screaming booming defiance.

'No Svea does that!' she said with panic.

'Goths,' I said. 'Bero, he wasn't fooled.'

'Or someone told him he had been,' she hissed, and I know she thought of Aldbert. She shook her head as she pulled on a tunic and a cloak. 'I don't blame you for loving him, for the trust. But I hate him. We should have asked someone to keep an eye on him,' she stated with a growl. 'You told me you would. You should have asked Ceadda—'

'You said you don't blame me! We cannot know—'

'He didn't want us here, did he?' she hissed. 'Probably been promised a heap of gold, or after he helped you hurt Maino just his life if he helps them. He's a coward.'

'How could he sneak off to the woods to find Goths? He is as adept there as a drunken grandfather.'

'I think none of us know him,' she said. 'But we have no time now to think about him. Dress!'

I pulled on my shoes, listening to what I thought was a thick melee somewhere near, but the lake carried sounds very well, and so perhaps it wasn't near. We'd see soon enough. 'We can blame him, of course, but how is it the Svea let them in to surprise us, eh? Agin's men know the land, no?' I cursed and shook my head as I knew none of it mattered then.

She looked furious for a moment but also calmed her temper and spoke evenly as she pulled me up. 'They make mistakes like any man, husband,' she said testily and slapped my chest lightly. 'Get your weapons. See what is happening. I'll fetch the Saxons.' She took the ax, and I had my hand on the hilt of Hel's Delight.

'Meet you here, in a bit,' I told her as I rushed to the main hall. There were servants there, looking utterly shocked and before I could accost them a huge shadow filled the doorway as Agin burst in. He wore chain mail, darkened, crudely made, and looked dangerous with his ax. He pointed a

230

thick finger at me. 'Someone betrayed us,' he said, and I saw he was tempted to blame me.

'I was enjoying a night with Saxa, not skulking in the woods,' I insisted.

He took deep, angry breaths and shook his head. 'Yes, I know it was none of you. I had you and the lot of the Saxons guarded.'

I bit my lip but asked anyway. 'Did you place a guard on Aldbert?'

'The poet?' he asked, staring at me blankly and that was the answer. 'But he's a damned fool. Anyone can see it. How could he lead them here? Would probably get lost on his way to the shithole.'

I shrugged, and we both froze as there was a long scream drifting on the morning air. I stepped closer to him. 'How bad is it?'

He spat and pointed an ax to the woods. 'Someone did betray us, and I'll have that one's ball-sack hanging on my shield. I have some eighty men from the closest settlements who were coming this way. They were surprised out there, on the march. We are lucky they happened to heed my call so fast, or we would all be waiting for your relatives to decide on whom to hang first. I have more coming, but that won't help now, will it? And there are over a hundred Goths creeping for the village. Your Bero leads them, his damned standard was seen in the midst of a horde of Goths.' He ground his teeth together, frustrated how the hunter was turning into the hunted. 'I'll go and lead my men. Perhaps we can keep them out. You take my sister and go! Hild!' he called out and I turned to see the völva, who took a hesitant step forward from the shadows. 'Take them to Gunnvör's village. Tell him to guard them, and do not stray! Can you do this for me?'

Hild nodded carefully, her shifty eyes twitching and Agin grunted at me. 'Take care of Saxa, will you?'

'I'm married to her, aren't I?' I said harshly.

I grasped his outstretched forearm and he left, roaring orders to the surprised Svearna who had gathered. His standard with red antlers was carried by a young man, perhaps his relative, for the man was as wide as a hillock. I rushed back to the hallway with Hild in tow, where the pack of hungover Saxons were standing, holding their new shields and framea ready, their eyes glittering in the darkness and I noted how they hovered around Saxa protectively.

Ceadda spat and spoke harshly. 'What, lord? They came here anyway?'

'They did,' I said. 'Someone ... led them here.'

'Bastard,' Ceadda said and looked around. 'Your friend's not here?'

I didn't say anything and the Saxon's eyes glinted with a promise and I begged Aldbert would not meet them in the woods, even if he had nothing to do with our predicament.

I pointed to the end of the hall, where there would be a doorway out. 'Let's find someone to blame later, and now we shall have to go. Hild here,' I said, 'promised to take us away to a safe village. Who is Gunnvör?'

'He is a lout,' Hild said softly, 'but loyal to Agin. Fat bastard living in a valley to the west. Half a day of running, at least.'

'We shall run, then,' I told them. 'Out that way and we shall see what comes out of this.'

'Shouldn't we get a boat and go home? We did what we promised?' Njord said with a frown, but Ceadda pushed him in the face so hard the taciturn Saxon stumbled, and so Njord nodded sullenly and rushed to the west end of the hall, cursing all the way. We followed him, pushing in the tight hallway until we reached the side doorway and a small room where we grouped up. I gave Saxa a brave smile, and she returned it and gods, I prayed to them and begged she would stay safe and not end up a plaything to a relative of mine, though the truth was she was married, and Maino could never change that.

Unless she was widowed, I allowed and nodded at Njord.

He sighed and yanked open a doorway, and then fell under an onslaught of flashing fang and slavering jaws. A trio of savage dogs rushed in from the open doorway, and Njord was fighting like a man in the jaws of lindworm, his eyes bulging with horror. He was trying to keep their slavering maws at bay, but then the masters of the hounds appeared, and they were Goths. An arrow smacked in the head of one Saxon, a spear took another and then ten Goths pushed in and ran into us, and I could see the surprise on their faces as they realized the hall was filled with spears and men who would not hesitate to fight back. Ceadda didn't waste time on niceties, but stuck a spear in a man's chest, and screamed. 'Kill the dog-whores, strut on their shit!' he yelled and savagely kicked off a dog from Njord's side, killing the beast. A desperate, close melee ensued. Spears flew from Saxon hands, and two Goths fell, one wounded in the side, one mortally with an open chest that pumped blood crazily. Clubs went up, then came down and I joined the nasty fight, the push and pull and tear of the battle with my sword stabbing. I tried to keep my feet in the sudden press, and surged forward as a large Goth slapped a Saxon down with his shield, ready to stab the man with a framea, but he did not quite manage it when my sword snaked forward. It punctured the man's eye, and he fell like a sack of hay. I stepped on him as hard as I could, but he was already on his way to Valholl, and Ceadda followed me and killed another Goth. I flailed around me in the press, slashing bearded faces, and saw the Goths were looking back, giving way. I slashed open a grimacing, young face. I pushed over a Goth to the waiting spear of Njord, who was now standing, bleeding from bites and claw-scratches and struck my blade up through a man's gut so hard we fell out of the door into the morning's light.

All around the village, a battle was being waged. Goths were probing the many houses and longer halls, trying to find resistance, rich loot, cows and food, and ultimately us. There were some fires in the structures, a blacksmithy was steaming, its wet thatch burning lazily, and there were many horses galloping around. In the bushes and small fields before the halls, older men were being speared, and women were dying and being captured.

And then I saw Maino.

He was seated on a shaggy gray horse, guiding his men to a neighboring hall sixty feet away and with him, were Bero's champions.

He had not noticed us, and I cursed awfully when I saw Aldbert standing near him, looking meek, sheepish. He was wringing his hands, nodding for the hall, and I realized that while he had betrayed us, and gods know why, but he had guided them to the wrong hall. Maino thought he would capture me like a rat, and had set other men in our hall, but Aldbert would pay for the deceit. My eyes met Aldbert's.

His mouth moved, his face was white with worry, and he shook his head weakly at me as if to explain his foul actions, but I couldn't guess his reasons or any of his actions, and I spat in his direction.

Inside our hall, the Saxons were winning. A few desperate Goths were still fighting, but had been pushed to the corners where they were being speared. Some Saxons were dead, one spitting blood from a slashed lip, and then Ceadda came out, bloodied and fey, like a vengeful, thin bear crawling out of its pit after killing intruding hunters. I looked around desperately and then Hild pulled at me. 'Gunnvör's village is half a day away. We need a distraction to get away.' Maino was still sitting on his horse, entirely oblivious to our presence as we crawled away from the doorway, begging no more dogs would be skulking around.

That would not last. They would see us.

I saw many of the villagers running southwest and west and then I nodded at her. 'I'll be the distraction.' Hild began to argue, but looked at the savage champions of the Goths, and nodded reluctantly. 'You get her, and the confused herd of pirates to safety, and ...'

'You will survive,' she said softly. She looked to the west, and there, far, were two tall hills. 'That is Saxa's father's village, Snowlake, right there on those hills. 'I'll take them,' she thumbed the others, 'to where they will be safe, and I'll find you. Head for the two hills, hide in the woods to east of it, and I'll find you and take you to safety. Tell her goodbye, for you have to go now.'

'Thank you, Hild,' I said, crawled to Saxa and kissed her long and hard and my heart was hammering with fear at the thought of losing her. 'Ceadda, take care of her,' I said and noticed the Saxon had no objections. 'Follow Hild, do as she says and then guard Saxa. I'll make sure Maino takes after me.'

He was now looking at Aldbert with a vengeance. 'That bastard, eh? Why would he—'

'He will pay,' I told Ceadda with a brave smile. 'Go.' I grabbed a spear, a shield, and two javelins and walked from tree to tree, spying Maino. I turned to look behind, and the Saxons rushed to the lakeside after Hild, where they fought with three Goths, very surprised men guarding the boats and I noticed there were some Goth boats there as well, the ones they had used to bring Maino's men to the village during Bero's attack. The shouts of a brief scuffle at the muddy lakeside led Danr to turn his head that way and to take steps my way, trying to see past the shrubs.

Then he noticed a wounded Goth crawling out of Agin's hall, and I saw his face go white as he turned to Maino. I prayed to the gods, hefted the javelins, well made with strong iron points, and jumped forward. Danr's instincts told him something was happening, or perhaps he saw a glimpse of movement. His face betrayed shock as he turned and then the javelin spun in the air. The champion fell on his rear, but the weapon was not aimed at him.

It spun towards Maino, and so did the next javelin.

The beefy cousin of mine turned his horse, no doubt stolen from the Svea of the Wolf Hole, to look at me in horror, then fell flat on his horse and one javelin sailed over him and disappeared into the woods. The next one struck his horse's neck. The beast fell, whinnying wildly, and spilled the fool heavily over its head.

Gasto and Eadwine were pulling axes and swords, grinning at me ferociously as Danr rushed to see to Maino. I did stay to see if he was alive, but sprinted off. There were yells, screams and warnings, as the Goths began the pursuit. They sounded like a happy hunting party, encouraging each other to kill the fleeing bear, and so perhaps most of the village would survive as they now had sight of their true prey. Eadwine, a younger man was sprinting in his heavy chainmail, flitting through the trees near me. Maino was screaming now, as furious as a downed god as he tried to reconcile himself with the loss of more face, and I heard him hollering like man with a bee-stung nut. 'Get him to me! Drag him to me by his ankles! I'll skin his legs and piss on them. And get her here as well! She is with him, surely! Get me another horse!' I grinned at the small success, and then blanched as Eadwine jumped over a boulder right next to me, a happy, victorious smile on his bearded face as he reached for me.

He grabbed my hair and yanked, but cursed as he slipped on a wet stone and fell heavily. I pulled from his grasp, kicked him in the jaw and left him spitting blood and bits of teeth. I lost my spear and grabbed Hel's

Delight, but hesitated as he turned a ferocious look my way, and then I ran off. I spied higher ground to the southwest, noticed some women running that way and went after them, sliding in mud, ripping through ferns, begging Donor to protect Saxa and her Saxon escorts. Horns were blowing behind, screams could be heard, but now, one rose above the others. 'Dusk! Gloom!' the voice screamed, and I knew Gasto had more dogs to send after me, and I sobbed. 'Fetch flesh!' the man added. I hazarded a glance behind and saw tall men rushing forward in the pine woods, holding javelins, shields, spears; Bero's Goth's coming for me. Eadwine was with them, so was Danr, and finally, there was Maino as well, running unsteadily and without a horse, half his ear missing, and his leg apparently still hurt by our duel.

I did not see Gasto.

I had heard him, but I did not see him, and that made the situation much worse. The sounds of battle began to fade, but I heard my breath rasping as I surged on, hoping I'd find a sustainable rhythm, and nearly fell on a hidden root, cursing the gods foully for putting it there.

Then I glimpsed a speeding cur to the side.

It was sniffling the shrubs, the thing unaware of me and as I looked behind, I saw the Goths were all running a bit to the northwest, perhaps having mistaken some poor Svea fleeing the village for me. The dog kept on sniffing and I begged Frigg in her eternal mercy to keep it guessing. Gasto would be close, his other dogs as well, but for some reason I seemed to be doing well.

I picked up speed, little heeding the roots and mossy stones and rushed for green-covered craggy hillside, jumped over a muddy stream and scrambled up the unsteady side of a hill, and then the wind blew into my face and as I looked back I saw the dog stare right at me, all through the woods, shrubs, and shadows. It lifted its head and howled and the far shadows of the Goths turned abruptly, and I heard Gasto whistling. The wind had changed, or the evil beasts got help from some bastard wood spirit but they were onto me. I saw the dog yap, growl and then Gasto, his broad chest heaving with the exertion of the run appeared next to it and spied me pulling myself up the hard hill. He yelled, 'Here! The rat's climbing!'

A dozen Goths surged in unison and followed Gasto's finger.

I cursed with despair and climbed on. 'At least no horse will get up here, unless I missed some trail,' I spoke to myself. I hoped the dogs wouldn't make it up, either. I reached the top, stopped to retch from fear and fatigue, and looked down to see Eadwine, his face bloody, scrambling up, pulling himself up with such gusto that greenery was flying and I wondered if he would burrow his way through the dirt in his single-mindedness. The dogs were down there, looking for a way up and Gasto had picked up one, while starting to climb.

'Shit, Woden, for once, help me and let them break their necks,' I whispered, nearly vomiting as I tried to catch my breath.

'Come down, Maroboodus!' Danr yelled, hefting a thick spear. 'We'll make it easy on you. We won't kill you, only take you back to be judged. I doubt Maino would dare to kill you for Hulderic would have feud, no?'

'Yes, he would. He tried already!' I screamed back at them and ran off to the west. I ran and ran, blessedly getting into a rhythm I could hold, and weaved my way on the hillside, then down it, the decline being much gentler than the incline and jumped into a lazy river. I swam over, feeling the pull of an undercurrent, my shield helping me to stay afloat, and I made it across. I ran for an hour, shivering with cold, puffing desperately, hoping beyond hope to make it to some Svea village, but there were only huts that were empty, or the occupants hiding and so I'd have to make it to Snowlake, where there were no friends and where I was to hide. But if the dogs had my scent? I would not be able to.

I chortled to myself, snot flying. The dogs would catch me much before I made it anywhere near Gislin's unwelcoming village. Perhaps the legendary dverger could show me a hole to their underworld? No holes presented themselves and so I began to accept I'd have to fight.

When running in a thicket full of spider webs, and what I thought would be midday, I heard a dog growl very near, the sort of a half-escaped sound one makes when pounding over stones and slippery surfaces. I didn't think. I acted.

I pulled my sword, threw the shield over me and fell under the weight of a dog and just barely avoided the fangs that snapped closed before my eyes. I pushed my shield up, and the dog fell to the side, and I was damned afraid. A ferocious, killer dog is a thing to note. It's fast, so fast, and relentlessly powerful. It knows how to rip flesh apart, how to make sure the prey doesn't go anywhere, and like it would herd and savage a moose for Gasto, this one was doggedly determined to rip my legs to shreds. It lunged for my limb, and I was kicking at it frantically, but never fast enough because it was following every move with speed to match and I begged Woden for help. My sword swished at it, but it saw it coming and changed tactic. It jumped over my shied, the claws burrowing into it, had one leg on my face and turned to latch its fangs on my shoulder. I rolled away, avoided the bite, but fell to my belly, as the sword again struck weakly at the brown-gray mound of trouble, and the beast grabbed my forearm. I lost the sword, foolishly, but when such a foe has a hold on you and begins to shake its head, you will not be able to hold your weapon unless you are made of stone. The shield was stuck on my left arm, and I used its rim to pull myself up while the dog was biting down hard, and I screamed with pain.

Then another dog jumped on my back.

It tore into my side, tearing and jerking and pulling at my tunic and a bit of skin and I felt the blood flowing from my side as it pulled me over.

I managed to drop the shield. I latched my hand over the snout of the dog pulling at my arm. I pushed it, squeezed the furry face and all I managed were to make it look comical as its skin rolled over its eyes, but the fangs stayed in my arm, and it bit even harder, and I yelped and wept and then, I pushed my fingers through the wrinkled skin and into its eyes.

It was harder than one might think, but then the fingers slid into the slits, something popped and broke, and the creature shuddered with pain.

It let go.

It fell away, yelping piteously and rolled in the mud and grass, its legs twitching. It was making dreadful, terrified howls but I ignored it as I turned to the dog on my side. I grabbed the sword, fought with a desperate need to hack wildly, but I endured the dog's bite as I calmly placed the blade on its neck and stabbed down. The dog twisted, its sleek muscles taut with pain as it bowled me over and I rolled with it as its paw was stuck in my tunic. It was barking loudly, clawing at me, biting weakly and I managed to pin it with my hand, and pressed the sword into its throat, twisting it around and then I pushed down. It made a meowing noise, its claws still scratching my belly, and it died.

I got up, panting, eyeing my wounds which seemed surprisingly small, when things turned even worse.

Gasto surged from the thicket, his red shield flashing.

He saw the dogs, my shocked face, and then he raged. 'I'll rip your head off and hide the body, boy! You took my prized bitches!'

He pulled a dark club, and ran for me, his chain jingling, his face red, eyes bulging with a rage that would not disappear by begging or surrender. He had loved the creatures and evil tongues around Marka often claimed he preferred them to his sons and daughters. I turned to face him, trembling with the shock of seeing the dangerous man charging. I was covered in blood, and I was sure I'd be covered with my brains in a bit as the club went up. I prayed to Woden, and as the enraged champion got close, I charged for his leg. The club sailed past my back, as I surged around the limb. We fell heavily, he lost his shield, but not the club as he swatted it down on my back, but it had little power as we rolled. He lifted the club again, and I bit down on his leg. His eyes widened in shock as I tore into the flesh and we rolled painfully down a small, mossy bank, and ended up in a muddy pond. He swatted me across my ears as I kept biting down, but finally struck my ear so hard I had to let go. I saw red dots as I tried to find my footing. Gasto backpedaled from me, but went deeper into the pond and nearly floundered as it turned deep very suddenly. I had lost the sword while we tumbled, but I grasped under the surface of the water, found a fist sized, jagged rock and as Gasto made his way up, now holding a dagger, I whipped the makeshift weapon into his face. He looked shocked, but strangely not so hurt. He was, in fact, but like a real champion of dozens of terrible fights, he thought of his honor instead of his wounds, and still lifted the dagger. He opened his mouth to spit, and teeth fell out, and while his pain was evident, his refusal to give up made me despair. I cursed and danced to his side, dodged a clumsy slash and struck down again, and the rock dug deep into his skull with a sickening crack. He fell on his side with a splash, his eyes staring like a dead fish's, his hair floating in the cold water.

I panted, delirious, shaking, surprised by my survival as I looked down at the dead one. I had killed him. Like Ludovicus had been, he was a lord of war, a ring-giver and famous man with songs and poems and wealth. He had been a terror of a shieldwall, a Goth champion.

I staggered to the beach and grasped Hel's Delight. Had Hulderic been right? Was I the bane of the worlds, at least, that of the Goths? I looked at Gasto, whose brains poured into the water, and that made me vomit. My belly heaved, I gagged, and I wept as I looked at the jagged hole in the skull of the man I had been allied with once, a man who had greeted me kindly when he met me and like Ludovicus, this one had not hated me before I had decided to defy Father. It had been my choice, and the Norn had woven the tapestry, and that weave had pulled hundreds into a headlong, desperate battle for their lives, and now, some life-strings had been cut. Gasto's boys and daughters and their boys would be waging a feud against me until the end of the ages, and it would extend to Hulderic, as well. I wiped my mouth and took a deep breath. 'Wyrd, mine and yours, eh?' I asked the corpse, but it had nothing to say on the matter. It had been a nasty, terrible fight for my life. I hoped he would understand, even if his family never would. I spat his flesh and blood from my mouth. I staggered my way up the incline and took up the red shield.

Not too far, Maino burst from thick woods, with ten Goth warriors.

'Give me a damned break, Woden!' I cursed the god for his unfairness, but of course the Goths would be there, hot on Gasto's heels. There was a surprised, brutal grin on my cousin's face, but then one of puzzlement as he gazed at the familiar shield. 'You looking for your lapdogs?' I yelled and kicked a dog's corpse and flashed my sword at him. 'All three are here. Bury them together!' I yelled and pointed at the dead Gasto. Their eyes followed my sword, and I could see the astonishment on their bearded faces. 'Burn and bury him and let the poets sing of Maroboodus, the Blood

Maw!' I wiped the blood off my lips, laughed deliriously and ran off as they spread out, their incredulous looks changing into enraged ones.

'Bring the bastard's bloody maw to me, and I'll bloody it properly!' Maino screamed. The Goths took after me, and I thought them terribly predictable. I was in a fey, strange mood, and for some reason didn't fear as much as I had. We raced through the woods and patches of old blueberries. My side was hurting, my head was aching and my arm was throbbing with festering pain. I prayed Saxa would survive even if I didn't, and yea, the damned Saxons as well.

I stumbled on, hearing the Goths gaining ground on me. I heard a man yell with surprised anger, then pain as he fell, but the others came on, heedless of danger. In fact, there were many others out there, running through the Svea woods and hills, Maino's men who had spread out and further on more as the Goth war bands were organizing, though most were far and I had a hunch Bero would not approve of Maino's relentless chase. Horns blared, and I begged for the Svea to intercept as many of Bero's men as possible. Eadwine and Danr were jogging, the latter holding a javelin, his eyes gauging when he might dare to throw it. Ten more men were apparently getting closer, not showing much fatigue under their hard looks. Their Suebi head knots were bobbling, beards swinging and all clutched their weapons with the certainty of seasoned warriors. I begged Woden for intervention, and then, miraculously, after an hour of exhausting, tortuous running, I received it.

I stumbled out into a field.

Before me rose two wooded hills with palisades on top and smoke was rising from the roofs of beautiful, long halls, solid structures. There was a glittering lake, swampy woods and there, between the hills was a village with many burned up remains of halls. Snowlake.

There was a warparty of ten Svea riding in. There were two women on horses. One was clearly Hild.

And there, also, was Saxa.

She was being escorted to her father. Something had gone wrong.

There was no sign of Ceadda, not at first, but then I saw twelve men jogging after the Svea and I saw they were the Saxons. They had lost some men, and I realized Hild had betrayed them. Her intensity, her strange questions the night before, her look as she regarded me. There was something about it. She was going back to Gislin, and she was bringing a grand prize with her. Saxa.

I looked behind me, and knew I'd not be able to hide. I didn't want to. None would fetch me to safety. I burst into a run. I could not scream, I could not do anything but keep my legs pumping, and my lungs felt like they were bursting out of my chest. My wife reached the village, and I saw men rushing about, some on horseback and spears were glinting. The Saxons were hanging back, hesitating and I cursed them for failing to protect her, though likely it was not their fault.

I looked behind as I ran. Some horses were now emerging from the woods, and Maino sat on one sturdy beast, having commandeered one from his men. A Goth was running faster than the others, unburdened by armor. He held a javelin, and he threw it. It sailed near me, embedded itself in turf and I kicked it as I ran. He was a good runner, young man of Bero's dominion and apparently had spared his stamina to capture me, to gain fame and honor in front of the gods. He was grinning, puffing and fingering a thick seax, a dagger of crude make. The Saxons were pulling at each other and I thought I saw Ceadda pointing a finger at me.

I ran for them, but let the Goth get closer. I stumbled and cursed and heard him laugh hysterically, sensing his kill, his capture, his fame. I felt him right behind me.

Then I turned, lightning fast, agile as a lynx, and stabbed upwards. The blade pierced his chest, and he fell on the edge, which I ripped out as we fell.

The Goths were closing, and I got up to my feet. I saw there was a field right before me, and a rut dug around it, and I jumped over the rut. The Saxons were coming for me, and the Goths were nearly there and it would be desperate.

Someone in the village pointed a long sword our way. It was an older man. Gislin. It had to be, and the man I had planned on killing, would perhaps be our only hope. He would help, surely, against the Goths. But he would not spare the Saxons. Or me. Unless Saxa made it so. She would try.

I thought I saw her there, arguing with the old man. Then someone rushed from the side, pulled at Saxa, held on to her. They grabbed the man, and Saxa was holding on to him as well, and would not let go. She struggled, was talking to the man and I felt my head spin as it was Aldbert, whom they finally tore from her. They kept them apart.

Had he escaped Maino? How did he end up in Snowlake?

I turned to stand and faced Maino's men across the rut. It was a muddy, nasty field, and I held on to my shield ferociously.

The pack of beastly warriors ran at me, encouraging each other, but now Ceadda was there for me and his men, all carrying hide-shields spread around. I wept, laughed, and cursed. They guarded the ditch and Ceadda grabbed me. 'Not a Lord Pup anymore, eh?' he laughed thinly. 'Looks and smells like a proper Saxon, no?'

'Woden and Donor thank you, bless you,' I wept. 'Saxa?'

He swallowed and looked at the village. 'Some Goths caught up with us. Had to fight, and while we won, that whore völva … she had men waiting for them. Probably had fetched some during the night to grab Saxa. I'm not sure who betrayed Agin and us, Aldbert or her, but neither are friends to us. I'm sorry. They knew the land and we gave chase, but—'

'You've done more than we agreed on,' I said, swallowing the unreasonable need to blame them.

'Yes, we have,' Njord said, but smiled to take the edge of the comment. 'It's Ceadda's fault. Got lost in the woods, the idiot,' he added.

'First we deal with this,' Ceadda barked. 'Then we get her back. Shieldwall!'

We formed one. We had six men in two ranks, and we held the ditch. The Goths across from us cursed, some twenty of them now. Some men had ridden in, and they dismounted, looking at the village with apprehension, but Maino was beyond caring about the Svea. He pointed his ax at me. 'Bring him to me. Slit the bellies of the others. In fact, slit his belly as well, but do it well, so he lives a while, holding his traitorous entrails.'

'She is safe, cousin,' I told him. 'Safe from you. Married to me, by the way.'

243

He grunted as their shieldwall formed. Eadwine was on one end, Maino in the middle and Danr on the other end as they crouched behind their thick shields, their eyes gleaming over the rims. They were eying the ditch, and yes, they could jump over to our side, but we could kill many as they did. Maino growled at me and looked across the field to Saxa. 'She is safe for now, cousin. But I'm not giving up on her, no. Never. Know that in your death. We will wage war with them after we deal with Hughnot's Black Goths, the hall-burning bastards. We'll hump their skulls like I will hump yours, and she, Maroboodus, will be a widow, won't she? In a bit. I have time. Just wait and watch from the afterlife.'

We braced our feet. In Snowlake, dozens of men were gathering, shields could be seen, spears flashed, but there would be no help coming our way for a while. 'Come, cousin. I already killed dogs today. One more won't feel any different,' I said and tried to hide the despair in my voice.

'I'll hang your ugly face from my standard,' he grinned, and so they marched forward, hitting the spears on the rims of their shields. They stopped at the edge of the ditch, so close we could nearly touch them. They were hesitating, and that is when the six men in our second rank grabbed rocks and began pelting the enemy. One struck a man in the mouth; another bounced off Danr's shield to scrape his face, and that is when Maino roared, in his battle rage.

They jumped over. It was a mad, crazy move that nearly caught us unaware.

They crashed into us, pushing us back, some fell into the ditch and flailed as they tried to get over and then we pushed back. Three Goths fell to the spears, our second rank pushed the first rank, our backs, and we bowled them all into the ditch, Maino included and there, above that rut the killing began. We stabbed down. They slashed and pulled at our feet and blood flowed. A shield rim caved in a man's face, a seax cut one's nose, but then two Saxon fell and were dragged to the damned ditch and there Maino and Danr hacked them to death. Then another Saxon fell as javelins were thrown at us by men who had stayed across the ditch and we answered with rocks. I slashed at a wrist that was reaching for me and the man howled. Another pulled me on my knees and Maino ripped at my shield with his hands, his face enraged beyond all sense. I slashed the sword into his helmet, then to his shoulder, drawing blood, and so the terrible battle went on until Eadwine jumped over to the side and ran his sword through a Saxon throat. He turned to kill another and Ceadda turned to face him and then things changed.

An army rode out of the woods. They carried a standard of crows and I nearly shat myself as I saw it was Hughnot. Hrolf was there, Ingulf, and Ingo as well and they looked splendid as two hundred men marched behind them. Two hundred, at least.

Hild was screaming, and rode her horse past us to meet them, gesturing at us wildly, but Hrolf pushed her aside with no remorse and she fell from her horse. He ignored the holy völva and that deed made everyone flinch and make signs to ward off evil luck. Hughnot's army didn't care. Maino climbed out of the ditch, so did his men and they turned to look at the newcomers. Now, Svearna were also running across the field, fearless in front of the vast army of Goths, and we retreated to them. I looked on and saw how Maino walked to Hughnot, showing his fist to the man. Danr was pulling at Maino, but the mad berserker didn't care.

Hrolf dismounted.

He pointed a finger at Danr. Six archers rode out of the army and raised their bows. Danr lifted his shield, but it didn't matter. Arrows ripped into his body and he fell to his knees. Hrolf swung a sword and Danr's head twisted to the side and he fell, his chainmail blooded.

Butchery began. Eadwine slashed his spear in a grinning foe's face, and then ran at another. He was caught by a rider, who slammed a studded club in the back of the champion's head. Maino fought valiantly. I almost felt sorry for him, but he attacked a man, pulled him from the horse, broke his neck with his foot and vaulted on the horse. He slammed another man from a horse, but that man fell and hung on to Maino's saddle and then my cousin was dragged down and beaten by six men. The others ran away, but were brutally hunted across the field.

I pulled at Ceadda. 'Go, and run. You have done your bit.'

'You are going to fall here!' he said, too loudly and the Svearna, who formed a shieldwall near us, scowled at him. A man with nearly iridescent eyes, an older man with braids running on each side of his head nodded at me. Saxa had been speaking with him. It was Gislin. 'They should go.'

Ceadda hesitated, and Njord pulled at him, and the six men still alive pulled away. They looked at me, long and hard, trying to see a way to save the day, but there was none. I waved at them, and they ran for the woods and I prayed they would see their home. I turned to look at the old man. He was looking at the Saxons run. 'They fought well, and deserve to leave. But you are my daughter's man?' He looked at Hild, who was getting to her feet in the field. 'She told me a most spectacular tale.'

'What did she say?' I asked.

'She said you tried to join Agin, my son and hoped to kill me next year,' he chuckled and looked down at me. 'Hild failed me years past. This is her way to come back home. Saxa merits her that. But she said you are important. They are here for you, no?'

'They are,' I said hollowly. 'What will you do?' I asked and cursed because there was nothing to be done. There were only fifty Svearna, and there was an army of two hundred men approaching.

'You love her?' he asked with a thin smile.

'Yes,' I answered.

He smiled wistfully. 'A pity. Young love. So rash. So quick. I was like you. My wife died of a cough six winters ago.'

'I am sorry, but I do not wish to lose her,' I told him warily, eyeing Hughnot's army forming up and marching for us. We were in a sturdy line, but there was no hope. 'Should we retreat up the hill?'

'No,' he said dryly. 'We'll stay here.'

He was a believer in the gods. Perhaps he thought the gods might spare him and us. I saw Hrolf's eyes as he stared at me and wondered how much bad luck could one man have in a single day. There would be no gods sparing us then.

Aldbert appeared. He walked behind Gislin, and my eyes followed him. He had a guilty look on his face.

Gislin spoke to him. 'This is Hulderic's son?'

'Yes, he is,' Aldbert said huskily.

'I sent you there as a child to keep an eye on their family. Now a member of that family is here. They will ask for him; I know,' the Lord of Snowlake said. 'Is there a reason he should be spared, son? Hild said he wanted me dead. Plotted to kill me, even.'

'Yes,' he answered with fear. 'There is a reason.'

I stared at Aldbert in shock. 'What?' I asked softly. 'What does he mean? And what reason?'

Aldbert looked sheepish. He fidgeted and flushed and walked to me. I resisted the impulse to kill him, as he pulled me to the side and spoke to me in hushed tones. 'It's a long story. And I am your friend. I always was. I betrayed you to Ludovicus, and I left them a sign they missed. I sneaked out to find your father from Wolf Hole. I'm sure he is out there as well. Hild had gone to fetch men, and hoped to take Saxa while you slept. I ran into Eadwine. He found me and I lied to them about the hall, didn't I? Trust me, I didn't want to hurt you.'

'Why?' I asked, wanting to understand. 'Why all these lies?'

'I didn't want you to come here. Ever. The Bear? Remember? Your family? This is the other family. Our family. The family of those gods who cursed Woden's first men. But while your family tries to bury the curse, my father wants to set the Bear free, and you have been doing well at it. They wish for you to rampage across Midgard, and he set me in your hall to see what I might find. To see if there was anyone in your family who might show signs of this madness.' He was swallowing. 'Then there was that night I tried to fool you. That was real. It was a warning. A goddess or a god warned you. Me. And you didn't heed. The Bear wouldn't.'

I stared at him and felt the need to push him away like an asp. 'You have spied on us?'

'He has not,' Gislin said dryly, having listened. 'He fell in love with your family. But he is here to save you. Are you saying Maroboodus is the Bear?' His voice betrayed disbelief.

Aldbert shook with indecision but finally nodded. 'He is,' he answered. 'The god spoke to me.'

The lord's face twitched. He looked shocked, and then his brow filled with sweat. Finally, he turned to Aldbert who bowed before him. 'You are not lying, are you? Signs and gods, eh? Finally? Finally, we might have one of the unlucky ones?'

'Perhaps,' Aldbert said sadly.

'In that case, we will see. We'll ask the spirits, and gods rage, if you lie,' Gislin said. 'You have betrayed and failed us before.'

'I am sorry, lord.'

'You came here to save him,' the man said, smiling thinly. 'But he'll not enjoy it. Take him.' I turned, but I was too tired to fight, and fell as three men pulled me down. I heard Saxa screaming, but they were not trying to hurt me, as they tied me up expertly, and stood me up roughly.

'Your Grandfather Hulderic,' Gislin said. 'Has he spoken to you of Woden's Curse?'

'The prophecy, yes, but—'

His eyes glowed with intensity. 'Then know we work to see it come true. The god that cursed Woden is jealous, and my family come from the breed of this other god. And now you shall serve his will. Aldbert did fail, but only because he loved you. Oh, the irony.'

'I will not help—'

'You will,' he smiled. 'I see your greed, you are relentless. I feel and taste it. You'll stay with me now, and I shall think on how to employ your curse if you are the one. Gods are watching, and I had better not fail.'

'Saxa is mine, and I shall live with her, and heed no prophecies,' I told him bitterly. 'But these Goths shall kill us if you don't—'

He laughed bitterly. 'You will not get Saxa,' he said and walked forward to face the Black Goths. 'And they'll not get you.'

Hughnot greeted Gislin. He sat on his horse, slouched, tired, and eyed me. He pointed a finger at Saxa. 'I tried to save your daughter. The Saxons would have sold her to our lord, but I attempted to snatch her from my brother Friednot. I had a plan. This man betrayed us.' He nodded towards me.

'Doesn't matter,' Gislin said, cocking his head at him.

Hughnot went on. 'Doesn't it? But I expect our alliance, nonetheless. The Boat-Lord still wishes for it.'

The Boat-Lord? Was he working for the Boat-Lord? 'You—' I began, but a Svea slapped me.

Hughnot looked at me and shrugged. 'I grew tired, Maroboodus, of Friednot. I made a deal with our old master. I'd give him back the Ring and the Sword, and I'd return to his rule. That Friednot died, was just a bonus. I'd prayed for it for so long, that when it finally happened, I was so surprised. Perhaps I helped it along a bit as well, eh? That Friednot learnt of the deal between Gislin here and the Boat-Lord was unfortunate, and how he snatched your Saxa from the Saxons, was a cursed nuisance. But it's all fixed now. The Black Goths shall rule the coast under Boat-Lord's banner.'

'And what of your banner flying over faraway lands?' I yelled at him. 'Liar! Maggot!'

Hughnot shifted in his saddle, angry. 'Hrolf will take her to the Boat-Lord,' he said. 'And I'll hang you.'

'No,' Gislin said simply.

'No?' Hrolf asked with anger. 'Why not?'

'Your Boat-Lord still needs us to conquer the coast. You and him alone? No, you might not make it. We will ally, and do what we planned. Saxa goes with you.'

'No!' I screamed.

Gislin ignored me. 'And I am in a happy, generous mood, lord Hughnot, since you delivered to me something I had not expected. Something we have sought for ages. We will help you in your wars to make yourself a Thiuda of a great nation, we will reap the profits of such wars and greed, and you shall be thanked.'

Hughnot grunted. Then he pointed a finger at me and my belly filled with ice-cold fear. 'And that something is him? Why?'

'I shall not speak of it,' Gislin said quietly. 'It doesn't concern you.'

Hrolf bellowed. 'That traitor? Him. I want him. He lied to us, he betrayed us. He made a fool of Hughnot, Father, our lord and I will have his head sent to his father Hulderic.'

'No, lord,' said Gislin and I looked balefully at the traitor Aldbert, who had apparently both betrayed and saved me. Gislin would not let me go quickly. Not ever, in fact. 'He has his uses here. He shall be mine, not unlike a tamed bear—'

'He is not to be tamed,' Hrolf grunted. 'He is a wild pig. Stick and reward will not teach him, and he'll escape! He'll come after Saxa.'

'She is my wife, you dung-chewing weakling,' I yelled. 'We are married. Properly married.'

Hrolf's eyes flew open, and he stammered, as his men looked at him snidely.

Hughnot sighed. 'See, he is dangerous.'

'We have ways of taming such as he, my lord, we do have them, never worry,' Gislin said and smiled at me. 'We will take him to my haunt, deep down the hill and there he shall change into a tool for my god. He will eat a heart, and man flesh and such a fare will change a man. Trust me, lord.'

Hughnot glowered, not happy with the decision of Gislin. He evidently considered ordering a butchery, but took a deep breath, knowing the Svearna, especially Gislin, would be needed in taking care of the Goths of the coasts. Then he nodded. Gislin whistled and men rode out of the village. They were leading Saxa forward on a horse, and the happy girl I had known briefly was cold and sorrowful again. Hughnot sat up in his saddle. 'You have just been divorced, woman. We shall take you to meet the Boat-Lord. He might or might not marry you. Or perhaps he will marry you to a chosen warrior. He will guard you.' He nodded at Hrolf, who glowered at her, unhappy and I prayed to gods she would not suffer at his hands for my words. But she would, of course. 'Send me a thousand men when we begin, Gislin, and you shall gain lands and fame and sit in my Thing as an ally. You will always be welcome in the Spear Hall, my home.'

'It sounds proper, rich, and what I desire, oh great Goth,' Gislin said smoothly.

Hughnot turned his horse around and his army rode away. I stared after Saxa but she did not turn, until at the very end, and her cool, cold composure cracked and as she turned to look at me, her eyes filled with tears and fear and I struggled against my guards. I felt a blow on my back, then another and fell down amidst Svea feet. I crawled but Gislin stopped me from doing so as he placed a foot on my neck.

'Take this Bear to Himnhall, the Dark Below. Get him to a cage and see to his wounds. I shall need a sacrifice to give to the gods as we prepare. We'll make sure he is what we think he is. Then we shall seek guidance. Gods will whisper lies, but I know spirits that shall aid us in helping the Dark Walker escape his prison. Let the Ragnarok come. At least we have finally found the strand, the beginning of the end. Finally.'

Ragnarok. End of the world. I spat on his foot, and he wiped it on my face.

His eyes looked across the field. 'The champions are alive,' Gislin said. 'Some of them. Go and find which ones and bring them along. They will make fitting feed for us, won't they? We shall sacrifice one for our answers. The higher, the better.'

Men agreed with grunts and moved to obey. Some grasped me and pulled me along. I saw them knocking over Goths, killing many wounded ones and then they carried Maino and Eadwine out of the piles of wounded, both alive still.

They blindfolded me and after a long walk in a moist, cold place that was underground, they locked me in a cage and ripped off the hood.

I was not alone. Maino and Eadwine were in the same cage.

BOOK 4: Dragon's Tail

'We have her. We will have Gislin's Svea. We have the ring. The sword. You go home, and wait. The end will come soon enough.'
Hrolf to Maroboodus.

CHAPTER 15

I stared at my two fellow prisoners balefully, but they were in no condition to pick up our fight. Eadwine was not well at all, it was clear. He was throwing up in the corner, his hair matted with blood, and Maino was holding his side, face down on the wooden floor, breathing harshly, though he would occasionally look at me, mouthing curses. The Svear had retreated from the cages. I looked around to see a natural cavern of some sort, with sputtering torches, and shingles set on alcoves, and shadowed faces looked at us from many points in the cavern. They were not human, but stone or faces carved hideously from mud.

I banged my head on the bars.

Saxa was gone. Aldbert had tried to help me, and he'd suffer for it.

And Hughnot? A traitor. Filthy traitor, worse than I was.

I banged my head on the bars again, this time so hard I winced and Maino looked up. 'You shit,' he whispered. 'Can you at least suffer silently?'

'No, you murderous pig-faced maniac,' I countered, and didn't really care if he'd be riled up. I'd welcome it, in fact.

He grimaced at me, in no condition to throttle me then and there. 'Coming from the killer of Ludovicus and Gasto, that is thick as reindeer stew. You've doomed us all,' he panted, 'and yet you still live. Gods must have something worse than this in store for you, eh?'

'Shut up,' I spat. 'It's been a long two days. I'll slit your belly later. I've lost a wife, and you would do well to keep your trap shut. I'm past fearing you, cousin.'

The astonishment on his face made him look like a child caught stealing mead from a cellar. Then the child disappeared and the animal took its place and he sat up, cursing, hoping to get up, and I stretched my legs, readying myself to fight. Some Svear moved in the shadows, nervous and alert.

Eadwine got up with a groan, grabbed Maino's shoulder and shook his head. Maino fought the grip, but the powerful warrior kept him still. I stared maliciously at the fool, spite shining on my face. 'Lord,' Eadwine said sternly. 'We *need* to work together. We are all sitting in the same pool of piss, our fates tied together. We will settle our scores later, if we can.'

'We aren't going anywhere,' Maino hissed, 'so might as well do that now.'

'Perhaps this time you won't end up on your face or under a horse?' I coaxed him. 'Hughnot would laugh, he would, seeing you sputter and make a fool of yourself.'

'He would smile when I rip your throat out and spit down your neck,' he growled. 'To imagine you have managed to betray every Goth on the coast? Impossible. But at least you ended up trapped in the end. If you ever step out of here, Maroboodus, you'll have to travel far if you ever want to find people who utter your name without a curse. I'll rest a bit, and then I'll—'

'I doubt they will let you touch me,' I told him as a pair of hulking Svear came forth with long spears and a hook attached to a spear shaft. 'They look like they know their business.'

'Why did they lock us up in the same cage anyway?' Eadwine grumbled as he let go of Maino carefully.

'Probably for the entertainment,' I said and spat out of the cage. The Svear grinned as Maino slouched and leaned on the bars, while glowering at me.

'I'll find a better time and place, then,' he said sullenly.

'Is your father out there?' I asked. 'Or did he get lost? Went home?'

Eadwine answered for Maino, trying to keep his voice from dripping with accusation. 'Lord Bero led the main force. We ran off without leave. Gods only know if Hughnot surprised and killed him. We heard nothing of the sort as we chased you, and surely some would have seen it, but if he is alive, he is in danger.'

255

'That would make *me* the lord of the gau,' Maino said smugly and both Eadwine and I looked at him dubiously.

'It would make you a shitty lord prisoner whose gau is defended by my father, and …' I began and clamped my mouth shut. I had spied a shadow deeper than the rest, and it had moved. It had been squatting there, right next to the cage, listening, and I frowned at it. 'They put us here so they can learn of us. Who we are. If *you* are important.' My eyes didn't leave the shadow and then a small man rose to his feet and walked to where there was light and guards. He pointed a finger at Maino, who blanched visibly at the unwanted attention and a guard scampered off. 'I guess we just told them you are important indeed.'

The man came forward and squatted near our cage. His hair was ragged, a sweaty thing of grease, his bones shone beneath his skin and he looked like a sick, strange man, or a corpse.

'What are you, I wonder?' Maino said arrogantly. 'An animal or a man?'

'I'm called Whisper,' he said, and indeed his voice was one, a soft whisper like a distant wind ruffling trees on a hillside. 'I'm vitka of the Dark One.'

I snorted. 'Is this about the Woden's curse again?'

Whisper nodded vigorously. 'It's *all* about it, boy,' he said, his voice slightly excited. 'All our lives are tied to it. Yours too.'

Maino moved from the bars to sit at the center. He grabbed a pebble and tossed it at the man. 'I don't give a damn about your curses and I don't care for your face. What will you do to us?'

'We'll see if Aldbert is right,' Whisper said to me, ignoring Maino. 'Gislin thinks he is, he felt the stirrings of the dark one when he saw you, and so we'll ask the gods if they agree with Aldbert. We will sacrifice and find the truth. I'm good at truth-finding. Like Aldbert, I see things. I'm no charlatan like Hild.'

I shook my head. 'I will not be convinced by strange tricks. Your Aldbert tried it already.'

'Your Aldbert,' he said with a sad smile. 'He told us. The twigs and the skull? You saw these things already? And a rotten hull?'

I felt my jaw tighten. 'There are skulls, twigs, and rotten boats all over the land.'

'Yes,' he laughed. 'But you believe him. I see it. Aldbert is your friend indeed. Tried to help you, but you didn't want that, did you? He tried to hide you from us, but no, you came after all. Poor fool failed left and right. He was sent to you as a boy. A talented one, he was, like Gislin. Like me. Saxa and Agin never had the gift, but Gislin and his father before him have sent men and women to serve and live near your family, here and in the islands. In times past, there have been others like you, other Bears and we have tried to get our hands on them before. We always failed. But we try, and Aldbert was sent, but he was too young. He turned Goth. Now? He is here. Gislin's not happy, but you are here, and that balances things.'

Eadwine snorted and rubbed his head. 'Poor boy, this Aldbert. Not much to look forward to in his old age if he has to lick your stinking feet. Will they let him live?'

The surprisingly sane vitka shrugged and kneaded his shoulder, uncertain. 'He served the clan well, finally, and when he was touched by the spirits, that night he sang the galdr with you, Maroboodus, he knew he could not run from it. I don't blame him for trying. He tried indeed, but couldn't run. It's too bad he loved you so much. He might have left the land on his own.'

'Is Agin alive?' I asked, swallowing my guilt over Aldbert.

Whisper smiled. 'His village, the Wolf Hole? It's gone. They say he died to Bero's men. Others say he led many men away after the loss. It's sad business, really. Not all Svearna agree with our clan, very few worship the Dark Sleeper, and while most respect and obey Gislin, Agin's been a growing power and a painful, ever growing thorn in our backsides. You did us a favor by getting rid of Agin for us. *If* he is gone. We don't have his body. We've sent men to seek him.'

I walked to the bars and looked down at him. 'What exactly do you need? Of me, that is.'

He got up to eye me. He was filthy, spoke of sacrifices casually, but didn't seem as unkind as one might have imagined. 'I don't know, son. If Aldbert failed and lied? If you are a nobody? You'll die. Gislin will want you given to the Sleeper, but if you are what Aldbert said you are, what Gislin believes you are? You will live here. Perhaps they'll let you out of the cage, even.'

'To *what* end?' I hissed at him.

He shrugged. 'That is the thing. We know not. We know you herald the end of the world. That it starts with you. What else is there? We will find out. Little by little we shall coax the spirits for what the curse means, what your part is.'

'Mad lies, all of them,' I said.

He shook his head. 'Boy, this is an old story. Your family is ancient, so is ours. It has lived in Gothonia, the islands, for long and long ages, longer than any, and since Woden gave life to your ancestors, you also carry the responsibility of upholding his honor. By staying true to family and honor, by being brave, the very best of men, you stave off the curse some gods put on you. And if you are not the very best of men? The curse says it leads down a dark road, with wars, death, and the end.' He shrugged. 'That's not much, I agree, but there is this line. It's all we know. It says the Bear will roar, and the Raven will find the way. We know little more right now. There was a seer here once. They say she knew much, very much about this, and goddesses gave her the full lines of the curse the Dark Sleeper cast when your kin was born. Those lines give hints of this curse, but she fled, fearing the lines, and Gislin sent people to find her. None have returned. But we know there is the Bear, and the Bear comes from your blood, and will herald the calamity that is to come.'

'And you welcome such calamity?' Maino spat. 'Madmen.'

Whisper glowered at Maino, and I half hoped Maino would push a bit more, enough to tip the Svea's patience over like an unbalanced barrel of water, but Whisper ignored the fool and spoke to me. 'See the difference between you and him. He is of your blood, a wretched, if valiant thing, much like most warriors who stomp the land of Midgard. You would never know he has a god's blood running wild in his veins. He's not that special.' Maino looked ready to refute the claim, but Eadwine slapped his foot to keep him silent. 'The blood is there, but its just blood. Yet you, Maroboodus, son of Hulderic, you decided to change everything. And you have. Blood, war, misery follow you, and such are the paw-prints of the *true* Bear. There have been others.'

'Others?' I asked him, cursing him, and myself softly. 'Before. The men you have spied through our past?'

'Yes. Your relative, the Boat-Lord? He is the rightful head of your clan, and long has he kept your family in Gothonia, as his father before him, and many others like him. There were harsh men in your family like you before, men who thought differently, obeyed little and our family has forever tried to catch them. You do know many of your kind died miserably at the hands of the vitka of your family?'

'I've been told,' I said darkly.

'Hulderic. Your grandmother,' he surmised. 'But they are no Boat-Lord who would have hung you quickly. You are ours. And no, Maroboodus, I do not embrace the fate Midgard will face. I'd rather your family had stayed in Gothonia where we could not find you easily, but Friednot and Hughnot rebelled, and stole your family sword, and the ring, and opened up a dangerous door.'

I stared at him, wondering how he knew such things. 'Stole? How do you know?'

He waved his hand. 'Hughnot told us many things when he visited us last Spring.'

'How is this Boat-Lord related to us?' I asked him.

He chuckled. 'Why, he is your great grandfather. Old as shit. Your grandfather and Hughnot are his sons. They left Hogholm without his permission, and while he *had* given Friednot the ring and the sword, he never approved they be taken away from Gothonia. He was very upset. But so was Friednot. He hated the Boat-Lord. They had had a smaller brother once, a young man, whom your Boat-Lord had given to Donor for being reckless, possibly another Bear, and Friednot and Hughnot had never forgiven him for that. Even the mighty families fall if they squabble.'

'And Saxa is to marry *him*?' I breathed. 'This ancient man?'

'At least he can't get it up, eh?' Whisper laughed, but sobered. 'But no, I think he will give her to Hrolf. The key is that he will do the gifting. He is the master, see? Did you see how upset Hrolf was when you told him she was your wife? Jealous.'

'Curse him, may a spear rip his ass out,' I sobbed and struck the cage and the Svea tensed, but only for a moment, as Whisper waved them back.

'Gods only guess if that is possible with them holding all the advantages,' he smiled. 'Hrolf and Hughnot are going back home, and the sword and the ring they stole will be given back as soon as Bero dies, and Saxa will cement their alliance to Gislin. Gislin will take back much of our lands on the coast. It's a good deal for everyone except for Bero and your father and the other Goths further south.'

'I'll not stay here,' I said slowly. 'If you don't want this fate of your god to come to pass, why don't you—'

He blanched. 'I dare not rebel. No. Why would I give away my position here? I fear the future, but I fear hunger more. You'll be ours and perhaps you won't want to leave either,' he said with a sad smile. 'We will ask the gods, a high man shall die,' he said and looked at Maino, who cursed, 'and you shall change, slowly, but you shall. No man stays defiant forever. You'll live here, and we'll let the gods decide how best to use you, Bear, while you suffer your way into weeping obedience.'

'I doubt it,' I hissed. 'I'll not turn a Svea. Nor obedient.'

'True Bear, eh?' he chuckled. 'Free as the wind, selfish as a storm. You will, no matter if you want to or not. We will keep you until gods speak plainly. Only your cousin here shall go to Hel's tables, and that one as well.' He nodded towards Eadwine. 'And you'll eat their flesh. After they are gone, the flesh of others. That also changes a man. It drives some mad, others obedient, hungry for more. It's what the Sleeper would eat, and you will be closer to him. His heart. You'll eat it tonight.' He looked at Maino meaningfully.

I looked at Maino as well, and the fool's face was white with terror. 'I doubt he has a heart.'

Whisper barked a laugh and turned to go. 'Heart. You'll eat it and we'll speak to the gods. His blood is royal, and very loyal, even if he is dull as a lump of rock,' Whisper said and scratched his armpit. Maino's face went slack with fear and I cannot say I was not tempted to see him die. Eadwine smiled ironically as he eyed the brief, if happy look on my face and Whisper shrugged, ready to go.

'What is this Dark Sleeper?' Eadwine asked tiredly. 'We do not know this god.'

'You do, my friends. He is also called the Trickster, the Spirit of Shadows.'

Maino breathed hard. 'Lok?'

Whisper nodded, approvingly. 'There, he is not so stupid as he looks. Has listened to old women and drunken poets, even when they do not sing of heroes, but the villains.' He walked away, picking his way carefully in the dark.

I nodded and Maino looked at me with terror. We had indeed all heard of Lok, the demi-god, the friend and foe of the gods, friend to the jotuns, father to monsters, and the one who will march on the gods when the end is nigh. Of course we had. I sat down, and held my head. 'So,' Maino slurred. 'We'll be dead. You'll be a cannibal. Didn't see that coming.'

'Neither did I,' I said.

'I don't want to go out helpless as a fool,' Maino cursed. 'I'll fight.'

I looked at him, and shook my head. I had been promised life, but what kind of life would it be? One full of madness, sorrow, suffering?

Saxa would certainly suffer.

Father would die. And so, I agreed with Maino. We'd fight, but not the way he would have fought.

'Listen,' I said, and they did. It took some convincing, some arguments, and when Eadwine agreed with me, so did Maino, finally.

Then we waited, allied for once.

CHAPTER 16

They came during the night. I heard them talking and saw them enter the cavern, and they were carrying a cauldron filled with burning wood. Otherwise it was fairly dark in the cavern; many of the torches and shingles had burnt out, which didn't seem to bother the Svea who lived there. There was more light in the cavern than there should be, I decided. Perhaps there was a strange glow in floor below? I squinted as I looked up and noted a hole where the light of the Mani streamed inside. It was not a strong light, but it lit up a tree trunk that had been set upright in the middle of the lower hall. There were Svear standing in the shadows by the trunk, silent, figures out to witness the magic of their leaders, who were descending a path for them. I saw Gislin, wearing a helmet made of a fox face, black tails swinging on each side, then there was the vitka Whisper, naked, painted white, and he carried a stone ax with a sturdy handle. His hair was spiked with mud, his eyes dangerous and fey and he pointed a finger to the cages. Hild came last, wearing a white dress, and she carried a hlaut vessel, used to gather blood. They looked eerie in the light of the fire in the cauldron.

'Shit,' Eadwine said. 'It's happening.'

'I don't like it,' Maino said nervously. 'We should just fight, and—'

'Shut up,' I said brusquely. 'Fight now, and you'll hang from that trunk for sure, beaten and broken,' I spat and Maino nodded sullenly, swallowing his fear.

'I'd not go there willingly,' he said in a terrified whisper. 'I don't trust you.'

'It will work,' I told him angrily. 'Are you ready?'

'I am,' Eadwine growled. 'Don't fancy this place too much. Wish to get out of here, no matter the way. Even if it means my life will end.'

'We can only try. And do not die, Eadwine, before you kill at least half of them,' I joked and he laughed softly.

'They will tie us up,' Maino said as if to an idiot. 'We will be helpless.'

'They will. Though not for long,' I said with confidence I didn't feel. 'But if they don't cooperate later with my plan, then it has not been a pleasure knowing you. I'll eat your heart and probably break a tooth on the lump of cold rock.'

'May rancid dogs hump you, Maroboodus. I—'

Men approached the cage. There were ten, and they had long spears and the dangerous looking, spear-like hooks. A tall warrior approached us, holding an ax and a shield, wearing a fur cap, his beard long, greasy, and braided with silver. He stepped near the cage. 'Coming peacefully?'

'We haven't eaten,' Maino said sullenly. 'Perhaps later?'

The man smiled and thumbed one of the hooks. 'Come or be dragged. We don't mind which.'

'We are coming,' I told him and got up. The cage was opened and I inched my way out. They grabbed me roughly and held on to my arms, and men stepped forward.

They tied my hands.

The cords were looped around my wrists, and when the others exited the cage they were as expertly tied. Maino's face twisted with a hint of his battle rage, but I held his feral eyes, and summoning every shred of sanity, he let them finish. Eadwine smirked at the Svea, who were not overly gentle and the knots were very tight. They placed a rope around our necks and I could only imagine how pitiful we looked as we were pulled towards the trunk, and what was likely the temple of Lok. *Like cows to the slaughter*, I thought and grunted, and Maino growled fearfully as the specter of his death approached.

'Bring the meat, our sweet guests here,' Whisper called out and so we followed the warriors, unable to disagree. They dragged us behind and we took a precarious, rubble filled path to the middle of the cave and I squinted as Mani's light was bright there.

I spotted Aldbert. I had missed him before, but perhaps he had been there all along, alone in the dark. He was standing near Gislin, looking down, but he was dressed like a lord in a fine tunic and well-made pants and held his hand beneath his cloak. Hild pushed forward and pointed out our positions around the trunk, and she had Hel's Delight on her hip.

We stood still for a moment, unsure what would follow. Whisper and Gislin were looking at us quietly, as if looking for a divine sign to start. Men were dragging the wide metal cauldron next to the trunk, and there was indeed wood inside, burning brightly, lighting the whole trunk. The cauldron was quite ominous, and I thought they'd burn the heart there, or anything they took out of Maino. Shadows danced on the floor and walls, and even the ceiling, and the high Svea still looked at us.

Finally, Maino spat with defiance and fear.

That was enough, apparently, to break the spell, because Whisper shrugged and walked to Maino. He grasped his meaty face, turned it left and right and smiled. 'Spirited. Good. Be like that as you die, son of Bero. This is a special day and you are a very special man. Woden's rage rushes in your veins, it does. The moon is full, spirits are awake, watching, the gods are talkative and so we shall learn great things today.'

I nodded and spoke ferociously. 'Kill him already.'

Gislin raised an eyebrow. 'You have accepted your lot, then? And that your blood-relative will be sacrificed?' He nodded at Maino.

'I wonder what,' I chuckled, 'would you have done had Hughnot killed him in the battle? You have no other blood from our family living here, do you?'

'We would have taken his heart from his dead body,' Gislin said with a vicious smile. 'The dead are no different from the living. But we are lucky and he is fresh and yes, it is more appropriate. And there are high men, of high blood, even if not of yours here, men who failed,' he said and glanced at Aldbert. 'Gods would have welcomed his blood, no doubt.' Maino was shaking his head softly, eyeing the evil looking trunk where thick rope loops would hold him high up, his arms stretched to the sides, his legs dangling, ready for his evil fate. Judging by the darker wood at the bottom of the trunk, there had been bloody and violent deaths there before. Many of them.

'I'll not—' Maino began but the large warrior pushed him and he went silent, eyeing me with bloodshot eyes. He would not stand for such treatment for much longer.

'So, let's hang him up,' Hild said. 'Gods await.'

Gislin snapped his fingers. 'Strip his shirt and gag him, make him fly.'

Whisper took a step forward, the Svea grasped Maino, and he finally fought, but to no avail. A pack of Svear ripped into his clothing, and Maino howled, as a leather gag was pulled over his mouth. I heard sibilant prayers fill the cavern as Maino was dragged and raised on the trunk. Men were standing on ladders as he was lifted, and not even his savage strength helped, when the enemy overwhelmed him like ants would a carcass. He was wheezing in terror as they untied him for a moment, but only long enough for them to force his hand past the leather loops, which they tightened deftly. He was finally left to hang painfully from the trunk and the warriors retreated. Whisper, the vitka who was used to offering sacrifices took a hesitant step forward, sweat running in rivulets down his painted face, streaking the skin. He was praying, begging to gods and Hild was chanting with him. 'Take the son of Bero to you, Lok, Sleeping God, the Imprisoned One, let us feast, bless us with your wisdom, Dark Sleeper, the great god of the night and tricks. Give us direction and send a spirit to guide us in our eternal quest. Tell us, Lok, tell us Sigyn, his wife, if Maroboodus is the one to release you, one day?' He approached Maino, who moaned in horror as the ax was raised.

Maino's eyes sought me out, pools of terror. I grunted, disgusted by the plan I had devised. Sparing Maino's life was as desirable as dipping my cock in an anthill. I stepped before Whisper, nontheless. 'I should do it.'

He looked like he had snapped out of a trance, batting his eyes like an owl chased out of its hole during the daytime. He swayed; having let himself swim deep to the nightmare of murder and slowly, very slowly he pulled himself out of it. Aldbert blanched as he looked at me, and fidgeted. 'You?' Whisper asked. 'Why you?'

'I'm the beast, *the Bear*,' I growled. 'I'll eat his damned meat. But a man doesn't eat what he hasn't killed. And more, I hate him. I swore in Woden's name I'd kill him one day. You are robbing me of my vengeance. Give me this, at least.'

'I'm much more a beast than you are,' Whisper said, but the ax in his hand grew lax. 'I know how. And you don't.'

I snorted. 'How? It's butchery. I've killed men this past week. Many men. It's easy. I'll just open him up from his throat to his belly and then you can do your divinations,' I stated. 'I'll carve his damned heart out.' They stood there, ten strong, and all turned to look at Gislin. He hesitated. All he had to do was to refuse. I spoke, pouring all my malice into the words. 'I hate him.'

'Let him,' Gislin said after time, tiredly. 'Doesn't matter who does it. Hild?'

'Lord?'

'Cut his bonds. And then hold a knife on his shoulder. If he turns to fight us, cut a tendon. The Bear will roar without an arm.' The lord's eyes glinted and I cursed, as the madwoman approached. She stepped before me, considering the ropes around my wrists, and then pulled my sword and cut them. She nodded and Whisper stepped forward.

'Do it,' he said huskily. 'Here.' He handed me the ax. The warriors stared at me carefully, their hands on their weapons, and the spears and the hooks were turned my way. I grasped the weapon, and Hild stepped behind me, very close, and the blade was on my shoulder, cutting the skin. She put a hand around me and stroked my belly nearly lovingly, ran her fingers inside my pants and chuckled as her hands touched me where she should not go, and I cursed the mad bitch, while I shuddered with disgust. I squirmed from her, though she followed, holding on to my belt, as I stepped forward for Maino. I lifted my eyes to my enemy, saw the pain and terror there and swallowed away the bile of fear at the terrible situation.

A knife rested on my shoulder. The men around us were tense.

I raised the weapon. It was a good weapon, sharp, sturdy, and my only ally.

I swung it. The sword moved away for a moment to allow for me to strike.

Instead of finishing the strike and opening up Maino's chest, I slammed my elbow on Hild's already ugly face. She fell back with a shriek, the knife clattering across the stone. I turned and kicked the cauldron over and the burning bits of wood scattered over the floor. Shadows sprung up as much of the light fled and I swung my ax at Maino's bonds.

It struck true. One leather bond was severed and the man hung from one arm, his toes touching the ground. 'Do it! The other one! Hurry, you bastard!'

I heard screams and yells, and a spear flew past me, and I heard Eadwine bellow a challenge behind us.

I saw Hild from the corner of my eye, up on her feet, coming for me with Hel's Delight, her snarling, bloodied face intent on killing me. Men approached, Gislin amongst them, his face twisted with surprise and anger, trying to stop her. I could not deal with them, not if I had to release Maino. And without him, we'd die. *Woden, let them trip*, I begged.

I turned my back, and hacked at the other binding.

It snapped, drawing some blood from Maino's wrist. He fell from the trunk onto his knees and I gritted my teeth, waiting to be stabbed mortally.

It was no Woden who intervened, but Aldbert. He saved me. Or rather, Saxa and Aldbert did.

Saxa's axe, the one I had given her flashed in the semi-dark as Aldbert charged the völva. He was surprisingly fast, put all his strength into the swing and Hild's skull cracked sickly as she sprawled on the floor behind me. Aldbert's face twisted with disgust and then agony, as the shadow of Gislin pushed him aside brutally, steel dagger flashing. Aldbert screamed, wounded in the back, and I turned and attacked the Svea lord. His fox-face helmet fell from his head as he stumbled away, his eyes huge with fear, but I cared not for his fear as I swung the ax, and hit the mass of his body before me.

The weapon bit deep, chopped through his arm, slammed into his chest and he fell on his back, screaming, and blood was flying from his nose. There was a huge wound across his chest.

The shadows around me were cursing and moving with confusion. There was a shriek as someone fell, another as a Svea stabbed a spear at a man that I took to be Eadwine, who was yelling with pain as he struggled with many of the enemy. I saw Whisper's face in the moonlight, not far. 'Take him alive! Kill the others!'

I laughed spitefully and rushed him.

The ax came down, split a Svea shield that had appeared out of the dark to save Whisper and then some men tackled me. Whisper was dancing behind them, praying to his gods. I managed to whip the ax into a man's foot, and it was neatly split in half, bone showing. Then two men sat on my chest, one struck me with a fist and I swooned from pain.

'Get up, you damn weakling,' a familiar voice growled and one of the Svea made a choking sound as he disappeared into the embrace of a huge man and that man was Maino, who slammed his fist in the Svea's throat. Eadwine appeared, bleeding from many wounds, panting, and kicked the other one in the head, and I was freed. I heard there was a fight somewhere close, where Svearna had apparently started to fight each other in the dark. Whisper retreated to the deeper shadows, skittering up the hill.

I got up, gave the ax to Maino, grabbed Hel's Delight, and then the Svea chief who had fetched us stumbled to us. His eyes enlarged with surprise at seeing us armed but to his credit his ax came down fast. Eadwine grasped him in mid-swing and they fell to the floor, rolling in the dark, grunting. Shouts could be heard where there was a doorway higher up, and more men carrying torches came in. I looked at Maino, who nodded, and went like an avenging spirit to the dark to help Eadwine. 'Here,' Maino shouted and a shriek was heard, and he came back with Eadwine, the enemy chief dead.

'Hope he was a high one,' the champion said with pain, and held a spear and a shield. 'Good luck to kill a warlord.'

'Good luck to have killed Gislin,' I said and kicked the twitching corpse and spat on Hild. 'And that bitch. We have to move.' I witnessed Whisper running up a small incline for the doorway where the newly arrived Svea were, and nodded that way. 'We go through that door. Or not at all. Now's your chance to show what you are made of, cousin.'

'What of him?' Eadwine slurred and pointed his spear at Aldbert, who was gasping on the floor.

268

I gazed at his glistening eyes. 'We'll fight first. He deserves to be saved from this filthy hole of Lok.' I moved forward with Eadwine, but Maino did not follow. I turned to look at him and his resentful eyes burned as he stood over Aldbert.

'He betrayed us, didn't he? He gave us the wrong hall. So many died because of that bit or treason. So I'll worry about him now,' he laughed and swung the ax.

'No!' I screamed, but I was far too late and the ax entered Aldbert's belly. My friend made a squealing noise and I stared at him in stupefied shock. Whisper shrieked above as if he had seen the deed.

'Take them! Take Maroboodus alive! They have to pay, and they shall!' he yelled, dancing on top of the stairway. 'Gislin is dead!'

The warriors, eight to ten, bellowed, wide and fur-clad, and turned to charge down towards us, to the dark shadows, their torches burning lazily. They probably didn't see well, only shadows. Maino went past me; laughing like an evil spirit set free, and Eadwine hesitated, and went after him.

I kneeled next to Aldbert, swallowed my rage, and looked down at my former friend, who was twisting in pain. His guts were spilling from the wound, entwined on his tunic, and he looked like a mother holding a baby as he tried to keep his belly in. It was a death that was coming slowly, and so I lifted Hel's Delight. He nodded for the ax by Hild. 'Saxa gave it to me. She had hidden it. Sister, imagine that. Told me to hide it as well. Said I could finally do some good, and—'

'I am sorry. I didn't mean for this,' I whispered and he seemed to nod again.

'We failed each other,' he said weakly. He grasped my hand. 'The twigs, the skull, the hull. Next, a girl and a choice,' he grimaced. 'Choose wisely,' he added, biting back a scream of pain, and so I prayed to Woden as I pushed the blade into his chest and he fell silent.

I turned to look up the incline.

There, Whisper was holding his head, half out of his mind, his eyes pools of madness. He went to his knees. I hesitated and wondered what that meant, and then I looked at Aldbert, and wondered if the gods thought my friend was a fitting sacrifice, and the damned bastard had had a vision, a sight?

If he had, he wasn't running, and that was too bad for him.

I ran up the shadowed, near dark path, behind murderous Maino and Eadwine, and we would hack our way through the Svea. Shadows shot up before us, and I saw Eadwine roar, slam his shield forward, toppling a Svea, stabbing down at the writhing mass. A boy-sized Svea stumbled into Maino's path and howled as my cousin slapped him down so hard bones cracked. He was in his rage now, careless, brave, and mad, and despite the burning hate for him, I knew he might get us through the enemy. I pressed next to him, Eadwine ran after us, as we all roared out defiance at the Svea. They lined their shields across the path, unsure where we were, the spears rested on the shield rims, clubs and daggers and axes were hefted, but Maino didn't care. This is why I had left him alive, and despite the fact it had cost Aldbert his life, Maino's rage saw us through the battle. He roared and slapped spears aside, growled away a club strike and then he was in the midst of the enemy. His ax split a tall, older Svea. He rolled and came up lightning fast, laying about him. Chunks of meat and bits of shields and broken spears flew. Men tried to spear him, but he moved like a drunken wraith, never still, dreadful, and threw his enemies around like a wounded boar. He growled away a slash on his forearm, another on his leg, but his ax slammed down, opened a face, and then beat a neck open, leaving a Svea on his knees, gasping with terror. Another crawled to the darkness, and Eadwine speared him.

And I fought as well. I wanted to get to Whisper.

A chief, clean-shaven and thick-boned attacked me with a younger man that looked like his son. He probably was too. They came at me, spears slashing forward and with luck they went under my armpit and shoulder, as they got in each other's way. I pushed the sword down, and the younger man's side opened up. I grasped the shield of the older, horrified man and pulled him towards me, hoping to kill him easily, but he let go of the shield and grappled me. He had a dagger in his hand as we rolled and I raked my hands across his eyes as fast as I could and butted his mouth so hard his lips bled and his eyes rolled in his head. He didn't move. I felt blood all over my face as I got up from the comatose man, and spotted Whisper, still on his knees, not far. The vitka was clutching his face, moaning and I charged up, dodged a confused Svea, whom I pushed down where Eadwine killed him and got to Whisper. He looked up at me, horrified as I kicked him onto his back.

Eadwine appeared on the other side. 'Don't kill him!' I screamed.

'Why not?' Maino, covered in gore demanded. 'I want him dead. He won't boast of having Maino of Marka stripped on a pole, will he?' He grabbed the little man and I put a sword to Maino's throat. 'What are you—' he began.

'You shit,' I growled. 'We *need* him!' I turned to Whisper. '*You* are getting us out of here.'

'They will never let you leave,' he said with a wistful, tearful smile. 'You killed Aldbert—'

'I didn't! I didn't want his life,' I hissed as I looked at Maino's mocking eyes. 'But it is done, and now I will go after Saxa and you will help me.'

Whisper smiled. 'His death, I felt it. I had a vision. Lok spoke, boy, in his slumber, whispered and dreamed,' he said and looked on in terror as Maino finally dropped him, stalked to the side, and broke the neck of the last enemy in sight, a wounded man trying to crawl away. 'You are the one, indeed. The Bear. But it will be the Raven who will serve our god most, perhaps. The raven! Yes. You will push the Raven into madness and beyond. This escape? It is as it should be. We didn't fail. If you get away, if you survive long enough in your life, you will serve Lok well.'

'Who is Raven?' I asked him, scowling.

'Your son,' he smiled. 'A bastard like you.'

'Will I be proud of him?' I asked. 'Will I have him with Saxa? Will I—'

He cackled. 'With Saxa? I'll not tell you. But know that you will hate him. He will hate you. He might die. I saw he would be in mortal danger many times in his life. You might die as well. But all is possible. Our god might be released. You will see. Our kin in the south will help—'

'I'll stay here in the north, Whisper,' I told him with a growl, 'and I shall spit in your mouth if you don't stop talking about it. I'll rape Lok with this sword if he shows up, now or later. Get up. We shall leave.'

'Why ask him?' Maino yelled and grasped him. 'We'll just take him.' He was right, of course, and then he threw the vitka across the floor, kicked him so hard Whisper yelped like a dog, and we gathered shields and weapons. I took one of the strange hooked spears, and the others were ready as well. 'We go out, and we don't give an inch,' Eadwine said grimly. 'There will be many men there. Better to die fighting than get locked back in here and tied to the log. We are more seasoned warriors than they are. We might make it.'

'Indeed,' Maino hissed, still totally under his berserker's spell. 'I'll never go back that way. Never. And I will not forget what you did—'

I pushed him and he stared at me mulishly with red eyes. 'Nor I what you did. But now we have a long way home. And a war to fight.'

'Hrolf and the twins,' Eadwine growled. 'Ingo and Ingulf. For Danr and the others. As long as they live, Maino, we shall not touch Maroboodus.'

'As long as he holds Saxa, your fight is mine,' I hissed.

'So be it,' Eadwine said and stared at Maino, who slowly recovered some bit of his senses from the fogs of Woden's rage.

'So be it,' he said hollowly and grabbed Whisper. 'Shall we see our way out?'

The tunnel was short and we stumbled forward, carefully looking at each nook. Outside, there was silence.

They were there, nonetheless.

We stepped into the moonlight, and dozens of Svearna of Gislin's dark clan stiffened and banged their shields together. Many wore chain mail, the apparent champions of the village, and one wore Maino's, another Eadwine's and yet another Danr's. We grasped Whisper before us and Maino growled in his ear, as we eyed the multitude of the enemies before us. 'Tell them to put their weapons down,' Maino hissed. 'Now.'

'I'll do no such thing, fool,' he answered. 'None of it matters. It's in the hands of the gods. You'll see.'

'You are going to die—'

'Of course I will,' he said, smiling with bloodied gums. 'There are others in the family to take this burden. I care not for it. And I shall see you die, perhaps, son of Bero, before I go.'

Maino grunted, looked at the determined, savage, fur-clad band and casually snapped Whisper's neck. 'You won't,' he spat. Whisper's body fell to the mud before us and the Svearna murmured with rage. The shieldwall came closer, and I glanced back to the tunnel. 'We must hold it. The tunnel.'

'They have routes in,' Eadwine said. 'They will just overwhelm us or smoke us out. I think we should just die well, then.'

'I won't die here,' I shouted.

'He did say,' Maino told me with mad relish, 'that you *might* die after all, despite all the fucking prophecies. We'll go together.'

Whisper had said that. He also thought I would escape that night. And he was right.

Perhaps Lok guided allies to us as Saxa's brother arrived.

A mass of men ran in the dark. Spears glittered, shields made a hollow noise as they struck each other. There were sixty men with Agin, all angry, all swift as shadows of the night. The men on the Snowlake's shieldwall grew alert, stared around uncertainly, looked behind them and saw the mass of men charging for their backs. We stared in stupefaction as javelins flew, arrows whistled and cudgels and axes fell on men's backs.

The men in the shieldwall broke and ran.

There were thirty men of Snowlake, all sturdy warriors, but they ran for their lives, the better armed ones pointing at the tunnels beyond us and so they sought safety over us. 'Back off!' I yelled, and we fled to the tight corridor. The Svearna were thick, dark and hulking beasts as they pushed after us. They carried heavy spears, thick shields and were the best warriors in the strange clan, and we might have died fast.

Eadwine did.

He fought in the middle of us. He held his spear low, and the first enemy warrior rushed at us, thrusting with his seax but he missed the low-held spear and rushed into it, impaling himself. He made a meowing, pained sound as his brothers pushed past him and we managed to block their mass with our shields. They were pushing and hacking at us, we beat them back, but Eadwine was too slow to let go of his spear and a club caught him in the face. He fell forward and before we could stop them, one of the huge, hairy champions stomped on his back so hard his neck broke, and he died a brave, but pained death.

We backed off slowly. We fought and hacked and struck with our weapons as hard as we could, punching at the relentless enemy. Our shields thrummed with hits as fingers tried to pry them out of our grasps. Maino slashed the cheek open of one champion; I killed a lesser man that tried to sneak by us and lost my spear in his throat. I pulled my sword, and with desperation born out of fear of death I hammered the weapon on the wounded champion trying to kill Maino. He howled, his cheek flapping open as he fell away, but such heroics did little as we were finally pushed through the tunnel into the cavern, where we would die from the sides.

They didn't care to kill us.

The enemy clawed past us, cursing, some fled to the darkness and the tardy ones fell under stabs and thrusts of spears. The men of Wolf Hole appeared. We stared at Agin, the huge man who scowled at us. 'Where is Saxa?' he asked darkly. 'Is she alive? Speak, Maroboodus!'

I took a step forward and clasped his shoulder. 'She is being taken away with Hughnot. She will marry another,' I told him. 'Hughnot is working with the Boat-Lord. Always was.'

'She is not here?' he said in astonishment. 'Hughnot is allied to my father?'

'He is, he visited here in secret last spring. And Saxa. I told you, she is gone. She—'

'They have nearly two hundred men,' Agin said. 'But I shall sacrifice every man of mine to regain her.'

'I'll help,' I said.

'Of course you will. You are her husband. We will all go. And so will he.' He nodded at Maino, who said nothing, while stripping a champion of his precious chain mail.

I grabbed the body of a man I had killed, a wealthy champion with Danr's mail and pulled him to me. I also began to peel off his chain mail. 'We have some men to kill,' I whispered.

Agin was looking around. 'Where is my father? And Hild. I want her ugly head.'

'They are dead,' I stated coldly. 'Gone to their Lok.'

Agin made sure it was true. I went to fetch Saxa's ax and we left Snowlake burning. I kissed Saxa's ring as we ran, and begged gods give her back to me.

CHAPTER 17

To mirror our desperation, the weather was taking a turn for the worse. We were running through whipping wind, being pummeled by icy rain and everyone, including the hardy Svear, many of whom had wounds, was shivering uncontrollably as they jogged on. Some fell behind, and gods knew I would have loved to just lie down beside a mossy boulder and sleep. To make up for the men we started to lose, Agin was receiving reinforcements, but there were no more than some eighty men with us.

Agin was staring ahead as I jogged next to him, and he spoke of the battle in Wolf Hole. 'The Goth, dog-humping bastard of Bero brought his men to us from two sides.' He looked at me with respect. 'Your Saxons did a good job with some of them, though. We found their victims all the way to Gunnvör's village, where we learnt Hild never went there.'

'Have you seen them?' I asked, worried for the few that were left.

He smiled. 'Boy, they probably went home. They paid their debt, right? Anyway, Bero surprised several families, even clans running to my banner that morning, but they also slowed Bero down. In the end we fought shield to shield, but they broke us and we fled. They killed forty men and took many women and burned the village. Luckily enough half took after you and we managed to pull out.' He looked down at me. 'You killed my father?'

'I killed him,' I said, puffing along, hot and shivering, wondering if he was bothered by the fact.

'It was his time,' he said steadily. 'Too bad I wasn't there to do it. He sent Saxa to our enemy.'

We passed a village that had been emptied, some halls burning after the passing of the Goths. Apparently we were on the right track. 'Do you have any idea where Hughnot's army is?'

'Ahead? Someone will,' Agin said, squinting at the wooded hills. 'I've sent word to my chiefs and my people know how to track. But we'll look by the Long-Lake. Hughnot had a lot of men. Some will have come over with boats and they'll have to leave with boats anyway. Hughnot's Spear Hall cannot be reached by walking across water. They'll go out by boat.'

'They had many boats in Marka,' I panted. 'Let's hope they didn't land too near your lands, but have to march across land some.'

Agin nodded to the hills ahead. 'We run past Wolf Hole, cross the Three Forks, and start looking for them along the coast, and hope they haven't left already.' He didn't sound hopeful.

Of course they would have left, as fast as possible.

He went on, speaking tiredly, knowing it was likely so. 'Be that as it may, I have scouts running up and down the hills, looking for signs. We are not sure of anything, but we will find out.'

'And if they get back to Hughnot's lands? Reach his damned Spear Hall?' I asked. 'Shall we go over the Long-Lake?'

'Then,' Agin said sadly, 'we will die trying to get her back and yes, we'll go after them.'

'Damned madness,' Maino spat behind us. 'I'll not go there after her. I'll find my father.'

A Svea pushed him and Maino nearly fell, and was left behind, where he was pushed back to the column. 'Brainless Goth,' Agin grumbled. 'I can see why you left your kin. That bit of fatty gristle would make anyone lose joy in life.'

'We are not friends, and I rue the fact we are related,' I said, and looked back at Maino, killer of Aldbert. I had restrained myself from attacking him after Agin's rescue, and I was not sure why I had, but I was starting to regret that restraint.

Agin spat and coughed as we ran, having read my mind. 'You did well not to. He will be useful, won't he, if we meet his father?'

'Exactly,' I answered and nearly fell on a patch of mud.

'What happened to my father?' Maino asked from behind as he regained our lead. 'Did he—'

'Tried to gather his men,' Agin spat. 'We hurt them enough to slow them down and when you, boy, led half his men and nearly all his champions to chase after Maroboodus here, I think you might have forgotten his orders. He was left behind. If Hughnot missed him, he is alive still. If not, you can blame yourself for his death.'

'I—'

'You left him for your revenge,' Agin laughed. 'We'll find him, dead or alive, but Hughnot first.' He looked hard at Maino. 'And you shall *not* go and find him on your own.'

Maino clutched his ax, but relaxed his grip, knowing better than to challenge Agin there.

We surged through thick woods, and navigated the land, led by skilled Svea who knew the mosquito-plagued hills and valleys as well as their own halls. We could see the Long-Lake, then Wolf Hole, but there was no sign of life there. We kept going, crossed the Three Forks after hours of running, and we made good time after that, wet and cold.

Then, finally, a sweaty, leaf-covered Svea ran to Agin.

He was muddy, scratched, and out of breath and the column jogged slowly forward, as the man spoke to Agin, while trying to catch his breath. Finally, Agin clapped his back and went quiet, thinking hard.

'What did he tell you? Where do we go?' I asked him miserably. 'We cannot run for much longer.'

'No, we cannot, but we must,' he said and squinted up to the hills again, as if expecting Donor to race across they sky in his flaming chariot, and provide us with answers, but he spoke, half to himself. 'I hope they camped for the night.'

'What do you mean?' I asked. 'Did you find them?'

He pointed his spear at a hazy string of hills on the horizon, by the lake. There was smoke rising from it. 'That there is called the Dragon's Tail. It's a series of hills that squirms around a lush valley full of blueberry bushes and there are holy woods there, dedicated to Freya. The man said there are many boats on the shore by it, a dozen at least, and something strange is happening around one of the lesser hills. He said there was a small battle.

Now there are smoke pillars rising, and the man said he thinks they are camping.'

'How can he be sure they are camping?' I asked. 'You think Saxa is there?'

He grunted. 'Smoke. There are no halls that can be burnt. That means they are camping, no?'

I felt relief, then elation, and finally so impatient I wanted to pass Agin and rush there headlong, but the column kept running at a sustainable pace and Agin slapped a hand on my chest as I tried to take the lead, and I brooded as we went on. 'We must rush!'

'We'll go. In a bit we'll exhaust ourselves. This is excellent, hopeful news,' he grumbled happily. 'This means we will have a chance, at least a chance. Gods sometimes drop men some small, sad morsels from their table, and now we'll thank them and go,' Agin said grimly. 'We will be there, tired as dogs in the summer heat, half-starved, outnumbered by two to one, but we will be there.'

We ran, and found Hughnot.

And we also found Bero.

CHAPTER 18

Sunna was hanging low in the sky, giving no warmth after a dreadful night. The rays of the divine thing were blood-red through a hazy net of thin clouds, and there were some bright lights in the sky, twinkling coldly. We had lost men during the night. Some had been too hurt to go on, others had gotten lost, others deserted, but we still had seventy men and just before we reached the Dragon's Tail, we found a tall, gaunt man barring the way, rising from a patch of blueberries. He wore the furs of Svearna, and with him there were fifteen men. Agin stopped, and leaned on his knees, gasping and gagging, shaking on his feet, and the troop fell left and right, groaning, cursing softly, the stragglers arriving far behind in ones and twos. I was one of them and cursed profusely at the chain mail I had liberated. It had been a horrible struggle to hold on to it during the night. I fell behind Agin, and vomited next to him, though my belly was mostly empty.

'That the Goth?' asked the newcomer Svea, staring down at me. 'Looks weak as a newborn.'

'That's him, Fox,' Agin said weakly. 'Husband to Saxa.'

'Trust her to find a man that unsuitable,' the warrior snorted, and I entertained a vision of him hanging from a tree. 'Looks like something I voided after a terrible hangover.'

'I don't seem much better,' Agin complained. 'Give him a damned break. This,' Agin said with difficulty and nodded at the man, 'is Fox. He is one of my warlords and apparently knows how to think on his own, as he is here. You have been following the Goths?'

'You sent word. I spread men around and yes, we found lots of Goths,' he said, still looking at me with disgust. 'There is—'

'Tell me,' I gagged and struggled to my feet as I interrupted Fox. 'Is Saxa out there?'

He shrugged, sucking in his breath. 'Saxa? There are some women with them. As for her? She might be. I don't know. Can't be sure. I know none has left since they arrived. There are nearly twenty Goth boats on the shore by the hill, and they could have rowed out yesterday, but they decided to stay, and not one boat has been rowed out.' Fox was smiling ferociously. 'Why, you ask? Because they are besieging a fool. It was that bastard Goth that attacked our village, Crow Bero. This lot was heading for the boats, and Bero was caught napping near Wolf Hole. They fought a skirmish back there,' he nodded to the west, 'and were chased off. The huge band of bandits took Bero's boats in Wolf Hole, a great many of their boats joined them in there, and here they finally cut off Bero's retreat. They had chased him by the Lake, and through the woods and Bero could not run anymore. He has some fifty quivering Goths on the middle hill and the Lord below him, I think Hughnot, is a happy man. We saw him dance when Bero was surrounded. It looks like the Goths aim to kill each other. Who would have guessed? I know they have feuds amongst themselves, but—'

'Hughnot has nearly two hundred men, though?' Agin interrupted, scratching his chest. 'Why hasn't he just attacked and killed him?'

Fox looked genuinely astonished. 'Why? Do I look like a Goth lord, privy to their councils? Do I sit there and give them advice while they serve me mead? No, they do not, and I do not,' Fox said forlornly. 'That shit-rooting Bero is negotiating with the turd Hughnot, in case you wish to know why they haven't killed each other yet, but I don't know what they are blathering about.'

'My father would not negotiate with him,' Maino said through gritted teeth, his face red from both the rigors of the run and the accusation. 'Never! Not if his life depended on it. He is—'

'A damned coward,' I concluded and ignored the red-faced fool. 'An indecisive bastard.'

Fox scratched his chin. 'Well, lots of Goth adelings in the woods today. Bero's son? Looks confused, doesn't he? As for negotiation? He is a dead man if he doesn't. He is croaking and begging. His life depends on the mercy of Hughnot, and he is negotiating. Lost his nerve. Your father, eh?'

Fox spat. 'I don't know what they are talking about, but it's not likely the harvest.'

'We have to find out more,' I insisted. 'Any way for us to get a prisoner?'

Fox looked at me blankly. 'A prisoner? I doubt a simple Goth commoner would know anything more than I know, and I told you I'm no seer. The guards don't know what they talk about up there, nor will they ever. They'd just gossip like girls.'

'Are they all on this side of the hill?' Agin asked, looking at the streams of smoke rising from below the hill.

Fox shook his head. 'No, no, of course not! Bero would walk out, and it wouldn't be called a trap, if it only had one wall, eh? I know there is a standard of a raven's wings on this side, but there is another on the other side of the hill, where Bero is hunkered down. They have them well-surrounded, a near hundred on the west and east side, a dozen to scout the sides, but the raven standard on the east side was taken up the hill yesterday, and perhaps it will go up this morning. There, at the camp over the hill, there is a great young noble bastard who seems to do the talking for the hunters, and he doesn't look like the sort of a negotiator who discusses terms, but tells them to surrender or die. Blond, broad chin, the man has. Sword, chainmail. He rides up in, arrogant as a king.'

'Hrolf,' I stated, and Maino frowned. 'Hrolf commands the east camp. Hughnot the west one, and the old bastard guards the boats as well. Probably Saxa. He will not go far from the boats and keeps Saxa near as well.'

I sat down, and Agin looked at me shrewdly. 'What are you wondering about? You had a look like this old man Gunther when he tried to dye old fox skins and sell them off as the very best quality, though he was always roaring drunk and got caught every time.'

I shook my head and looked at the lake that was glittering in the morning light. The waves were lapping on the muddy banks, and I could smell the burned timber. 'Well, I know why they are negotiating.'

'Blurt it out, you damned bastard of a dog-lord,' Maino yelled. 'My father is in danger!'

'I'd piss on him if I could,' I told him cheerfully. 'But what part does Hughnot have in Boat-Lord's plans? He'll be going back to the old man on the island, but they needed you, the Svea and Saxa for alliance.'

'To kill your family,' Agin said. 'To conquer lands in the south.'

'Yes,' I said. 'The Boat-Lord and Gislin both wanted our land. But Whisper knew a lot about our family, spoke with Hughnot last year. The Boat-Lord's greed aside, he wants something Grandfather, Friednot stole from him. Something they took away from the islands.'

Even Maino understood. 'The sword. The Head Taker.'

'And the ring,' I said darkly. 'Both are on that hill there.' I thumbed that way. 'The Boat-Lord hates our family for leaving Gothonia, but more for taking the family heirlooms with them. Hughnot wanted to wrest them from Bero's cold hand; they wanted to make sure they could, with the Svea. With the turmoil I caused and Bero here without most of his men, he can. He was lucky, and found Ber, floundering around like a wingless duck.'

Maino blushed. 'You had better watch out, Maroboodus, how you speak of my—'

'You watch out, you simpleton,' I said, and we both clutched our weapons. Agin slapped both.

He spoke after we let go of the weapon hilts. 'That's right. He got Saxa, but more, he found a chance at victory here in the woods. Hughnot is about to get all he desires soon, an alliance with the Svea for glory and lands later, and now even the items he hardly dared to hope would be so easy to—'

'Gislin is dead, though. Many of the men in Snowlake as well. There is no leader in the west for a long time, probably. Saxa is worthless as a hostage, perhaps,' I said and regretted it because I realized she was in grave danger. Maino's eyes glittered with malice.

'True,' Agin breathed. 'If he touches her, I'll touch him. And he won't enjoy it. But for now, he doesn't know Gislin is dead, and let's keep it that way for the time being.'

Maino stared at me blankly and shook his head. 'Draupnir's Spawn. He wants My father's ring. The sword. But why negotiate? Why not just take them? What's stopping him, eh? Just march up the hill, slit their bellies, get it over with? I'd—'

I shrugged. 'The ring, at least, can easily get lost in the battle, no? Bero might threaten to destroy it if his terms are not met. If he has any terms. He's probably witless with fear. But in theory, all Bero has to do is to bury it, or toss it away.'

Maino spat at my words, and I read such bloodlust and a wish for revenge in his eyes, I knew we'd soon be enemies again. 'Now we have to figure out how to make the best of this messy situation.'

Agin opened his mouth. Fox as well, but both went quiet, brooding. Maino pressed his hands on his head, thinking, and I wished Saxa were there because she'd come up with an idea.

We stood there, silent, and wondered and soon the Sunna was higher, the fog was dissipating around us in the woods, men were crouching, eyeing us, and finally Maino pushed me.

'We need to get up there and help him,' he growled. 'We cannot let him face all of them alone. It's as simple as that. We all go up there and then we'll fight.'

'Like you helped Aldbert?' I whispered in my frustration but shook my head. 'He doesn't have the balls to fight them,' I told him. 'And his ego won't let anyone else lead. He is the ring carrier, no? He holds the Head Taker. How would we help him, if he were already resigned to giving up? Why else didn't he try to leave the hill in the dark? He should have gone last night, taking losses, but running and escaping with what he could have salvaged. No, he stayed because he is listless with worry and about to cave in. We go in there; he might just sell us out to sweeten the deal.'

Maino opened his mouth to refute the claim but shut it so hard his teeth made a chomping noise. 'Perhaps,' he allowed after a time. 'But the fact is he needs me. He'll listen to me. We could sneak past and add our men to his after I speak with him.'

'No,' Agin said tiredly. 'Our men on the top will not help. We are barely a match for one camp. We have to surprise them. Surprise them so that they'll not recover. We cannot fight fairly. We have to attack them together, at the same time, from front and back. But Bero won't help, will he? It won't matter if you speak with him, boy.'

'He is helpless, like a limp cock,' I said, perversely enjoying the look on Maino's face. 'His champions are dead, he has no advice, few heroes left.' I rubbed my face.

Agin sighed and nodded at Maino. 'Do you have a better plan, though? Get him there, I say. Make a plan if Maino leads them.'

'Finally words of sense,' Maino said with hope. 'Yes.'

'He might lead them if Bero cannot,' Agin said. 'The men up there must be enraged at Bero's cowardice. Come, let's agree on a plan. How do we—'

'How well is their camp guarded?' I asked Fox while looking at Maino. How I enjoyed the look of hope on his beefy face, his hands shaking with eagerness.

'It's a small bit of hill there,' Fox said and pointed a dirty finger on a hazy, wooded elevation at the middle of the Dragon's Tail. Dragon's Tail was a series of humps, with lower valleys in between the humps. 'They have men north and south as well, but only guards. Hughnot's is in a field below the hill, on this side, and they guard the boats, as I said. There are tracks that take them quickly to the shore of the Long-Lake, a dozen men guard the boats, and the tracks up the hill are very well guarded,' Fox said carefully. 'But I can get a few men anywhere.'

'Fine. We'll go there, up the hill. I'll find a way and an opportunity,' I said. 'Surely Hughnot's men are also tired, having run in the woods for days. They won't be at their best. I'll be fine.'

Agin raised his eyebrows. 'You two go? No, let Maino go alone and we wait for word. Fox will go with him, in fact, and will wait below the hill. What guarantees do you have Bero won't slit your gullet and leave you wallowing in the dirt? That's why they came here after all. Quite a risk.'

'It is,' I said and stretched, groaning. I wiped some lingering bits of vomit from my beard. Then I pulled my sword and put it to Maino's throat. He moved uncertainly, his face gray. 'But Maino won't go.'

'What—'

'Shut up, Maino. Fox and I shall go up the hill. He'll show me where the guards are, and I will go all the way. You will stay with Agin here. That way Bero won't disagree with me, or grow too timid when I suggest we fight Hughnot rather than run away or surrender. He loves his lovely little boy, doesn't he?'

'You would dare?' Maino asked his face white, and I saw the rage in his eyes. He surged up and met Agin's fist and fell like a limp sack of wheat.

'Wanted to do that,' Agin muttered and pointed a finger at some men. 'Tie him up like a roast leg of goat.' They grabbed him and did a thorough job. 'How will this help with Saxa?'

'Risky,' I murmured as the birds started singing around us. It would be. It would be terribly dangerous. 'It will have to be well-timed. I have an idea. Just like Maino's plight will force Bero to fight for us, we will need something to keep Saxa alive when we attack. She might die if we just simply charge them. She won't be far from Hughnot and he is no fool. He'll have her skewered before we get anywhere near rescuing her unless my idea works.'

Agin rubbed his face. 'So, how is battle going to help her?'

'We need to have something Hughnot values,' I told him. 'Something he loves enough to stay his hand from slaying her, something he cannot do without.'

'His cock?' Fox said with a frown. 'What would he value enough?' Fox asked. 'You Goths mystify me.'

'Did you say Hrolf is the one going up there to negotiate?' I asked Fox.

'Yes, why?' he asked, confused.

Agin blinked. 'You wish to—'

'Yes,' I said. 'We'll attack Hughnot together. You from behind, and we'll come down the hill. Hughnot will see Hrolf is a prisoner. We'll fight; he'll let the spears decide, and Saxa is safe until the battle is decided. If she dies, Hrolf dies. Hughnot will not risk it. He has no other son.'

Fox spat, finally understanding. 'You fucking Goths. All shit. He is a negotiator. He cannot be touched.'

I spat. 'I don't give a damn. I'll touch him.'

Agin was rubbing his forehead. 'It's your fame and honor. Fine. We will fight then, and you will go now?'

'We will fight,' I said simply. 'We will go to them, fight like the wild spirits of Svartalfheim, and we must win. If we lose, I'll leave Hrolf alive. Perhaps Saxa will survive, then, as well. But we must win.'

Agin nodded. 'We'll make our way there. We'll be ready.'

'You'll see us coming down the hill,' I told him. 'Fight well for Saxa.'

'If you die up there,' Agin said, preparing his exhausted men for one more battle, 'I'll send Maino after you.'

I smiled wickedly. 'Thank you.

CHAPTER 19

We crept through the thicket, and I lost my way more than once, until Fox set me on the right path, cursing under his breath. The ground was surprisingly dry until we approached the edge of the hillside, and soon our tunics and pants were completely wet. We passed patrols of Goths, crawled quietly as mice, sneaked around the hill where Bero was holed up and made our way to the large, eastern camp where Hrolf held sway. Finally, we were close, and I stopped when Fox pelted me with a pinecone. I turned to look at him and saw he was squatting under some thick branches. He waved at me and pointed at silhouettes of men nearby, carrying wood. We froze, and saw they were Goths. I had totally missed them, but then, I nearly always did. They went away with their firewood, and Fox crawled to me. 'They have near hundred men there, just beyond sight and more are nearby. It's a small clearing. They patrol the hill's edge, but this is Hrolf's camp, right over there. We don't have to see it. They won't offer us breakfast anyway.' He nodded towards an opening in the trees, shadowed by high ferns. The drone of voices could be heard, then the whinnying of a horse. 'The main camp is over the hill as I said. But it's here or nowhere. We'll wait until Hrolf goes up? If he goes up again,' Fox said.

He would, I thought, hoped, and prayed for. I squinted up the hill, saw shrubs, ferns, and heather fields under thick pines. There, surprisingly, I saw a Goth leaning on his spear, looking down, his eyes following the men who were carrying wood. Beyond him men walked, eyeing down the wooded hill lazily.

'They seem at ease,' I said. 'As if they're going to a feast.'

'Your Bero's probably ready to give up,' Fox growled. 'No loss of face for the men, only the leader and they get to go home. Maybe.'

'When is he going up? Hrolf?'

288

He banged his head on pine. 'Again you ask me something I cannot possibly know or guess. How in Hel's name would I know that? Do I call the Goth dog-humper a friend? Do I toast him in the feast, and does he come to me with his troubles? No, I am here, and you are sitting in rabbit shit,' he told me, and I cursed profusely as I noticed he was right. He nodded towards the camp. 'He was up there last evening, and he will go up there this morning if the gods are kind to us. We wait. There,' he said and pointed at a trail that led up the hill, not all that far. 'That's where he came down. I saw him, riding under his standard. Perhaps you should try to sneak near there now?'

'There are a dozen men up there,' I said. 'They will see me.'

'I—' the Fox began, but went quiet, as there was a loud yell near. There was a drone of voices and a horse neighed again.

'Perhaps he is going up now. When he does, that will flush out all the men on the hill,' I said. 'A bit closer, then we wait.' We inched through some berry bushes, hoping not to crack any dry wood. Fox followed very close to me, and we slithered forward, sure there would be Hrolf's guard with a spear standing over us in a bit. There were none. Perhaps they were all tired of the campaign, or perhaps, indeed, Bero had indicated willingness to surrender. Slowly we got closer to the camp of Hrolf, and I got some glimpses of his men. There were men lounging, laying about, fixing spears and drinking, a starving-looking bunch, but Hrolf was there; I twitched with hate as I saw him.

The arrogant adeling of the traitors was mounting.

He had three hulking Goths with him, their long beards were dirty and riddled with brambles, but Hrolf himself looked as savage as always. He led his men forward, apparently to meet with Bero on top of the hill, once more. He rode, his ominous crow wing banner bobbling up and down as a lanky young man carried it after him on the uneven terrain. They headed for the small trail up the hill, and as I had hoped, all the guards walked up to greet him. Fox and I both saw them, coming out of the bushes. Their brooding eyes followed the adeling of the Black Goths, hoping for a glimpse of him, to catch a sign of favor from him. There was something, I thought, about his arrogant smile. There was a smug sense of victory in the man's face, the superior, thin smile of a conqueror. It was almost a glow around him. I nodded at Fox. 'Right. I am going in.'

'Good luck, Lord, and try not to piss your pants,' he said.

'I'm lord of this sword,' I said and patted Hel's Delight. 'Nothing more. But I will bring Saxa back, and perhaps I'll merit such a title when I do,' I told him.

'I'll go and tell them to get ready?' Fox asked with a smile and gave me a frightening, foxlike grin and shook his head forlornly. 'All this. For a girl?'

'For love. For Saxa. And for all our futures,' I told him and pushed up.

'Let it be so, Lord,' Fox called after me. 'The gods will help us if your heart is right.' I hesitated at that, cursed him under my breath and sneaked on.

If my heart is right? What is that? Should I not want power for my family? Are meekness and obedience a pair of virtues above all others? I cursed Fox's words. The Bear or not, I was in a just cause, and also in love, and I would rule, and rule well.

The guards were still moving out of the shadows to salute Hrolf, who steadfastly ignored them, eyeing the higher part of the hill where Bero waited. His party followed him, and I sneaked from one shadow to another, flitting in and out of the dark places, hoping not to get caught. I felt constricting fear as I neared one guard, who was eating something near inedible and tough, eyeing the adeling. I saw Hrolf was riding faster and knew I'd have to hurry. I gave myself to Woden's care and brazenly walked past the guard, praying to gods he would ignore me. I felt him turning, heard him move with surprise, but I also heard he was still eating. So I kept walking. No alarms were shouted. Nobody charged after me. The guard probably thought my chain mail and sword and natural manner marked me as someone important and more importantly, someone who belonged there.

I kept walking up the hill while Hrolf was riding up arrogantly, his shield a red spot of color amidst the leaves and branches, his standard high in the air behind him. I stopped halfway up the hill and eyed the lord's progress. Bero's Goths began to appear in droves. One pointed a spear

Hrolf's way and the standard-bearer called out his lord's name, so it echoed in the woods. 'Hrolf the Ax! Hrolf the Ax is here! Fetch your leaders!' he yelled. Men, some Bero's high nobles, and Friednot's old warriors walked down and greeted the enemy champion and adeling. Up there, I saw Osgar, Friednot's old champion twirl around, probably going to fetch Bero. I sneaked on, staying quiet, pushing blueberry bushes out of my way and finally saw the flatter top of the hill, where many fires burned; Bero's war party was eating what they had left. I walked past some men, and kept my face down, joining the growing party that walked around Hrolf, curious to see the exchange between Bero and him.

Then, there was Bero's guard up ahead, and the Lord of the Bear Goths got up, tying his pants. He had been sitting in a thicket, voiding himself. He looked sickly, probably worried out of his mind and when he walked to meet Hrolf, I nearly felt sorry for him. Hrolf's party stopped, the men who followed him did as well, and we who followed him stood uneasily to see what would take place.

Bero gazed up at Hrolf, and his and father's plans had all but dissipated into thin air. There would be no Bear Goths. Bero would never rule. It could be read in Bero's nervous face. Hrolf was higher than Bero, both because he sat on a horse, and because there was no strength left in the man before him. Finally, Hrolf waved his hand around the multitude. 'You agree? Or do not agree? We have no time to ponder the matter longer. These are hostile lands, the Svea will want us gone, and gods grow impatient. Give us what we want, the items which we would have taken from you later anyway, or refuse, and we come and take them today.'

'The men were eating,' Bero said. 'We have not decided—'

Hrolf snorted. 'Eating? God damned fools. What are your men eating? Bark and thistles?'

Bero was eyeing our relative with deep hostility and resentment, but he said nothing. He was tilted to the side, as usual, and apparently felt sick at the horrible situation. I noticed many former men of Friednot's were unhappy, ready to support whatever Hughnot and Hrolf suggested.

'Some humility, boy,' Osgar growled, and that lifted Bero's spirits a bit.

291

'Come down from the horse, friend,' Bero finally called. 'I would not speak to you as a slave to a master.'

Hrolf snorted and leaned down to address the Lord like he would a child. 'In your home, which was Friednot's hall, actually, did you speak to me as equal? As you remember, Father asked you to serve me. You refused, spat and acted as if you had been insulted. Nay. I'll just sit here, and you can look up at me until your neck snaps, as I ask your surrender, one more time. I gave you this ultimatum yesterday, and you said you needed just a bit more time. Now that time has been spent, and still you fidget. Will you submit? Or will you not? You will not leave this hill unless we have your word, your ring, your sword, and maybe your head as well, if you will not make up your mind.'

'I—'

Hrolf spat at Bero's feet, making all the men around twitch with indignation. 'You will give me an oath on your knee, lord Bero, that you shall support me. And what we discussed goes to Hughnot. That sword,' he nodded at the Head Taker on Bero's hip, 'and the ring. Right now. With them, the Boat-Lord will be happy. With Saxa, the Svea will join us. Nothing will stop us from gaining all these lands for ourselves, and more. It's time to stop this divide and for the stronger branch of the family to finally rule the weaker. You'll live, and know your place. Below the Boat-Lord, below Hughnot. And below me.'

Bero fingered the thick golden band with flowers and animals carved on the surface as if trying to weigh its worth against his life. He looked around and attempted to catch the eyes of his men, who seemed unable to support or advise their Lord. Osgar wanted to, I saw it, opening his mouth and gesturing for Hrolf, but he didn't as Bero looked away. They were beaten men, their spirits crushed. It was a sad state of affairs for such a strong and powerful tribe, and they wanted to find face-saving ways out of it. Bero spoke. 'Maino.'

'I told you,' Hrolf said tiredly. 'He survived. He'll be home when things are to our liking.'

Liar, I thought. Hrolf's men had beaten Maino and then left him for dead, or Gislin's sacrifice. All they wanted was the ring and the sword. I had a hunch Bero's funeral had been planned already, no matter what he decided.

Bero's face betrayed his relief, though, and he hoped to see Maino again. 'On my knee?'

The men around me whispered, again angered by the humiliation demanded by Hrolf, and some growled because of Bero's meekness. They muttered, and scowled, and it was not lost on Hrolf, who spat and gazed over the men imperiously. 'Yea. On his knee. It is how families rise and fall, men. The lords live if they are humble and meek and serve, or they conquer by the strength of arms. He has no strength in him, not without Hulderic, so he will have to be humble and servile.' He scowled at Bero. 'On your knee. Then, later, when we have taken the Svea girl and your treasure to our relative, the Boat-Lord, you will come with us. You will attend my wedding to Saxa of Svearna, and you shall govern when I make war all along the coasts. You will deal with trade, and bow your head. We shall all live in Gothonia once again, grow into a Suebi nation of strong arms, and our ancient family will be one again. One knee on turf is worth this, no?'

'It is a painful thing to do,' Bero said, his eyes moist. Gods, I hated the turd.

'Maino will return to you, one day,' Hrolf said smugly. 'He was left alive. Painful or not, you will forget it when you see your lost son.'

There was a soft thrumming of a spear on a shield as some men supported Hrolf's words. Bero stammered and asked one more thing. 'And Hulderic?'

Hrolf shrugged. 'Hulderic's son is also a prisoner with the Svea. Maroboodus shall not survive that ordeal, or perhaps he shall? One day the woman-stealing dog might be freed as well, and perhaps Hulderic will be happy with that? Perhaps you shall both serve the family and us again. But Maino, my lord, will suffer if you make life hard for us. And do remember we can just simply push up this hill. And then your head will be brought to Hughnot, who shall make a cup out of it.'

'You may try, boy,' Bero said weakly, the suffering man pushed to show some defiance. 'But it will be a hard climb.'

'But one,' Hrolf said quietly and clenched his fist, 'we will finish. We'll have an orgy on the hill,' he laughed. 'And the crows will have one when we are done. Gods won't save you; the vaettir won't aid you. Your champions are nearly all dead.' He looked at Osgar spitefully, but Osgar only grinned back at him, his back straight.

Bero staggered forward, fighting with nausea, and went to one knee, then another before Hrolf, whose face lit up with a bastard's joy. I had wanted to see Bero do that. I wanted men to witness it. If we survived, he'd been shamed forever. And to survive, I had to act.

'They aren't all dead, snake-face,' I said darkly from the group of men. They all parted from around me, eyes full of wonder. 'Not all the champions of the Bear Goths are dead. Osgar is there. And I live.'

Hrolf turned slowly to look at me. His sharp, savage features froze with a look of utter shock as he spied me. 'You,' he said and nearly fell from his horse, breathing the names of the gods, thinking he saw a dead one walking, a draugr out for vengeance.

'No, Hrolf, do not shit your saddle. I'm alive,' I said and walked forward, holding my sword. 'I'm just fine, in fact.' I looked at Bero, who scrambled to stand up. 'Your moose-brained son is with me.'

Bero's face brightened for just a moment and then he blushed from the indignity I had just witnessed. 'Maino? Where exactly is he? The others?'

I stared at the fool. I wanted to blame him for all our trouble, heard a voice in my head, one that whispered I was also to blame, but I ignored the voice. Hughnot would have betrayed us in any case, but had Father led? We would not be on the fucking hill kneeling to Hrolf. 'Danr and Eadwine are dead. Gasto is fish-food,' I said bitterly. 'I killed Gasto,' I said, and the men around me rumbled, some angrily, others in awe. 'I killed his dogs before him. He,' I said with a threatening hiss as I pointed a finger at Hrolf, 'killed your Danr. Eadwine died when we escaped. But Maino? He thrives. Gods do not want turds in their halls, and so I have him.' I looked at the men, and my face broke with anger and sorrow. 'The rest of the men with Maino died. They murdered them when they tried to surrender.' I lied, of course, but the men believed that lie quickly enough. The warriors around us began to shout. They had relatives, sons, brothers, uncles who were dead by treachery, and they all eyed Hrolf murderously. They didn't look as beaten as they had before.

'All dead?' Bero asked, and was left swallowing. 'While surrendering?'

'Of course they are dead,' Hrolf yelled, his eyes betraying fear as the mob around him clutched their weapons with white knuckles. 'That is so. Yea, they are all gone. And they weren't surrendering! Maroboodus lies! They fought like men. And died like men!'

'Shut your mouth, you corpse-faced coward,' I told him and he grasped his sword. Hrolf sat there, silent, and pondering what I was doing there. His eyes went downhill, and then over the lake, his animal-like cunning working on a plan on how to survive.

Bero took a tentative step forward. 'I will want to see him. Maino.'

'Maino,' I said thickly, 'serves a higher purpose for now. He is, alas, held.'

'You hold him?' Bero yelled so hard the forest echoed, and his voice carried across the lake. 'You damned whelp! Tell me what you wish with him!'

I kicked dust his direction, and his face went blank with indignation. I pointed the sword at him. 'I want something with you. You quivered like a grandfather when Hrolf said he held Maino. Now you shout? Trust me, I'll be no less merciless to the bastard if you don't calm down. Maino is with my friends. He is alive. And he waits for you.'

Bero slumped down to the tree stump, his face gray as ash. 'Me?'

Hrolf spat. 'He wants to make a man out of you, threatening to kill your boy if you don't fight us. He dares not kill Maino. Who shall you choose, Bero? Join a vagabond of no worth, or the Black Goths? The latter is the easier road; I tell you. And if he will kill Maino,' Hrolf said while looking at me spitefully, 'you can sire new sons.'

I cursed Hrolf. 'Spoken like a true bastard. This is what you would ally with? I don't pity Maino, Uncle; I hate him. But I'll spare the one-eared shit if I must.'

Hrolf opened his mouth and laughed cruelly. 'For the girl?' he asked slyly. 'You'd spare your enemy for a girl?'

'For her, for us all. For my wife,' I said. *For me, as well*, I thought.

Hrolf had a gleeful glint in his eye, and was about to say something hurtful, something terrible to stab me mortally, but thought better of it and spoke to Bero at length. 'Maino or no Maino, you are strapped like a cow to a post. We have over two hundred men around this hill. And it will end badly for the lot of you. I'll ride down, I'll send word to Father and we'll kill you, and Maino as well.'

I looked at Bero, who was licking his dry lips. He rubbed his face tiredly. His eyes sought mine, hoping I might have an answer. I had one. I prayed to the gods, walked forward and pushed past his men to stand next to Hrolf, who looked down at me disdainfully. I pointed the sword at Hrolf while speaking to Bero. 'He'll take the ring, the sword, and the only reason they haven't done so already is because they fear you might throw the ring away before they put their tiny, greedy claws into it. No, Bero, you must fight.'

'We cannot win!' he yelled.

Hrolf snorted and looked down, enjoying the strife. 'No, you cannot.'

I took a deep breath and steeled myself.

I pulled the sword back, saw Hrolf's eyes widen, and then I moved. I stabbed at the young standard-bearer. The blade went to his chest, the man gurgled and fell with an astonished face, and he gave a sad, child-like wail as he lay there, sprawling on the fallen crow-wings. Hrolf pulled at a sword; the men around us stepped forward in horror and I stabbed at the horse Hrolf was sitting on. The beast whinnied, reared, Hrolf fell from it and screamed as his horse rolled on him. I jumped on the thing and put the sword on the man's throat, but I had spears surrounding me now and Bero was pushing men aside, his face a thing of terror.

'You … you are damned! The vitka shall judge you, Maroboodus!' he screamed.

I laughed. 'Did I fear your vitka when I defied you in Marka? No.'

Osgar, former champion of Friednot's, grabbed Bero and tried to reason with me. 'Do not kill him. If you do you will be skull-nailed to an oak and left for the spirits to feast on!'

'I'll skull-hump Hrolf before you make a move,' I growled at the men around me, all hesitant, some apparently hoping to try to pry me off the shivering horse and Hrolf. Hrolf's two remaining men were near, holding their spears, contemplating attacking me, and so I emphasized my words by placing the sword tip just under Hrolf's eye.

Bero was wringing his fingers. 'You attacked my guest! You have brought doom to us!'

'Doomed you all,' I said with a grin. 'Or saved you. They would have killed you the moment you gave them that ring and sword. Can't you see that?'

'Damned right we'll kill you lot,' Hrolf yelled, pained and shamed as he stared up the sword-blade his father had once given me. 'We will if you won't gut him now! Do that, and all is forgiven!'

They moved. I saw it in their fearful eyes, and I pushed the sword into Hrolf's skin under the eye. He howled and yelped, and they froze. I looked at the lot of them. 'Hear me now,' I said, terrified I'd fail, but I did have their attention. 'There is only one way for this to end if you take his deal. The Black Goths will rule, you will lick their shitty shoes, or you shall die anyway here on this hill. They will have the ring, and our families will fall. They will purge us. They will fear the vengeance of sullen, bitter men and they will slaughter you all later, if not today. Instead, we have brave men here. And they are divided. Their camps are split. And we have him.' I nodded at Hrolf.

'He is an emissary!' Bero yelled, and ripped at his dark beard. 'You cursed us all in the eyes of the gods. We are all going to be fed to the dogs of Helheim.'

'Let us fill their bellies first with Hughnot's men. I have warriors down there,' I told them and that piqued their interest. 'They are Svearna, who love Saxa and wish to see her free. They are ready, down below. We will take this bag of shit down there. We will strike at Hughnot. We will do it fast, and we will do it from two directions. It will be an even fight as those bastards are holed up on too many sides of the hill, won't it? We will go down there,' I said and nodded for the small clearing where Hughnot was camped, 'and then we'll butcher them. We'll dance on their yellow guts.'

'You—' Hrolf began, but I twitched, and the sword moved, and he gulped down his next words. I smiled maliciously as ants were crawling on him. 'We take him and his fucking standard and surprise them.'

'That is hardly honorable,' Osgar said from the crowd, but I was beyond caring.

'It will be as honorable as the poets will make it sound. And when Hughnot is swinging from a branch, you will feel much better about your honor,' I told the multitude. 'Be brave, and be like a fox now, and only in the battle think like a bear.'

Bero looked at me with resignation. 'You give me the same options as Hrolf did. Maino's life is at stake.'

'Except I have the bag of shit under my blade. He doesn't,' I told him. 'And there is more at stake here than that ugly liar. It's our tribe. Let's surprise the enemy.'

They all looked down, feeling shame. None wanted to take the blame before the eyes of the gods for the actions I suggested, even if most saw the plan had possibilities. They all waited for Bero.

'You damn me, Maroboodus,' he whispered. 'Hulderic was right. You are dangerous. The Bear, though I never believed in the curse. You are a dark blot on our honor.'

'Where is Hulderic?' I asked him.

'He refused to help capture you. He rode away that night we found you missing. He was wise.' Bero took a breath and looked me in the eye. 'Very well, dark blot. We shall go down together, then.'

I pulled the sword from Hrolf's eye. 'Ready the men. I'll lead us down.' I pointed at the two men of Hrolf's. 'Tie them up. And beg the gods we will succeed. Now we have hope.'

CHAPTER 20

The crow banner was bobbling as the fifty men slinked down the path for the west. I kept my eyes on the men leading Hrolf on Bero's horse, which was nearly the same color as the warlord's dead one. Hrolf had been bound, his legs were tied under the horse, his mouth gagged and a man was walking on each side, holding a spear to his back. Osgar, the last champion of Friednot was walking near, wounded to his belly in some earlier fight, but holding himself erect as he walked, grinning to himself. 'You seem to be the only cheerful soul in this pack of vermin,' I murmured as we stepped across some wet mossy boulders.

'Oh, yes, Lord Maroboodus,' he said sarcastically. 'I mind not smiling. It is better to fight than to bend a knee. Your honor is gone, but at least we will go fighting. Lord Bero,' he said, eyeing the gaunt man walking nearby, 'would have dishonored us as much as you did.'

'I think Woden,' I said mirthfully, swallowing fear as I saw our scouts slinking ahead down the hill, 'would approve of a few twists. I'm merely stirring a wonderful stew, Osgar, not willing to give every advantage to a superior enemy. Woden is a tricky god, is he not? Has he not taken disguises, like a Jotun, and fooled his foes with lies?'

'Gods have their own game, Maroboodus. And the children are expected to obey the rules,' Osgar said like a student of the gods, his eyes wide as he contemplated the strange ways of the Aesir and the Vanir. 'He lied, by the way.'

'Who? Hrolf?'

'Bero, when he said your father refused to join your hunt. He wanted to, but Bero wanted to capture you on his own. He distrusted Hulderic and sent Hulderic away. He rode away like a damned man.'

I eyed the gaunt Lord darkly. 'I hate him. I always wanted Father to lead, but Hulderic is gutless as well.'

'He is not,' Osgar said reproachfully. 'He is obedient and humble. Unlike you. I don't like Bero either, Maroboodus, and I know what men often say of him. Many would have liked to see your father lead. Hulderic is the best of us.' He looked like he was ashamed. 'I serve Bero now, he took my oaths, but there it is. I wanted to give them to someone else.'

I looked at some ferns below and saw the scouts wave at each other. There were five, and they were holding bows and javelins and had probably spotted the enemy. 'Let them be lax,' I whispered.

'They will be,' Osgar said with a bloodthirsty voice. 'They have no reason to think Bero would fight. And the standard,' he added and looked up to the fine crow-wing pole, 'will confuse the shit out of them.'

And so it did. We marched on and soon three Goths approached, wearing furs and smudged tunics for having been lying low in some berry bushes. They waved at us, and I waved back, pointing at Bero's standard that was behind the troop and held my hands up jubilantly. I heard Hrolf squeak, but then he went quiet as spears prodded his rear. The Goths came forth, confused. 'Lord Bero,' I yelled at them, 'has surrendered! Hail Hrolf the Ax!'

And they did. They cheered, which I cursed, as it would be heard in the main camp below, but they didn't cheer for long, as when they got near, javelins flew. The scouts acted, Hughnot's men looked shocked, two fell silently, and one let out a piercing wail, but only until two of our men clobbered him brutally in the face and head. He fell silent, a feast for the night animals.

We walked on, past the dead.

'Pray to gods,' Osgar said reverently as he kicked one corpse he was stepping over, 'that the rest will go down easily as well.'

'Pray other guards didn't see that,' I whispered.

'Too much praying,' Osgar added. I looked down, and behind the pines, I saw flashes of movement. I did pray one more time, and for Agin to be ready.

We marched on, down the slope, the men tense, even if they had been instructed to look like a relaxed, humbled party of men, instead of a troop readying to form a cunus, a boar's tusk bristling with spears, trying to kill the men down there.

There were warning yells downhill.

They had spotted massive movement. Perhaps they had heard the cheers? And the man dying?

Our scouts were waving at the men getting up in Hughnot's camp, pretending to be their guards. Dozens of men were moving down there, some wiping their hands after eating a meal, others drunk on mead, some probably looted from Svea settlements. They clambered towards us, cheering Hrolf's brave standard, though some looked thoughtful. I noticed the terrible twins Ingulf and Ingo. There would be well over a hundred men down there.

Then I saw Hughnot.

The old warlord exited a large skin-tent, and was soon walking forward, head cocked as he buckled on his sword. His war standard was being carried behind him, almost similar to Hrolf's, if taller. There was an odd silence, and while most of the Black Goths smiled and nodded at our procession happily, Hughnot was hesitant, Ingo was fidgeting, holding his shield's rim tautly in his hand, and Ingulf, he was walking briskly for Hughnot, dragging out his two-handed ax.

They would spot Hrolf's gag in a second. I eyed Bero. He was praying, his mouth moving as he tried to gather courage. Hughnot turned to Ingulf. Ingo was pointing at Hrolf.

'Cunus!' I roared, and Hughnot's eyes widened in shock. Men pulled Hrolf out of the saddle and dragged him back as agreed and the rest of us?

We charged in a thick mass, spears bristling, shields overlapping.

The hesitant men turned into vengeful hammers, bent on breaking their enemy. Many were brave only thanks to ale and mead. We gave ourselves to Woden, roaring our defiance at the Black Goths, our one-time allies, and men who were even family tied to many of us. The common blood did not matter then, but the feuds that grew from the battle they later called the Dragon's Tears would carry on far into the future. Our fifty men charged, we tightened the block of men as we went, Bero's largest warriors taking the point and then javelins flew down at the enemy as many men on the sides stopped to throw them, the best hunters. Black Goths howled in surprise and pain, and Ingulf was shrieking orders. The Black Goths reacted, some too slowly, but many running to cover the Lord with their shields, as spears and javelins rained down at Hughnot. Men fell, bearded faces twisted in agony, and I could barely register what was happening as the dense mass rolled over some of the enemies. Beyond them there was an incomplete wall of shields in place, the leathers painted with wondrous beasts, stars, and symbols. Nervous grimaces and looks of hate flashed over the rims, then javelins fell amongst us, even stones, and some men fell in our ranks.

We all collided in a battle to make Woden and Freya weep.

The terror of the mad charge and the shieldwall after.

To fight for your life in such a tight place, with panting, desperate men before and behind you and dying men flailing at your feet? You remember little of it but the fear and the confusion. Our thick cunus hit the middle of the thin, barely formed enemy line, bowled over a dozen men into ruin, shattering their shields and I could see Hughnot's eyes widen with horror. It could have ended right there, right then.

But for the champions.

Ingo and Ingulf stopped us, and heroics were what such men were all about, anyway. Few heroes live to see old age, and the ones who did were often sad cripples. The two terrible men of Hughnot's rushed in and met us. Bero's men had pushed through the first of the enemy, crushing and stabbing Black Goths, and then met the champions, who were covered by shields on all sides as desperate men streamed from the sides to save their lord. I saw Ingo's ax go up, heard his roar and saw the weapon come down and split a skull. It went up again with gore flying high, and he killed another.

Ingulf's attack was worse. The two-handed weapon cut a man in half, and that gruesome sight nearly halted the attack, and at least bought the enemy time to form.

The champions were pushed back to a new shieldwall, men fell in both ranks, and there the momentum of our charge ran out. Men were panting, clutching weapons, pushing, getting pushed back and our cunus flattened on those steady shields. It flattened bloodily as our men fell to prepared spears and we formed into a shieldwall to match theirs.

Agin. Where was he?

There was only silence in the woods beyond the battle and the tents.

I was in the second rank, nearly fell as men crashed into my back, everyone clawing to find a place in the wall, and the enemy wall was building at the same time. For a moment, I couldn't breathe as I flattened into the man in front of me. The enemy faces were so close I could smell their breaths over the shoulder of the man before me. Ingulf was nearby, his huge ax coming down again with a crash. Splinters of a shield flew high into the air, a man screamed. I struggled to raise my spear on top of the shoulder of the man before me, who was panting as his shield pushed at the shield of the foe. I managed it, despite the press of bodies and so did others around us. The spears stabbed, many without great force, but some punctured enemy faces and throats and so did mine. A man disappeared, another took his place. The next enemy was struggling mightily with his shield, and did not see the spear coming as I pushed it in again. His eyes went round with terror as I reached forward and the blade went into his mouth. He gargled a bloody scream and fell back to the mud, and the man behind him stumbled on him and fell as a spear flew from the side to hit him in the chest. I could hear little, and I was not sure how long we kept stabbing at each other like this. Out attack had surprised them, certainly, and dozens of men had died for the fact. Their shieldwall was still incomplete, broken in places, thick in others, but Ingo and Ingulf held the line while Hughnot screamed for men to rush around our sides. They had the men to do it. And perhaps Hrolf's men were coming over the hill, alerted by something?

'Where,' Bero roared somewhere near, 'are the Svearna?'

I turned to answer and curse him, and then disaster struck.

Ingulf attacked in a frenzy, having heard Bero's question. He was cursing, wounded in the face, but seemingly indomitable. He pushed at the shields in front of him and shrugged off hits from axes and clubs. He held his huge ax one-handed and then jumped on the shieldwall. He was muttering, spitting, barking like a dog, and the already dulled ax spun left, it spun right, and meat and blood flew high in the air as his vengeful wrath felled the best men of Bero.

Then he fixed an animal's eye on Bero himself.

Ingo joined his brother, his massive shield covering the maniac's back as the terrible twins ripped through a shieldwall. I saw Bero's face, holding his shield with trembling hands as his men tightened around him. It was a mask of naked horror. He was shaking like a leaf. On the sides, there was a battle tightening around our edges, men getting pushed, so we were about to be surrounded, and our men began to lose hope.

I cursed Agin, I cursed Fox, and prayed they would still appear.

You could nearly feel it, smell it, amidst the blood and shit and vomit. The defeat. It was there, almost readable in the very air around us. First, we had nearly won, almost grasped victory. Then, in the next moment, the gods took it away.

I cursed and pulled myself towards Bero. Ingulf would be there, very soon, ready to slay the Lord, and no matter how gutless Bero was, he was fighting now, fighting well, and his death would ruin us. Bero's men were throwing rocks and spears at the champion, who took the hits stoically. His ax went up and split a shield in half. I clawed myself past warriors and reached Bero just as the enemy champions did. I cursed Osgar, who was nowhere to be seen and prayed, as Ingo's shield appeared before me, protecting his brother who was grabbing Bero's shield, growling away a spear in his shoulder. I dropped my spear, useless against the great shield, and pulled the sword and cursed as I dodged under the shield and saw Ingo's legs. He was shuffling forward, hacking with an ax at a man on Bero's right but he did not see me.

I stabbed the sword forward, and it went deep into his leg.

I felt flesh and leather resisting, and then I felt bone and tendon split on the blade, and he dropped down on me, and his shield's rim struck my neck. I screamed with pain, seeing black, but I also saw a man on his knees next to me and so I stabbed up at the mass, and Ingo fell on his side, his side bleeding, screaming his lungs out. Ingulf faltered, saw Ingo and then me and cried vengeance.

He went for me.

304

He moved like a vaettir of the night, and tried to kick me, but someone pushed him over his brother, and he fell amidst their troops. He was soon up, I was as well, and I slithered to his wounded twin. Ingulf surged forward, but too late and I stabbed the sword down at Ingo's throat, and the man didn't even gurgle. Perhaps he had died already, but that didn't matter to Ingulf. I spat at Ingo's face in my battle frenzy, hoping to taunt the foe into a horrible mistake and Ingulf went mad indeed. He charged and bowled me over. Bero and his men tried to kill him as I punched with the blade at the man's face. A fierce fight was being fought over us, and I saw Hughnot's angry face near, holding a spear. The weapon went forward, and Bero howled above me as I struggled to keep Ingulf's fingers off my throat.

It didn't matter, I thought. Only the way I died matters, I hoped. We were going to fail. Woden, spare Saxa, give her a good life, I prayed in my head. Half of our men had fallen, at least. Then Ingulf slapped me so hard I saw red and dark, and he pulled a dagger from his belt, hovering above me. I swatted his face weakly, he stabbed down and my mail saved me. The hit hurt like hot coals, my chest was bleeding, but the blade was thick and wide, and he didn't hit any vitals, though there would be a terrible wound.

He pulled his arm back. 'For Ingo. For him,' he panted.

Then, finally, Agin attacked.

He and his men charged from the harbor road, a line of bristling spears, and they struck fear in all of us with their guttural, animal-like, screams. They were bleeding, wounded men aplenty with them, and I knew they had met more Goths as they'd tried to move in. Ingulf looked that way, shocked, Hughnot's mouth fell open and then there was a general chaos as our enemy turned to face the new threat, which was a threat to us as well.

The Svearna were slaying Goths indiscriminately.

They bowled men over, felled a dozen, then ten more, and Ingulf rushed away, screaming orders. I slithered back, bleeding, and saw how Hughnot joined in shouting warnings to their men. Near me, Bero was being pulled back, wounded, as our men turned to create a thin wall against the wild Svearna and the Black Goths alike. I cursed, for everything was going to Helheim. I saw Agin pulling at his men, screaming at them with a red face, pointing his ax at Hughnot. Slowly, they obeyed and attacked Hughnot's men alone, giving us some time to breathe and so the battle churned around the tents. I was looking around desperately, and then I saw men dragging a struggling woman to Hughnot's standard.

'Saxa!' I screamed but lost sight of her as dust filled the air where Svearna and Black Goths fought savagely. 'Charge them! Now!' I screamed and then caught a sight of Hughnot in the dust, now holding Saxa in an iron grip. He was looking my way, grimacing. I pointed Hel's Delight to where Hrolf would be. 'Hughnot! Leave the girl alive and I'll spare your son!' I screamed.

His eyes flashed, and he hesitated, growled, and pushed Saxa to some of his men, and went to battle.

'Charge them! Now!' Bero screamed weakly, as they dragged him away. Bero's men hesitated. Most had broken weapons, many were wounded and shocked by the butchery, and I cursed them.

'Form a fucking battle line. A shieldwall!' I screamed. 'A shieldwall! No, charge! Kill Hughnot! We have to kill him! He is the key to the fight!' Some of the Black Goths were turning to look at us warily, but took the opportunity to press on to kill as many Svearna as they could while our side hesitated. Some Black Goths were blowing horns, and soon, no doubt, Hrolf's men would discover something was amiss. We had to hurry.

I gave myself to gods, rushed forward, bereft of a shieldwall, and thanks be to Woden, Bero's men followed and pushed for Hughnot. The enemy lord and many of his best men were at the edge of the raging battle with the Svearna, and I thought Hughnot was hoping to escape. The way to him was clear. Some of the Black Goths around Hughnot fell to Svearna, and I knew I might catch them. I'd kill Hughnot, save Saxa.

I surged forward.

Then a man pulled me around. 'Not now!' I screamed, pushing at him.

'Lord! Bero!' he yelled, and pointed at the man who had pulled the lord away from the battle, and it was Osgar.

Hrolf was with him, ungagged, unbound.

I staggered and realized many things at the same time. Osgar had worked for their side all along, and he had not lied about hating Bero, that he had wanted to give his oaths to another, though obviously not to my father as I had assumed. He had protected Friednot that fateful day and failed, probably on purpose. Perhaps he had made sure Hughnot found Bero in Wolf Hole as well. I'd never know, and I realized what Hrolf was doing.

Hrolf was pulling at Bero's finger, tearing at the ring. Osgar was guarding them, though our men were near now, pointing spears at them.

The ring came off. The enemy lord kicked Bero and pulled out the magnificent Head Taker and hissed at Osgar, who was nodding, backing off.

'What shall we do, Lord?' the man who had stopped me asked desperately as Hrolf left, Osgar in tow, running around the battle for the boats. I took running steps after them. The ring, the sword, and they must not get away, ever with the treasures. They were fast, I was tired, and so I stopped. Aldbert's lines drifted into my mind.

To choose between a woman and a noose? I chose a noose, the ring? Over the woman?

I turned to look behind.

Hughnot and Saxa were gone.

I roared my anger, standing there like a fool.

The boats. That's where they would all go. Saxa and the ring and the sword. All would go there.

'Break them and rush their boats!' I yelled, and turned my eyes away from Bero. I charged the scattering Black Goths; Bero's men after me and many of them struck the backs of the Black Goths, who fell between the Svearna and us. Blood flowed, chaos reigned, Hughnot was roaring somewhere beyond my sight, Ingulf was cursing, and many Black Goths hacked down the exhausted Svearna to escape from the trap. I forgot about my pains, exhaustion, and fears, and pushed forward, killing and wounding many men. There was no line now, only running men, a chaos where warriors fell indiscriminately.

I saw Agin.

The huge man had spotted Saxa. He was running in the chaos, far ahead of me. He had hammered down a man, and I saw Ingulf turning, and that's where Saxa would be. I prayed for my friend as I dodged through groups of fighting men, and as Agin's huge ax went up, I was sure Ingulf would die, wounded and obviously exhausted as he was, and Saxa would be safe, and all would be well.

It would have been, but for Hrolf.

The bastard appeared, and he barreled in and pushed at Agin and the two men rolled on the ground.

'Agin!' I screamed, trying to slay my way through the fleeing ranks, but I saw Agin crawling in dust, his eye bleeding, looking for his ax. He found it, toppled a Goth, and hammered the man's throat with the ax shaft, but then Hrolf appeared next to him, and I despaired as he held the Head Taker, and the weapon came down. The huge Svea shuddered; fell on his face, and Hrolf's savage laughter echoed through the ranks as he waved the bloodied, famed sword in the air.

The Svearna moaned.

They howled and despaired and some fought, but many retreated, their heart lost. I saw Fox being carried away, bleeding and delirious.

Suddenly, so suddenly, there was calm on the field.

The Svea were going, and we, the Bear Goths stood there, but a mere ten strong. The enemy was still far more numerous than us, and many turned from their flight to regard our ragged band.

I saw Hughnot pointing a sword at me, speaking to Hrolf. I saw Saxa beyond him, her face shining with love and fear as she tried to rip free of two Goths.

What would have happened? I don't know.

They had some forty men left, all shaken and many wounded, but many of their lords were alive. Osgar, Ingulf, grievously wounded that he was, Hughnot, Hrolf, all were there, pulling at their running men. They could have rallied, probably won the day, and we would have been wolf-feed, the lot of us forgotten.

But the gods threw their dice, and finally, the dice fell favorably for us.

Everyone stopped, as horns were blown up on the hill. An army emerged from there. Hughnot howled in triumph. He danced with glee.

And then his face fell.

It was a bloody army, recently fought, and they emerged from where we had marched down not too long ago. There was a standard, one I knew well. On top of that pole, there were rows of bear fangs. Hulderic had arrived with hundreds of our men. His warriors roared defiance at the sight of Hughnot, their voices echoing over the lake and across the hills and they rushed down and attacked.

The Black Goths ran.

We ran after them, hearing Hulderic roaring at his men to give chase. They took after the enemy with us, having routed Hrolf's camp and joined us and then, finally by the lake, pandemonium reigned. Goths killed Goths, men surrendered, some drowned in the lake, some fought on valiantly, but some escaped on one ship.

In that boat, Hrolf, Hughnot, and Ingulf were standing. A dozen men were pushing and pulling at the boat, some standing in the water and the boat was soon out of the shore, oars treading water. We tore into the guarding few oathsmen of Hughnot with vengeance and desperation. 'Saxa!' I screamed, and she heard me as she climbed to stand in the boat. Hughnot was pointing a finger at me, but Hrolf was shaking his head. He showed his father the ring and the sword. 'Saxa!' I screamed, desperate. Hrolf looked at me disdainfully.

I stood there and cursed and wept. Men were going silent around us as we stared at the departing enemy. There was victory, but it was a hollow and useless one, and everyone knew it. Saxa was leaning on the prow, held by Hrolf now.

I raised my sword at him. 'Come back here!' I said, without any power to make it so.

Hrolf laughed. 'We have her. We will have Gislin's Svea. We have the ring. The sword. You go home and wait. The end will come soon enough.'

Then I heard a cursed voice. Maino. He stood, his hands tied, not far from us. 'Gislin? Gislin is—'

'No!' I screamed.

'Dead! Your allegiance is useless!' he finished, and I felt the cold claws of doom rip at my guts. Hrolf's eyes sought his father's. Hughnot rubbed his face and spoke to Hrolf, and when the bastard turned to look at me, I knew what would happen.

Hrolf grinned at me like a baleful monster. 'Maroboodus. You killed my men, mocked me, and dishonored me. And now they say there is no Lord of the Svea to ally with? If that is so, then she is useless to us, indeed. I'll marry someone more worthy. We will finish you all without the Svea. Takes longer, but we will.'

'Gislin lives!' I yelled.

Maino was laughing. 'He died! Maroboodus killed him!'

Hrolf spat in the gray water of Long-Lake and picked up an anchor stone. Saxa didn't move. She didn't show fear. She raised her eyes to the sky as Hrolf tied a rope around her throat and I rushed to the water. I cursed him, spat in rage and then he pushed the stone overboard.

She was gone. There was barely a splash and she disappeared under the waves.

Hrolf spat after her. 'At least she had a real man before she met the gods!'

I heard nothing more. I went under as well, hoping for the water spirits to bring her to me, but all I felt were hands pulling me back. I was coughing water as Harmod pulled me out of the water, helped by Dubbe. But it was Ceadda who spoke, sitting next to me, holding my head on his lap. 'Easy, boy. It's done. Do not throw your life away.'

'I did everything for her. For the family!' I screamed. 'They took her away.'

'And we shall pay them back,' he said. Father was nearby, his blade bloodied, and he didn't argue with the Saxon as Hrolf's laughter drifted across the lake.

BOOK 5: Hogholm

'A fine joke, a grand jest! Is this your idea? Hughnot's?'
The Boat-Lord to Hrolf.

CHAPTER 21

Marka seemed half empty.

It was not silent, though. There was a steady drone of weeping from nearly every hall, brief howls of anguish as the wounded were tended to, and even the gods were weeping, since it was raining forlornly. Men of Timberscar and the southern villages had lost a few men, but Bero's warbands were decimated, and the lord himself was in his hall, wounded and feverish. I had spent hours looking for Maino, but he had gone into hiding. Ceadda had forced me to abandon my quest, though he had needed Njord to aid him. They had sat me down, held me there, listened to me sob, curse, and rage, all the while forcing mead down my throat, until I had willingly drank myself senseless. After that, I had slept for two days straight. I had not even woken up to having my wounds sewn.

Now I sat on the beach, looking at the islands, the wet cliffs, and dully wondered at the slowly gliding sea fog of that morning. There was a strange ethereal look to the sea, and it matched how I felt. The anger was there, lurking under a heavy blanket of denial and exhaustion.

Mainly, I blamed Maino. Of course I did. He was filth, had caused the deaths of Aldbert, and also Saxa. He had. He had known what he was doing. He had been the spear in the hands of death.

However, there were other such spears. I blamed the plotters and the weaklings, men of both brave and weak hearts. I basically blamed everyone, I realized and smiled bitterly as a gull swooped down to the sea and lifted a herring away, beating its wings furiously. Yes, I blamed Bero, and Osgar, cursed Hughnot and the damned Boat-Lord. I blamed Father as well.

But my anger was also fueled by self-loathing. Like the cursed lines of Aldbert had predicted, I had chosen between the noose, the Ring, and the girl. I had.

I had gone after my family treasure, even if for just a moment, and so given Hughnot time to slip away, and even if I had repented, turned around, it had been too late. Gods be cursed for their wicked games.

I blamed myself. Perhaps most of all. I shivered and hugged myself, trying to see a way forward. I needed something to think about, other than Saxa's face.

I took some stones in my hands, letting them roll on my palm, slipping between my fingers. I had wanted power, glory, like any man would. Instead, I had seen my wife die. I had seen Hrolf take the ring, gloat over the sword.

Hrolf.

Had he raped her? I placed my hands on my face and squeezed so hard I felt blood flow down my forehead from the stones still in my hands. Hrolf. Killing him. That was a worthy goal to live for. If only I could pick myself up and find the energy to try.

And then I heard steps, and dared not look up. Someone was standing there, and for some reason I expected Aldbert to speak, to say something awkward but comforting, but no, I had let him down as well and he'd never be there again. The bastard had been protecting me, I had distrusted him, but wasn't it his fault as well? If only he had told me the truth.

I had been a terrible friend, though.

Something metallic fell on the rubble-plagued beach, startling me from my wandering thoughts. It rattled and clanged dully for a moment and I saw it was Hel's Delight. It was glinting, its edges sharpened, kinks taken out of the blade and I looked up to see Njord there, frowning, not his usual carefree self. 'Will you pick it up?' he asked.

I didn't. To pick it up meant I had a purpose in my life. Revenge? Yes, that was a purpose, perhaps, but perhaps I *shouldn't* have one. I didn't deserve one. Who else would die if I got up with a sword, striding to kill another man? Father? The rest of us? I shook my head.

'Gods, really?' he breathed. He went to his haunches and joined me in the scrutiny of the sea. 'Like my girl, you are. She is three. Four, sorry. Perhaps five? Matters not. She sulks and mopes like you, especially when I have to leave. Fisila, my wife, says she stays that way for days, until she has to eat, eventually. Then she forgets me. When did you eat?'

I had no answer.

He went on. 'Not eaten. Perhaps all that mead we forced down your throat keeps you going. It was pretty fulfilling, I bet.' He smiled guiltily. 'I drank down the rest of if. There was a lot. And told your father it spilled.'

'What is Father doing?' I asked him dully.

I could almost sense his pleasure for having made me speak, and I felt I had betrayed my sorrow. 'Hulderic? Well, he is putting together a defense. He is calling all oathsmen from the gau, leaving south almost undefended, and there will be a thousand men here very late in the summer. He is gathering boats, sending out spies, taking stock of the supplies. He is doing what great men do when faced by war. You still outnumber the Black Goths. Yea, your champions are half dead, but war makes new ones, eh?'

'Hughnot will have the Boat-Lord,' I reminded him. 'His men will eventually overwhelm us, even without the Svea.'

He grunted. 'Yes. But when will they work together? Your old bastard of a relative probably heard of this loss of the Svea. Perhaps he fears treachery? He doesn't trust Hughnot. And he has probably heard how Hrolf took that golden loop and the sword. If they want an alliance, for the Boat-Lord to send his men over the sea, I bet they'll have to give him the ring and the sword back first, no? No alliance or forgiveness before that, is there? That's what I think and I'm a bastard and know how bastards think. Even Ceadda thinks I'm right and he usually doesn't.'

'Yes,' I agreed. 'They will have to give them over first. Probably so.'

We sat there and there was a sudden stiff wind blowing from the sea. The trees on the islands before the village were bending, their light-green leaves waving softly, living on, unheeding the misery of the humans, and I envied them. 'Take the sword,' Njord said.

'Why?' I whispered.

'I made a bet with Ceadda. I told him I could pull you from your misery, and I don't like losing to the morose bastard,' he chuckled. 'We bet a cow, the very best we have, and I want his cow come winter. I'll make a feast of it, and serve him the head. He'll eat and weep, won't he?'

I chuckled and shook my head tiredly. 'I cannot take the sword, even if I wanted to.'

'Why? You turned coward? Will you weep for your mistakes forever? Don't you deserve to live again? Oh! Wait!' he was batting his eyes, holding a hand on his chest like a surprised girl. 'You are afraid I'll die if you go back to war? Yes, you are afraid you are cursed and you might lose your precious Njord as well. I'm truly touched.'

I looked at him with anguish and anger, and opened my mouth to tell him he was a damned fool. For some reason, a hint of a smile made its way to my lips and I looked away swiftly as he grinned victoriously. I raised my hand to douse his joy. 'Father told me he'd have me skewered if I make any more trouble. They *all* hate me, you see. All of them. Even Dubbe. They say Bero tried to have me hung when he woke up yesterday. And the families of the dead will all heap accusations on my neck. They'll line up against me in the Thing, and Harmod mentioned they will spend days just to sort out who shall go first. Ludovicus's family, I hear, don't even want wergild. They want my skin. I mean exactly that. My *skin*. They say they will make a rug out of it for the dogs to sleep on.'

'Well,' Njord said languidly. 'I know how that is. We have several feuds with some of our neighbors.' Then he brightened. 'Though two died in the battle by the beach with Cuthbert. I didn't realize.' He shook his head and concentrated. He nudged me and I frowned at him and he was whispering like a girl to another during the feast. 'Hulderic is sending us home.'

'He is?' I asked. 'Why?'

'Well, considering we found him marching after Bero and Hughnot, and had seen how Bero was trapped on that shitty hill, he does owe us something.'

'I'm surprised he doesn't let you die to appease Bero,' I spat. 'I bet he's still keen on licking his brother's hairy, weak balls.'

'He isn't as happy with Bero as he used to be,' Njord said neutrally. 'Too many things happened. Perhaps too many for Hulderic to forgive. Perhaps too many for him to handle,' he added, and I knew he thought we'd lose the war.

We?

Not I, I realized. I had nothing left in Marka. *Or in Timberscar.*

'Changes nothing,' I said forlornly. 'It is far too late to save my skin from the malice of my own people. But I wish you happy hunting, friend.'

'We'll row out this night,' he told me and hesitated. 'I'm ... we are sorry for Saxa.'

'I'm ...' I said and shuddered, fighting the tears.

He was nodding. 'We miss the girl. And so, here it is. Listen. I was with Cuthbert in Hogholm.'

I was confused by the change in subject. 'You were? In Boat-Lord's land?'

'Your grandfather Friednot had spies there. So did we. So does everyone in these shores. The place is a virtual fortress, a cove on the western side of the islands.' He pointed in the general direction of Gothonia, and I didn't doubt his skill in navigation. He went on. 'The Silver Anvil, his hall is high on the cliff, the villages sprawl under it, but the whole place is ringed by rocks, and there's a harbor with a fine pier. Stone, thick timber. Rich trade. We all know the Boat-Lord hates you lot for taking off from under his thumb, but he also detested that your grandfather partially cut off their trade in furs from the west. You have grown rich on furs, you know? But now, that is changing. Hrolf will be going there to crown their re-established relations, to plot for your demise. He will go there soon. The loss of the Svea alliance will be a hard blow, but they will win without the Svea. But if Hulderic attacks them before they have the alliance? No, Hrolf will row his boats there very soon. For now, they are starving for furs there, though, and so, perhaps we'll take them some?'

I shook my head, and tested his forehead for fever. 'You'll take them furs?'

He slapped my hand away. 'Indeed. Hear me out. To sail to Hogholm's cove, you need to know people. And the man who sold Cuthbert this information about the Svea girl, about Saxa,' he said with a tight voice, 'he is the master of the fort, the man who taxes ships who come in and out, and I know he'd love some fox furs for his wife. He'd ask few questions, he would,' Njord said steadily.

'You wish to go to Hogholm?' I asked him dully. 'But where would you get the furs?'

'It's not on the way home,' he snickered. 'It's fall and the sea can be dangerous. But we didn't make much of a killing on this trip, and perhaps we wish to do some trading?'

'*Where* will you get fox furs to trade?' I insisted. 'And what would you be trying to do there?'

He leaned closer to me. 'Bero has a warehouse full of them,' he said with a wink. 'His personal wealth. We'll take them. Why not? He's very few guards left. You remember you wanted to join the crew if Saxa betrayed … well, she didn't. But the offer stands.'

'You could just take the furs, and not go to Hogholm,' I said, understanding what they were offering. They'd join me in my revenge.

He slapped me gently. 'I told you. We liked her well. I say we go and kill Hrolf, we'll gut him like a salmon, feed his eyes to the gulls, bet on how long he lives without his guts, and row south. There you shall find something worth doing, I'm sure. And perhaps someone worth knowing, as well? We have pretty girls aplenty, and some might be as brave and clever as Saxa was. She'd hate to see you suffer like this forever.'

I didn't say anything to that. It was too early, no matter how wise the words. Instead, I wanted to make sure he wasn't drunk. 'How would you take the furs? It's guarded,' I said slowly, so he'd understand the issue. 'Surely it is. You say he has few men left, but he has dozens. You think they—'

He smiled and pushed me. 'Let the thieves do the thieving bit. Be here at the evening. We'll deal with everything, don't you worry. There's still some of us left and we know how, eh?'

I looked at the sword and the fog had cleared. There was the sea, gray, cold, vast, and the horizon was dotted with islands, their ghostly silhouettes whispering of new tales.

There would be lands. New places to see. Father would have sent me there and I hadn't been willing. Now I was. I grabbed the sword, felt its weight, the risk it brought of more trouble, but would I stay there, and die after a Thing? When Hughnot arrived?

No.

I got up. I'd go and see the Saxon lowlands in the south.

But before that, I'd visit Hogholm with the thieving Saxons.

CHAPTER 22

I had always rowed a boat in near the land. There you knew where you were going, and while the whole coast was dotted with islands far to the sea, it felt strange to row out from the Marka. The past seemed suddenly distant, insignificant, as if my life had been locked in a box before, and suddenly that box was left ajar and behind me. The Saxons were in good spirits, singing lustily, laughing. Ceadda was happy with the calm sea, and I ventured a smile when they clapped my back, and understood the strangely comforting freedom that the open sea gifted men. I had nothing left, nothing but opportunity to build something new, and while the sorrow followed you everywhere you went, being far from where the sorrow was born made breathing easier and the pain lighter to bear. Rowing away was healing, it was hopeful, and I loved every splash of the oars, even if I was terrified we'd get lost, or a storm took us. Our exit had been easy, people occupied, and not one of the men that had been sent to watch me made so much as a squeak as I waded to the waiting boat the Saxons had pushed out. Likely, they wanted to be rid of me. I had not even said farewell to Father. Perhaps I didn't want him to fare well at all? Or perhaps I had feared he'd not let me leave and I'd change my mind.

For some reason, there was a huge pile of furs in the boat. How they did that, I could not guess.

I was shaken from my contemplations by a wave that slapped my face and I sputtered, lost my rhythm and my oar clanked to the man's oar before me who cursed profusely.

'He looks like a Saxon,' Njord said. 'Shivering and salty, hungry and bitter! Like he was bred down south. Only if he knew how to row.'

'And can't see worth a shit,' Ceadda added. 'We'll row out, and try to find this island, that's not too far. We'll spend the night there, and then we cross the open water in daylight. With luck, a day of sturdy oarsmanship, and uncomfortable night, and then, by midday, we will reach Hogholm, unless we get lost.'

'Very well,' I told him. 'We will see what's what. Just don't get us drowned,' I said and went white with the stabbing pain of loss, as I thought of Saxa, sunk under the water of Long-Lake, her body never recovered.

Ceadda saw it and nodded at me, sharing the pain. He thumbed over his shoulder, 'Perhaps Hrolf is there. Perhaps not,' he said and shrugged. 'But he will be, won't he? He has to be. If not? We have time.'

'He'll be there,' I said bitterly. 'I'll see his eyes as he dies.'

'I know a great silversmith, boy,' Ceadda said. 'He can make a brilliant cup out of the skull.'

We rowed, spent a cold, windy night on an abandoned beach, and rowed the day, then slowly that night, while half slept. By the next morning, my blistered hands were bleeding.

As predicted, Ceadda smirked at midday the next day. There were islands and a larger mass of hazy land. Slowly it grew, the smell of land drifted across the waters, the birds grew many, and I saw the land we hailed from, Gothonia, our own land, the land where all men were born. We slowly rowed past beaches filled with great rocky pillars, unearthly, unnatural and likely made by jotuns when the world was young. We gazed at the rich pastures filled with cows, towns and villages, and then entered a calm waterway between two lush islands and finally spied a rocky hill far, and on top of that there was a long, brown hall. Below it, a town sprawled, and a tall, thick wall of timber guarded the hall and the town. There was a harbor, ringed by jutting rocks and small islands and the only navigable way to the harbor was guarded by a huge, jutting rock from which ran a thick chain to a small island, where there was a small, earth-walled fort.

We slowly rowed next to the chain, a rusty, thick thing with dried seaweed hanging from the barnacles that covered its length, and all of that was heaped with bird shit. We approached a bit of sturdy pier on the fortified island, and the winch from where the chain was lowered and raised. Men walked out of the fort, bored, yawning, isolated guards far from the comforts of the town across the water, and I looked up at the huge hall where Friednot and Hughnot had grown, the Silver Anvil. That's where Bero and Hulderic had probably visited often as boys, hearing tales of the past, and perhaps they had even lived there.

In the harbor, there were fine ships pulled on the shore or tied to the pier.

One was familiar, the one Hughnot had used to row to Marka. Ceadda's eyes flashed my way, and he gave me a baleful grin and I nodded at him. Woden had brought us all there, in Hogholm, and there many debts would be paid in full. 'I bet it's Hrolf,' Njord whispered. 'If it's Hughnot, we'll kill him first. We have time.'

Hughnot. I had not thought of that. Perhaps Hrolf was home, and Hughnot there? Gods, let them both be in Hogholm, I prayed as I stared at the ship. It was a well-made thing, suitable for thirty men, had decorated sides, rich-red hue, and tall prow. The Saxons had pushed it to the sea the day we had escaped Marka, but it had been recovered and looked fine. I cursed my eyesight, fidgeted, sweated, and then I saw Hrolf.

It was he.

His long, blond hair was like that of many men in the north, but his pose, erect, and arrogant, his wide shoulders and rich tunic betrayed him, and I felt the tears of relief roll down my cheeks. They were busy, all of them. Hrolf was obviously giving orders, and then he marched off, taking a winding route that led up to the hall. Men were left working the length of the boat, carrying their gear to a nearby hall with an odd roof, where grass grew. Ceadda crouched next to me as Njord hailed the men standing on the pier. 'Yea. It was he. That's called Hraban's Kiln. A tavern, a smithy. They have rooms, and sailors get to eat and sleep on the floors.'

'Hrolf will likely sleep up there?' I asked and nodded for the huge hall on top of the rocky path. There flapped a standard, near the hall's doors, of a rampant bear painted in red over a black field. It was the standard of the Boat-Lord, our distant relative. It beckoned for me, for some reason, and I thought it a much finer herald of glory than what Hulderic sported, the bear jaws.

'Perhaps he will, perhaps he won't,' Ceadda said. 'It's not too long ago they were enemies. See, there are a lot of men in the town. The Boat-Lord doesn't trust Hrolf's men.' Indeed, Hrolf's men were surrounded by dozens of idle warriors, all lounging easily, but with spears nearby.

'Just like Marka, when Hughnot arrived,' I said.

'You there!' a tall, gangly man was yelling. We turned to look at him, and it was clear he had been napping. He was a mid-aged Goth with a red, useless eye, long blond beard, and he was thin as a wand as he raised a hand to stop us. The guards flanked him. 'A sorry-looking bunch of traders, aren't you?'

'Rich enough,' Ceadda said, struggling to stand near Njord. 'We bought something really nice from some Svea.'

The man's eyes took us all in. I avoided his gaze, but he saw my sword, the chain mail, and that of Ceadda, who had received one in thanks from Hulderic. I pulled up a deep hood to cover my face and his eyes passed me and went to the covered pile in the middle of the boat, the thick pile of precious furs, and probably enough to make a man rich. 'Furs?'

'Black fox,' Ceadda said proudly, smacking his lips.

'You are Saxons?' he asked. 'I've seen Saxons before.'

'We are both Saxon and Chauci. One is a Langobardi,' Ceadda lied. 'All dumb as oxen. We would trade in Hogholm. Or do they have too many furs this year?'

The man hesitated and eyed the pier. It was nearly full and the many boats pulled on the beaches were larger than ours. 'There aren't many fox furs from the west this year, or any year. I give you that. A man can make a rich profit with them. But the town is pretty damned full.'

Ceadda went to the pile, pulled away the cover and the man twitched visibly. Heaped there were some of the best-looking furs I had ever seen. They glimmered in the light, the tails and skins thick and dark. There were at least sixty of them and I again wondered how the Saxons had managed to steal them from under the noses of Father and Bero.

'How many?' Njord asked with a bored voice as the guards next to the lord of the harbor began to whisper to each other, making wagers on how many we were to be robbed of.

The man snapped his fingers and Ceadda threw him one. He looked at it, stroked it like he would his favorite hound, and looked down at us, greed chiseled on his features. 'I'm wondering if these were taken from a Goth?'

Ceadda cursed. 'They were taken from the Svea. We'll give you ten.'

'Thirty,' he said, having masterfully estimated the sixty furs. 'Or you can be on your way home.'

Njord snorted. 'Did you know Cuthbert is dead?'

'The Saxon lord?' the man asked, squinting.

'Yes,' Njord said, whispering confidentially. 'There is a new chief. He would like to know who led Cuthbert deep into the Svea lands. Who gave him such advice?'

The man twitched and shrugged. 'Who did?'

'Someone in Hogholm?' Ceadda said darkly. 'He visited here, didn't he? Sent his men to buy information, and did that every spring and summer. It was information that sometimes got Goths killed, no? Do you know who spoke to him of the Svea princess and the alliance your Boat-Lord was to have with them? That bit of news drove Cuthbert mad with greed. Our new lord will want to know who lured him to that kind of a trap. The new lord is related to Cuthbert, you see? It wasn't you, was it?'

The man twitched.

The chain was lowered, and we rowed to the harbor with our fifty furs. We went past the pier. The Saxon eyes scourged the rich Goth boat, where last of the gear was being carried away. There was no sign of Hrolf coming back. We beached, jumped to the water, and pulled the boat high onto the beach where it settled in the muddy stone beachfront easily.

Njord nodded at me. 'So, we are here. What's the plan?'

'I suppose we'll ambush him when he comes down the path?' I asked, feeling disappointed by such a simple punishment. Perhaps I'd feel better when he was dead?

'Let's go and ask some questions about what's going on up there,' Ceadda said and pulled me with him, while Njord and the men stayed behind, making sure the boat was secure, and to unload the furs. We walked the length of the shore, and reached Hraban's Kiln. It was busy, mead's sweet scent drifted out of the doors with that of sweat and piss, and we pushed inside past men crowding the doorway.

There in the main hall, the huge room was surprisingly well lit, the fire-pit was high with roaring flames, and a short Goth was arranging for room for Hrolf's crew. Men lined the walls, some slept under the tables, but there was a strange sense of order amongst the chaos. Still, there was no sight of Hrolf. No Ingulf either, thankfully, though I thought he might have been too hurt to travel so soon anyway.

Ceadda pulled the sleeve of a man, who looked horrified before my friend had uttered a single word, waving his arms around, showing how there was no room, but we had no intention of staying, only eating, and that went down well enough and they began to bargain. I looked around, saw some familiar faces in the Goth ranks, the men who had helped kill Saxa. They were carrying gear, walking to find a place for them, and then I saw a large chest being repositioned, well-carved out of pinewood and decorated with animals and strange symbols. It was sword-sized. 'Ho, what's that?' I asked a young man carrying it.

'Gifts for the Boat-Lord,' he said cheerfully. 'Best not think of stealing it. Hrolf the Ax would make you a head shorter, he would.'

'Is the famous Hrolf here?' I asked him with a smile under my hood.

'Up the hill to make ready for the evening's Thing. They'll give the old lord mighty gifts,' he said, winked and clapped the chest and dragged the thing away with his friends. They set it down in the middle of their men, and turned to fetch drink.

The sword and the ring. They were surely inside the trunk.

Ceadda appeared. 'Hrolf's—'

'Up the hill.'

He nodded. 'He'll be feasted up there, said the tavern keeper. He'll come back down here to gather his men later. They'll be giving oaths to the Boat-Lord. And probably the ring and the sword. We will kill him as he comes down. Probably not well guarded, eh? If he is, we wait for the night. We'll find a way.'

'I have a new plan,' I said.

'A new plan?' he asked nervously.

'I want more than his death. I want to see him suffer,' I said thickly.

325

Ceadda was scratching his hair. 'Boy. It's a fine thing to dream of. But common sense says we just gut the bastard, eh?'

I shook my head. 'No. I want to try something. Look there. I bet that's where the sword and the ring are,' I said and nodded at the trunk. 'I'm sure that's it.'

'Why do you think so? Granted, the size is right, but—'

'Because,' I said, 'Hrolf wouldn't dare to wear them when he meets the cranky, murderous old man. He wishes to make a ceremony out of it, and not give the Boat-Lord any excuse to get itchy about the alliance. No, they are there.'

'Well,' Ceadda said. 'Shit. We can't get to them. We'll have to plan how to kill Hrolf anyway. Forget them.'

I shook my head. 'That's how we kill him.'

'Eh?'

'Hughnot's men like to light fires, don't they?' I said. 'So we'll show we can as well.' I turned to whisper to him, while the tavern keeper arranged for food to be taken to our men. Ceadda shook his head at first, then more, but finally squinted his eyes as he looked around the tavern, and shrugged.

'Perhaps. It's a damned mad idea boy,' he said. 'Damned mad. Can't be sure you get anywhere near, fire or not.' He smiled thinly. 'But why not? We're all dead men anyway.'

CHAPTER 23

We stood by the beach. Ceadda was wearing his war-glory, and Njord and the others had new shields and spears, and sturdy clubs. They had sold the fox-furs in the afternoon, and fetched a hoard of fine weapons and precious iron ingots in return, and it had been a trade to make any man rich. The Hraban's Kiln was busy as ever, while most of the village had settled into sleep. Dogs were barking in the lands around the town, their howls heralding deaths that night.

There had been no sign of Hrolf yet, and Njord had ran up and down the hill to check the hall of the Boat-Lord, and claimed they were feasting up there. A great many old chiefs were seated next to the master of the land. Hrolf was the guest of honor, poets were reciting stories of heroism, and so they would take a while yet to get down.

'Do it,' Ceadda growled.

I gazed at Njord, wishing him luck. He paled, nodded and he and two Saxons walked after him for the great mead-hall. They went in, I saw Njord turn right, the other two left at the door, and gods knew if they might succeed, but if someone could, it would be Njord.

'There's a storage room to the right. A large one,' Ceadda said. 'It's going to be lit with fires, because they make the food and fetch the drink there. Yes, there will be fire burning in there. Njord will do well.' He sounded dubious. 'His slippery tongue wags, and they will be so confused they'll do anything to be rid of him. Yea, he'll succeed, unless he forgets his mission and finds free mead.'

'The two men make trouble, and he slips in to the storerooms?' I asked, though I knew that was the plan.

He grunted, as nervous as I was.

Some minutes later, we were rewarded by the sounds of a fight. There was a crash, and men roaring. Someone yelled in pain, a victim of Saxon malice. Then there was a huge uproar, guttural shouts, slapping sounds as men ran. I saw someone was at the doorway, clinging hard to the frame, then more men beyond him, and a punch threw the man from the doorway and he fell to the mud outside. It was one of the Saxons, grinning happily with a bloodied nose. A thick man followed, and he was howling and holding his jaw and a crowd came soon after, pummeling another Saxon who looked a bit torn, but he was calling the Goths nasty names, laughing while he did, protecting his face. There was no sign of Njord. I nodded as Ceadda, who tightened his belt, roared orders and cursed and walked to settle the fight with the remaining Saxon at his side.

I turned and took to the other end of the hall, where there would be rooms and a doorway.

I made my way there, found a drunken man in a doorway, and gingerly stepped over him. I had a long, furry cloak, similar to what Hughnot had given me and I also wore the hood, and made it into the better end of the hall, where men guarded their lord's rooms. One would be Hrolf's perhaps, but I didn't care about that, only the chest. However, one of the men inside cared about me. 'Hey, what are you about?' he called as he took a step towards me. He was a tall, well-built warrior, armed with a short spear and clad in leathers. I hesitated, raised a hand towards him apologetically, and turned to the drunk. 'Just getting my friend here,' I said and bent to revive the drunk.

The warrior stood there, uncertain. 'Be swift, then. All the rooms are taken by Hrolf the Ax, the lord's relative. No vagrants allowed.'

'Perhaps you should lock the door, then?' I retorted and kept pulling at the comatose man, wondering if I'd have to risk killing the guard, who was taking angry steps towards me. There were other men behind him in the corridor and I cursed my luck.

Then there was a booming noise.

While fires often begin stealthily, whatever Njord did in the end of the hall was anything but. There was a wave of air that staggered us, a sound of something wooden breaking, and the walls were shaking and groaning,

328

and then there was a cloud dust billowing down from the rafters. The tavern keeper was yelling hysterically and it took only a moment for smoke to start billowing across the roof. I grasped the drunk, the guard spun on his heel and ran to the main room, and coughs and shouts of terror echoed from there. I unceremoniously dropped the man in a pool of mud outside, and rushed back in and across the room after the guard, all the way to the end of corridor, nearly to the main hall.

There were flames smiting the main hall from the end of the room, where the kitchens had once served the customers and the drink had been stored. The wall at the end of the hall, the one separating the storage area from the main hall was a wreck, the roof was tilted, smoldering, and flames licked the ceiling. Men were throwing water on flames, some were rushing out, others back in, and calls for more water could be heard when the flames began to lick the pillars and the benches, driving men away from their attempts to save the place. The tavern keeper and his lot were desperate, and begging for the warriors to help.

All Hrolf's men were there, either helping, or trying to get out or in.

Save for the guard.

The diligent, nasty bastard came to sight, pulling at the chest. He was dragging it across the floor, towards the corridor, hoping to save it, and I swiftly sneaked back, all the way to Hrolf's room. I was cursing the man, and taking deep breaths, trying not to cough. I heard the man's grunts and curses as he dragged the thing across the uneven floor. I waited, nervous to the bone. I had hoped there would be no fight, but of course, it hadn't been likely. I thumbed the ring of branches on my finger, Saxa's ring, preparing.

I pulled Hel's Delight, kissed the blade, and waited.

I heard the scraping sound coming closer. I heard the puffs, the curses. Then the man's ass appeared, he was pulling the trunk mightily, then the face and the eyes turned my way. He had expected an empty room, and instead found a deadly blade coming for him. I moved fast as a wraith and punched the weapon to his chest. It impaled him, he screamed briefly, and I pushed it all the way through him, embracing him desperately, twisting and pulling at the blade. I looked to the main hall, and nobody could see us. I had succeeded and I laughed wildly, and then disaster struck.

The man didn't die. He was impossibly tough, and pushed back with a maniac's strength and we fell into Hrolf's room. I struck him across his face, breaking his nose, but that didn't matter to the dying man, who raised an arm.

He held a seax.

It came for my throat, and I twisted my blade in panic. That made him scream with pain, and instead of impaling me, the blade struck my side and I howled, as the chain mail split. The wound was deep, though perhaps not lethal, but it weakened me immediately, and I felt blood flowing. I grasped him to me, kept a hold on Hel's Delight and we stayed thus, in a deadly embrace. When he finally stopped moving, I pushed him aside. I was seeing dark spots, and while fighting nausea, I pushed and kicked the man to a dark corner and threw a blanket of cheap furs on him.

I staggered out. The smoke billowed thickly across the hallway, and I heard men yelling. I kneeled next to the fine chest, ripped it open, and did my evil deed as fast as I could. Then I retreated to the room, as I saw shadows, coughing specters of warriors rushing nearby. I hid behind the wall, praying they'd not save anything of Hrolf's from the room, but they stumbled on the chest, took it out swiftly and finally, after coughing terribly, I dragged myself out of the hall that was soon a sea of flames.

Later, we looked on as Hraban's Kiln burnt. People were dousing fires in the nearby houses and it felt somewhat appropriate to end Hughnot's schemes like they had started. I grasped Ceadda, and wondered at Njord whose beard had burnt, his clothes had blackened, and who had a terrified, huge-eyed look on his face. He waved towards the flames. 'There was a tub of liquid. A lot of it. I just dropped a burning log into it to douse it after I had used it to start a fire in a stack of kindling,' he whispered.

'Why,' Ceadda asked thinly, 'would you bother dousing a log you just used to start a fire with?'

He shrugged. 'I don't know. I just did. I like the sound when fire goes out. But it didn't go out, oh no. It went *boom*. I was thrown through the wall.'

330

'Ignore him,' Ceadda said desperately. He was looking at Hrolf, who had rushed down from the top with the Boat-Lord's guards, and they were organizing the chaos. The precious chest was carried to the side, and there was a great deal of commotion as they counted men and found some missing and then, after half an hour he ordered the chest to be picked up, and they started up the hill.

'Wait for me,' I said weakly and walked after the Goths.

'We'll wait for you,' he said and turned to make our boat ready.

It was time to see a murderous lord fall.

CHAPTER 24

The Silver Anvil of Boat-Lord was eerily like the Bone-Hall. Friednot, having no imagination, had tried to emulate their father's house, but had succeeded only partly. Where the Bone-Hall was a ghastly, smoky affair, the walls of Boat-Lord were painted white. It was an oddly clean hall, the slaves well dressed and healthy, and the only contrast to all of this finery was the man sitting on the wide throne at the end of the hall, under the most gigantic antlers I had ever seen, stretching left and right across the wall in all its bone-white glory.

The man was ancient.

His hair was gone, and only stubble remained. His belly was round and large, while his chest looked fragile, and his face was lean, but there was an ample amount of extra skin under his chin, suggesting he had once been corpulent, but was sick and old now, holding a weak hand across his stomach.

And that, of course, was why Hughnot had wanted to ally with him, I thought.

If Hughnot, a lord as high as any in the land, would return to the fold, he would rule vast lands when the old man died. He would deal with the lords who had served the Boat-Lord since Friednot and Hughnot had left the island. He'd scheme, he'd have power, because he was the son of the Boat-Lord, no matter how errant. Perhaps his dreams of power across the seas had not been lies after all. He could have it all, even more if he ruled Hogholm. I stood near the gigantic door that was guarded by men both wide and vigilant. Rows of warriors stood to the sides. Lords—well-armed and nervous—looked at Hrolf, who stood tall as a young god in the midst of his men. The Black Goths had tried to rub the soot from their skin, but had failed. They were an impressive party, nonetheless, over thirty men with long spears and wide shields, many dressed in leather armor. I swooned with weakness as I stared at the hated murderer of Saxa. Hrolf was now walking forward to the unkind-looking host, my great grandfather, ancient as a moldy rock, and Hrolf was bowing his head, gesturing for the men to bring forth the chest. It too, was blackened in places.

My plan was suicidal. Mad, even.

I had not fully shared it with Ceadda, but I begged the gods would show him their favor, and he'd escape. I might not be able to. I'd probably die there. He knew it, I was sure.

I'd not leave before Hrolf stopped breathing, no matter what it took.

They'd be fine, I thought. Their job was to capture the chain and the fort from the sleepy guards, and there would be a rowboat for me, but it was not likely I'd use it.

I watched behind the guard's backs as the hated enemy of mine walked forward. His men crowded after him and were stopped just shy of the throne, as our great grandfather gestured them to kneel. They put down the chest, and went to both knees, which must have irked the proud Goths terribly, but Hrolf went down also. And then he spoke. 'This, Lord, is the beginning of a new start for our families. Let the wound mend, finally. My father erred in following Friednot, and freely admits it. Much harm has come out of it.'

The ancient man nodded, but could not resist a dry barb. His voice was like the grating of whetstone on a spear blade, and he waved his hand weakly. 'I'll want to hear it from his lips one day. For now, this will do. Allies again. So be it, though I lack the Svea woman hostage.'

'I lack a wife, but Gislin is dead, and Tiw knows who rules them now. Yet, I know we shall win together.'

The Boat-Lord grunted. 'Yes, we shall. But it shall be costly. This Saxa died in the battle, they say?' the old man asked with a wry, evil smile.

Hrolf was not shaken by the question. He shrugged. 'She drowned herself. Did so after hearing of the loss of her brother and father. She had a weak, cowardly heart. And I would agree to marry a woman of your choosing, great Lord, if you tell me whom,' Hrolf said smoothly.

I had to stop myself from entering the hall.

'Sad,' the Boat-Lord uttered, not believing a word about Saxa. 'She could have been useful, despite the loss of her father. If her bothersome brother died, she actually might have ruled them. With a good husband, it would have aided us all. Now many Goths will die, when we could have had the Svea take the losses when we take the coast.'

I felt tears fill my eyes, and pushed them away angrily. I clutched a weapon under my cloak and smiled at a guard who glanced at me, and turned back to the hall.

'It is truly sad she did this to herself,' Hrolf said with barely hidden satisfaction. 'I failed to expect it,' he added, but I could hear from his voice he relished the memory. He had enjoyed the pain he had inflicted me. He no doubt was thinking about it right then and there.

I'd enjoy his pain in a moment, if things worked out like I hoped. I had been very lucky already.

The Boat-Lord grew impatient. 'So, come and show me. I wish to hold what should never have left the islands. The ring and the sword. Let me have them.'

Hrolf nodded at two men who got up and lifted the chest. They walked forward, until the Boat-Lord's guards took it from them and they carried it to their lord, who slowly climbed down from his throne. His face was flushed, spotted with excitement, and the joy for the ancient man could not have been greater. His hands were twitching, shaking, he indicated where the chest should be set, and they did, right before him. 'Long, so long have I waited. Your men should be rewarded for saving them from fire.' He fixed an accusatory eye on Hrolf. 'And you should be whipped for allowing the treasures to be in danger.'

'They were in no danger,' Hrolf said smugly. 'They are eternal and precious, and what you find in the chest, you have richly deserved, my Lord.'

I grimaced and held my breath, and so did every man and woman in the hall. The old man struggled with the lid, struck it with a thin roar of anger, and the guards rushed to yank it open.

They retreated with the lid.

The lord leaned in.

He stayed in that position for a long while. I half thought he had died there, looking at the treasures inside.

When he finally reached in, and took out Hel's Delight, bloody and plain, and then the ring of branches Saxa had made me, his face could not have been more disbelieving. 'Lord Hrolf?' he asked so quietly I could only barely make it out.

Hrolf looked like he had been ass-speared. His face sought answers from his men, who all looked as horrified as he did. His eyes were red, his cheeks puffed out and the veins in his neck stood out so hard it looked like he had worms crawling under his skin. 'This is---' he began.

'A jest, a joke?' the Boat-Lord asked, holding his chest. 'A fine joke, a grand jest! Is this your idea? Hughnot's?'

And so it was my time.

Before Hrolf could answer, I stepped forward and screamed, wincing from the pain in my side. 'There is an army by the shore! Hughnot's men! They aim to kill you, Lord! They'll kill you all! Fight! Kill the traitors!'

And that was enough.

What followed was a savage battle. Hughnot's Goths were bloodied, tested fighters, and while the wealth of the Boat-Lord's men were evident, the thirty men of Hrolf made a heap of bodies in the hall. Warlords fell, men were terribly wounded. The Black Goths fought like maniacs, and died in the midst of the craziest melee, and the white walls were awash with crimson. Screams echoed, men rushed from the dark to the hall to aid their lords and I retreated, walked down the path to stand under the magnificent bear standard, and turned to look inside. The scene was rewarding, near magical, a dance of death of the men I hated.

The gods gave me one more favor, the one I had begged for.

Hrolf, roaring in rage, pushed out of the ring of enemies. He howled as a club caught him in his face, and while spitting teeth, his ax hacked left and right, and few battered men pushed after him. They slaughtered a woman on their way, but his men fell behind as their enemies gave them chase, but the bastard lord charged the two remaining men in his path out of the door, and he fought so very well.

335

The guards were armored in leather, their tall spears reached out for him, and one pierced his shoulder. Despite the pain, and the fact he probably had nowhere to run, he fought and killed a man on the left with a savage hack to the neck, then slashed the blade at the man on the right, hitting his leg, toppling the fighter to the dust. Then Hrolf staggered to the door, chased by the frenzied shouts of the Boat-Lord, but his men still fought and Hrolf laughed, looking back, then across the town, seeking darkness where he might hide. His strong face was covered in blood, but the man's grin and arrogance was unchanged, so like it had been the day Saxa had died.

He rushed forward, and I staggered to meet him and he saw my shadow.

He raised the ax, gathered determination for one more fight, and I flipped back the cowl. His eyes enlarged in horror, disbelief, and he understood what had happened in the hall. He wasn't a coward, never had been, and though he saw his death in my eyes, he charged forward. 'Join the whore, you draugr. She moaned, Maroboodus, when I—'

I whipped up Saxa's ax and stepped forward.

His ax came in and struck my chainmail in the chest, but my ax swished in the air with a deadly, nearly hungry purpose and struck his temple with a bony crunch. I jerked the weapon off his skull, and was rewarded by an astonished, frightened look as his life fled, and then his corpse fell to my feet. I spat blood, having bitten my lip in pain, and I felt fire in my chest, where the wound by Ingulf had opened. My side bled profusely. I dropped the ax, pulled out the Head Taker, and struck the man's throat. I struck again, like a butcher and the head rolled free. Then I grabbed his head and staggered weakly. I saw a shadow, cursed, yet happy because I had killed the murderer, but saw it was Ceadda. He grabbed me, looked over my shoulder, and pulled me as we rolled downhill to the darkness, as Boat-Lord's men came rushing out.

He pulled me along as we made our way down to the harbor. 'You fucking idiot,' I said as I collapsed into the rowboat.

'Yes, my friend, I am,' he said with a laugh. 'But I had to see it. It was a great use for a weapon. Best I ever saw.' He nodded at the head. 'And you didn't lose the ring?' he asked.

'I didn't,' I said, as I thumbed Draupnir's Spawn. It felt heavy, supposedly one of the first spawns from Draupnir, Woden's magical ring that spat out nine such rings every eight days, but it also felt bitterly disappointing to hold it, and I knew I would never enjoy it without Saxa. It granted men power in the north, but what was a man without his woman? *Perhaps I'd find a new one,* I thought, and smiled.

Ceadda lifted my head, smiling. 'I'm taking this to my kin in the lands of the Saxons. They hate it, and I'll be famous for it.' He thrust the great standard of the Boat-Lord in my lap, and laughed like a demented spirit as we roved to the chain, which had been lowered. Njord was busily loading the ten fox furs he had reclaimed from the greedy bastard in the small fortress, and we rowed out, short one man who had died taking the fort. I held on to Hrolf's head, until it began to stink and in time, delirious with fever, we reached the Saxon coast.

RAVENNA (A.D. 37)

I t was late when Marcus got up. We had been sitting thus for days, drinking, him writing furiously as I told the story, and while I had been reluctant to speak of my past, now I found it annoying when he wanted to stop for the night. Marcus had an annoying habit of sleeping, where I could go on indefinitely, especially fortified by wine. He paced to the windows, and sniffed the surprisingly humid night air, for while Ravenna was often saved from the plague of summer's warmth by the refreshing winds from the sea, it had been oddly hot the past days.

'You left the land?' he asked. 'You became a Saxon?'

I smiled and stretched. 'Well, no. Not really.'

'But Ceadda and Njord—'

'Ceadda,' I cursed. He had been having terrible trouble with the names of my people, and while in the beginning I had got perverse joy out of seeing him curse and fix what he made a mess of, now it was just annoying.

'*Ceadda*,' he said, 'took you in. Right?'

'No,' I said. 'He helped me, but I didn't become a Saxon.'

'Why not?'

'Because, just like it is in the Roman world, *pater* is the tyrant of the family. In all matters, big or small, Father rules. And Hulderic was my master still.'

He sat down to write that bit down, but looked puzzled. 'But he let you leave Marka? You did indicate the guards didn't care if you left or stayed. That they hated you. And you said you hated him. Blamed him, even? That you didn't even tell him you would go?'

I snorted. 'Well, it turns out Father had found he could be a bit dishonorable after all,' I said. 'Listen. After we arrived at the Saxon coast, I was taken to a hall. It was Ceadda's hall, and their Saxon women and

338

Chauci slaves took care of me. I was nursed to health and when I awoke one day, I had a visitor.'

'Your father?' he said with astonishment.

'Yes,' I agreed heavily. 'He was there. He was there with Harmod, Dubbe, Sigmundr and many of his men. And Erse, of course. This is how our adventure ended.'

'Tell me this, and then I'll go to sleep,' he said tiredly, wiping his brow.

'Try not to make mistakes, if you can,' I chided him.

He nodded and I let him write.

***

My eyes opened that morning to a curious sight. I was aching, some of my wounds were red and infected, and while they had told me I'd live, I still thought I was feverish. Ceadda was there, and he looked down at me. That was nothing. That was normal. What was not, was that Hulderic clasped his shoulder and the Saxon disappeared, looking guilty, and Father sat down on my bed, brushing away hay. He held a gleaming white skull with a fractured side, where Saxa's ax had splintered it. The top was cut off and there was a silvery gleam inside it. He saluted me with it, drank from it. 'To Saxa,' he explained and gave it to me. 'Drink.'

I took it weakly and noticed I no longer wore Draupnir's Spawn. My eyes traveled to his hip, where on a thick belt was the Head Taker in a new sheath. I was about to protest, but thought about it and finished the mead, running my hand across the polished bone.

'*You* gave them the furs. And they gave you the ring and the sword.'

'I did,' he said simply. 'Though I took a risk. There was no way to know they could retrieve the weapon and the ring at all. But you and they did. They even parted with them willingly as I arrived. Strangely honorable, they are. Oh, don't blame them. They love you well. If you must know, they wanted to go to Hogholm even without making a deal with me.'

'You tricked me,' I accused him.

'I did. You lied to me. And betrayed me. You thrust all our lands into chaos. The Bear. He came and made a complete mess out of our lives.'

'I won't go back, Father,' I told him bitterly.

He shrugged, his brutal face scowling. 'There is *nowhere* to go back to, boy. After what you did, there is *no* place for our family there. Nowhere in Gothonia. They all hate us. Not only you. Us. So I made the deal with the Saxons, let you get your revenge, if you could, and I gained the mighty items, because I will not let Hughnot have them, and Bero doesn't deserve them.'

'I said I'm not going back,' I shouted, not really understanding what he was saying.

He snorted. 'I have Dubbe, Sigmundr, and Harmod out there with a dozen men.'

'I'll fight them,' I said with all the strength I could muster. 'I love them, but I'll pummel their fat heads—'

'Shut up! Listen! We don't have a home! I'm not taking you anywhere!' he roared and slaves ran out nearby. He slowly calmed himself and then leaned forward to look me closely in the eye. 'I feared you. I fear you. I fear what you are. I see why the Boat-Lord disliked our family leaving the islands. The curse. It truly is real. I believe that, I always did, but even more now. I'll have to keep an eye on you, and I shall. We shall go and seek a new home.'

'You are leaving the north?' I asked him, finally comprehending what he was saying.

He shrugged. 'Yes. I tried to unite the gau. They were quarreling. Unable to meet my demands. Thought I was to blame for your deeds. Yet you are my blood. We are here because I fear you, and because I fear for you. Because I love you.' He looked away, his face dark with anger. 'Your sorrow broke me. Saxa's loss, what it did to you? And still Bero and Maino expected me to condemn you. Still, they wanted me to lead the men in war. To serve with Maino? And Bero, who is a damned fool? Your tragedy made me hate Bero more than I thought possible. I couldn't keep pretending I respect him, and while I cannot fight for him, I cannot kill him either. I promised Mother, and I keep my promises.' He had a wistful look on his face. 'It's too bad he survived the Dragon's Tail. Too bad. When I left him three days ago, I kneeled next to him and told him I'd kill him with the Head Taker if he came after us. I told him to rule, to rule well, to fight

Hughnot, and to take care of our mother, who would not come with me. I came here, because I didn't wish to kill you. I came here because I trusted Ceadda, and for the ring and the sword, and for you. And now, we shall flee to the south. We have no home here. I don't want one here, no more.'

I looked at the ring and the sword and felt the bear rearing inside me. Had not Saxa seen me happy, a lord of men, and a king? And she had seen the ring and the sword as well.

Ceadda came to the hall. 'All good, lords?'

'All good, friend,' Hulderic said tiredly.

'I'm good, you liar,' I told him and he grinned at me widely but then his mood changed and he fidgeted, and we both saw he had news. 'There are some things you should know.'

'Well?' I asked.

He sighed and waved to the north. 'A trader came in after you, Lord. He visited Marka. He says there is an army of Goths there, ruled by a madman, a raging crazy lord and he thought it was Hughnot. The man lost his mind after his son died. And there is more. They took Timberscar. Your mother is dead.'

Hulderic's shock was evident, and guilt shone on his face. 'And my brother?'

'He fled, with his family, though his wife died,' Ceadda stammered. 'They say he has declared a blood-feud against you. Calls you a thief and father of Hel's spawn.'

'So be it,' Hulderic said heavily. 'I warned him.'

Ceadda bowed. 'There is more. The trader said there is a man called Ingulf, who has vowed to fetch that cup from you.' He nodded at Hrolf's skull. 'And to make one just like it out of yours, friend.'

I looked down at the cup and nodded at Father, who smiled at me ironically, as we had a common enemy to survive. 'Let them come,' I said.

Ceadda scratched his neck. 'He is already here. Our new lord is feasting him.'

I stopped speaking and nodded, indicating I was done, despite Marcus's incredulous look. He spoke. 'Well?'

'What followed, I think, is a new story,' I said, mulling at what took place that winter on the Saxon shores. At that, Marcus smiled, wrote the final words, and got up, dragging the parchments with him.

'You wintered there, at least?'

'That, and more,' I said darkly. 'There is much more to the story.'

He laughed and walked to the door, where he turned to look at me. 'There is, no doubt. And worry not, Maroboodus. Tiberius has not yet sent word you must die. He must be relatively well for now. We have time. You tell your story, Lord. But mind you, Maroboodus, that a man can only escape so many traps. Like a cat, your lives will run out. Perhaps yours are at an end? Enjoy our time together, relax as best you can, and let us finish the story, but do not fool me. I will not be happy if the story is over long and becomes too unbelievable.'

'I told no lies,' I told Marcus. 'And I'll not die in Ravenna.'

He smiled, bowed. and left, and I poured myself more wine.

Soon, Marcus would be back, and I'd tell him how we fought that winter, and fled from the lands of the Saxons, and survived Ingulf and the Boat-Lord, and even Bero, all of whom hated us.

And I'd keep trying to find a way to survive the wrath of Tiberius, and his advisor, his assassin Hraban, my son, the one who hates me.

- The story will continue late 2016 with the book: The Bear Banner -

Thank you for reading.
Do sign up for my mailing list by visiting my homepages. By doing this, you will receive an occasional and discreet email where you will find:

News of upcoming stories
Competitions
Book promotions
Free reading

Check out the rest of the stories, and especially The Hraban Chronicles, the adventures of Hraban, son of Maroboodus

Grab them from my AMAZON HOMEPAGE

SOME THOUGHTS

Writing a story that takes place so far in the north, entirely out of scope of the Roman historians of the time, is both a challenge and an opportunity. While the tribes living around the Baltic Sea were probably not all Germanic, nor did they all share gods and customs, or even speak each other's language, I had to make some shortcuts and assumptions so that there would be enough common nominators for them to co-exist in some sort of a cultural and geographical harmony. Suiones, Svear, probably *did* have stormy relations with the Gothic (Gutes) tribes of the time. Generally, Goths occupied the southern part of Sweden, the Suiones, or Svear the central and gods only know what was way up north in Sweden.

The story of Maroboodus takes place in these borderlands between the Goths and Svea, and his family is a brave group of settlers from the Gothonia, Gothland, rogues who broke off from their family against the wishes of the family patriarch. They are an enemy to their relatives, and they are also in constant competition with their robbed neighbors the Svea and the other Goths who had already built powerful nations further south.

Who were the Saxons, then?

Again, very little is known of their origins. They might have been several different tribes who inhabited Holstein, Denmark, a loose confederation or no confederation at all, especially 30 B.C. when this story takes place. They are mainly mentioned as raiding the Franks and Britain in later times, but just like most of the Germanic tribes, they raided their neighbors for their livelihood, and probably and most likely raided not only the west coasts of modern Holland, but also the south, the north and the east as well. Cuthbert's Saxons were the ones to turn their eyes to

Sweden, where the tribes across from Denmark lived, namely the Svea, Goths, or whatever was there during his time.

And that was enough for them to be regular visitors to the shores where the story takes place, though it was probably too far for them to bother.

Also, what is Long-Lake? There are plenty of places you could pick for such a body of water on the map, west of Gotland, and I'll keep this one my own secret. I visited it once, and while it is nowhere as large or takes one as far to the interior of Sweden as I make it in the book, those shores and rivers I visited had a mythical, magical, ancient feel to them, and I could easily see the Goths and Svea fighting over the shores of these waterways.

As you see, we have a lot of room for imagination here. One must remember this is fiction, not accurate historical study, and I dare say it is no better or worse than many of those non-fiction works claiming they can prove a theory in an era where so little has been written of the subject. This book touches lands the Roman's didn't conquer or know. Sometimes we have to let our imagination take the place of science, especially when there is no way to prove what is the truth. I like to trust the laws of likelihood, if nothing else. It is likely there were many Germanic tribes in the area, and that they all shared trade, intermarried, explored, and shared gods and beliefs.

As for the family of Maroboodus and their belief in them being the first of men, their belief there is a curse set on the blood of their family? One that might bring Midgard to an end, as well as the gods and the Nine Worlds themselves? All fiction, of course. Aska and Embla were rumored to have been created in the northern shores by Woden (Odin) and his fellow gods, so I make that shore to be Gothonia, and since Lok was deemed the enemy of the gods after the death of Baldr, it made for an intriguing storyline to create this curse originating from the trickster. It will be mostly solved in the *Hraban Chronicles*, but will plague Maroboodus and his relationship with Hulderic in the coming books of Goth Chronicles as well.

One more thing. The focus of Germanic warfare rests on the shoulders of the champions, heroes of the warbands. Such men were the speartip of ancient warfare, half-professional fighters who led the warriors of the lords, and I introduced plenty of them in the book. Did it go overboard? Probably a bit. But then, every good fight needs a famous death, and since the book had plenty of good fights, I needed many famed men to fall. After so many famous deaths, Maroboodus has no place in the world of Goths after Dragon's Tail.

And I am sorry for Saxa. I needed something to break Maroboodus, to make him colder, less idealistic, less happy, so there is something for him to brood over in the coming books. Saxa's death did the trick, sadly. He'll love again. Too many times, perhaps.

That's it. More to come, hope you enjoyed the book. I tried to paint the world and the characters as believable as they might be. It's no tale of Viking raids, though it was probably not too different, to be honest, no matter the difference of eight hundred years. It was a violent, hungry world, after all and the Goths would not later conquer the Roman world if they had been content and happy in the north.

CPSIA information can be obtained
at www.ICGtesting.com
Printed in the USA
FFOW03n1433200317
33698FF

9 781530 690336